# HUNGER

# FRAN QUINN

Hunger
The Blighted Empire Series: Book One
© 2025 by Frances Quinn

ISBN: 978-1-0685040-0-6
EBook ISBN: 978-1-0685040-1-3

Cover Art by Hampton Lamoureux.

Contact information:
franquinnwrites@gmail.com

First Edition: April 2025

First Sentence Publishing

for my parents,
you have done more for me
than I could ever repay

# CHAPTER ONE
## RUA

T he wait was always the worst part.

When Rua finally heard hoofbeats and the unmistakable march of the Hounds, she ignored the uptick of her pulse and smiled in the dark before letting out a low, long whistle like a bird. The familiar response rang out and made her smile widen, sharp and elastic.

This was what it meant to be alive.

The road they were on was little more than a dirt track through a wooded area, but Rua had taken full advantage, hiding her gang of thieves in the only part of the route that had cover. When the Hounds appeared around the bend in the road, almost invisible in their black trousers and dark armour, Rua whistled again. She heard the familiar twang of the bow and a flaming arrow flew past her ear, closer than she was comfortable with, and hit the ground in front of the Hounds. Fire exploded in a blinding burst of light. The horses pulling the wagon reared up. Another arrow ignited the second line of oil behind them, trapping them. Two Hounds grabbed at the frightened horses while the others circled the cart with the precious food.

Rua strolled from her hiding place, blade glinting orange in the flames. "*Mo chairde*, we can take this from you easy, or we can take it from you at the end of the sword."

"We are sworn to protect the Table," someone growled. "This belongs to them."

"*Chuig an mbord*," another Hound replied, drawing their weapon.

Hounds rarely spoke Éirely's native tongue. The Table had long forbidden it. The only thing they had allowed to remain was that horrible proverb. Said now at funerals and over drinks; a snide declaration to the cruelness of their legacy.

"End of a sword it is, then."

When she moved, she knew the others would follow.

Rua lashed out and caught the second speaker on the side of his head with the hilt of her dagger. With a clang of armour and a gruff grunt of shock, he dropped to the ground unconscious. The clash of swords rang through the cold night air as the others joined the fight and the Hounds remembered they were armed as well. She lost herself to the noise and the speed. Heat poured off the flames, illuminating them in golden light. The adrenaline made her heart pump so hard she felt it in her fingertips. It forced her to focus until she became nothing but this fight, this moment, this crash of violence. She twisted under a punch, stepping out of range of the swinging arm, and quickly glanced around, checking on the others. They mightn't think they needed her help, but she wasn't willing to let any of them get hurt. Not if she could help it.

Conor fought two of them at once, dodging blows and landing punches to the weak part of their uniform. As a deserter, he had the unique knowledge of where those spots were, and his size gave him an advantage as he battled with the smaller Hounds, easily pushing aside their attacks.

Hearing the clash of movement behind her, Rua twisted just in time to duck a blow from a mace that would've taken her head off. She fell and rolled quickly away from the hulking man's stomping boot. Escaping under the cart, she waited, and when he reached in to get her, she stabbed a dagger through his hand. He screamed. The hand disappeared.

By the time she crawled back out, Aoife had kicked him in the side of his head. He didn't move again. She helped Rua stand.

"Try to stay on your feet."

Rua smirked.

Only Seán still fought. Rua leapt in, throwing off the remaining Hound's rhythm and undercutting her with a swift punch. Seán swung the blunt side of his axe and the woman dropped.

He scowled. "You know I had that, right?"

Rua shrugged. There was no point explaining she wanted to protect him.

Seán shook his head and went to unshackle the horses.

Conor appeared at her side, feet as light as ever, and helped her tie up the Hounds. They gathered any weapons and coins scattered across the unconscious bodies, stole their boots and warm layers. They left the armour because it was impossible to sell and even harder to melt down. Working in silence, they finished quickly. The oil finally burned away to nothing but a trail of ash blowing away in the wind.

"The fire was pretty, I thought," Rua grinned.

Aoife snorted. "It was useful, was what it was."

Rua checked the Hounds were still unconscious. "Let's transfer that to Aurnia's cart and get going. We've two hours before sunrise and we need the food hidden by then."

"We have done this before, you know," Seán said as he tied one horse to a tree. He attached the other one to their cart. "You'd swear we were amateurs."

"And you don't need to include yourself in all our fights," Aoife sniped at Rua. "We had a plan. And it wasn't you jumping in front of everyone else."

Rua rolled her eyes. "I helped, didn't I?"

Aoife snorted. "*Amadán.*" Idiot.

Moving quickly, they loaded cornmeal, beans, peas, rye, some rare slabs of dried meat and even some flour. The annual Masquerade Ball that would be held in the Síochain's manor on New Year's Eve meant the food was better than usual. After filling their cart, they packed their bags, sitting after and having a quick meal with what they couldn't fit. Most of them had joined Rua's little crusade so they would no longer have to go hungry, and she respected that by making sure they never did. In the year that they had been doing this, they had all lost the skeletal look that dogged most people in the country. It was a risk, since it made them easy to spot in a crowd, but Rua didn't begrudge them.

It had been a long, hard eight years.

"Conor, you're okay with the cart?"

He nodded, and stood, cracking his back. No one pushed him to talk. They had all suffered but he had suffered the most.

"Everyone else back to camp," Rua said. "I need to get this mud out of my hair. It's itchy."

Rua had learned the hard way that her bright red hair was too identifiable on nights like this, so they had gotten into the habit of slicking it back with handfuls of mud. Combining the fiery hair with her green eyes and pale, freckled skin meant she stood out in any crowd, and they needed to make sure no one suspected her as anything but a homeless famine survivor who was slightly better fed than everyone else.

Crouched on the ground, searching through the abandoned armour, Aoife grinned. "Oh, yes." She waved her prize around. "Whiskey."

Conor disappeared, the echo of hoofbeats playing on the silent air.

"We'll light a fire when we get back." Rua grinned. "Maybe we can convince Seán to tell us a story."

4

"My sisters were better listeners than you lot ever are," he complained as he pulled the bow and arrows he had used to set the oil alight down from a tree. He threw them across his back with his axe. "You all interrupt too much."

Aoife linked arms with him, dragging him into the forest. "We promise to listen really, really well."

Rua paused for a moment in the silent clearing, watching the unconscious Hounds breathe and the snorts of air mushrooming from the agitated horse. She walked into the woods after the others, exhaustion from the fading adrenaline crawling along her skin.

In the distance, a wolf howled.

# Chapter Two
## WOLF

Wolf stepped back from the sword, twisting away from the steel that sliced through the air. She let her momentum carry her as she swung her blade up and caught the woman opposite her with a rough strike to the side. The woman fell back a few steps. Wolf followed her. She attacked before the woman was steady on her feet, swinging her blade again and again until the woman fell under the barrage of blows.

"Yield," Wolf said, sword at the woman's throat.

"Never."

Wolf sneered down at her. "You're dead."

"A member of Righteous Death does not yield."

"Well, you have your honour, and now you're dead." Wolf took a step back and sheathed her sword. "Well done."

The woman climbed gracefully to her feet. "Don't get cocky just because you're almost ready for your final test. Death is always waiting."

"Let her wait," Wolf responded.

She glanced up at the sky and grimaced. She was late. She shouldered past her opponent and stalked across the practice ring. The other apprentices who had been put forward as suitable for this job were already lined up across the courtyard, waiting. Wolf joined them, wiping sweat from her face with her top and tightening the ponytail that kept her hair from her eyes. The rest looked like they had washed and raided the costume room. Wolf looked like she had been rolling around in dirt. Which she had been. If looks were what he was after then Wolf didn't want the job anyway. The nun at the top of the line glared at her as she settled into position. The four other women beside her were whispering to each other. No one considered including her. Wolf had long been an outsider in a group of outsiders.

A carriage pulled in through the stone gates of the convent. Despite the training they had all undergone, the women scattering the grounds paused momentarily to watch it. Two black horses pulled it, and the sudden silence meant their hooves echoed across the yard like the fall of hammers. With an almost coordinated movement, the nuns training the apprentices and assassins gestured as one and the yard fell back into its normal activity. There was no real noise though; most of the assassins were trained in silence and the apprentices were punished for noise. Wolf had broken bigger rules than that when training and would continue to do so until someone decided she needed punishment. She had just survived her training in the Silence. She had no real urge to go back, but she did have a desperate need to prove her freedom through tiny rebellions.

The door of the carriage swung open. Wolf watched the man stroll across the yard, decked out in the Hound's black but with a cape of rich burgundy. A warning sat in his straight back and broad build. The dark shadows of his hood hid most of his face. Only his sharp jawline remained visible, covered in short, brown stubble.

*Liam Cogadh.*

The county was named after his family. Cogadh was a bleak place with little help for the poor and too much for the rich. Liam Cogadh was as bad as the landscape; harsh, hard and unforgiving. A Coimeádaí Síochána, the keepers of the peace were referred to casually as Síochain throughout the country. But peace was not a thing they kept, at least not without violence and fear. Liam Cogadh kept his county under control through harsh punishments and a heavy Hound presence in every town.

He walked the line, examining them one by one. Wolf stood at the head of it, waiting to feel the cool, disinterested sweep of his eyes. If he picked her, he just had to point and she would go running like a good little assassin.

She didn't officially have a name. None of them did.

When someone wanted to speak to them, they called *you,* or *her,* or *that one,* or *amadán,* while pointing at the person whose attention they wanted. Wolf had long ago decided that as the best, she had earned a name. Even when she wasn't the best, she thought she deserved one. Everyone outside the convent had a name. She had heard little children being called them by their parents, and adults greeting each other with them. It didn't seem like it should be so hard to have one, and since no one else could know she had a name, she admitted only to herself that it wasn't a very inventive one. The wispy memory of her father held a warm lap, strong arms and a nickname.

*Mac Tíre Beag.* Little Wolf.

It seemed an easy thing to steal from the man who'd abandoned her.

And really, she preferred to keep her imagination for more interesting pursuits. Like the best way to murder a man using only her feet, or how many times a person could be stabbed before they lost too much blood. Once, during a questioning, she managed to cut a woman fifty three times before she had no more blood, or answers, to give. That had helped her learn where the most blood was stored in the body, and which cuts caused the most pain, but the least bleeding. She didn't think it enjoyable, but there was a smug satisfaction in the work.

The Síochain reached her, and paused.

She didn't preen and tense her muscles like some of the others did. She continued to stand serenely, staring into the distance, and considered how quickly this man would fall if she stuck her knife into his throat.

"This one." The male voice grated over her nerves, too used to the women who guided her. "She's scrawny enough to pass for a famine child."

She ignored the insult since she had just been contemplating his murder.

"Yes, sir." The nun stepped forward and nodded at Wolf to follow.

Wolf had long acknowledged that her life meant walking behind people with more power and allowing them to lead her to whatever ends they deemed fit.

She was so sick of following.

Still, she left the line, one step behind as always.

# CHAPTER THREE
## RUA

The next morning found Rua on her way to Scíth to visit Aurnia. She insisted on a visit from at least one of them after any job so that she could see for herself that they were safe. She wouldn't have been able to meet Conor when he had arrived with the food, would have been stuck inside behind the bar serving the Hounds that drank in her inn, but he would have easily hidden the food in her stores before sneaking out of the township. Since Rua had drawn the short straw, instead of training or planning her next robbery, she strolled down the muddy paths to the main township in the county.

If the world was a fairer place, Scíth would have sat at the crossroads of a trade route. Aurnia's inn had been first; a place for travellers and merchants to stop and rest before heading on to the next destination. Aurnia, charming and trustworthy, convinced more and more to stay, settle and trade. She built the town, and was the unofficial mayor. Obviously, the Table allowed no one to question their authority, but in this regard Aurnia had the power. She dealt with disputes, she haggled prices and she kept the town working even as the famine stretched on with no end in sight.

She had also introduced Rua to most of the others, and was the one who had helped her plan those earliest robberies. She had stitched up their injuries before Oisín came along, and acted as a distributor for the food they stole with merchants she deemed trustworthy. Rua adored her. When she had been at her lowest, Aurnia had lifted her up and given her purpose again. A gift so great, Rua could barely articulate it.

She had to push into the inn; starving people desperate for a bit of warmth crowded the fire to get away from the winter chill. The heat eased away the hungry bite of cold nipping at her fingers. Aurnia always had a huge vat of soup bubbling on the fire that anyone could eat from but the scent of it wasn't enough to dampen the stench of unwashed bodies and old beer. Rua wasn't quite sure how Aurnia managed to stay open without any real customers. Except that sometimes she disappeared for days at a time, and Muire, her wife, would be fretting and scared until she returned — rarely injured but often enough that Rua suspected she carried out jobs of her own. She never pried though. It wasn't even a sniff of her business.

Rua shuffled around the crowd, hating the feel of ill and dying bodies pressed against her, all sharp bones and papery skin. She made it to the bar, nodding at familiar faces and ignoring the clench in her gut at how many were missing. Each loss reminded her of all that had been stolen from her.

"Rua." Aurnia scanned her for injuries. "You're late."

She shrugged. "Last night…" She stopped talking, aware of the crowd around them. "Can we talk inside?"

Aurnia nodded and led her to the back room that was their living quarters and the inn's kitchen and pantry. Two battered chairs sat by the fire. Well-worn books sat on slightly slanted shelves, and there were paintings on the walls; one of Aurnia and Muire wearing beautiful gowns and smiling at each other, others with intricate designs containing warnings and blessings written in the old language, and a picture of the inn. A pile of clothes covered the table. Flowers sat in a chipped vase adding a spark of bright colour. A low fire burned in the grate. It smelled like madeira cake and herbs, and comfort. It had invited her to settle, to relax and recover since the first time she had set foot here.

Rua walked to the fire to warm her hands. "Conor got the food to you?"

"And I've already dispatched it. What's bothering you?"

Nerves clattered across her skin, pulling tight at her grief. She held on to her wavering control in tight fists and watering eyes. "Nothing, I'm fine."

Aurnia quirked an eyebrow.

She gazed down at her rough hands. "I had a nightmare and I just miss her. I miss my sister."

Aurnia closed the gap between them and wrapped sturdy arms around her. "You have lost so much. Nightmares are expected."

Rua snorted. "I've lost no more than anyone else."

"Suffering is not a competition." She leaned back and caught the tears gathering in Rua's eyelashes. "What you are doing is a good thing. You are saving others in her name. Sometimes that is all you can do to honour the dead."

"It was my fault; I shouldn't have brought her to that place."

They had had this conversation so many times, Aurnia knew her lines by heart. "You were starving, *mo leanbh*. Desperate."

Rua's raw nerves couldn't handle the endearment, *my child*, and she buried her head into the crease of her neck to avoid answering. She should've known better, should've known that any help from the Table was a dagger dipped in poison. But they hadn't eaten in over a week and she had insisted they go to the workhouse. Saoirse hadn't wanted to, because their parents had always warned them off such places, but their parents were dead and they would soon follow. Rua was the oldest, she knew what she was doing. She had gotten sick a few weeks after they had arrived, and when the fever had finally broken, the stench had woken her. Saoirse was already gone. Rua had left that night, ready for death, but Conor had found her. He had saved her life and she had spent the last few years trying to make it up to him, to Saoirse, to everyone who died in a workhouse.

When she had calmed the ache to manageable levels, she pulled away from Aurnia and wiped her eyes clean. "Thank you."

"You know I'm here for all of you." Aurnia may have only been thirty five, but she had taken on a hoard of orphans, and made it clear she would protect them from anything.

Rua nodded. "Has my friend been in contact?"

"A letter. Usual coding. You can sit in front of the fire and work." Aurnia rooted through the drawers in the dresser and pulled out an envelope sealed with melted wax. "I hate to think of you in those woods."

She took the envelope and sat by the fire. "We're warm and safe."

Aurnia nodded, watching her for a few moments before she left, squeezing her shoulder as she did.

Rua lost herself in decoding the words. It had taken them over a year to create the secret communication. Before they even began, her friend had needed to teach her letters and then reading. Now, not only her, but all of them could read and write. Only she knew the code though. One of the many stipulations they had for working together.

As always, the letter started with their familiar greeting, a joke between them and a reminder of how far they had come, before getting to the information.

*Thursday, and you were wet as a dog.*
*The next shipment docks in thirteen days. It will be travelling the old way, along the road through Scíth. It is mostly linens from what I can attain from the Síochain's desk. Little food. I'll try to*

*find more information. But, we must meet. There is something*
*happening here that means I must speak to you in person. He has*
*gone somewhere. I don't know where but I do know this: the*
*Síochain is searching for you.*
*Stay safe.*
*I will meet you again on long lost roads at forgotten times.*

Rua read it three times to be sure she remembered it and
then threw it into the flames. She would meet them at the lake
at midnight, two nights from the day she received the letter.
Another message built into the last line. She gnawed her lips and
stared as the paper curled away from the flames, watching as the
edges burned black and then faded to ash. The Síochain was
aware of what she was doing. That would make her life much
harder but she wouldn't stop. No matter what.

# CHAPTER FOUR
## WOLF

The carriage rocked along the uneven road, making Wolf's stiff muscles ache. Sparring before they had left the convent had been a bad idea, but she had never missed a chance to show the others up. The cart dipped into a hole in the road, shifting suddenly. Wolf fell into the nun beside her. She pushed herself back up, touching the nun as little as possible, and ignoring the judging eyes of the Síochain on the other bench.

"I'm sure we taught you basic balance a long time ago."

Wolf gritted her teeth. "Yes, nun."

Not rolling her eyes took more effort than it should have for an almost fully trained member of the Sisterhood of Righteous Death. She leaned back, locking her muscles in place so she wouldn't fall again, and stared out the window.

Brittle, frozen grass shone white in the weak light. Winter gripped the country, making it glitter; beautiful but harsh. *Púdar dubh*, the Hounds' explosive of choice, scented the air. A cottage burned; the thatched roof illuminating the morning like a rising sun. Hounds sat on horseback watching as the family tried to save what little they had from the burning building. Forced evictions were the Síochain's harshest tool against the growing numbers not able to pay their rent. Destroying the house stopped the families sneaking back in. He would rather destroy something than let people have it for less than he believed it was worth. Running her finger up and down the blade she had hidden in her sleeve helped calm the quiet rage burning in her stomach.

Strategically, Wolf understood the action.

Personally, she thought the Síochain was a bastard.

The sun had dropped low in the sky by the time they reached the Síochain's looming estate. Windows blinked in time with the shine of the armour of the Hounds standing along the tall walls surrounding the manor. A training space took up half the yard. Enclosed by a short fence, two women circled each other with practice swords. Wolf longed to join them and ease the strain from sitting for so long. The nun climbed from the carriage like a predator. Wolf stood one step behind her right shoulder. The Síochain emerged and gestured for them to follow him.

The Sisterhood wasn't complex; the apprentices were in training to become assassins; the assassins went wherever the Table wanted. The nuns were retired assassins who trained the apprentices and helped anywhere else they were needed.

She hated the fact that the nuns didn't have names either, that even when they were no longer at the beck and call of the Table, they remained unknown. They claimed it was a gift to be part of the Sisterhood, to be a disciple of Righteous Death, but Wolf knew lies, recognised which ones were meant to keep them quiet as children. They didn't spend their lives training and reading and learning to then go and buy into the casual mistruths that people told. Wolf's loyalty to The Table had been beaten into her, and it was all she knew, except for that fuzzy memory of a man, holding her and reading a story.

Wolf didn't remember when she had decided to leave the Sisterhood. She didn't know if it had been a lightning strike of a realisation or a gradual wearing down of her dedication.

Sometimes she thought it was because her father hadn't let her go until she was five when everyone else went to the convent at three. No one else had memories of a home, knowledge they were once more than what the Sisterhood had made them. The reasoning didn't matter though. Not to her. All that mattered was that in the final test the apprentice got to decide whether to stay or leave. Wolf already knew what her decision would be.

No assassin, but one, had ever chosen to leave. After fifteen years and fifteen tests, it was an honour to complete training and become an assassin for the families. The woman who had left hadn't even chosen freedom at her final test. She had decided later and no matter how much she searched, Wolf couldn't find out any more information, but whispered rumours, and brief memories from when the woman had sent a shockwave through the convent.

Hollow opulence hung across the house in a way rarely seen outside of Ríthe, the capital city that held the Table. The six families had ruled for as long as Éirely had history. They controlled the land, forcing farmers onto smaller and smaller plots that could only grow potatoes. Wolf knew it made sense; the more they divided the land, the more rent the landlords received, and the less likely it was that they would turn on the Table. It worked well until the potato blight arrived on the island. Now most of the country was starving and no one could pay their rents.

Wolf had *thoughts* about how the Table should have handled the starving masses, but she rarely even articulated them to herself.

The Síochain's footsteps echoed off the walls and the high ceiling. Wolf made no sound as she stole every detail of the manor. Pretty artwork hung on the walls but the tapestries falling from the rafters were beautiful. Grand scenes of lush farmlands and people toiling in the fields, images of war and blood and death, and one that drew her in and held her still. It showed the Table in dark shades of grey and ruby red. The eldest siblings who were destined to rule by birth sat on high backed chairs, power written into the shape of their shoulders and their blank faces. Each had a dagger in front of them. Behind them stood their other siblings, dressed in advisers' robes or the dark garb of the Síochain.

The eldest ruled. The middle advised. The youngest kept the peace.

A clearing throat brought her back to the hallway. "Beautiful, isn't it?"

The fact she had not only paused to examine the floor to ceiling artwork, but had been snuck up on by the Síochain, made her stomach churn. He stood so close she could feel the heat of him. She almost leaned in just for the closeness of another human being. She took a tiny step back. She still couldn't see his face under the shadow of his hood but his harsh jawline was just visible. His mouth was flat. There was *maybe* a curve of amusement at the corner.

"It is." She kept the words calm despite the pounding of her pulse. Every member of the Sisterhood was well versed in small talk and inane chatter even as they panicked over the punishment they might receive from such a stupid mistake as stopping without permission. "The craftsmanship is astonishing."

The nun stood behind him, glaring.

"Are you ready to continue on?"

Ignoring the shine of murder in the nun's eyes, and the hint of mirth at the edges of the Síochain's flat mouth, she bowed her head respectfully, hiding her fear where they wouldn't find it, and followed once more.

Mahogany wood, leather chairs, and more artwork made up the room they entered. A blazing fire burned in a huge fireplace that stretched above her. Light streamed red and blue through the stained glass window behind the desk. Dust motes danced on streams of sunshine. She knew the Síochain watched her still, despite not being able to see his face, and she wanted to cut out his eyes. She stared straight ahead, back straight and arms pulled behind her. She fiddled with the sharp point of her blade.

Technically, they weren't meant to be armed when they weren't working, or when they weren't training. Technically, Wolf had not been without a weapon since four girls decided that incapacitating her would be easier than beating her in the test when she was eight. The nun that found them unconscious had given her the first knife she had ever owned. She never left her room without it. No one had attacked her in three years. Not since she killed the last one who'd attempted it. It was sort of sad how little the others tried now.

She rarely felt challenged anymore.

"Thieves have been stealing food meant for the Table." The Síochain sat at an oversized desk, covered in papers and maps. A glass of wine sat on the table beside a metal plate of half-eaten meat.

Hunger gnawed at her stomach. Thirst made her tongue fat and heavy.

"These thieves," he continued, "have been getting bolder in their actions."

She forced her mind away from how good a few drops of water on her tongue would feel,

The nun stood beside his chair, watching Wolf with eyes that missed nothing.

"We need you to identify this group of people, infiltrate them, and find out who the informant is."

"Informant?"

"We've been changing the delivery routes, the times, but they are still managing to intercept them." The Síochain's voice sounded rough and brisk. It reminded her of the draw of a knife across a whet stone. "To betray the Table means death."

Wolf nodded because *obviously*.

"The largest town in the county is Scíth. You can start there," the nun added. "You will be given very little. You must blend in with the people."

"I can be ready to go in an hour."

Nun tilted her head towards the Síochain, but he shook his head. "Tomorrow is market day. Most of the county attends it. You are sure to find them there."

Something about the confidence in the Síochain's voice niggled at Wolf. She pushed it away. It wasn't important if he had more sources than he was telling. That wasn't her business.

"You can go at first light tomorrow."

Wolf's back was to the door but she registered the new presence when the hairs on the back of her neck stood up and the air in the room shifted just the slightest bit. She didn't acknowledge them, but she did shift her balance to the balls of her feet.

Uncomfortable with the weight of the Síochain's full attention, she asked, "Why not just kill them?"

Heavy silence filled the room, stretching on and on, weighty with her failure for questioning a member of the Table. She felt the drag of the Síochain's eyes as he examined her.

"What is it you want?"

The question caught her off guard but she didn't let it show on her face. "To complete my final test."

She hated that he would have known her response without even having to specify the question, because what else could an apprentice want but to complete their training and become an Assassin of Righteous Death. The tests started when they were six and ended when they were twenty one. Wolf would do anything to ensure her success in the final test, and her chance at choosing her freedom. She knew it was possible to escape the reaching fingers of the Sisterhood. Even if it meant she had to leave the whole cursed island behind. She could make money by choosing any jobs she wanted. Maybe even ones that didn't include death.

He tilted his head in agreement to her obvious answer. "If you find me this informant, I will give the Sisterhood my blessing to allow you to complete it."

Sponsorship was the only way to take a test early. It meant freedom now, instead of having to survive another ten months at the convent.

"I'll bring you the informant."

Nothing would stop her.

"And then you may kill whoever is left of these thieves." He tilted his head towards the door. "She will bring you to your room."

Wolf nodded once and gladly turned away from him.

A woman waited by the door, dressed in black. A tight plait pulled her crimson hair off her blank face. She stood with her back straight and arms behind her, a mirror image of Wolf's stance. Wolf would almost have mistaken her for a Hound except for the confidence in which she stood. That wasn't the stance of a Hound. That was a Sisterhood bodyguard. Trained from an older age and less highly than the full initiates, they were still a formidable force.

Just as she reached the door, the Síochain coughed pointedly.

"*Chuig an mbord*," she said, managing to keep the bitterness from her voice.

"*Chuig an mbord*," he repeated. *To the table.*

Sacred words oft used. Wolf hated them.

# CHAPTER FIVE
## WOLF

**W**olf followed the younger woman from the room, tensing when she heard the nun excuse herself.
"A word."

Wolf froze at the ice in the nun's voice. She stopped, facing her and falling back into the resting posture. She heard the woman step away from them, either for privacy or to avoid the nun's attention.

"I do not know what has gotten into you in the last few hours; falling in the carriage, getting distracted in the hallway, questioning your orders," she hissed. "But this is not *acceptable behaviour* for an apprentice who is one test away from full membership to the Sisterhood. It would do you well to remember that." Shorter than Wolf, barely reaching her shoulder, the nun radiated power. She had her dark hair shorn close to her head, and her brown eyes stripped Wolf's confidence like teeth ripping meat from a bone. "You may have passed your last test, but we can always put you back. It is not just for testing."

Wolf fought the shudder crawling across her skin at the threat. She did not want to go back there. Not for anything. She nodded, "Yes, nun."

With one last scathing examination, the nun went back to the Síochain's office.

If she had been alone, she would have taken the time to let her heart calm down and her breathing return to normal, but the woman waited, so she locked it up where it wouldn't show on her face, and waved at her to lead the way.

With a nod, the woman led her through the hallway and down a staircase. They cut across the entrance hall, and down another steeper set of stairs. They walked through a bustling kitchen, alive with the shouts of an old woman ordering around scurrying children, pots boiling on four separate fires and the smell of herbs and warm bread. Wolf's stomach ached, so flashing her eyes over the kitchen staff, she grabbed a still warm roll off a serving platter. A pouch of water eased the dryness of her throat. She easily managed to steal an apple and a thick slice of cheese as well.

Pleased with the haul, she chewed and examined the woman. She had a plait that almost reached her lower back. The red hair deepened to brown in the dark hall. Muscular and well fed, shadows of the famine still rested in her slim wrists. Survival hung off her like a second skin; this woman had done terrible things to stay alive, and Wolf knew she had no regrets. Wolf recognised the instinct. She held her own survival as a physical thing, as a warning to *stay back, this animal bites.*

The clothes the woman wore were similar to the Hounds outside; black trousers and a long sleeved top. No armour. They were taught to survive with their wits, their weapons and their bodies. She carried three knives that Wolf could see and a garrote disguised as a bracelet around her wrist. Her footsteps were light but not soundless.

Wolf considered correcting her form but instead asked, "You're one of the new recruits?"

The woman shrugged.

"Where'd they get you?"

"Poor house." Her voice held the same heavy lilt that the cook's had; she hadn't managed to drop her accent yet.

Wolf could imitate any accent, but mostly she sounded neutral, untraceable and unmemorable. Everything about her was designed to be forgettable, from the dull brown the nuns had dyed her blonde hair to the way she carried her lean body. Her eyes were her only failure; a pale, icy blue, they were the most memorable and identifiable thing about her. She had learned to duck her head when working. "Family?"

"Dead."

"Name?"

She glanced back with a shrewd expression. The newer recruits, stolen from families and workhouses, had names, and then had them beaten out of them with trials and training and sometimes a wooden lash. She would have to be a whole new level of stupid to give Wolf her name, but still, *a name*. Wolf didn't know why anyone would give that up.

"Alright then, I'll call you Pup." It suited her; fresh off her training and so clearly eager to please.

This made the woman stutter in her steps and swing around. The plait took longer than the rest of her to come to a stop. "We do not have names," she hissed.

"I'm not throwing things at you every time I want your attention. It'll be our secret."

"There are no secrets in the Sisterhood."

Wolf took a step forward, levelling an even gaze at the woman. "There are only secrets in the Sisterhood."

Pup stared at her for a moment, muscle in her jaw ticking with unsaid words before she twirled around and kept walking. She opened the door to a small room.

"You'll be staying here tonight."

Two beds were crammed into the tiny space, barely a foot between them. One was clearly slept in and had the bedding from both piled on top of it. This far below the house, the cold seeped in through the stone walls. The floor was beaten earth, flat and brown. A door sat to the right and a chest of clothes to the left.

Wolf pointed to the other door.

"Stables." The woman stood, feet shoulder width apart, hands behind her back. "My bed, your bed. I guess you can have some of the blankets."

"I won't be sleeping." She didn't share her sleeping space. She had never trusted anyone enough. "You know the estate well?"

"I've been here five months," she said, drily.

Wolf grinned. "Well then, you won't be sleeping either. Show me everything."

The Síochain's lands spread over fields and fields of browning grass and broken stone walls. Trees edged along the north corner; a forest which stretched on until it reached Scíth. The main house was surrounded by high walls, broken up by Hounds' posts and large torches lit in the dulling winter light.

It took Pup until they were walking the perimeter to finally ask the questions Wolf could see sitting at the corners of her mouth. "I've never met an apprentice before. How long have you been in the Sisterhood?"

Wolf didn't answer. She always got more information by allowing others to fill the uncomfortable silences that she helped create.

"When they trained us, we knew about apprentices obviously. Because you were always the thing we would never become." Bitterness soaked Pup's words. "We were just the spares, the bodyguards. They still trained us and fed us. That was all that mattered."

Wolf could almost laugh; the nuns spent the whole time belittling the apprentices, making sure they knew how completely useless they really were, and yet, they told these stolen children that the apprentices were the goal.

The chill grass crunched beneath Pup's boots. Wolf made no noise, left no tracks.

When Pup said nothing more, Wolf asked, "Why do you want to know?"

She gestured to an old gate, locked up and plaited with ivy, that they were strolling past as if this was a simple winter's walk to escape the stuffiness of the big house. "That leads to the old stables. They built stone ones in front of the old wood ones and did nothing but lock the gate." Pup glanced over at Wolf, examining her face for a long moment, before admitting, "I just want to understand the Sisterhood."

"Regretting the unquestioning loyalty?" Wolf asked drily before pointing up at the Hounds on the wall. "How long do their shifts last?"

"Six hours on, six hours off. They do two shifts a day. Work with the same team of sixteen in groups of four that change constantly so no one slacks. I have lists of names, ranks, and friendships." Pup kicked a rock and watched it tumble through the grass. "I don't regret surviving. I just like to understand what it is I'm using to do that."

Wolf appreciated the idea of someone using the Sisterhood instead of them using everyone around them. She liked the idea so much she saw no harm in giving Pup some of the information she wanted.

"After the apprentices are trained, they become assassins. They go where the Table wants them to go and do whatever they want us to do. We are loyal to the Table but the families sit at the Table so..." she trailed off, uninterested in filling in basic politics for her.

Whoever sat at the Table changed, but the Table itself never did.

Wolf noticed a slant in the ground and headed towards it. There was a hole just on the edge of the woods lining the estate, and when Wolf brushed the long grass away, there was a thin tunnel almost lost in the foliage, made of loose earth and held up with rotting wooden beams.

She gestured to it, annoyed. "Did you know about this? Where does it let out?"

"The cells."

Wolf stared at her, face blank.

"I knew about it, okay?" Pup glanced away. "Sometimes you have to have an escape route."

"There is always an exit," she agreed, a long held lesson. "Even from the Sisterhood."

"The Sisterhood saved my life. I'm loyal to them. I just want to know… more." Pup pulled her plait around and fidgeted with the ends. It took a second for her to catch what she was doing, and when she did, she shook herself like a cat, dropping her hair and straightening her spine, transforming back into the Síochain's bodyguard. "I know there are six Síochains, one for each county. Each has an army of Hounds but they don't know we exist. The Sisterhood is the Table's secret sword. And they are loyal to the Table. *Any* member of the Table, including Liam Cogadh, which is why you're here."

"Do you have a question in that long list of facts?"

"I'm just trying to understand what my life is going to look like if I don't use the tunnel."

Wolf pointed to the dark entrance sitting between them. "I'll follow you down."

Pup stared at her, but when Wolf didn't move or respond, she sighed. "Fine."

She disappeared into the dark but Wolf didn't follow her straight away. Instead, she examined the shadows between the trees. They were only a few feet from the tunnel but Wolf knew that she had only noticed the entrance because she had been looking for discrepancies in the grounds. She made sure Pup had not left any noticeable tracks, made sure the tunnel stayed hidden and then climbed down into the dirt.

# CHAPTER SIX

## RUA

The sun had cast long shadows across the cave floor by the time Rua dragged herself awake on market day. The dead, desperate for company, had stalked her dreams. They reminded her of all she had done wrong, all she was doing wrong. She had relived the fight, an oozing parody of the adrenaline and violence, except this time she had failed to protect the others. They had all died, her sister Saoirse along with them, swinging from trees as the Hounds held her back and made her watch.

It had been dawn before she had finally settled into an empty doze and she woke with a pervading sense of guilt. The doubts were the same as always, inviting the others into her mess was going to get them killed, and she had to do everything to protect them. This time when the doubts rose up she had the visuals of her friends' lifeless bodies behind her eyelids to remind her of her selfishness. With a shuddering breath, she pushed herself up and pulled on her boots, but didn't bother getting changed from her sleepwear yet. Every pile of blankets was empty, except for Aoife and Oisín, who were curled around each other like a two-headed creature.

Light brightened the low entrance of the cave into a gaping mouth. She had to drag herself forward on her stomach to get out. Their camp sat inside a hollowed out mountain with intersecting passageways and caverns big enough for all of them. Outside was hidden by bushes and stacked with leaves and other debris. Anything to throw off searching eyes.

Seán and Conor were huddled together next to a fire pit, watching a pot bubble. Building it lower in the ground with a rough covering of branches and a tunnel for the smoke meant when they lit fires, no one knew where they were. One of Seán's parents' tricks. Conor's broad shoulders made Seán look smaller in comparison. Sitting, he only came up to Conor's ear, and he had never gotten rid of the harsh shadows of starvation. Conor had lost the dogged frailty quickly, filling out his wide frame and making his sharp, brown face handsome again, but he never quite managed to get rid of the emptiness in his grey eyes.

The air smelled of damp rot and the warm scent of stew. Black clouds darkened half the sky; a startling contrast of dark swallowing light.

Rua sat down on a log. "Who's on watch?"

"I'll go in a second." Seán's black hair, usually wild around his face, was pulled into a bun on his head and his sallow skin was warm in the barely-there sunlight. He nodded at the pot. "There's food."

"Thanks."

Rua dished up some stew, relieved to see the vegetables swimming in the pot. They all knew the months of empty broth that was more water than soup, or the nettle soup they often had to resort to when there was only boiled water and whatever plants could be put into it. She hated seeing the dead bodies along the roads with green staining their mouths from their desperate devouring of weeds to fill the chasm of hunger in their straining stomachs.

She worried about food constantly. Even more since she had put Seán in charge of it; Seán had lived off the land his whole life, and his parents, uninterested in the growth of towns and trade, had kept their family to themselves, teaching him and his two sisters about herbs, hunting, which plants could be eaten and which would kill him. Seán had only left to do his apprenticeship in carpentry. When he had come home to visit, his family was gone. He had never stopped looking.

After a few bites, Rua said, "This is good."

Seán gave her a *look*.

"What?" She swallowed more broth. "It's a compliment."

"You can just ask about the food stores, you know," Seán said.

"You'd make a shite interrogator," Conor griped.

"Yeah, well, I'm trying not to get involved. You all told me I had to share responsibilities." She scooped the last of the vegetables into her mouth. "Are we training today?"

Conor shook his head. "Market day."

"I'll finish this and go, so."

She swallowed the broth, putting her bowl by the pile of dirty dishes, and glanced longingly at the pot, wanting another bowl, but knowing it was better to save some for later. Just in case. Even after a year of steady food, she still expected it to disappear again.

Conor was watching her when she glanced back up, a terrible understanding on his face.

"Make sure to get some training today," she said to fill the silence.

He nodded.

She knew that was all the conversation she would get out of him today.

She changed from her sleeping clothes to her day clothes, which were pretty much the same — brown trousers and rough long sleeved tops with a heavy knitted jumper, the only thing she had left of her mother — and woke the others.

Market day was a must for all of them. Oisín needed supplies for his healer's bag. Aoife needed a new whet stone for sharpening her knives. Seán wanted more charcoal and paper. Conor didn't want anything so Rua tried to grab him something anyway. He needed reminding that even in the middle of all this death, life still continued.

Rua, Oisín and Aoife were the ones who always went to the market. Twins who refused to be separated, they had only joined Rua when Aoife had been sure Oisín wouldn't have to do any fighting. Since he had the skills of a healer, Rua had agreed. He kept them safe in a different way. The twins had the same dark skin and hazel eyes, but the similarities between the two ended there. Aoife rarely smiled, always searching out the next threat while being wildly protective of her brother, whereas Oisín was a quiet, thoughtful man who smiled softly at everyone, and was always willing to stop and talk. She kept knives. He had herbs. They were best friends.

The walk to Scíth was quiet; each lost in their own heads.

Aoife tugged on Rua's plaited crimson hair as they approached the town. "We need to cut that again," she said. "Someone is going to grab it and slit your throat."

"Thanks for that imagery first thing in the morning," Oisín complained, poking his sister in the ribs.

"Ow!" Aoife gasped and elbowed him back. "It's not even morning anymore."

Rua hid her grin in her shoulder as she glanced around to check the road.

They separated when the gates of Scíth came into view, staying close enough to help each other if something happened, but far enough away that no one would realise they were together. They were too well fed, too obviously not dying of the starvation that was killing everyone else. Hounds watched the crowd as if fearing a riot, even though most people barely had the energy to shuffle along. Grass stained people's mouths green. Rua could see ribs and hipbones, distended stomachs and sagging skin, through the rags that covered the starving bodies. The stench of death made each breath burn. She stepped forward, hand on her knife when a Hound grabbed a man who had stumbled into him and shoved him into a ditch. A cool hand encircled her wrist. Oisín shook her head when she glanced over at him. She nodded. He dropped her hand.

When they had left camp, Rua hadn't been planning on doing anything today but keeping her head down and buying what she needed. The sight ignited her reckless need to *do something*. Casually, ignoring the glare Aoife threw her way, she slipped across the crowd. Once she was beside the Hound, she reached out and grabbed the coin purse that hung from his belt. Most Hounds only carried a couple of coins for lunch but it would be enough for Rua to help some people. She slipped back into the crowd, purse up her sleeve, before the Hound even glanced her way. The small rebellion helped calm the pulse of anger that fuelled her. Some days she worried it would eat her alive.

She wandered the crowd, placing the coins in people's gaping pockets and before she had even reached the market the money was gone and the purse was buried in the mud. She nodded at the others as they disappeared into the crowd. Aoife stalked behind Oisín as they made their way around the market, ready to hurt anyone who dared to touch him.

Irritation still burned under Rua's skin so she moved between stalls, relieving any Hounds she met of their coin purse. She had a hat pulled low over her face and her bright hair tucked into the brim of it. Her drab clothes helped her blend in and she moved through the crowds with ease. She had been trained for this long before the famine hit.

Rua never understood how people allowed cruelty to

continue. Her mother had raised her to believe you protected those weaker than yourself. Even when it meant breaking the law.

"Laws are nothing, *mo leanbh*. Laws are what the Table uses to control us, what the Síochain uses so his Hounds can stop us from taking back our land." She could easily remember her mam's hands running through her hair and resting on her neck. "Laws are not always right. You have to question them, make sure they do no harm. Remember, you help people first. You make sure they are fed and safe and housed."

"But what about you and papa and Saoirse, mama?"

"Our blood is written across this land, and we protect our own."

"Our own?"

"Anyone who needs it, *mo leanbh*."

Rua pushed the memory away, and gazed up across the stalls. It gave her time to blink the tears from her eyes. She found Seán his supplies and picked up a book for Conor. She didn't steal from the stalls. Innocent people trying to make a living were never her targets. Small sacks of corn, shipped straight from Ríthe, were guarded by more Hounds. The queue for them laced its way around the market. Most of the people were here for the free food; the hope was it would keep them alive for just one more week. Everything was lived in moments now. One more week, day, hour, minute.

Help was coming. Help had to come.

Eight years was too long to wait. Six years had been too long but it was when Rua had started this little campaign of hers. Feed as many people as she could for as long as she could. And she wasn't done yet. She took three more purses and one dagger before she felt eyes on her.

She didn't freeze despite the instinct. Didn't even glance around. Just wandered the crowd until she could see who might be watching her. It took her longer than usual to identify who it could be. There was a woman; skinny but not famine thin, with muscles that spoke of strength, and a way of holding her body that told Rua she knew how to fight. She wasn't actively watching Rua, but every time Rua glanced up, the woman was closer. Waiting until a large push of people blocked her from the woman's sight, she headed further into the crowd, dipped low and disappeared behind a stall. The others would find her in Aurnia's when they were done. It was their usual meeting spot.

# CHAPTER SEVEN
## WOLF

**B**y the time Wolf left the Síochain's estate the next morning, she had a full stomach, her knife and a thorough knowledge of the house and surrounding lands. She knew every secret passage and false entrance, knew the guards' shifts and how often they changed up, how many there were and most of their names. She slipped out one of the side exits and crossed the dewy field to the road. She wore the rags she had seen so often across the country, and had no shoes, an annoyance since she had to walk to Scíth.

Before she had left the Síochain had given her vague descriptions of the thieves from the Hounds they had left alive, told her they may turn up in the town, that he didn't trust the Innkeepers, Aurnia and Muire, and that she was to join their gang, gain their trust and find out the information he wanted. He had also given her a dire warning not to fail him. She had nodded, and managed not to show the impatience she had felt at his stark words, already thinking the thieves incompetent. The first lesson apprentices learned was that dead people couldn't talk. Leaving the Hounds alive allowed for a risk this gang couldn't control and the carelessness of the action irked her.

Pup had, at least, been useful. Better than some of the others. The Sisterhood had long stolen children, and the younger the recruit, the easier they were to mould. Only in the last eight years had they begun to take older ones. The Table needed protection for their Síochains; unrest was growing across the counties as the famine dragged on and the lower members of the families needed to be kept safe. It was a waste to give them a fully trained apprentice, so they stole older children, trained them hard and fast, and sent them out knowing just enough to keep their wards alive. Wolf hadn't ever trained with them or eaten with them. They kept the true apprentices separate because their identities had to be a secret. No use being a secret assassin in a secret organisation if everyone knew who you were.

She easily convinced a man with a cart to give her a lift to Scíth; he was too thin, muscles wasted away and knuckles that tried to break from his skin as he clutched the reins. The horse looked better fed than him.

He must have seen her staring because he laughed, a harsh bark of mirth. "If only I could live off grass. Fields of it and not one potato."

Wolf rooted in her bag and offered him one of the rolls she had stolen from the kitchen.

He shook his head. "You need it more than me. I'm already on my way out." He coughed a wet, heavy noise and a shudder passed through his skeletal frame. "I'm just selling this ol' thing in the hope my boys can get a ship off this forsaken rock."

She nodded but kept her mouth shut.

Wolf wasn't allowed to talk about the Table being wrong but she very often considered thinking about it. This famine seemed like a problem easily solved. Keeping the citizens happy meant no unrest, meant no rebellion, or robbery, or distrust. All the Table had to do was feed the people and none of this would be happening. Watching this man, hardly older than the Síochain, struggle to breathe made something ache in her stomach. Not stopping the hunger seemed like a poor strategic decision. It irritated her.

"Why are you heading to town?"

"A job."

He frowned. "Family gone?"

She nodded, hating the sorrow in his voice. Her family had abandoned her a long time ago.

"Try Aurnia's place, she'll know if someone needs a bit of help. And she always has a bit of extra food she's willing to share. Tell her Frank sent you."

She liked his name; it held strength and security.

He pulled to a halt in front of a market square. Cottages made up the edges of the space and stalls waited in front of them, leaving a small pathway for people to get into their homes. Most of the stalls were abandoned but there was a queue of people winding its way towards a stall guarded by two Hounds. The other stalls seemed to be selling everything but food. A stage and gallows sat starkly in the middle of the square.

Wolf watched the queue, examining the ones who sat or leaned against walls, too weak to support themselves. Hounds strolled down the paths, watching everything.

While Frank concentrated on finding a safe place to pull the cart up, she stuffed two rolls and the cheese into the bag at his feet. It was all the food she had, but if she needed anything, she would steal it. She jumped off the cart and waved her goodbye, and wandered into the crowd, examining the people that shuffled around. It was on her third pass that she noticed three individuals who stood out; they were well fed, better dressed and clear eyed. Two walked not together but close enough that Wolf knew the woman was protecting the man. Both had weapons concealed in the sleeves of their well-worn but sturdy jumpers; she could see the outline on the man's, and the woman's hand went to her forearm every time someone approached him. The third was the most interesting. She walked through the crowds with an ease that spoke of practice. Each time a Hound passed her, she reached out and stole their coin purse. The action was so smooth, so well-practised, that not one person picked up on it.

Wolf was impressed. It was a rare feeling.

As if sensing eyes on her, the woman disappeared into the crowd. Wolf left the market and scanned the crowd until she saw the woman emerge and stroll down the streets like she hadn't a care in the world. Wolf followed at a distance.

Scíth was a town built on a crossroads. Wolf knew the superstitions around crossroads, knew restless spirits roamed them lost and confused. The thought some people would believe such stories almost made her laugh. She knew there was nothing more monstrous than humans.

She strolled down the thin streets, eyes darting about for exits and hiding spots but always flitting back to the woman. Tall, wooden walls stood guard over the cottages and shops and inns that made up the township. Hounds guarded the four entrances, tracking who came and went with watchful eyes. It was at the very centre of the county and the Síochain liked to know exactly who was travelling along his roads.

Wolf's main impression was the smell; a loamy, musky stench that invaded her nose. When she tried to breathe through her mouth, it coated her tongue and caught at the back of her throat. She acknowledged the discomfort and then ignored it. Allowing it to have power over her was unacceptable.

The second thing she noticed was the noise. The further she walked from the market square, the more people there were. They called to each from windows, carts, horseback, and the roadside, from the ground and from roofs. Though none of them were healthy, most with protruding collarbones and ribs visible through thin clothes, they still acknowledged each other, chatting, laughing and joking. They bustled around her, banging into her and falling into each other. The worst were the starved bodies leaning against walls, too weak to talk. She glanced down an alleyway; crows were picking at a dead body.

The convent was mainly quiet. Just the drawing of swords and the grating of metal on metal. Silence was a weapon as useful as all their others. It had been a year since she had last infiltrated a place so alive and she hated how it clanged in her head like morning bells.

Mud and puddle water squelched between her toes. She forced back the shiver that trembled beneath her skin and walked slowly behind the woman. Rain clouds sat low on the horizon like a fat grey house cat sprawled on a windowsill. She watched three Hounds stroll down the street, saw how the crowd parted for them and heard the whispers that followed in their wake. Nothing they could hear clearly but enough to let them know they were unwelcome.

An old woman, hunched and starved, walked past Wolf, muttering, "*Na fealltóirí fola.*" The bloody traitors.

She caught the woman's eye, and nodded, before continuing on her way.

Aurnia's Inn sat on the corner of the crossroads. The woman disappeared inside it. Pup had explained that Aurnia had set up her inn first, long before Scíth was even a named town. She kept the records and mediated the fights, while always making sure the Hounds had a place to drink.

The inside of the inn was a more condensed version of the streets outside; people crowded every inch, huddling around the fire and into each other, swallowing down bowls of soup or queueing up to get some. The smell was intense, catching in her throat and almost making her cough. She was glad now for her lack of shoes. Few people had them and she would have stuck out if she did. Rough wooden floors with soft hay caught most of the mud being dragged in. Frank's cart and horse had kicked up dirt onto her clothes and she could feel it crusted onto her face as well. She fit in as easily as anyone. Especially since she had lost so much weight during her last test and hadn't had a chance to put it back on.

She slipped through the crowd, snagging a stool by the bar when someone stood to call out to a friend. They glanced down at her, shaking their head at the cheek but allowed her to keep the seat. Despite the crowds and the smell, the pub was nice. Dirty white walls held paintings of the town, candles sat lit on each table and the warmth of the fire spread a certain cheer through the space. Most of the people seemed almost content to be away from the weather outside. With careful glances around, she searched for the woman she had been following, but she couldn't find her. She was gone.

"What can I get you?" The woman was dark skinned with broad, curved hips and a soft, round stomach. She had tight braids across her head that led to a long, dark plait down her back. She rested her hands on the wooden bar. They were rough with calluses. When she smiled, her whole face softened. "Do you have money, loveen? The soup is free if you don't."

Wolf rooted in her pocket for a coin, eyes scanning the space behind the bar. At the end of it, there was an open doorway. She couldn't see much but a lit fire. The woman had to have disappeared into it.

"Pint." She handed over the money and took the metal tankard filled to the brim with honey coloured beer. "Are you Aurnia?"

"Muire."

"Frank told me to come here. That Aurnia could get me a job."

Muire nodded and shouted, "Aurnia, you're needed."

Aurnia was darker than Muire and more muscled. She

moved with a careful grace that reminded Wolf of the nuns and set her nerves on edge. When Aurnia smiled, it didn't soften her face. It just made her look more like a predator. But then she glanced at Muire, and everything about her became gentle, from the curve of her shoulders to the hard set of her jaw.

"You called, *mo stór?*"

Wolf tried not to flinch at the affection in the words, *my love*, so easily given.

"This woman is looking for work. Frank sent her." She pecked Aurnia on the cheek. "Be nice."

"I'm always nice," she replied softly before her eyes caught on Wolf, taking in her raggedy clothes and mud-stained skin. What sort of work are you looking for?"

"Anything."

"What have you been doing before this?"

Wolf shrugged. "Surviving."

Aurnia grinned. "Aren't we all? Drink your beer and I'll have a think."

# CHAPTER EIGHT
## RUA

Hidden in the shadows of Aurnia's kitchen, Rua watched the woman from the market. The room usually contained a warmth she basked in but now all she felt was nerves racing along her spine.

This stranger had been following her; Rua had noticed her twice as she made her way to the inn. Not that it had been easy. The woman moved through a crowd like smoke, disappearing and reappearing with startling ease. Rua needed to know why she had been singled out, wondered if this was someone the Síochain had sent, or if it had just been a coincidence.

Rua watched as she chatted with Aurnia, some story about needing a job. Aurnia and Muire disappeared into the cellar beneath the bar and Rua decided that that was her chance. Aurnia would be angry if she knew Rua was taking such a stupid risk, especially after the contents of the last letter, but reckless need still drove her and she wanted to know why this woman had followed her.

She left by the kitchen's side entrance and walked across the deserted yard. The inn had two stories, with rooms upstairs for the merchants who rented them on their trips, and the kitchen that was stuck on the side like a fat mushroom. It must have been a later build, because the stones had less wear, and it was only one story high. Stables lined up beside it like Hounds waiting for inspection, but with the clouds threatening rain, there was no one about. Voices carried out of a storage shed in the corner, interrupted every few seconds by the sounds of horses. She slipped back into the entrance of the inn like she had just arrived.

She sat on the stool next to the woman. She had dark brown hair and sharp eyes, with a mouth holding too many secrets. Rua felt her eyes on her while she pretended to scan behind the bar for Muire or Aurnia.

"They went to the cellar." The woman's voice held no accent. Not even intonation. The words were flat and emotionless. "I'm watching the beer." This time a slight hint of amusement coloured her words.

Rua studied the woman in her peripheral vision; up close it was even more obvious that although she was skinny, she was nowhere near the usual famished bodies she saw. Lean muscles threaded up her arms and across her strong shoulders.

"Aurnia must trust you if she asked you to do that."

"It's a test." The amusement disappeared, replaced with a hint of annoyance. "She's checking if I'm trustworthy."

"And are you?" Rua asked, caught in the cold blue of her eyes.

"Trustworthy?" She shrugged. "Maybe. Aurnia seemed to think so."

Rua wet her lips and grinned. "That sounds like her."

"You know her well?"

"No one knows me as well as they want to," Aurnia answered, appearing from the cellar and dropping a barrel of beer at her feet.

Muire, coming up behind her, snorted. "Dear, stop with the dramatics." She kissed her on the cheek, hoisting the barrel up and carried it to the other side of the bar.

"What are you doing out here?"

Rua shrugged. "Making friends."

Aurnia stared at her, unamused. "Go back to the market. Find me something worthwhile."

She knew a dismissal when she heard it. From the way the woman tensed beside her, so did she. Rua glanced over at her once more, stealing as much from her as she could, before she nodded at Aurnia and left the inn. The last thing she needed was for Aurnia to realise that Rua may have been noticed when pickpocketing. Aurnia had a simple rule about robbing in Scíth: don't. She left, neck prickling, and she knew the woman still watched her.

# CHAPTER NINE

## WOLF

olf had to wait long minutes before she could leave the inn without alerting the two bartenders that she was following someone that they obviously cared about. She finished her pint. She listened to the woman playing fiddle in the corner. She slipped out as soon as Aurnia disappeared into the back and Muire turned around to grab something from the shelves that lined the back of the bar. She strolled from the inn, casually checking left and right, before heading back to the market. She had been walking for barely a minute when a shout echoed down the street.

A small crowd had gathered, and between the heaving bodies, she caught a flash of the woman from before. Jogging up, she broke through the small line of people. Frank lay on the ground, gripping his ribs. Mud splattered across his face mixing with the blood that poured from his head. The woman stood in front of him, defensive. Three Hound's stared at her. One gripped his bag in a tight fist. The food Wolf had given him scattered the ground. She had a sudden flash of unease that she had caused this situation.

"He stole from the Table. He must be punished." The Hound talking was a gruff woman, armour straining where it covered her thick arms. "The Síochain has decreed that thieves get sent to build the roads."

The other two stood silently behind her. Both were tall but they had their hoods up so Wolf couldn't tell who they were. They were big and well fed; a sight made worse by the starved bodies around them.

"He said he didn't steal it." The woman's voice echoed like a sword being drawn. Her eyes glinted in the darkening light and the hair that had fallen from her hat shone like fire. "Give him his bag back. Leave him on his way."

The Hound stepped closer. "Who are you to talk to me like that?"

Wolf suddenly knew exactly what would happen. The woman already had one hand up her sleeve, and Wolf knew someone reaching for a dagger better than she knew her own mind.

With a sigh, she said, "I gave it to him."

Frank stared up at her with fear creasing his brow.

The rhythm of her heart missed a beat when she realised the fear was *for* her. She had never met so many people who were willing to help a stranger so quickly and for no reason but kindness. The woman stared as well. She opened her mouth like she was going to speak but the words failed to form.

The Hound scrutinised her with hooded eyes. "And where exactly did you get it?"

She did not like that tone of voice. Not one bit. She took a step closer. "I stole it from the Síochain's house."

Silence fell.

Wolf watched as the red headed woman moved closer to her, a pleased smirk shaping her lips. They stood in front of Frank like a human shield.

"That is…" the Hound stumbled over her words. "You're a liar."

"And if I'm lying, you're going to have to punish me for talking against the Síochain, and if I'm not lying, you're going to have to punish me for stealing from the Síochain," Wolf answered, a bright spark lit in her chest. She so rarely got to talk back to those in charge. "So, how about you let this innocent man go, and see what happens when you try to punish me."

Everyone was staring at her now.

The Hound tossed the bag aside, a scowl creasing her brow.

The woman caught it before it hit the ground and gave it back to Frank. "Head down to Aurnia's. Get yourself some food."

His hands shook where he clutched the bag. "I can't be leaving you to fight my battles."

"Trust me." She found someone in the crowd she must have known and gestured at them to help. "Go on."

Wolf said nothing.

The woman glanced at her, brow furrowing, and said, "Go on, we'll be fine."

Someone put a skinny arm around Frank and led him away.

"You are going to hang for that." The Hound closed the distance between them, and the others followed, hands already on their blades.

As much as she would enjoy the fight, Wolf knew beating up three of his Hounds wouldn't keep the Síochain's favour, or more importantly, his sponsorship. She glanced at the woman. She was balanced on the balls of her feet, knees soft and shoulders relaxed with a hand resting up her sleeve. Ready for violence. Wolf knew better than to let it get that far. Even though she found herself interested in studying how the woman would fight, how well she moved and how competent she was with a blade.

Wolf nudged her shoulder and asked quietly, *"Cé chomh tapa is féidir leat rith?"* How fast can you run?

"*Tapa go leor.*" Fast enough.

Wolf smiled.

The Hound stared at them, anger rising in a red flush stretching up the woman's neck. "We do not speak that language here. By order of the Table."

The woman tilted her head and grinned a mean shape. "*Chuig an mbord.*"

She spoke the words in a way Wolf had never been allowed to; full of scorn and disrespect.

Wolf grinned and kicked dirty puddle water into the Hound's faces. They spluttered and wiped their eyes, blinded. A crack of thunder erupted above them, the clouds finally broke and the promised rain fell in sheets of water.

The woman smiled brightly and they both took off running.

# CHAPTER TEN
## RUA

They raced through the pouring rain, ignoring the shouts of the Hounds pursuing them. Rua let out a howl of laughter and grabbed the woman's hand. She dragged her between two houses, leading the hunt through crowded and rubbish-lined backstreets. When they were far enough ahead, she stopped and grinned at the woman, breathless.

"How's your climbing?"

She rolled her eyes before hoisting herself up the side of the house.

Rua paused, scanning the tight space for anybody watching them. She saw no one so she climbed the wall and lay beside the woman on the thatch. Only a couple of seconds later, the familiar clank of armour and swords sounded beneath their hiding place. Sheets of rainwater lashed down and her clothes stuck to her skin. The chill soon turned the burn of adrenaline into a harsh shiver. Blackened clouds stole the remaining light as dusk fell early.

"Pick fights with Hounds often?" Beneath her almost-nothing accent, she sounded amused.

Rua observed the woman; she had her face to the sky, eyes closed. She wasn't relaxed though. Tension roped its way through her body, and she played with a knife, turning it over and over in her hands as it glinted with raindrops. Rua couldn't help but be drawn to this stranger, this woman who had followed her, only to help her. Maybe she had been too quick to judge her as a threat. Maybe she was another kindred spirit. Someone just trying to right the world when it had fallen into so much wrongness.

"You're the one who picked the fight," Rua reminded her. She hadn't actually meant to cause trouble, but she wouldn't let an innocent man be taken to the roads because of some food he sorely needed. It didn't matter if he had stolen it; people had to eat, and if they couldn't afford it, then they had every right to take it. "I just politely asked them to return Frank's bag."

"Something tells me you rarely do anything politely."

Rua snorted. "Maybe. Do you have a name?"

The woman shrugged. "Most people do."

"Are you going to tell me?"

"Not today. Maybe next time." She sat up, making the knife disappear in a motion so fluid, Rua would have missed it if she hadn't been watching. "Do you come to town often?"

"Once a week."

"I guess I'll see you in a week then." She walked to the edge of the thatched roof, footsteps light as air. "Try not to pick any more fights." She disappeared down the side of the house.

Rua lay back down and grinned at the sky.

Rua had given Aoife and Oisín a very direct nod to get them to leave when the trouble with Frank had started so she wasn't worried about meeting up with them again. Dull light lit her way back to camp, but since it was winter in Éirely, she knew it was closer to afternoon than evening. The cave was closer to Scíth than she would have liked, a long walk for sure, but a walk all the same. But the caves were perfect for hiding and the need to be close to supplies and Aurnia trumped the need to be further away to avoid association with the town. She was glad of the cover when she reached the forest line even as drops of icy water slithered under her collar. It took her another long hike through the trees to reach the camp. The others had retreated into the cave, leaving the clearing surrounding it untouched. No hint of their existence remained.

Conor and Rua had been together for a year before they found the cave, moving every night before that, constantly aware and stressed about every noise. They had been doing little jobs, enough to keep them fed, but it had still been too dangerous to stay in one place. Aurnia came into their lives after they had settled in the cave and *Scíth* became their local town.

Finding it had been pure luck.

Conor had been searching for some berries when he had pushed the hedgerow aside and discovered the hole in the side of the mountain. Sneaking in without telling Rua meant she had spent a desperate hour sure he had been lost to the Hounds. He had finally emerged covered in spiderwebs and leaves, muck across the front of his body and soaking his feet. Grinning so wide the gaps in his smile sang with every breath, he had grabbed Rua and forced her into the dank, dark space.

"This is it," he had whispered, as if terrified to break the spell. "This is where we set up camp."

Rua had stared, uncertain.

There were puddles as deep as her thigh and spiderwebs hanging like loose straw from the ceiling. Wind seeped in through gaps at the top of the walls. But Conor had saved her life more than once, so Rua nodded, and did everything Conor told her to. Within a month, the space was free of spiders, drafts and puddles. They had filled the holes in the ground and the roof, had caught the webs with brushes made of branches and straw and had managed to build a firepit which let the smoke out on the hill side. It dried out the cavern and allowed them to bring in blankets and food. When Seán joined them, he built a long table with chairs in one of the caves off the main cavern, and candle holders now lined the walls. They still had to patch leaks more often than not and air out the blankets regularly, but it was home in a way most of them never thought they would have again. Even if the spiders still made frequent visits.

Rua paused for a moment, the hairs on her arms standing up. She listened to the sound of rain hitting leaves, and the howl of wind, making sure the noise of the others didn't carry on the night. She glanced around, sure no one had followed her and yet unwilling to ignore her instincts. The woman had disappeared when she had climbed off the roof and Rua hadn't seen her anywhere in town as she walked through it. She stood still for a long time, waiting. The feeling slowly faded. It was probably paranoia after the day.

When she was sure all there was were wet trees and creeping silver fog, she shook her head like her dog used to do to clear the rain from its fur, feeling silly for her suspicions, and crawled into the entrance of her home. The main cave was empty so she stripped out of her wet clothes and changed into some dry ones. She slipped on the thick, woollen socks Muire had knitted her and padded across the floor to the smallest side cave where they had rigged up some clothes lines. She threw her sopping wet clothes over them, flinching when little droplets hit her face.

The woman with no name wouldn't leave her thoughts alone; the warmth of her hand, the cocky smirk before she disappeared down the side of the cottage, the steel in her voice when she spoke to the Hounds. Rua's cheeks heated up as she remembered.

"What the hell was that today?"

Rua didn't jump, but it was a near thing. "I thought you were on watch tonight, Aoife."

"Conor took it." Aoife shrugged. "Said he'd done it in the Hounds enough that he didn't mind a bit of rain."

"He said that?"

"Not in so many words."

Rua grinned. "What's for dinner?"

"Stew. *Seán* made fresh bread and he saved you some. I didn't think you deserved it since you fucked around in town. Again. If we told Aurnia, she'd kill you." She examined Rua. "Did you have to start another fight?"

"It was only a small one."

Aoife shook her head. "Try to keep your head down once in a while," she scolded and ducked out of the cavern. "The others want to play cards. Oisín got a new book on his rounds too, and he said he'd read it to us all later."

At the other side of the main cave, a small, warm cavity had been made into a meeting room. It held the long table, piles of blankets scattered about the floor, weapons lying in a corner — not as neat as Conor would have preferred — and books haphazardly thrown into piles. Ever since they had been taught to read, it had become a competition to see who read the most, and the fastest, and who did the voices best when they read out loud. It kept them entertained on the long waits between jobs.

She filled a bowl with stew, grabbed two rolls of still-warm bread and lowered herself into a pile of blankets in the corner. The others were arguing over the washing up, a hated job in the winter, but one that had to be done every evening. Conor had traded his turn at it to take the even worse job of watch during a storm, so now they needed to decide who would take his turn.

"I'll do it," Rua called to get them to stop talking.

"But you're meant to do it tomorrow," Aoife replied.

"This is why you're not meant to switch out jobs, Aoife," Seán snapped.

"I'll still do it tomorrow. Stop arguing. It's sorted."

Seán opened his mouth like he was going to reply, but then he huffed and fell into a pile of blankets. "Yeah, fine," he said, which was about as much of an agreement as they were going to get from him.

Rua took a breath and said, "I've to meet with my friend."

"When?" Seán demanded. He didn't agree with her keeping the person who helped them secret. He thought they should all know who they were trusting.

"Two nights from now." She didn't mention the fact the Síochain knew that it was one group doing all the robberies. They used to space them out enough that it seemed random, but with winter, the desperate need had grown. Now they took any opportunity they could to get more food to the people. "They think they have some information coming through on another delivery."

"Because of the Masquerade Ball? It's only a few weeks away," Aoife said, glancing up from the scarf she was knitting. "They've got to be stocking up on the food by now."

Rua nodded. "I think so. Last year there were a lot of extra deliveries."

Aoife glanced at Oisín, and away quickly. "Are we still safe?"

"I'm always safe with you, Aoife," he said, knowing exactly what his twin was worried about.

Seán snorted. "Are you okay meeting up with them alone?"

"They've gained my trust over and over again. I'll be fine." Rua unplaited her hair and ran her fingers through it, helping to unknot the damp strands. "They're not going to betray us now, Seán. Why would they?"

"I don't know, do I? I don't even know why *you* trust them, so how would I know why they'd betray you?" He picked up his paper and slashed charcoal across the page, glaring at it. "Just be careful. You can't know what would make a person betray you, and if they do, *we're all* in danger."

Rua nodded and, trying to change the subject, asked Oisín, "So you're reading tonight?"

He agreed, and when no one had anything else to say, he told them about the book he had been given on his rounds, and who had died, and who was dying, and Rua tried not to let the fiery rage that had been burning since her sister had died eat her alive.

At least the stew tasted good.

# CHAPTER ELEVEN
## WOLF

Wolf easily stalked the woman through Scíth with the crowds of starving, homeless people filling the thin streets and thick sheets of rain making visibility poor. Leaving the town behind made it harder. They walked a dirt road surrounded by open fields and burned out houses. The downpour helped because it meant the woman tucked her head into the collar of her jumper and practically jogged through the mud.

She expected the forest. It was the most logical place to hide.

Evergreens stretched high above her but did little to keep drops from slipping through their branches. Mud slopped across her toes, and rocks dug into the soles of her feet. Shivers wracked through her, but she ignored them. Roots thicker than her arm lay hidden under debris of the overhead trees that padded any noise she might make. She watched the woman stop to whistle. A returning call sounded from high in the trees. They were smart enough to have someone on watch. Something about that pleased Wolf. The woman walked up a slope to a mess of hedgerow and overgrowth, pausing for a brief moment to glance around.

Wolf froze.

Shaking her head, the woman slipped behind it and

disappeared. When she didn't reappear, Wolf carefully left, keeping an eye out for the overhead watcher. She didn't find them and that gave her pause. Few people were as good at hiding as an apprentice, and even fewer stayed hidden from one.

Wolf was sure she had found the thieves with what she had seen today; a hidden camp, daggers up sleeves and people keeping watch. It bit at her again how easy it had been to find them with only the Hound's descriptions and the Síochain's certainty that they would be in Scíth. She knew he would have spies around the county, he would be a fool not to, and Liam Cogadh was anything but a fool, but it still seemed too easy. He had requested an apprentice for a job any competent Hound could do. It made no sense and she wanted to investigate it, find out all his secrets and then exploit them, but she knew that was a dangerous path to tread. She pushed aside the niggling uncertainties and decided to return to his estate; if the informant had access to his desk, she needed to find out who had that privilege.

It made more sense than having her out in the wilds.

Cold, wet and uncomfortable, she trudged through the forest. She had been trained to ignore such frivolous discomforts but she refused to when a warm house was available. She used the half collapsed tunnel Pup had shown her. It let her out near the cells. Two women sat huddled near the back of one, wrapped around each other but otherwise still. Wolf wasn't even sure they were breathing. Ignoring her unease at how thin they were, she crept through a side door, and out to the stables. Better to avoid the Hounds and the house.

She had been told not to come back without an answer, but if the Síochain thought she would keep wandering around without shoes, he could jump in a lake. Winter made the ground hard with frost in the morning and muddy with rain at night. She would either lose a few toes to the frost, or end up losing half her skin to the constant wet. The nuns would not be best pleased about that; the apprentices' bodies were considered another weapon and they were expected to treat it as they would any blade. It didn't help that the eighth test she had taken had involved water and wetness and freezing damp. She had never recovered from the dislike and even the stable room with Pup would be better than that.

Wolf knew she was nothing if not contrary.

She broke into Pup's room just after the midnight turn of the guards. She crept in through the dark and straddled the woman, knees on her wrists and knife to her throat. Pup's eyes flew open.

Wolf snorted. "You shouldn't be this easy to sneak up on."

"What are you doing back?" The words fell from her mouth, slurred with sleep.

"What? Didn't you miss me?"

"Like a knife in the gut."

Wolf snorted and climbed off the other woman. She stripped off her wet clothes and stole a blanket off Pup's pile. Pup tightened her fingers on the rest of them but didn't react otherwise. Still shivering, Wolf sat on the bed and wrapped the rough cloth tightly around her naked body.

She ignored the unsubtle examination and asked, "What's been happening since I left?"

"I don't report to you."

"Of course you do. Apprentice," she pointed at herself and then at Pup. "Bodyguard."

Pup tossed another blanket at her. Hard. "Your lips are going blue."

Unsure of the generosity, but pleased, Wolf nodded her thanks.

"Not a lot of change. The nun has stayed so I'm training with her. The Síochain hasn't left the estate. There have been people crowding the gates every day begging for food but he's not giving any out. It's grotesque."

"The people or the Síochain?"

Pup didn't answer the question. "I've been doing my rounds. The Síochain's apprentice arrived back from Ríthe with news from the Table. They had a meeting but I wasn't allowed in the room."

"So what did they talk about?"

Pup grinned. "The famine is worse. The blight has destroyed the crops again, and the Table is getting frustrated with the unrest in the country. A Síochain in Farraige almost got killed when people tried to overrun his estate. The Hounds sorted the rebels out pretty quickly though."

Cogadh. Farraige. Talamh. Teanga. Draíocht. Seanchaí. The six counties of Éirely.

Wolf had visited them all; had killed people and spied on people and gotten information from people in each of them. She had learned their customs in the convent. She had walked among their small villages and practised the lilting differences in their accents. The Table ran the country but each county was its own mixture of riches and poverty. Wolf had seen it all, and knew that Scíth was the mirror image of all the little towns she had visited. The only difference in them seemed to be how close rebellion itched beneath the surface of Scíth. Although it had been months since Wolf left the convent, and if what Pup was telling her was true, rebellion seemed to be a pot of stew ready to boil over all of Éirely.

"Hounds against unarmed, starving people? I'd hope they sorted them out quickly. How'd they even get through the gate?"

"They don't know yet but they think they have someone on the inside."

"A Hound?"

She nodded.

Wolf had little interest in rebellions and dissatisfaction. The Table had ruled for longer than they had history, and it would rule long after she was dead. "What about the Hounds here?"

"As far as I can tell all are loyal to the Table. Not even any grumbling or whispers in their own rooms."

"Good job, Pup."

She flinched, and glanced around as if someone could be listening.

"Has there been any talk of what I'm doing?"

Pup shook her head. "I know someone has been stealing food meant for the Table. I know you're meant to stop them, but no one has even mentioned you since you left."

"How did you find that out?"

"Whispers between the Síochain and the nun."

Wolf nodded, pleased by her work. "Don't tell anyone I'm here. I need to watch without being watched for."

She shrugged. "I'm just the stable hand. I wouldn't know anything about you anyway."

Wolf snorted. "You know, most of my covers have been servants, merchants, or landlords. Mostly in Ríthe. And now I'm wandering through muddy places that can barely be called a town. I wouldn't complain too much."

"I'm not complaining. The Sisterhood saved my life." Fierceness pulled her mouth tight. "I'm loyal to them."

Wolf shook her head. "Be loyal to yourself. They'll never be loyal to you. Not ever."

Pup stared at her, suddenly younger. She creased her brow and ran her hands through her hair. "Sometimes—" she started.

Wolf gave her an encouraging nod; secrets held power she had been trained to steal. Then the image of Frank, staring up, fearful *for her*, made her stomach clench, and she interrupted Pup before she could think on it. "Don't ever tell me something that can be used against you."

Her eyes widened at the implication. "You'd do that?"

"It's been drilled into my bones to exploit all and every weakness." She swallowed. "Warning you, it's the best I can do."

"We're on the same side."

A sudden chill licked up her spine and Wolf wrapped the blanket tighter around her shoulders. "For now."

\*\*\*

Wolf slept in a hollow in the rafters above an empty ballroom.

When someone called out, she woke instantly; a lifetime of threats making consciousness an easy thing to grab. She lay still, listening to the undisrupted quiet of the room below her, and the shouts in the yard echoing in the windows, and the bang of hooves on the stone. Sunrise glowed crimson and orange, making the room burn and flicker. She stretched slowly, allowing each muscle to warm up before she crossed the beam extending across the vast room. It seemed a ridiculous waste of space with high, slanted ceilings and a shining wooden floor. Carved mahogany tables stained a deep brown lined the edges of the room. They shone with polish. Tapestries hung along one wall telling the story of the Cogadh family. She had walked the line the night before, admiring the stitching and colours.

The Síochain only used the ballroom a few times a year. She knew of the Masquerade Ball, and that it was the social event of the season. Even while a famine raged through the country. The most important people in the county attended; the business owners, the landowners, and those in charge of collecting rent for them. They indulged in riches barely imaginable to the poor and at midnight stripped off their masks to welcome the beginning of a new year. The show of excess might have insulted the lower classes, but it reminded the rich that they still ruled. Wolf saw the strategic value of keeping the richest members of society loyal to the Table and the Síochains, but it still seemed a frivolous waste of resources. Each county had a ball, although the one in Ríthe put them all to shame. Wolf had never been but she had heard talk from the nuns who had. *Heard talk* meaning she had spied on them while bored.

The ceiling of the Síochain's house held rafters made up of interconnecting beams, dark with shadows and close enough that Wolf walked over them in easy strides. There were gaps at the top of the walls between rooms and hidden alcoves to settle in when she had no one to listen to. It was a massive lapse in the safety of the manor, but Pup was aware of it, and more importantly used it to her advantage. Wolf might tell the Síochain before she left for the final test, but only when he had guaranteed his sponsorship.

For now, it was too much of an advantage to give up.

She trailed the Síochain around the building, watching him interact with the head of the guard, his staff, and Pup. The manor stretched out below her; room after room of chairs and fires, books and tapestries. Three stories to explore with the kitchen on the lower floors, and the servant bedrooms in the attics. Servants cleaned and Hounds patrolled the hallway. Besides the servants, no one else lived there except the Síochain, but the guest rooms were regularly occupied with representatives from the Table, merchants, landlords and the nuns.

The doors of the manor burst open at midday with a clatter of noise.

A man strode into the entrance hall; he had on charcoal trousers and a burgundy top, the same colour as the Síochain's cape, and had skin so pale it seemed almost transparent. It gave him a wispy presence that belied the strong muscles lining his back and arms. Wolf recognised him. This was Luchán Cogadh, the Síochain's apprentice and nephew. Twenty-four years old with brown hair that kept falling into his hazel eyes, Wolf didn't think his name suited him, but she supposed naming wasn't an exact practice.

No one knew who a baby would grow up to be.

"Uncle?" he called out.

"Out riding, nephew? We did keep your horse well looked after, you know." The Síochain's voice was soft in a way that made Wolf's stomach ache. "You never did tell me how your visit went?"

"I updated you, Uncle."

"You updated the Síochain. You never told your uncle."

Luchán's posture softened and he shrugged. "I arrived. I spoke to my mother. I listened to their opinions. I tried, uncle, I did. But the *politics*." He smiled when the Síochain gripped his shoulder and shook lightly. "I know, I know. Politics is part of the job, but they just speak so much shite."

Liam Cogadh laughed, bright and easy.

Wolf's skin crawled, and she left them to it, deciding it was a good time to steal some food.

# CHAPTER TWELVE
## WOLF

Dusk had stolen over the manor in dull navy when she noticed a change in the atmosphere of the estate. Hounds raced along the corridor and Roisin, their leader, rushed to the Síochain's office.

"A Hound has gone missing," she said when he waved her into the room. Hounds slept in barracks by the stables, eating and sleeping in the long, thin building lining one wall of the yard, rarely leaving the estate except for patrols. "They didn't turn up for their shift and their bunk hasn't been slept in. We have a search party out."

The Síochain nodded, and waved her away. "Keep me updated."

The Hound's body was finally found two hours later with their throat slit and their uniform missing.

Wolf found the would-be assassin hiding in a small alcove.

The woman was sickly thin; skin stretched over prominent bones and covered in a dense red rash. She would never have been able to kill a healthy soldier alone, but had clearly been left to carry out this last part by herself. Wolf stalked above her, watching as she stumbled down the darkened hallway to the Síochain's bedroom.

Midnight had long since passed and the Síochain slept.

Wolf watched her creep through the dark towards the bed. Barely breathing, the woman raised her arm, her dagger shining in the moonlight. Wolf didn't care either way who lived or died tonight. The Síochain had sins to pay for, and this woman wasn't innocent either. But only one of them had guaranteed her sponsorship and freedom.

Sighing at having to reveal herself, Wolf dropped down behind the women, grabbed her scraggly hair and slit her throat. The body dropping woke the Síochain. He jerked up, knife already in his hand.

"You should be more careful," Wolf said almost cheerfully. "A man in your position shouldn't be so easy to kill."

He stared at her for a long, considering moment before glancing down at the steadily growing puddle of blood. "You had to slit her throat? The stink will never fade."

"You're welcome," she replied, mockingly.

"We needed to question her."

Wolf acknowledged that with a tilt of her head. "Next time."

"You shouldn't even be here." He wiped a steady hand down his face. Usually when people escaped death they were shaken, crying, hysterical. Wolf liked that he remained as calm as always. "You are meant to be finding me a group of thieves and an informant."

"I already found your thieves, but the informant is on your estate." She glared at the dead woman pointedly. "Be glad I was here."

He watched her for a long moment, held her tight in his gaze, before dismissing her with a wave of his hand.

***

Perched above the room and hidden in shadows, Wolf watched the next morning as the Síochain met with members of his council. Three women and one man; the head of the Hounds, an adviser from the Table, the nun from the Sisterhood, and a representation from the landlords.

Not that the others knew the nun, her purpose or her identity. The Sisterhood hid in the shadows, known only in the highest of circles. No one but the Table and the Síochains knew they even existed. Dressed in the garb of the Sisterhood, the nun wore black trousers and a black top, soft leather boots and knives strapped to both thighs. Wolf knew she had more knives than that hidden across her body.

The sight of her made Wolf's nerves thrum.

"I've found the murderer of your Hound, Roisin," the Síochain said, words as cold as the frost glittering on the grass outside. "She attacked me last night in my chambers. I have left the body for you to dispose of."

Wolf had watched Roisin, the head of the county's Hounds, walk the corridors with the confidence of ownership, hair tight across her skull, dark skin warm in the candlelight, and eyes glowering every time her actions were questioned. No matter her name, the only part of a rose she reminded Wolf of was the thorns, but a quiet admiration of her had grown the longer she watched the woman destroy each contender in the sparring square, or bite back at a stupid suggestion from a lower rank, or even go toe to toe with the Síochain when he made an unwise suggestion.

Roisin's hand went to the hilt of her sword. "You were unharmed?"

"I do have some skills with a blade."

It might have been Wolf's imagination but she thought his eyes flicked up to her hideout.

"Of course."

"After you deal with that, we'll discuss the fact that a would-be killer got that close to my bedroom. Quite a failure by your

Hounds?" He tilted his head. "But that is a conversation for us to have in private, I think."

The hand on the hilt tightened. Roisin nodded.

"Now, let's discuss the shipments for next month."

Wolf watched the people in the room for signs they were the traitor. None were given. They listened to the Síochain speak and kept eye contact as much as possible. No one watched him lock up his papers, or tried to learn more information than he was willing to give. There was no fiddling, or discomfort. No signs of nerves.

Bored, she played with her smallest dagger and hoped the meeting would end soon.

It interested her how little the Síochain cared about the attempt on his life. He continued as he had before. Meetings with his Hounds, with his advisers, with merchants, with landlords. He talked with Luchán that evening, indulging him as his nephew spoke his opinions freely, making the Síochain smile. It interested her how much Liam doted on his nephew, sharing a drink with him, talking about shipment routes and arguing over different policies in a light hearted way. Wolf was impressed when the apprentice pointed out some flaws in the delivery schedule, areas where they would be prone to attack.

She was cleaning her nails with the knife when the Síochain finally acknowledged her existence with a pointed cough.

"Have you left me alone at all?"

It pleased her that he had known she was there. She didn't reply.

He sat writing at his desk, not even peering up to speak to her. "I suppose you're the rats the cook has been complaining about?"

"Tell her to bake more rolls."

He huffed what might be imagined to be a quiet laugh. "Come down here. We have to talk."

She landed in front of him without a noise.

He kept her waiting for another long moment while he finished off a letter. While he did, she inspected his desk. The invitations to the Masquerade Ball rested in front of her; gilded leaf paper with rich gold ink declaring it to be the time for renewal and regrowth. There were no places for names. They just held a formal greeting for the guests. The simple lack of such an easy safety measure irritated her. She memorised the wording out of habit and tore her eyes away. Books piled on top of each other in one corner and scrolls weighed each other down in the other. She glanced back at the Síochain but he seemed unconcerned by her wandering gaze. He was allowing her to see this part of his power.

He signed off the letter and closed it with his personal seal, watching the burgundy wax bubble and melt before finally putting it to paper. It went into a drawer beside him. He cleaned away his writing materials slowly. The efforts to make her nervous failed. She had long forgotten simple nerves.

When he finally glanced up, the dark hood fell away. An intentional action, and yet, she couldn't help but take advantage of the opportunity. It was the first time she had seen his face with the bright light of the candles dancing off his skin. He was an attractive man, harsh and beautiful like the craggy mountains behind the estate. Wrinkles across his forehead and around his eyes added to the seriousness of his expression, and made him into someone who had known too much power for far too long. His mouth slashed like a harsh blade, ready to cut any who got too close. The shape dragged his eyebrows together and hooded his eyes. They were the blue of a winter morning. They were a frozen lake glinting in the dawn light.

Darkness hid beneath those icy depths.

Even though a trickle of unease climbed up her spine and buried itself in her scalp, Wolf didn't look away.

With a curve to his lips, closer to taunting than welcoming, he directed his gaze over her. "You're still smaller than expected. Do they not feed you?"

"My last test was capture and survival. It involves torture and starvation."

The twist of his mouth would have hid the shock that travelled over his face as quickly as autumn leaves blown in the wind from anyone but a trained apprentice. "I forgot how charming the Sisterhood often are."

"Training is necessary to ensure our survival," she replied, by rote and uninterested.

"Quite the loyal little thing, aren't you?" He mocked her with a sneer. "Do you have a single original thought in that useless skull of yours?"

She tilted her head and palmed her knife, hidden behind her back. "I could show you some of my more original thoughts, *a dhuine uasail*, if you like."

"We do not speak that language here."

"*Ní labhraítear, a dhuine uasail.*" No, sir, we don't.

This time the smile was a fox with a rabbit between its jaws, blood wetting its fur. "There you are."

She kept her face expressionless but her heart thumped. She rarely showed her true self to anyone, and she didn't understand how this man had taunted her into doing it so easily.

"I want you to infiltrate the gang and find the informant."

Wolf swallowed. "It makes more sense for me to search your household where the informant actually is."

He tilted his head as if acknowledging her point. "You know little about politics if that is what you truly believe."

She tightened her hand around the hilt of her knife. "Politics."

She ignored how he watched her as she ran through it in her head.

When she was sure she understood, she said, "You have a traitor in your house. A traitor to the Table. To betray the Table means death. But there is no guarantee the other families would believe you weren't part of the plan to steal their food, to weaken the Table and claim it for your own family. No one can know you know and no one can know you are searching them out. They'd run to the Table and spill a story of conspiracy." She stopped talking but she wasn't finished. She just hadn't spoken so much in a long time.

He nodded at the wine on the sideboard.

She wanted to roll her eyes. As if she would accept wine from him. As if she would show that weakness. "A strange woman wandering the estate will raise suspicion. Especially after the attack. You need to publicly renounce the traitor and prove your fealty to the Table or they'll kill you all. Like the Sagart family."

"Like the Sagart family."

Few people spoke of the massacre, or how there used to be seven families.

A ruling family decided they wanted more power. They almost succeeded in toppling the Table and claiming it for themselves before failing at the last moment. They were wiped from the map; their lands divided and wealth redistributed. They were a warning to children now. The moral at the end of the story. Proof of the might of the six families; of the Table.

*Stop that now before you end up like a Sagart.*

"I was there, you know, in their final moments. All the families were. They wanted to remind us of the might of the Table. Stronger together than apart." No tremor shook his words, and his hands were steady on the desk, but something told Wolf he was still a trembling child as he told the story. "We do not betray the Table. We do not betray their rules. You know a Síochain must give up any children he has to the Sisterhood?

A Síochain's apprentice must come from the sibling who sits at the Table. Everyone else's children become Hounds or assassins. It stops there being any claims to power."

Wolf said nothing but the confession made her skin feel tight.

"We do not betray the Table or everyone related to us by blood dies. Even those who do not know they are our brethren." He stared at her, eyes echoing a long held pain. "I need you to infiltrate the gang and find out who the informant is."

She nodded, and couldn't help but ask, "Is every apprentice related to a family?"

"No." He stood and walked over to the pitcher of wine. The sound of sluicing liquid filled the silence. "Some are stolen from their parents or sold to the Sisterhood. Some are unwanted. Some are unneeded. It is rare for a sheriff to have a child. We are raised knowing the consequences of such actions. You could be any number of things, but being related to a family is unlikely."

She swallowed away bitter disappointment and the shame that he had read her so easily. "I need you to arrange a shipment for two nights from now, and I need you to ensure everyone who could be the informant knows. Make sure there are more Hounds than usual. Make sure they are outnumbered."

"Why?"

Wolf smirked, unamused. "I'm going to play hero and let your thieves invite death into their home."

# CHAPTER THIRTEEN
## RUA

Rua gasped awake, jolting up and swinging into a punch before consciousness flooded her and she realised she was safe in the cave. She sucked in a rattling breath. There were many miles between her and the workhouse. Many years between now and her sister's death. She ran a shaky hand over sweaty hair and pulled her knees into her chest. Sunshine leaked in through the entrance; a thin stream mottled with the shadows of leaves. Grey light covered the cave, darkening into pitch black as it stretched into the high ceiling. Empty blankets littered the room. Murmuring voices outside echoed like birdsong.

"Workhouse?" Conor leaned against a wall, sharpening a knife. The harsh noise grated against her stinging nerves.

"They were taking her from me." She blinked the tears from her eyes. "I was too weak to stop them."

He nodded and tilted his head to his side.

She took the invitation and crawled over to him, feeling safer when he wrapped a strong arm around her trembling shoulders. Heat leaked from him like a fire. It chased the chill of the nightmare from her bones.

Neither of them spoke for a long time.

"Seán is angry at you."

"I know, but I can't tell you who they are. I won't break that promise."

Conor didn't look away from the knife as he said, "You made promises to us as well."

"Trust me," she implored.

"We do, but trusting a stranger now, after everything..." Conor trailed off, swallowing. "We've all lost people, Rua." He had had two sisters, and he had joined the Hounds after their parents had died, trying to keep a roof over their heads and food in their bellies. When he saw what the Hounds were doing, evicting starving families, burning their homes and refusing to give them aid, he had deserted. When they found him, his sisters were killed as punishment. "Trust is as rare as food these days."

He carried the guilt like armour.

If Rua had a death wish, Conor was the walking dead.

She nodded because she understood even if she didn't agree with him. "I can't tell you and I won't tell you. I made promises to them as much as I made promises to you. They'd be killed if they were found out."

He nodded and wiped the blade until it shone. When he pressed his thumb to the tip, a plume of crimson appeared. "One day, they'll have to choose a side."

"One day they will."

Conor nodded and rubbed soothing circles into her shoulder, an apology for asking and comfort for the nightmare. Stubble lined his jaw and the dark bags under his eyes made him older than twenty-three.

"You need to shave."

A small smile crept over his lips, lighting up his pale face.

"Do you ever wish we could do more?"

"We do what we can." The words fell from his mouth like rusty nails. "We have to keep them safe."

She nodded, but the guilt at not mentioning the Síochain's

attention weighed like a heavy chain around her neck. She knew it was better this way; they were already carrying so much, she would bear a little more if it eased their suffering.

***

The twins were packing their bags when Rua finally decided to face the day. Their mother had trained Oisín in healing while their father taught Aoife how to protect her sensitive brother. Now, they travelled the county and tried to help any way they could.

"Leave me alone," Aoife sniped at Seán with bared teeth.

Oisín shook his head, but an amused grin shaped his lips. "Can we go?" He stood up, hanging his bag off his shoulder. "We'll be back tomorrow or the next day," he said to Rua. "I've a couple of people I need to revisit."

Rua nodded, pulling her jumper tighter around her to fight off the chill. "You've enough food?"

"More than enough."

"I'm just saying if you packed the bag differently, you'd have more space," Seán said.

"I swear if you don't back up I'm going to stab you." Aoife whipped out a knife and swung it around. "Leave it."

Seán snorted. "I'm only trying to help."

"I packed the way you suggested and it helped," Oisín said, ever the peacemaker.

Seán grinned. "Oisín thinks it's better."

"*In ainm Dé!* Let's go. We'll be back tomorrow. If we don't come back, assume we're dead... Or he found a new patient," she added with a shrug.

Oisín laughed at her dramatics, and when she and Seán were distracted by each other, whispered to Rua, "Seán's still angry."

"Conor mentioned." She didn't roll her eyes, because she knew his concerns were valid, but she wanted to.

75

He nodded and went back to join his sister.

"Be careful," Seán said. "*Slán a* Aoife."

"Yeah, bye."

They disappeared into the forest, making sure to leave the ground as undisturbed as possible. Frost made the edges of the leaves glitter in the weak sunlight. Her breath mushroomed out, raising above her and fading into nothingness. Birds chirped and leaves rustled and the wind hummed and the world was so *alive, alive, alive.*

Rua felt like a ghost haunting the woods.

"She doesn't like him leaving the camp," Seán said after they had disappeared into the trees. "It's dangerous on the road. Being around people you don't know."

Rua gritted her teeth. "I know them. I know my friend."

"Well, you know us better. Maybe you should trust us like you trust them."

"They don't know who you are, Seán," she growled. "I would never tell them that."

Seán took a step back and held up his hands. "Fine. Fine. I'm only trying to help."

"By convincing me no one is to be trusted? I won't look at the world that way. I won't."

Seán scrunched his eyebrows together. "That's not what I want, Rua. I know that's not who you are but you keep making these decisions for us, big decisions, and we have no input. It's not how this is meant to go. We can't help people if only one person's point of view is being listened to."

"But we are helping people." Rua stepped back and leaned against the cool bark of a tree. "Seán, I need to protect my friend. Same as I need to protect you."

He stepped forward and cuffed her gently on the head. "You have to let us protect you back sometimes. You can't hold the world on your shoulders all the time."

She nodded but didn't reply.

As if knowing he wasn't gonna get anything else out of her, Seán said, "Is it not better if she brings more food? Oisín says she ends up giving most of it to the families anyway."

Rua smiled at that. Aoife would hate them knowing, and Oisín probably told Seán after one of Aoife's particularly caustic moods. "I'm sure next time when she sees how much Oisín has, she'll want to do it too."

Seán nodded, "There's some jobs need doing if you want to help."

Rua agreed and followed Seán through their camp.

# CHAPTER FOURTEEN
## RUA

Hours later, she stalked through the trees, wrapped in her darkest clothes with a hood hiding her bright hair. Dinner sat heavy in her stomach, eaten late because she knew she would need the energy. She moved through the roots and leaves and branches, climbing higher and higher up the mountain. The moon illuminated her in cold, white light and the deathly silence surrounded her.

The quiet of a forest at night was nothing like the silence of a funeral.

Rua knew both intimately.

The quiet of a funeral shaped itself like an absence, a void too big to fill. That silence wrapped itself around you and made you silent as well, inky black poison flowing down your throat until you were suffocating, unable to make a noise. The silence of funerals left a mark, stealing a little more of your voice each time.

She liked that the forest never really fell silent.

The sound of nature just became softer in the darkness. Owls and wolves called out, far enough away she didn't have to worry. Her boots found all the softest footfalls so she made no sound as she moved through the night like a wraith promising death. Sometimes she thought the quiet promised safety, and other times, it felt like a warning. Tonight, it felt like danger waited in every shadow and each echoing call of an animal.

She broke through the trees and there he was.

He sat by the water, skimming stones across the surface. The lake reflected the sky in an endless mirror. It seemed to Rua that with the wrong step, she would fall off the earth and drown in the stars. Trees whispered among themselves. The boulder where they met sat far enough from the shrubbery that no one could hide and listen. After the rain, the moon shone bright and his burgundy cloak looked as soft as a kiss.

This had been her place first, her and Saoirse. Their house still existed, just five miles in the other direction. Even if all that remained of her family home were three broken walls and a collapsing, burnt roof. The Síochain didn't care that they had been two children who had just buried their parents. They paid the rent, or they left. Burnt out from the home they were born in, lived in, lost their parents in.

They forced her to the workhouse, and killed her sister.

Rua swallowed the burning rage with easy practice. "Mouse."

"Hello, Red."

They had met in Scíth. She had tried to pickpocket him during one of her more desperate times. He had trapped her fingers in his and pulled her between two cottages. She had been sure he would kill her, but something had caught his imagination, and they had formed an uneasy alliance. They were friends now. Mostly. She had known him longer than anyone but Conor. It was hard to be friends with someone who supported the Síochain but he had earned her trust over and over again. She knew the others wanted to know who he was, but she had made him a promise, and she would keep his identity secret.

They were her family, but he was her family too.

He had his hood up, hiding most of his face. Only his

amused smile remained visible. "Terrible news about all the food being stolen."

"I, for one, am shocked."

She sat on a boulder and rooted through the stones lining the lake for the perfect skimming stone. The water lapped at the shore with the hush of a whisper. She and Saoirse used to come up here, spend the night. Swim in the water in the heat of summer. Eat food her mother had packed. Stare at the stars and make plans for the future.

"Nothing but *fealltóirí*."

He tilted his head.

"Traitors," she translated.

"Ah, yes. Such terrible *fealltóirí*."

She rolled her eyes at his awful pronunciation. "What do you think the Síochain knows?"

"Nothing that he's sharing with me but he does know something." Education made his words smoother than hers would ever be, closer to the stones they were skimming. "There's a new woman in the house. Older, but she watches everything." He dropped the pebble, obviously deciding it wasn't any use, and hunched down searching for a better one. "Some of the Hounds were talking about him leaving and arriving back with her and someone else but when I asked him he said they were new kitchen staff. Which is ridiculous because he would never go get new kitchen staff himself, but I couldn't push him on it." He glanced up. "Oh, and there was an assassination attempt on him."

Rua startled, suddenly hopeful. "And?"

"It failed."

"Not even a little stabbing?"

"No stabbing at all."

"Of course," she said, tiredly. "Do they know who it was?"

He skimmed his newly chosen rock across the water. Ripples interrupted the tunnel of moonlight. "No, but there was an attempted uprising in Farraige. They all died before you ask." He watched as her stone jumped eight times before disappearing into the dark. "How are you so good at that?"

"My father taught me and my sister before he passed. Before she passed. Before everyone passed." She picked up another rock, so smooth it almost felt soft, and turned it over and over in her fingers. "So nothing has changed and we continue to starve."

He came to sit beside her, heat reminding her how cold it made her to talk of her family. "There's a shipment coming in the day after tomorrow. I found out today."

"Earlier than usual?"

He grinned. "These are emergency supplies. You stole the last one." Pride shaped the words. "It arrives before dawn." He handed her a piece of paper, lined with place names and vantage points. "This is the route."

She nodded, examining the paper. "They'll know what to do. Will this lead back to you?"

"I'm careful."

"So you always say, but the Síochain is not a kind man. He won't hesitate to kill you."

"He is not all you think he is. There is more to him than this famine."

She pushed him off the boulder. He landed on the shore with a thump. "There is nothing more than this famine. There is nothing but the death they allow to continue. Remember that."

He stayed on the ground, knees up but loose, arms hanging over them. "I'm sorry."

"One day, you'll have to choose a side." She ignored his worthless apology, knowing it wasn't for tonight, but for all of the trouble the Síochain had rained down on them. "You know that, right?"

"One day is not today though."

She snorted. "Go to bed, Mouse. Before someone misses you."

He stood, wiping down his thick cloak and expensive clothes. He leaned over her and kissed her forehead. She got a whiff of red wine and musk before he pulled away. "Be careful, Red. Something is coming, and I don't know if I'll be able to protect you from it."

She snorted. "I've never needed your protection. I've nothing to lose. Not anymore."

He considered her for a long moment, eyes hidden in the darkness of that damn cloak. She hated not being able to read the expressions on his face. It was safer this way though; anyone passing by would assume they were lovers with disapproving parents. Not that there was anyone left to care. Not anymore. Not for so many people.

"Rua," he said her name so quietly, it traced across her skin like a secret. "You are something I would cry to lose. There are many people who feel the same. Try to remember that when you jump into your next fight."

She couldn't bear the pain lacing his words. "I'll be careful," she finally replied, but he had already melted back into the darkness. Like he already knew her response would be something he didn't want to hear.

She was glad. She had never lied to him and she didn't want to start tonight.

Not when she had another robbery to plan.

# CHAPTER FIFTEEN
## WOLF

The ditch smelled of damp earth and the cold bite of winter. She lowered herself down, managing to lodge herself onto a dirt shelf slightly off the ground, still covered but not sitting in dirty water. She had slept in worse places, but not by much. She just hoped the informant had done his job and passed on the information about the delivery. This was the only place along the route she had chosen that would allow them the chance to rob the food. All she could do now was wait. She wiped a spider off her shoulder, wrapped the cape she had stolen from a Hound around her, and slept in twenty minute naps.

The thieves arrived an hour before dawn. Four of them.

The night spilled across the horizon like ink running off wet paper. Darkness still held them in its grip and they cast long shadows while they worked. She watched, hidden from view, as they poured two lines of oil on the road about fifteen metres apart. Not a bad way to trap and confuse the Hounds. They hid in the ditches around the road, far enough away from Wolf that she wouldn't be discovered but she could easily watch.

Expectation pulled the night taut.

When the grind of the cart erupted over the quiet, Wolf ached for a fight.

The noise of the marching Hounds echoed loudly. The Síochain had done what he had promised. She could hear at least twenty people marching along the earth beaten road. They appeared above her and then past, walking straight into the thieves' trap.

A whoosh of fire illuminated the night. The woman from the market stepped forward.

"*Mo chairde*, we can take this from you easy, or we can take it from you at the end of the sword."

A ripple of laughter flowed through the group. "All by yourself?"

She shrugged; she looked fierce in the glow of the flames and Wolf was suddenly desperate to see her fight.

"As fun as that would be, I brought some friends." She twirled her sword as if testing the weight and asked again, "End of a sword, or will you allow us to take this food easily?"

The Hounds roared and attacked, swords glinting orange in the fire.

The clang of metal screamed out and the road devolved into a mess of shouts and grunts, dropping bodies and sarcastic comments. Wolf watched, studying each of the thieves' styles, noticing who'd trained properly and who'd learned from a hard life filled with violence. The two large men fought differently; the one with brown skin, dark hair and bulky muscle had clearly been a Hound, and the other, who fought with an axe, was all lean muscles and worker's hands. He had learned violence out of necessity.

Wolf realised suddenly that they weren't killing people, but knocking them out. The only blood being spilt was their own. A woman with dark skin fought with skill and speed, rarely staying in a spot for longer than a second. She would have made a great apprentice. They worked as a unit, fighting individually, but always making sure no one struggled. The woman that Wolf had spoken to jumped from fight to fight, barely protecting her own back to make sure the others were covered. Wolf wanted to shake her when she barely blocked a knife aimed at her gut.

Still though, with only four of them fighting, they were quickly becoming overwhelmed. They were too good to show their panic but it scented the cold night air. Mixed with the blood and dirt was the ripe stench of fear.

Wolf joined the fight in an explosion of movement, sneaking from behind them and attacking in a way that left the Hounds reeling. She didn't kill them, despite it going against every instinct she had. She incapacitated them, barely pausing as they fell before attacking the next one. The fire burned so hot, sweat rolled down her back.

"Who the hell are you?" The woman who could be an apprentice shouted as she battled off two at once.

Wolf didn't bother answering her.

She watched the woman from the market jump in between the bulky man and three Hounds. She helped drive them away from him without bothering to protect her back. A Hound snuck up on her, sword swinging. Wolf sprinted. She threw herself between the blade and the woman. She stopped the motion with two knives, allowing the weapon to get close enough to tear along her forearm, before kicking the Hound in the knee, and when he dropped, in the face.

"You need to watch your back," she grunted as the woman stared at Wolf, mouth slightly open.

"Where did you even…" She trailed off, dragged back in by another wave of attacks.

With Wolf at their side, the battle turned until only three Hounds were upright. They fought with the rage of failure, slashing and striking out, uncaring of injuring themselves. Wolf knocked out two, and the man with the axe got the third.

Heaving breaths and the copper scent of blood flooded the bright morning.

The fire burned itself out.

The man who had clearly been a Hound finally broke the silence. "That was a trap."

The woman from the market wiped sweat from her eyes. She closed her eyes and nodded, her mouth a defeated line. "They can't have known…" She stopped and studied Wolf. "Where did you come from?"

Wolf shrugged. "I've been sleeping in ditches, and after I stole a cloak from a Hound, I had to leave Scíth."

She took a step toward her. "You're bleeding."

"You're terrible at watching your own back."

"That's what I've been telling her for months. I'm Aoife." Her voice was hoarse from exertion and a cut wet her cheek. She bent over to clean her knives on the uniform of an unconscious Hound. "Seán, Conor, and you seem to know Rua."

The names were thrown out with a casual abandonment that made her jealous. "Didn't know her name."

She glanced over at the woman from the market, wanting to taste the shape of her name on her tongue. The woman's name was Rua, because *obviously* she had a name. Rua meant red so at least it matched her. Wolf wondered if her parents had caught sight of the red hair when she was born and changed whatever name they had chosen first.

"It's the second time I've saved her from Hounds." She startled when Rua's gentle fingers ghosted over her arm.

"Oisín will have to stitch this."

"Rua," Conor growled.

Rua glanced over to him, and they had a silent conversation with their eyes. Wolf guessed the gist of it; if this man had been a Hound, he certainly wouldn't be stupid enough to bring a stranger back to their camp.

"I'm fine. I don't really want to get mixed up in whatever—
" she gestured to the bodies on the ground, "—this is. I can find
someone on the road. There's rumour of a travelling doctor who
works for free. I'll search him out."

"Yeah, that's Oisín."

"Rua," Aoife snarled. "Stop. We don't know who this
person is."

"We know she can fight. We know she saved us."

"And why can she fight so well?" Seán ran his fingertips over
the blade of his axe as he spoke. He seemed unaffected by the
fight, more physically fit than the others, but his knuckles were
bruised and bloody. "How does she fight better than Conor?"

Wolf pulled herself onto the cart and rolled back her sleeve.
A long, harsh cut ran up the length of her forearm. She had
predicted the injury perfectly. It looked vicious but would heal
in a few days with some stitches. The easiest way to get people
to trust her was to appear weak and fragile. No danger here;
nothing but a poor, starving, orphan child. She grabbed a
moleskin of water off the back of the cart and washed her arm
down. Stealing a bottle from a small crate of whiskey, she poured
it over her arm, refusing to react to the sting.

The others watched her in silence.

"I trained with the Hounds. They taught me to fight. After
the great hunger stole everyone, I joined them, but burning the
homes of starving families wasn't for me. I deserted."

She watched as blood mixed with the water and whiskey,
turned pink, and then darkened again as it kept bleeding freely.
Out of the corner of her eye, she saw Rua having what seemed
to be some sort of conversation with Conor with just her
expressions. Curious but trying not to seem too interested, Wolf
rooted around in the stacks of food and found a long strip of
linen holding some jars tight together. She rinsed her arm again
and wrapped the linen around it, tight enough it stopped the

blood. She finished with a long drag of whiskey.

"Good luck with all of this." She jumped off the cart. "*Slán a* Rua."

She had barely made it a few steps up the road, heart thumping with the fear she had overplayed her hand and lost her chance, when Rua called out, "Wait."

# CHAPTER SIXTEEN
## RUA

Rua ignored how the others were glaring at her. The woman faced them slowly, shoulders not quite relaxed and one foot behind her like she was ready to run. She had a Hound's cloak wrapped around her, and looked dirtier than last time, more dishevelled. She had boots though, instead of bare feet, and more weapons. The cloak clearly wasn't the only thing she had stolen. She understood now why the woman had followed her; they were kindred spirits both trying to find a way to survive in a cruel world. She had probably seen Rua stealing from Hounds at the market and been interested. Most people didn't bother trying to take anything from a Hound. The way she had fought had been nothing short of beautiful. It made something ache in Rua's chest.

She pushed it away when the woman quirked an eyebrow.

"We steal the food to feed the hungry." She wanted her to understand. Not for her skills or her speed, but because of how she had looked in the rain while she played with her knife. "We don't kill them."

"You should."

Rua bit her lip. "You really believe that?"

"They would kill you given half a chance." She stood away from them, watching as the others tied up the Hounds and filled their bags with food. Seán calmed the horse, jittery and nervous even without the fire.

They hadn't had anywhere to hide Aurnia's cart, so they had to hope no one had noticed the procession in the early morning. If they timed it right, the nightwatch would have traded off with a new group of Hounds. Either way, they stripped off the recognisable tarp covering the food. Aoife retrieved the one they had hidden in the ditch and covered the food again. Threw an ugly blanket over the horse and chucked the expensive saddle marked with the Síochain's brand into a ditch. No one would buy it from them. They loaded wet but passable bales of hay on top of the cart. Enough that it would pass for a farmer's cart with market wares. Conor and Seán stripped out of their dark gear and into clothes more similar to the few farmers who remained. They removed most of their weapons, leaving only a hidden knife each.

The woman watched all this with quick, searching eyes.

Rua took a step closer, not missing how she tensed at the movement. "You've got no one?"

She shrugged as if it was unimportant. "What do you hope to achieve with all this?"

"Save some lives."

The woman laughed, although not a cruel sound. More disbelieving than hurtful. "So idealistic."

"You're not?" Annoyance bit at the words and she glanced away. The others were watching her. "Seán?"

He peered up from where he checked the Hounds for coins. "Not a lot here. Like they were warned."

"Trap," Conor said again.

Seán nodded. "We've still gotta go. I vote no."

Conor considered the woman in that piercing way of his. "Yes."

"Of course." Seán shook his head. "Let's get going. I'd rather not die today."

Conor took the reins and coaxed the jittery horse forward. They strolled away, not chatting but every bit a pair of farmers on the way to market.

Rua watched her.

She examined the blood staining the linen, but as if sensing Rua's attention, she said, "What do you want from me?"

"Join us." Rua kept her voice calm despite the sudden need to get to know this woman. "Fight with us."

"The only life I have ever protected is my own."

"And mine."

She tilted her head as if to acknowledge the point. "Die with you?"

"None of us are dying."

"So you say."

Rua huffed out an annoyed sigh. "Conor voted yes. Aoife, you get two votes. One each for you and Oisín."

"Can you climb?" Aoife asked. "Are you a good shot? Can you make arrows? Can you hunt?"

"Yes."

She tilted her head. "Which one is a yes?"

"All of them." She had no tells, no way for Rua to read her. "I also know which plants can be eaten, which are poisonous and which can make tea."

Aoife paused in packing her bag. "The Hounds teach you that?"

"An old woman I knew." A bitterness weighed down the words until they sunk heavily to the ground and shattered. *"Ba gheall le mathair dom í."* She was like a mother to me.

The use of the old language gave Aoife pause. The Table had banned it, refused to have it spoken, and insisted on the language of their neighbours to increase Éirely's trading prospects. It was a lie though; the poorer in the country spoke and read in the old language. English meant no one could read anymore, move up their station, or question the laws being passed.

Speaking it now counted as an act of rebellion.

Aoife considered her. "She teach you that as well?"

The woman shrugged and took a swig of the whiskey stolen from the cart. She handed the bottle to Aoife when she gestured to it.

"She's like Conor, but crankier." Aoife took a long drag and wiped her mouth with the back of her hand. "I vote no. We can't bring home every lost stray you find. Even though she seems to be able to keep you alive." Aoife sighed. "But Oisín would vote yes. He has a soft spot for lost puppies."

"I am not a lost puppy."

"Sure you're not. Here," Aoife threw a bread roll at her. "Eat up, puppy."

When the woman reached for her knife, Rua stopped her with a hand on her wrist. "You'll get used to Aoife. She always knows exactly what to say."

Aoife crossed her arms. "As always, it comes down to our fearless leader."

Rua ignored her. "What do you want?"

The woman shrugged again. "I've been alone for a long time."

She didn't say it as a plea, or as a preference. She stated it simply as a fact.

"What's your name?"

Where before the woman had been nothing but a blank canvas, ready to create any emotion she thought Rua expected, the request for her name evoked something real in her eyes. Some pride and defiance Rua knew made up a key part of who this woman really was. Like she had earned this name, and no one would ever take it from her. Like saying it was the first time it had been uttered aloud. Like maybe Rua was blessed to be given the gift of a name.

"Wolf." The word was a full stop, and an explosion of possibilities across Rua's skin. "My name is Wolf."

Rua needed to know how many layers there were to this strange woman, needed to know if she could learn them all.

"I vote yes."

# CHAPTER SEVENTEEN
## WOLF

Amusingly, they blindfolded her.

They also turned her in circles as if to confuse her, except they were walking towards the sunrise and stayed on the road, so even if she hadn't already been to their camp, she would've figured it out. Rua held her uninjured arm, whispering directions as her thumb rubbed the inside of Wolf's wrist in the most distracting way. Wolf wasn't used to gentle touch. She certainly wasn't used to how she felt electrified with each sweep against the delicate skin.

They reached the forest quickly, and moved through the trees quietly, muck and leaves soft underfoot. Only the murmuring of whispered voices let her know where the others were placed around her. They hadn't taken her weapons or bound her hands. Not that either of those actions would've stopped her from winning a fight, but the simple *trust* in the action made her skin itch. It seemed impossible that the same people responsible for disobeying the Table were also willing to lead a stranger to their camp with no bindings.

The whispering around her faded away.

"I need you to lie down on your stomach and pull yourself forward with your arms." Rua's breath tickled Wolf's ear.

"If you take the blindfold off, it'll make it easier," Wolf said.

Aoife snorted. "That'd ruin the surprise. Rua likes watching our faces. It's the only reason she even has you blindfolded."

A flare of annoyance burned through Wolf. She wanted to sit them down and explain how dangerous it was to bring a stranger back to their camp, and how blindfolding them should be the minimum requirement, and not an entertainment for Rua.

Rua stood too close when she said, "Don't lift your head too much."

Wolf nodded, smug at already recognising them by voice alone, and allowed Rua to help her kneel and then lie. As she moved forward, the light dimmed. The air tasted of dust and cold stone and smelled damp, reminding her of the convent. It was obvious when she pulled herself free because the air warmed and the others chatted around her.

"Can I take this off now?" She didn't move her hands. She had known too many punishments because she had moved sooner than allowed.

"No."

"Aoife, shut up," Rua snapped. "We already voted. You can take it off."

Ignoring the bickering, Wolf untied the blindfold and gaped in surprise at the cave she found herself in. Beaten earth beneath her didn't take away from the richness of the place; this was a home, one born of grief and love. The walls went up and up and up. She found herself craning her neck to see how far they reached above her but all she could see was the darkness above that echoed with their voices. Piles of blankets added a mixture of colour to the brown staining the space. Candles were spaced out, throwing flickering light over their staring faces. Portraits covered one wall. There were more caves leading off the room.

Wolf swallowed away a sudden, unexpected jealousy. They were her age, and yet they had all of this, while she had nothing but a cold room and the hope of a lonely freedom.

"There it is," Aoife muttered.

For the first time in a long time, Wolf wondered what expression her face held.

She had the uncontrollable urge to explore this wondrous place. Instead, she walked over to the pictures, examining the steady lines of Rua's face drawn in charcoal, until she got her emotions in check again. Nothing surprised her anymore. Rarely did she feel anything other than fear, relief, and a cocky smugness, but now she was almost overwhelmed by the emotions that had been dragged free from the dark corner she had shoved them long before.

When she felt steady enough to talk without the needy *want* showing, she said, "This place is…"

"We know," Aoife smirked. "Let him stitch you up."

A man pushed himself off the wall and walked over to her, almost identical to Aoife in his golden eyes, the amused curve of his mouth, and his dark skin.

"I'm Oisín." He spoke softly but with clear authority. "Can I check that out?"

She nodded, unwrapping the linen and holding it out to him. "It's barely a scratch."

He too touched her like she was delicate, a stark contrast to the nun who nursed their injuries in the convent. To be injured meant you'd failed and they were ruthless in letting you know how much failure hurt. Wolf had developed a higher than normal level of pain tolerance because she had no natural talent for close combat axe fighting, finding the weapon too heavy and wieldy in comparison to a knife or a sword. She had spent a lot of time that summer in the infirmary. She had eventually mastered it in the same way she mastered everything else; with gritted teeth and a dogged determination.

A scraping noise by the entrance had her standing in front of the boy, knife already drawn, but she relaxed when Seán and

Conor pulled themselves into the cave, nodding hello and rubbing dirt off their clothes. She put her dagger away. Aoife watched her with assessing eyes she didn't like so she turned back to Oisín who had a slight crinkle between his eyebrows. Wolf wasn't entirely sure why she had stepped in front of him but the instinct made her skin tight.

Oisín smiled. "I'm going to have to clear this with alcohol and stitch it up."

"She already did that," Aoife interrupted. "Didn't even flinch."

Wolf shrugged. "Better clean than dead."

Oisín glanced up from his examination "Should that be the motto I use with my patients? Think they'll like it?"

She knew he was teasing her but it didn't feel like he meant it to be mean. It felt like maybe she had been invited into the joke. "They will if they have any brains left."

Seán snorted from the ground where he was wiping the blood off his knuckles. "The hunger stole most of them. All we have left are the fools too stupid to die."

"Like you?" Aoife smirked at his glare.

Rua added another pile of blankets to the wall. "Wolf, you can sleep there."

"I don't..." She jolted as Oisín poured alcohol down her arm, wiping the blood away as he did. "You couldn't have warned me?"

"It's better when you don't know pain is coming."

Wolf had never agreed with a sentence less. "Please warn me."

Oisín shrugged. "Aoife, clean off your cut."

Aoife picked a clean cloth from a pile by a bucket. She dabbed it with alcohol and winced when she pressed it on her cheek. "Happy?"

"Thrilled," Oisín grinned.

"I'll sleep outside," Wolf said to Rua.

Conor watched her, sturdy arms folded across a broad chest. Wolf didn't like how much his eyes noticed, how his expression showed the list he made of all her reactions and quirks.

"I don't sleep around other people."

Rua shrugged and said, "Well, you're welcome in here if you get cold."

"I'm starving." Conor trapped Wolf in his piercing gaze, brows furrowing as he tried to read her intentions from her face. She held herself blank and still, but he must have seen something because he nodded slightly to himself, before saying, "I'm going to check the traps and make food."

Wolf wondered if his exit was a show of trust or a test.

Oisín muttered, "Needle."

It broke her skin with a sharp, cold pain. She watched him as he studiously stitched up her torn skin, uncomfortable with a stranger working on her. She would have preferred to do it herself. Seán had sat down and was drawing, barely glancing up as he sketched. He already had a streak of charcoal across his forehead. Aoife watched Wolf's hands, eyes flicking between them and her brother continuously. Wolf thought she understood her a little better; protecting her brother would get Aoife on side the easiest.

Rua lay on a pile of blankets, face half buried in the covers, but her one visible eye watched as Oisín completed his work by wiping her skin clean with more alcohol and wrapping it up again.

"Tomorrow let some air get at it."

Wolf nodded. "I usually survive with less gentle treatment."

He shrugged. "Some people are shitty healers." He packed away his satchel and grinned at his sister. "Race you to the stream." Only his feet were visible by the time Aoife jumped up, shouting as she chased him.

"I'll show you around," Rua said, a sleepy smile tugging her lips up.

Seán snorted. "I'm going to check if breakfast is ready." He dropped the picture by a pile of blankets and left.

Wolf startled when she realised the portrait showed her being stitched up by Oisín; he had captured the harsh set of her mouth and the tension along her shoulders, had included her knives and the bloody gash in her arm. It was just a charcoal drawing, but it made her uncomfortable to see the parts of herself she thought she had hidden reflected in the thick lines and smudged shading.

"He's good, right?" Rua picked it up, glancing between it and Wolf. "We insisted he put the nails in to show off his drawings. Makes it more like a home." She pinned the picture onto a nail, ripping the top of the page to hold it in place and paused to make sure it hung straight when she took her hands down.

Wolf wanted to rip down this proof that she had existed in this place.

Rua smiled softly. "What was your home like?"

"Nothing like this."

Rua nodded. "Well, you're here now." She started undoing the bun holding her hair tight, loosening the plaits and dropping dried flakes of mud as she went. "I should really do this by the stream but it's giving me a headache. This is where we spend most evenings." She led them to a side cave and casually waved her hand. "Books. Table. Although oddly enough we never seem to use it. More blankets. Living in a cave gets cold. You're welcome to all of them. If you can't read, we can show you."

"I can."

"Great. Food is down there but no one but Seán touches it. Don't worry, he's a good cook. Washing is in there." She pointed to another small cavern. Two ropes stretched across it with damp clothes hanging from them. "We can't leave it outside because we have to keep this place hidden." She bit her lip, expression suddenly unsure. "You won't tell anyone, right? Because I voted to let you in and if anything happens to them…"

"Why did you let me come here?" Wolf couldn't help but ask. "If it is so important to you? You don't even know me."

Rua shrugged. "You've helped me twice now."

Wolf glared. "*In ainm Dé*, Rua, you can't just trust people. Do you know how dangerous that is?"

"Why don't you want me to trust you?" Rua watched her, examining every little movement Wolf made. Seeing Wolf.

She hated it. Hated being observed. "I'm fine with you trusting me. It's everyone else I have the problem with. The world isn't as kind as you think it is."

"And it's not as cruel as you think it is," Rua snapped back. She took a shuddering breath and threw her long hair over her shoulder. "Wolf, you're safe here. No one is coming for you. Trust us."

"I trust myself," Wolf replied, and then said quietly, "But I will keep this secret for you."

Wolf glanced around this cave, this home, and knew she would still give the Síochain his informant, but she would do everything she could to ensure this strange, safe place survived.

Even if its occupants didn't.

Something of what she felt must have shown on her face because the tension fell from Rua like rain off a leaf. "Okay, good. Let's go get food."

# CHAPTER EIGHTEEN
## RUA

T he next morning started as a foggy, damp complaint. Rua dragged herself from the cave, aching from the hard ground and tense from more nightmares. She stretched, shivering when her jumper rose. The chill fingers of winter scraped along her stomach before she managed to tuck it back into her trousers. The day before had been a waste of naps, eating and relaxing. Everyone had agreed to take it easy, tired from the early morning robbery. Wolf had shoved herself into a corner and spent the day reading and watching. Her eyes had felt like a trail of fire every time they had scorched over Rua's skin.

She didn't want to know what it meant.

In the weak morning light, Wolf sat at the fire with Conor. Neither spoke. Conor poked a stick into the fire pit, making smoke leak from the tunnel connected to it. Wolf sat with her back slumped and her hands resting in her lap; a posture designed to put the observer at ease, but something about the way her muscles were bunched up in her arms made Rua think of a rope pulled taut, ready to snap. When she got closer, Rua saw that Conor had Wolf's knives in his lap.

No wonder she was tense.

"I stole that one from a Hound about six months ago. That

one I got from my father." Wolf's voice sounded carefully blank. "Before he died, he gave it to me."

"What about your mother?" he asked.

Wolf shrugged. "Never knew her. Just my father."

Conor held up another knife. "This one?"

"A woman." She scratched the back of her head, but again, it seemed like a carefully decided gesture rather than an actual tic.

He nodded, eyes searching her expression and then skitting over her waiting body. "And the one up your sleeve?"

The muscles in her forearms tensed. "I earned it."

"How?"

Holding eye contact with Conor, she smirked, "How does one earn a knife?"

A bird chirped and neither broke the stare.

Sensing an argument, Rua sat down beside Wolf on the cold ground, making as much noise as possible. The tension broke like a hive of wasps exploding. She carefully ignored the hum of violence hanging between them and smiled as she accepted the bowl of porridge Conor handed her.

"Where are the others?"

"Seán went to check the traps. Aoife and Oisín had some herbs to gather for his bag." Conor stirred the pot. "I don't know if other people are eating all the rabbits, or if they've started dying out as well, but none of them are biting." He rooted into the fire pit and retrieved a warm roll. "Saved you this. Wolf has a tooth for bread."

Wolf shrugged, gathering up her knives from Conor and pinning them back onto her body. "They said you'd want to take me to meet Aurnia. Again."

"Oh yeah, she'll want to assess you." That day in the rain flashed through Rua's mind, stark and crisp. She thought maybe she wanted to hold Wolf's hand again. "Make sure you actually bring something to her family of orphans."

"Family?" The word fell from Wolf's lips like something foreign and unknown. "You just steal food together. You're not even blood related."

Rua laughed. "Don't say that to Aurnia. She believes in finding your own family more than she believes in her inn. We can go if you're ready?"

Conor took the bowls to clean. "Wolf. Keep an eye on Rua."

Wolf nodded, jerky and unsure.

Rua started to say she had long taken care of herself, but he had already walked away.

They strolled to Scíth cloaked in a silence Rua was unsure how to break. When the town finally appeared, relief tore across her skin. They made their way through the streets in silence and pushed their way into the inn. People packed every corner of the pub; they had to when the weather made it impossible to stay outside without dying. Groups of starving children were hunched around the fire, empty soup bowls in their laps as an old woman told them stories of times before the famine. Rua realised with an uncomfortable jolt that most of these children would have only known starvation. Death was so familiar to them as to be a member of their ever shrinking families. She fought her way through the crowds with a lump in her throat.

Aurnia greeted them with a smile and followed them through to the back. She leaned against the table and watched as Wolf studied the room. "I figured you two would end up friends."

Rua quirked an eyebrow.

"Oh please, Frank sang your praises for days."

A heavy weight settled in her gut. "Sang?"

"Got word this morning. Him and his wife. They'd managed to raise enough money for his sons to leave but the Síochain took it from them as back pay on the rent." She delivered the news in a flat voice that belied how much she felt. "It broke what little spirit they had left."

"His sons?"

"Sent to work on the famine roads."

Rua kicked a chair. *"A dhiabhal, cén fáth?"* Damn it, why?

"Punishment," Aurnia replied, crossing her arms.

"You mean those roads that people work on for food?" Wolf stood in front of the fire, stealing heat after the cold walk. "What's wrong with them?"

Rua stared at Wolf, unsure if she was being purposely obtuse. "Are you messing?"

"The point of them is to allow people to work and earn what they deserve." She spoke slowly as if explaining something to a stupid person. "What's wrong with that?"

Rua snorted. "You don't earn the right to stay alive. The Table has a duty to its citizens to protect them and feed them. Endless work is just another tool they use to control us. Those roads are an insult, and just like this damn famine, they've no end in sight. They just build and build to nowhere."

Wolf scratched the back of her neck, uncomfortable.

Rua wasn't sure if she actually felt uncomfortable, or was faking it. Even barely knowing her, Rua got the impression that Wolf rarely did things without purpose. Even something as simple as scratching her neck.

Wolf said quietly, "I never thought of it like that."

Aurnia smirked, glancing between them. "Well, aren't you two fun to be around."

Rua blushed, and hated herself for it. Like what she felt had scrawled itself across her skin for anyone to read. "She saved us yesterday. We voted her in."

"She's injured."

Wolf waved off her concerned hand. "It's nothing. Barely a scratch."

"She might have stopped me from getting a little stabbed."

Aurnia smirked. "I like her already."

"I have a name."

"Oh yes, and what would that be?" Aurnia's sharp eyes studied her, cataloguing parts of her Rua wouldn't have even known to seek out.

"Wolf." Again that pride and defiance.

"And where did you get that name?"

"Where does anyone get a name?"

"I chose mine when I didn't want to be who I used to be."

"You chose yours?" Wolf stumbled over the words and this time Rua didn't think it was an act.

"Matched my eyes." Aurnia. *Golden lady.*

Rua glanced between the two and realised that Aurnia had already started getting to know Wolf. She had seen through her act even quicker than Rua had.

Interrupting the glaring, Rua said, "Is there anything for me?"

She didn't expect a message since she had only just met with Mouse. Neither of them liked to risk Tadgh, a Hound at the Síochain's estate who had trained with Conor, and helped Mouse slip the notes out to Rua when they turned up in his bunk. He didn't know who her friend was either but he agreed to help because of what Conor meant to him.

Aurnia finally let Wolf free of her predator's gaze and smiled softly at Rua. "A note," she said, shocking Rua a little. "Our messenger said he won't be able to get away as much because of recent happenings. Try to get what you can next time you see your friend."

Rua wanted to ask for clarification, but if Aurnia didn't trust Wolf yet, then she would wait. "I'll read it here. Are you going out to the yard?"

Aurnia's eyes roamed over Wolf again. "I've got to check if this one is of any use to you."

With one last look at Rua, Wolf followed Aurnia.

Rua sat in front of the fire and studied the coded letter. Hastily written, it had none of the usual neat curves and artistry of his other notes. She knew he just did it to show off his skill with the ink.

Two scant lines stared up at her.

Recognising the usual opening line, even when encoded, meant the entire message had only three words. Chewing her lip, she let worry eat into her gut for a short moment and got to work. She had just figured out the first word when Muire brought her a pint of beer in a heavy metal tankard which stole the remaining chill the fire had failed to take.

Muire kissed her forehead and patted down her wild hair. "Don't work too hard, *mo stór*."

"I won't." Rua relaxed into the casual affection. "How are they getting on?"

"Beating the shite out of each other. Aurnia seems to be enjoying it though." A shout called from the tavern. "Better get back." Muire squeezed her shoulder on the way out.

It didn't take Rua long to figure out the message.

*Meet me tonight.*

A ripple of shock shuddered up her spine. They rarely met. Most of the information was passed along in letters that arrived *mysteriously* in Tadgh's bunk and were delivered when he had a day off. It was only when Mouse had something truly important to tell her that he insisted they meet.

Something must be wrong, and she would find out tonight.

# CHAPTER NINETEEN
## WOLF

Wolf wanted to stay with Rua, but since she didn't like that impulse, and didn't like that she had even had it in the first place, she pushed the urge away and followed Aurnia into a fenced area in front of the stables. She climbed in and paced it to get a feel for the space.

Hard earth beneath her had no grip and would be painful if she fell. Not that she planned to fall. The heavy cloud cover meant there would be no sun to be aware of, but also no way to use it to blind her opponent. The air burned on each inhale; cold as an icy lake. It would be uncomfortable but wouldn't slow her down. She would have enough room to manoeuvre; the size of the ring was similar enough to the one she sparred in at the convent. Sleeping on the ground the last two nights had left her aching, but she had fought in worse conditions, and today she had a belly full of food which wasn't always guaranteed with the nuns. The only thing she couldn't prepare for was Aurnia.

The woman moved around the space with confidence. She folded her body into a deep stretch that belied the strength of the muscles lining her back and shoulders. Every inch of her spoke of control and purpose. Wolf felt a lick of nerves. She pushed it aside, useless and unneeded.

"Usually we train the horses here, or give them a chance to rest before we lock them in for the night." She stretched her arms above her head, pulling her body taut. "I use it for sparring too with Muire. Trained Rua and some of the others here."

Wolf felt Aurnia's eyes on her as she fell into her own stretches. She already disliked how much Aurnia *saw* and she had only been around her for a few minutes. "What do you train them in?"

"Everything."

When Wolf lowered her arms, Aurnia tossed her a pole made of smooth wood that was about six feet long. Dents gouged the surface, and Wolf learned why when Aurnia attacked her with a speed that was startling. They clashed and the impact shuddered through her arms.

Aurnia grinned when she managed to block. "Good. Rules are simple. Point is a tap to the chest. No hitting the face. Anything else goes. First to ten."

They fought viciously, neither willing to give ground.

Wolf hadn't been challenged like this since the morning before she went to the Síochain's estate. Aurnia moved lightning quick and with ease around the small space, catching gaps Wolf hadn't realised she had left. Each time she got close, Wolf learned and didn't make the same mistake again, adaptive and slick. The clash of the wood again and again shouted through the yard, mixed with the keening of horses and the rumble of conversation from the street. The muscles in her arms were shivering and exhausted by the time Aurnia struck her for the tenth time.

"Good," she said, taking the pole from Wolf, barely sweating. More glowing. "You did good. No one has gotten six hits before." Aurnia considered her. "Who trained you?"

Wolf wiped a shaking hand over her sweaty face. Her arms ached, almost refusing to lift and her heart pounded so fast, it made her fingers tingle.

"My father started training me at three."

She hadn't known that was true until the words fell from her lips. It shifted her foundation slightly to know she had memories hidden somewhere she couldn't access.

"And then?"

"Hounds. The road. Life." She shrugged. "Who trained you?"

This innkeeper had secrets. She shouldn't have been able to best Wolf.

Aurnia smirked. "Hounds. The road. Life." She threw a water pouch at her. "Drink this and we'll move onto swordplay."

Two hours later, Aurnia finally called quits. Sweat poured down Wolf's back and she ached in an almost primal way. The juddering of her knees forced her to sit down in the dirt and rest her head between her knees. She felt like throwing up. Training with Aurnia was almost more challenging than the tests she had taken at the convent.

Wolf wanted to do it every day.

"Your girl is good." Aurnia didn't even sound tired.

When Wolf glanced up, Rua shone as red as her hair. "She's not mine."

"Take her home. Let her get some rest."

Wolf watched Aurnia climb over the fence and called, "When can I come back?"

"Whenever you can raise your hands over your head again," she replied, not bothering to turn back around. Her quiet laughter chased itself around the empty yard.

Rua bent down and stepped between two bars before sitting in front of her. "No one's lasted as long as you have. My first time I failed out in under fifteen minutes."

This didn't comfort Wolf; she had seen Rua fight. "How'd Conor do?"

"Three hits off the pole." Rua sounded as proud as anything. "He lasted about an hour."

Wolf nodded, relieved. At least she had beaten him.

"How many hits off the pole did you manage?"

"Six," Wolf muttered, embarrassed and disappointed. She hadn't scored so low since she was much younger.

"Six? That's incredible." She pulled her crimson hair down and ran a hand through the shining strands.

Wolf suddenly wanted to touch it. She shoved her hands in her pockets. "Not good enough."

"Don't worry, it gets easier."

Wolf bit her lip, purposely innocent. "Who sent you the letter?"

"No one important. Just an old friend." She stood and held her hand out to Wolf. "We should get back."

Disappointed, but not really expecting anything more, she nodded and took the gestured hand, allowing Rua to pull her up. When Rua let go, she fisted her fingers to try and rid the tingling from them.

"I hope there's food ready. I'm starving." Rua climbed through the fence, waiting for Wolf to force her aching body through. "Let's go home."

Wolf scoffed.

She still couldn't believe that with *one vote* they were just letting her walk to and from their camp without being blindfolded. She had already memorised the route. Now, Rua was just inviting her to refer to that place as her... She had never had a home and this cave full of rebels suddenly wasn't going to become one.

"Home, sure."

Rua gave her a searing look but didn't say anything more. Wolf shook her head and followed her across the yard. Rua didn't know what she offered with words like *home* and *family*, because if she did, she would know it was nothing but a lie to comfort small children afraid of the dark.

Wolf had stopped fearing the dark after the fifth test.

# CHAPTER TWENTY
## RUA

With no moon to shed light, darkness settled over the lake.

He stood with his burgundy cape flowing around him in the gentle breeze. Something caught in her throat watching him; so young, and yet, he still held an innate power he had been born into. Sometimes she wondered what that would be like, knowing each decision you made was correct, because your father made the same one, and your father's father, and on and on forever.

Rua's mother had been a pickpocket before she met Rua's father. They had settled on his small patch of land to grow food and a family, but her mam had known that bad times would always come knocking, so she taught both her daughters to steal. She had always said taking from those with too much wasn't even really stealing, it was just making sure everyone got their fair share.

She wondered which was her real, true path. The stealing or the growing. The law breaking or the law keeping. Rua was talented at both. The adrenaline of a job or the simple joy of watching crops grow strong. She shook the thoughts from her head and watched him, cautiously. There were no skimming stones this time. Tension changed the lines of his face into something harsh. He bit a hangnail, contemplating something in the distance.

"Mouse?"

"Do you remember the first time we met?"

Rua nodded, confused. "I tried to take your coin. You shoved me into a wall. You could've had me killed but you didn't." She still remembered the fear. She hadn't gotten caught in so long, she had grown cocky, arrogant. Her mother would've killed her if she knew Rua had tried to rob from someone in the Síochain's colours. "Why didn't you?"

"You weren't scared." He still wouldn't meet her eyes. Shame sat awkwardly on a face that was unused to the shape of the emotion. "At least not enough that it showed on your face. You just bared your teeth at me as if daring me to do my worst."

Those had been the darkest days; the loss of her family still raw, and the guilt at making Saoirse go to the workhouse roaring like an unmanageable beast in her chest. It made her reckless, and destructive. Only Conor's stubbornness had kept her alive.

"I'd lost a lot by then."

"The Table doesn't care about ending the famine."

The words made no sense and she scoffed, "They can't control the potato blight."

As much as she hated them, even she accepted that much. No one would allow it to continue, not if they had the resources to end it. They were selfish with food, keeping it for themselves, but they weren't responsible for the blight.

"He has a barn. Full of food. Enough to feed the county through the winter." The clipped sentences were like splinters shoved into soft skin. "They all do, every county, and the Table has instructed the Síochains not to distribute it until the attacks around the country have calmed down. As a form of punishment." His voice cracked and anger radiated off him. "They are sending more food off this island than at any other time in the history of our damn country, lining their pockets, planning for the Masquerade Ball, all the while allowing people to die." He ran a shaking hand through his hair, and finally glanced at her. "They're allowing them to starve, Rua."

A throbbing lanced through her jaw. She forced herself to stop clenching it. "I don't understand." She took a step away from him. "They're punishing us?"

"And the Síochain, he agrees with them. The attempt on his life, the attack in Farraige, and now some ruckus in Seanchaí. He thinks the people need to *learn*," he spat the word out, disgust saturating it, "who is in charge and who provides them with a living."

"I..." Words wouldn't come. She grabbed a handful of stones and threw them into the lake, screaming. "That bastard."

The children huddled around Aurnia's fire, the skeletal bodies and hacking coughs, the dead falling to a resting place at the side of the roads and left to be eaten by crows, her family haunting her sleep. She screamed again.

"I'm going to kill him." She knew she meant it. She had never wanted to hurt anyone before but she would kill him.

He stared at her, worry and anger battling across his face. They stood in silence for a few minutes. She stared out at the lake, mirror-like and reflecting the waning moon. She thought suddenly of Wolf who acted so uncaring about death. Maybe she would help her kill the Síochain. Rid them of him.

The blood of her people drenched the land, and she would avenge them all.

"What are you going to do?"

Anger roiled like a storm in her gut. "I'm going to steal as much food from that barn as I can. Then I'm going to kill him."

He didn't reply.

"You can't still think there's more to him than this," she bit the words out, sharp as daggers.

He sounded exhausted when he said, "I don't know how they can all be so blind. The Table. The Síochains. If they just fed the people, all of this would stop." A quiet ache laced the words; privilege finally waking up to acknowledge the world as it had always been. "I tried explaining it to him, but he just kept saying how there had to be order. Had to be respect. If the people had forgotten who was ruling them, then we had to remind them." He sank down onto the boulder, cradling his head in his hands.

She threaded her fingers through his hair and tried not to be frustrated by his wilful ignorance. She knew his failings when she agreed to his friendship. "I know you didn't want it to come to this."

"It came to this a long time ago. I just didn't want to see it." He pulled his head free and rooted through his pockets, handing her a rolled up scroll. "This is everything I know about the barn. Where it's located, how many guards it has, when the food is delivered." He stood up, towering over her again. "I'm sorry, Red. I never thought they'd do something like this. He'd do *this*. I'll help any way I can."

She thought for a moment. "I need you to act like everything is the same. The information you get us, it's not something we'd get without you." She hugged him. "We'll fix this. All of us. We'll fix this."

"Stay safe."

She grinned. "I always do."

She pulled him back onto the boulder and they sat together for far longer than they usually would, searching for a comfort neither of them could provide. When they finally left each other, they still hadn't spoken, but neither of them could even drum up a goodbye. It was only after she left that she realised she had never mentioned the trap at the last robbery, had never even thought to ask him about it.

\*\*\*

Wolf sat at the fire pit when she got back to camp. Exhaustion sat heavy on Rua's shoulders, weightier than the simple hike should've caused.

She sat beside her before asking, "What are you doing awake?"

Wolf held up a dead rabbit. "Seán kept complaining he was sick of vegetables so…"

"That's surprisingly nice of you."

"I'm also sick of no meat."

Rua laughed and rubbed a hand down her face. "I'm so tired, Wolf. I never meant for it to be like this. I just wanted some food. I was so hungry all the time, and Conor did his best, but the land wouldn't give us what we needed. I never meant to start all this trouble for everyone."

Wolf cocked her head, listening without taking her attention away from the rabbit. "What did you want?"

"To avenge my sister."

"How were you going to do that?" She sliced the skin from the rabbit's knees and started pulling it away from the body.

Rua watched as it tore free from muscle, spatters of blood landing on the ground. "Before, I didn't know. I just needed to survive. I was nearly dead when Conor found me."

"Too stubborn to die?"

"Something like that."

Wolf laid the body flat and carved the skin from the stomach. She did it quickly, clearly practised. Sitting next to her, the sun creeping over the horizon and the methodical movements of her knife, eased the knot in Rua's throat. Wolf glanced up, clearly wanting Rua to continue her story.

"Aurnia says I avenge her every time I save another person who would've died without the food I steal. She says I'm honouring all of them."

Wolf finished the work and tied the body up on a branch by her head to drain the blood. She caught it in a bucket by her knee. Rua watched her wash the blood from her hands with water from a pouch. When she finished, she pressed into Rua's side, a line of heat that did nothing to remove the cold of the night's revelations.

"Do you agree?" Wolf finally asked when her hands were dry and tucked into her sleeves.

Softness draped around her like a cloak in the weak light. She wanted to wrap Wolf in her arms and keep her safe from everything the world had already thrown at her. She hated having to tell her the truth, to tell her that all she had lost was for nothing.

"I did when I thought the famine was bad luck."

Wolf stilled. "It's not?"

Rua shook her head, tears filling her eyes, and she let them fall, releasing some of the pressure in her chest. "They could stop it but they're too busy getting rich from it. Too busy lining their damn pockets."

Wolf sat frozen. "The blight?"

"Oh, that's real enough," she said, voice thick. "It's just that they have enough food in other crops. Just not crops they're willing to share with us."

"Oh."

Rua nodded. "I need to talk to Aurnia about this, to the others."

"This is going to…" Wolf stopped hesitant. "They're going to want to go to war over this."

"Don't you?"

Wolf stared at the blood dribbling into the bucket, a constant *plink plink plink*. "All I've ever wanted is to be free from them, from everyone."

Rua didn't know who the *them* were but she knew one thing for certain. "You can't be free from everyone."

Furrowing her brows, she finally looked at Rua. "Why not?"

"Everyone needs someone, Wolf. Otherwise, what's the point to any of this?"

Wolf didn't reply but Rua thought maybe it was more confusion than stubbornness. She had told Rua she had been alone for a long time.

Rua could wait for her to figure it out.

# CHAPTER TWENTY-ONE
## RUA

The night morphed into day like the lighting of a fire; small sparks that grew and grew until searing light burned away the dark. Frost sharpened the grass into blades that crunched underfoot. Dew moistened her lips and layered her jumper in a sheen of water. The boiling, burning heat of her anger wouldn't settle. It scorched her skin and forced her to remember all she had lost. She couldn't shake it from her skin and bury it with all the other things she refused to think about.

She finally left Wolf's unshakeable presence to wake the others. "Get up. We need to talk."

Aoife stuck her head out from under her blankets. "What climbed up your arse?"

Rua ignored her, kicking the others gently to wake them up. They needed to learn the truth and decide what to do with the knowledge. The Table were too powerful to stop but maybe they could help a few people before they themselves were caught or killed.

Conor watched her from his bed. "You okay?"

She shook her head. "Get them up please? I'm going to get Seán down from watch."

It took another half an hour to get everyone sitting around the fire. Wolf handed out the stew she made, and seemed embarrassed about how excited they were about the rabbit. She waved off their thanks, and sat close to Rua, discomfort seeping from her like a bad smell.

Rua waited for them to finish eating before she started talking.

"My friend found out something." She opened her mouth again but the words didn't want to leave her mouth. She didn't even know how to form them. Staring around at their expectant faces, she swallowed audibly and found Wolf's eyes.

Wolf tilted her head, considering her, and Rua saw the moment she realised that Rua didn't know how to tell them. Wolf pushed her thigh into Rua's and started talking. "The Table are lying about how much food is available. They're exporting most of it, and if they were so inclined they could end the famine." Silence met her words. "In case you haven't noticed, they are not so inclined."

The whisper of wind through the leaves eased the shocked silence.

Conor shot to his feet, kicking dirt into the fire pit. "They killed my... They..." Violence threaded across his arms and shoulders. He ran his hands through his hair. "I can't..." He stormed off, disappearing into the forest. A muffled shout disturbed the birds in the trees.

Rua stared after him, "I'm going to tell Aurnia. Soon. Today. It's okay if you all need time to sort your heads out."

"I've to go to town as well," Oisín said, sounding distant. "It's market day and I need to visit the stalls."

Rua nodded but didn't speak. She watched the others as they processed what she had said. Only Wolf sat calm in the riotous storm. It brought Rua some comfort to know that even this couldn't shake her steady exterior.

Seán scrunched his hands into fists. "They can't just get away with this."

"No. They can't," Oisín replied. Aoife gripped his hand so hard his fingers were twisted together painfully. "What are we going to do?"

Wolf glanced at Rua. "Tell them."

"The Síochain has a barn full of food. My friend thinks there's probably enough to feed the county through the winter. We're going to take it from him." *And then I'm going to kill him.* "But we need to talk to Aurnia and make a plan."

Seán snorted and released his hands. "So what? We walk up to this barn and casually take out carts of food? Even if we knock out all the Hounds, we don't have those resources. How do we distribute it without being caught? How do we protect the people who accept it? A little food here and there is fine, but this is an act of violence against the Table. They'll slaughter us."

"And?" Aoife asked in a dangerously quiet voice. "What does it matter? They've already killed everyone else we love. What does it matter if they kill us? Maybe our deaths will incite enough anger that they will finally learn the wrath of a country pushed to its knees."

Oisín rubbed a soothing hand up her arm. "She's right. They've taken so much from us, and they'll keep taking more until we stop them."

"You might be ready to die, but I'm not." Seán stood and glanced at Rua. "I vote no."

She nodded.

"I vote yes," Aoife said.

Oisín nodded. "Me too."

"I'm always a yes," Rua replied. She tried to grin but it barely lifted the edges of her lips. Exhaustion settled into her bones. "Wolf?"

Wolf startled. "I get to vote?"

Rua squeezed her wrist. "That's how this works."

Wolf blinked, startled. "I vote yes. But," she glared at Rua. "You have to plan it properly and make sure no one gets hurt. You can't take risks when we're in there. I mightn't be there to save you again."

Warmth crept up Rua's neck and she pulled her jumper tighter so no one would notice. "I'll stick to my own fight."

Aoife snorted.

"I vote yes," Conor said, emerging from the overgrowth. His eyes were puffy, and his face was stained red. "Let's go to war against the Síochain."

***

When they got to Aurnia's and told her, she responded better than the others. That didn't mean she responded well. Rua watched the rage flitter across her face as her hands gripped the knife she had been using to cut bread. She stabbed it into the wooden table and stood so suddenly her stool crashed backwards. Pacing the room, she threw out a low, violent hum of the old language. When she quieted, she shook out her hands and rolled her shoulders. The tension tightening her body fell to the floor.

She took in some deep breaths, and then rolled her head as well. "Okay, I'm fine. What do you want to do?"

"I want to take the barn."

Aurnia shook her head. "It's a bad idea." She lifted up her stool and sat, glaring at Wolf as she ate a slice of bread she had stolen during the commotion. "He'll have it protected too well, and it'll bring unwanted attention down on the county. What we're doing works because he can't tell the Table without them having to react. He'll lose their trust and he can't risk that, but if you take this, it will cause enough of a ripple that the Table will notice."

Rua shrugged. "I don't care."

"Rua…"

"What if we planned it properly?" Wolf interrupted. "No half-arsed robbery."

Rua glared at Wolf. "We plan every one of those robberies."

"You don't adapt." She glared back, a fearsome sight with blue eyes and her sharp blade of a mouth. "That last one had too many Hounds for you to deal with, but you still went ahead. You need to be willing to back out of a plan if it's not going to work."

"People don't have time for me to plan. They're dying."

"And what happens when you're dead?" Wolf snapped back. "Who avenges your sister then? Who feeds the people?"

Fury roared through her and it took her a moment to be able to respond. "My life doesn't matter. Helping them," she pointed out to the overpacked bar, stuffed full of people trying to escape the freezing winter rain, "that's all that matters."

"You're helping no one dead," Wolf snarled. "You need to use your brain as much as your sword."

Aurnia put down the butcher knife carefully and stared at Wolf.

Rua watched as Wolf shrank into herself.

"What?" Wolf asked, word like a rusty nail.

"Nothing." Aurnia's voice sounded startlingly calm. "You just remind me of someone I used to know."

All emotion fell from Wolf's face until she became nothing but a lifeless doll. "Did she also think using your brain was a good life skill?" The question came out monotone, stark in contrast to the passion from moments before. "Maybe we should find a way to introduce her to Rua."

Aurnia smirked an unfriendly shape. "You're very protective of Rua."

"She's the one jumping in front of blades. Risking everything." The sentences fell from her in awkward starts like she thought she should be quiet but couldn't help but to say her piece. "No plan or desire to live."

"I'm still here." Rua huffed, annoyed they thought she was incompetent. She had been running this for months. Long before she even knew Wolf existed. "I'm still very much alive."

Both ignored her.

"And what would you do?"

"Is this a test?"

Aurnia shrugged and picked back up the knife. She started slicing the bread again, placing a thick piece in front of Rua. "It's whatever you want it to be."

"I wouldn't trust second hand information." Wolf stared at the confident way Aurnia held the knife before glancing at Rua. "I understand you've been working with this person for a while but they messed up last time. Even Conor thought it was a trap. So how do you know they're still trustworthy? How do you know they haven't turned back? If someone can betray one master, they can betray the other." Wolf tapped a blunt nail against the table. "I'd set up a watch for at least a week. Maybe two. Confirm the information and learn how the patrol works for myself."

With the dull, neutral tone in her voice fading back into annoyance, Rua realised how much life her words had held the last few days.

"Is it better to attack at dawn just before the change of guard when the Hounds are most tired? Is it better in the middle of the night? Is it close enough to the barracks that if we do get caught, there are more Hounds that can back up the guard? Are the Hounds bored and lazy? Are they still doing everything right? There are intricacies, Rua." Frustration leaked into her tone, and for once, Rua didn't think she had faked it. "You're refusing to examine them because you're too angry."

Rua shot up, pointing a shaking finger at Wolf. "Don't you

dare tell me my anger is the problem. I started this because of my anger. I've been doing it for over a year because of my anger. I know what I'm doing."

"Clearly, you don't," Wolf sniped back.

"Where did you learn all that?" Aurnia asked, face a blank mask.

It reminded Rua of Wolf.

"I've been alone for a long time," Wolf snarled. "You adapt or die."

"Well clearly, you adapted." Sarcasm weighed down the words. She studied Wolf for another second before turning back to Rua. "You know she's right. We need to plan this. I need time to figure out how we're going to get that food around the country. It's bigger than what we're set up for."

Rua fisted her hands, nails digging into her palm. "They're starving. All of them. We can't wait."

"I know it's hard, I do." Aurnia took Rua's hands and pulled apart her fingers. Half-moon indents shaped along her skin. "But we have to plan this properly."

Rua knew she was right but that didn't stop the clench of her gut when she nodded. "Fine. Let's plan it properly."

Aurnia nodded, glancing at Wolf. "You wouldn't check on Muire for me? I haven't heard anything from her for a while."

Wolf nodded, face blank but eyes burning. "No problem."

Aurnia watched her leave, and only started talking when she had disappeared through the door. "I don't trust her."

"What? Why?" Rua didn't completely trust her either; they had only just met, but Wolf had helped her twice now, had sat at the fire with her, and had spoken when Rua couldn't find her words. She had wiggled under Rua's skin and she didn't think she wanted to give her up. "She hasn't done anything but help."

"That stuff she spoke about, it's not skills you pick up on

the road." She twisted the butcher knife in her hands. "It's not something a half trained Hound would know."

"Fully trained," Rua corrected. "She left because of what they were doing."

"She turned up in town two weeks ago and saved you, and then again on the road. Don't you think that's very convenient?" Aurnia scanned the room as if checking for spies. "Why is she here instead of Conor? He's usually the one you plan these with."

"After the news, he was upset. He told me if he saw a Hound, he'd…" She shrugged. "He needed to stay near camp today. Wolf volunteered."

"Did she now?" Aurnia watched the door. "I might be wrong. She may just be a talented, capable woman, but don't let your guard down just yet, okay?"

"She knows where our camp is." Her stomach rolled uneasily. "She saved my life."

"For now, don't worry about it. She's helping and you can still use her, but just, don't get too attached. Not yet."

Blood rushed to her cheeks. "I'm not attached."

"Okay, loveen." She patted Rua's hand. "Whatever you need to think."

# CHAPTER TWENTY-TWO
## WOLF

Furious, Wolf left the bar with the empty barrel Muire had asked her to bring to the storage shed. She had reacted to the words *Aurnia sent me to see if you needed help* like they were a code; busywork designed as a distraction.

Aurnia suspected something.

The woman knew too much, was capable of hiding even more, but asking Wolf to leave after questioning her had been a mistake. Wolf knew what it meant to be talked about when she left a room, to be suspected and planned against. She needed to dumb down her knowledge of strategy or she would give herself away, but when she listened to Rua make stupid plan after stupid plan, she couldn't keep quiet. She didn't know why Rua infuriated her so much, why she felt the almost desperate need to keep the fool alive.

The one thing she had from her father, the only possession that had come from before, was a bound book of yellowing paper and a scrawled note.

*Even in the worst places, beauty lasts. Find the beauty in this world, mo Mhac Tíre Beag.*

She had hid it behind a loose brick in her room at the convent and filled it with flowers, not poisonous ones, or edible ones, but ones she had thought were beautiful. Each one had a description of the day beside it, evolving from her childish scrawl to her perfected cursive. The forbidden activity had kept her sane on the worst of days. She searched for beauty wherever she went. Beauty and names.

*Find the beauty in this world, mo Mhac Tíre Beag.*

The words had never related to a person before, but the more time she spent with Rua, the more she realised that beauty came from more than just art and nature. She barely knew her but Wolf knew deep in her gut that the world would be a less beautiful place if Rua didn't exist within it.

She froze when she entered the shed, dropping the barrel gently and palming a knife. The air should have been still and undisturbed but a presence existed at the edges. When a floorboard creaked behind her, she twisted and flung a knife. It flew past Pup's ear, lodging itself in the wooden door and shivering with the force.

"You missed me."

"Now ask how I knew it was you."

Pup glared at her. "The Síochain wants to see you."

A dull irritation crawled across her skin adding to her frustration about Aurnia. She pulled Pup into the back of the shed, hiding in the shadows. Barrels piled high in the space. Cheap beer and wet wood scented the air.

"Hurry up and talk. They already suspect something."

Pup scoffed. "The Síochain wants to see you," she repeated.

"Why?" Wolf snapped. "Does he think I'm incapable or is he just trying to get me caught?"

"I don't pretend to understand the workings of that man." For the first time, maybe because she had left the Síochain's estate, her true feelings for him came out. Disgust drew her eyebrows down and her mouth tight. "He says jump and I say how high. I don't question his reasoning." For the briefest moment, Pup's sneer sounded like Rua's had in the kitchen but then she forced her voice back into neutrality. "He wants to see you. He asked me to tell you. Here I am passing the message along. How shall I respond to him?"

She rubbed a hand down her face. She trusted Pup enough to show her this tiny insight of frustration, but caught herself before she showed any more. Being around the others was making her careless. They just emoted all the damn time like it wouldn't get them killed eventually.

"Tell him I can't. They're still suspicious of me."

Pup crossed her arms and glanced around the small space, stuffed with empty barrels. "He's pretty adamant about you coming back."

"What did the nun say?"

"Nothing. Obviously."

Wolf wanted to shake her for the arrogance she hadn't yet earned. "Did she want to?"

"Slight tightening around the mouth."

Wolf smirked. "So furious."

"They've both been unhappy with me since the assassination attempt, and don't even pretend it wasn't you who saved his life," Pup accused, fingers tightening on her biceps. "So figure out a way to visit him, will you? Allow me a moment of peace."

Wolf didn't react externally but her heart twinged. She knew what it meant to be on the wrong side of those stares; she had spent the first three years at the convent catching up and all she had gotten was their disappointment.

"They're pulling a job in a few weeks, I'll get myself captured. He can interrogate me, beat me and let me escape. Not that I know anything yet. I followed her to the lake when she met her informant, but she chose her meeting place well, I couldn't get close enough to hear anything." She studied the tense lines of Pup's shoulders and the muscle jumping in her jaw.

"I'll come in. It'll probably work in my favour. Get them to trust me."

Some of the tension fell from Pup's shoulders. "Someone else made another attempt on his life. They didn't get further than the stables."

"Good work."

Pup shrugged. "I should have let her kill him."

"Don't," Wolf snapped. "If he dies, you die."

She froze.

"They never told you?" A quiet fire ignited in her gut as deadly as any flashfire. Just because it had a gentle beginning didn't mean it wouldn't burn. "You're a bodyguard. You're *his* bodyguard. Your life is forfeit. The only way you survive is if he dies from natural causes."

Pup swallowed. "What's another noose around my neck?" Bitterness made the words sting across Wolf's skin. "I'd already gotten used to the other one before the Sisterhood removed it."

"They should've told you. They consider it motivation."

"My survival is all the motivation I need." She closed her eyes for a long minute before she managed to wash the anguish off her face. "I'll tell him you'll get caught. That you'll come back."

"Have you noticed anything strange? Anyone coming and going at night?"

Wolf leaned against a cold wall and watched Pup think about what she would be willing to share. Pride and frustration warred inside her; Pup finally understood how precarious her situation was but Wolf needed her information as uncensored as possible. Something Pup thought unimportant could mean everything to Wolf.

"No one has come through the gate except those delivering food and decorations for the Masquerade Ball."

Pup's words forced her thoughts away from the camp and

Wolf took the respite gratefully. She didn't understand why she cared, why it made her gut ache to think of how upset they had been. When Rua had told her, she had been taken aback by the carelessness of the Table to allow the famine to continue, by the stupidity of them to even think about providing food and then deciding not to. She wanted to shake whoever had decided on that strategy because it was like laying down *púdar dubh* and hoping no one lit the fuse.

"I check the logs daily," Pup continued. "The ivy concealing the side entrance, the one behind the abandoned stables, was disturbed this morning."

Wolf nodded.

This must be how the informant left without being seen. Hanging ivy and the old wooden stables hid that entrance, unneeded since the stone stables had gone up. There were more than a few ways to get to it within the estate walls, and the area around it was so overgrown, it would hide any tracks. The perimeter wall sat close enough to the forest that it would be easy to escape the attention of the watching Hounds if a person needed to leave the grounds undiscovered.

"Do you think that's how the rebels are getting in?"

Pup shook her head. "I'd left strands of the ivy beneath some rocks, casual enough to look like it had fallen from the wall. Someone had moved it. Had to be from the inside because it prevented the gate from opening on the other side. They never put the rock back, but whoever did it knew the estate well enough to leave no other trace of themselves."

"Once is an accident, twice is a coincidence, three times is a threat."

Pup nodded at the familiar phrase, well known in the convent. "The head of the Hounds, Roisin, is angry with the Síochain, but is still performing her duties well. Landlords are angry that the rents aren't being paid, and so is the Síochain."

Wolf shrugged, remembering the barn and the food and Frank's starving body. "They choose this action, and so they must live with the consequences. No one can pay if no one can work if no one can eat."

"They didn't choose the famine."

Wolf considered her. "No, they didn't, but they chose to punish the people for it."

"Do you agree with your new friend's little crusade?" Pup cocked her head as if seeing Wolf for the first time. Amusement saturated the words. "Do you think I should let the Síochain die?" Her voice held a teasing note with none of the kindness that Oisín had when he made his jokes.

"I think that the Table will rule long after either of us live. Long after this famine has ended." Wolf matched Pup's tone but added cruelty. "We are inconsequential. And I think, Pup, you should watch how you talk to me if you want to keep your tongue." In barely a second, a knife was in her hand, and she had pressed Pup up against the wall, blade in the soft skin under her throat. "Do you understand what I'm saying?"

Pup hissed when she pressed the blade closer. "I understand."

"Good," Wolf snarled. "Now, run back to your master and tell him I'll come when I'm goddamn ready."

"I'll tell him you'll get caught." Even with the knife against her throat, Pup grinned. "I probably won't quote you word for word. He might not be too pleased."

This time the words held true amusement and Wolf bared her teeth in a shadow of a grin. "You might be right." She withdrew her knife. "Keep your eye on him. I'd be disappointed in you if you die."

Pup shook her head and her hair, wrapped in a high bun, slanted to the right. "I'm not that easy to kill."

"None of us are anymore." She crossed the shed, glancing

out the door, and finding the yard empty, gestured to Pup. "Go on now. I'm sure I'll see you soon."

"Hopefully no sooner than you have to."

She watched as Pup skirted the buildings and let the crowded street gobble her up. An earthquake rumbled Wolf's bones at how close she had been to showing Pup how she really felt, to trusting her with the secret of who she was. She thought she had trained herself out of wanting anything other than her freedom a long time ago, and yet the more time she spent with Rua, the more she *wanted*.

She waited until calm had settled back over her skin before grabbing her knife from the wall and leaving the shed. She had just wrapped her hand around the kitchen door handle when she heard a shout and the hush of violence. She would have ignored it, but Aoife's voice suddenly called out, quickly followed by the slam of a body on the ground.

Without considering why she shouldn't, she raced towards the market square.

# CHAPTER TWENTY-THREE
## WOLF

Wolf pushed her way through the gathered crowd easily but stayed behind a larger man to assess the situation. Aoife stood with her back to a wall, Oisín pushed behind her. Blood coloured his lips crimson. Aoife had a knife in her hand. Three men stood in front of them; they may have been impressive once, but the famine had stolen that from them. Tall but gaunt, wasted muscle hung off too-prominent bones. There were bald patches where their hair had fallen out and a harsh red rash across their arms. Wolf knew that their desperation and anger would make them fight harder if she allowed them the chance.

"He should've saved them," the man in the middle spat, voice guttural with grief and rage. "They were just children."

"And why aren't you starving like the rest of us?" The one furthest from Wolf practically swayed where he stood. He would be easy to take down. "Where are you getting your food?"

Aoife snorted, ignoring the swaying man and watching the middle one. He must've been the one who hurt Oisín. "My brother is a healer. Not a miracle worker. Maybe you should take your complaints up with the Síochain."

The man closest to Wolf had a knife, and even though he clearly didn't know how to use it properly, it could still hurt

Aoife if he got too close. Wolf moved through the crowd like a wraith until she stood a foot from him. Hating how messy this would have to be to keep her cover, she ran at him, shoulder first, and collided with him hard. As he fell, she easily relieved him of the blade, his grip too loose to hold on. He landed hard on the other man and they both hit the ground with a thump. It took nothing for Wolf to knock the third man down with a punch to the stomach. When the man in the middle tried to get up, Wolf kicked him again and stepped on his throat.

"You're lucky I didn't just leave you to Aoife." She ignored how he struggled under her weight, hand flailing for grip on her shoe as she pressed lightly down. "For daring to touch her brother, she would have slit your throat and walked away whistling "

The man she had punched gulped in some air and whispered, "His children died."

"My condolences," she said, managing not to sound sarcastic. "But we do not attack the healer. You understand?" She pressed her foot down until the man nodded. "They're not your enemy. The Síochain is. Turning on each other won't help anyone." She spoke loud enough that her voice carried across the gathered crowd. "If anyone touches Aoife or Oisín again, I'll kill them myself."

Silence fell at the truth weighing down her words.

She released the man and he struggled up, grabbing his friends and fleeing into the crowd. A hand landed on her arm and she whipped around, knife already raised.

"Let's go," Aoife muttered, eyeing the knife for one second before pulling her along. "We need to get out of here before the Hounds arrive."

Wolf nodded, glancing back at the crowd. A flash of red hair stood out stark in comparison to the dull clothes before muttering people swallowed it up. She would have to hope that Pup thought the fight was all for show.

It *was* all for show.

For once, Wolf wasn't sure she believed her own lie.

"Oisín, go tell Rua what happened and meet us on the road," Aoife said when they reached the inn. "Keep your head down. I need to get Wolf out of here."

He disappeared inside with a nod.

Aoife pulled Wolf around the side of the building, past a row of cottages and into a thin alley. They walked in silence until they reached a small, square yard. Checking it was empty, Aoife pulled back some of the wooden beams on the tall wall encasing the town.

"Only way out that avoids the Hounds."

Wolf followed her through, emerging in a field. Long grass skimmed her hips and stretched towards the forest in the distance, grey sky sitting heavily on the dull day. After Aoife had put the beams back in place, they set off at a jog, across the fields, avoiding the road until the town disappeared behind them.

"We should wait for Rua and Oisín here," Aoife said when they stopped to catch their breath. Neither spoke for a minute and then, "Why did you do that?"

Wolf shrugged. "The man closest to me had a knife so I knew I had to disarm him first, and he had nothing to him so I figured if I hit him hard enough he'd fall and knock over the other one for me. The third man was very clearly weak so I knew he'd be easy to take down."

Aoife stared at her.

"I knew you'd be able to handle them if that's what you're mad about, okay? I just thought with you needing to protect Oisín, you were at a disadvantage."

"*A dhiabhal*, Wolf. I meant why did you help us, not why you attacked them the way you did."

"Oh." Wolf supposed that made more sense. "Oisín was bleeding."

Aoife's shoulders dropped and she let out a light laugh. "You're so weird."

It sounded like a compliment since the words were spoken in such a gentle way so Wolf shrugged. "Are you okay?"

"I turned my back for one second."

"It's not your fault."

"I'm meant to protect him." The words came out thick with tears and anger. "I'm meant to keep him safe."

Unsure, Wolf squeezed her shoulder. "Aoife, he is safe. *You* kept him safe. You could have taken those three men easily but you put your body between them and Oisín." She didn't know if what she said helped but she continued when Aoife's hands stopped shaking. "Protecting someone is never easy. There are too many unknowns. Too many things that could go wrong. You shielded him. You never would've let them touch him again."

She shook her head, blinking away tears. "Over my dead body."

"Wouldn't have happened. You're too good."

"Better than you?"

Wolf laughed, a bright noise that burst free of her. Something cracked and lightened in her chest, and she wanted to scurry away from the freedom it promised. She let the amusement fall from her face and replaced it with the blank mask as familiar as her knives. "Not as good as me."

Disappointment had seeped into Aoife's words when she said, "You've a good laugh. You should use it more often."

Before Wolf replied, a shout interrupted them.

"Aoife!"

She whipped around and ran towards Oisín, wrapping him in a hug when he came close enough. Rua walked past them, and when she reached Wolf, she took her hand and squeezed it.

"Thank you for saving them."

"It was nothing."

"It was everything," Rua insisted.

Wolf's skin burned at the contact; fingers laced together, palm to palm, Rua's pulse fluttering against her wrist.

"We should get back," Wolf managed, pulling her hand back and burying it deep in her pocket. "Better to not be on the road."

Rua nodded, and waved at the others to follow them. "Aurnia agreed with you," she said as they walked. "We'll start watching the barn tomorrow night. Try and get as much information as we can before we go in."

"It's the best thing we can do," Wolf said.

Rua nodded, but didn't respond.

They were silent all the way back to camp.

Wolf could not stop thinking about Aoife's question. She didn't know why she had stepped in. It would be better for the Síochain if she hadn't and Rua had two less people to help her. Without a healer who had no connections to the Table, the county would fall in line much quicker than when they knew they had support outside the reach of power. Aoife had skills; a dangerous fighter with something to lose and a stubborn protector who wouldn't give up. Getting rid of either of them made sense. Only weeks ago she had been ready to kill them in their sleep for the Síochain. She didn't understand why she had saved them. She knew there was no strategic benefit to it. All she knew was that someone with as soft a touch as Oisín didn't deserve to bleed, that someone as loyal as Aoife didn't deserve to lose, and she wasn't willing to let that happen to either of them.

When she got back to camp, everyone started praising her, complimenting her, *thanking* her. It made her skin tight and her heart riotous. She eventually escaped, sitting by the fire pit, ignoring how cold and lonely she felt under the stars.

"What you did today was a good thing."

She didn't react when Conor spoke but it was a near thing. A man his size should not have been capable of such gentle movements.

"Anyone would have done the same," she replied.

"Any of us, yes." He dropped a blanket over her shoulders, and then sat beside her, picking up a stick to stoke the fire back to life. "Anyone else, no."

Everything in her head had become a dangerous mess that she didn't know how to clean up. "I'm trying."

"I know you are." He didn't touch her, but moved a little closer, sharing his warmth. "Do you want to train with me tomorrow?"

She let out a relieved breath to be back on familiar territory. "Please."

He laughed. "I promise no more talk about today."

"It's just... I'm not used to..." She swallowed away a sudden lump in her throat. She hadn't cried in years, and she wasn't going to start tonight. "They're so grateful, so full of praise. It's too much."

"Not much praise where you come from?" He stared at the fire pit as he spoke which made it easier to answer.

"Not much of anything," she admitted. "Except a hard stick and harsh words."

He nodded. "You don't have to go back there again. You're with us now."

Wolf had to blink tears from her eyes because of the overwhelming longing cascading through her. She nodded. "What do you want to practice tomorrow?"

Clearly amused, he still allowed her to change the conversation to easier topics.

# CHAPTER TWENTY-FOUR
## RUA

"How long until the next patrol?"

Conor shrugged. "Any time now."

The waning moon was almost completely invisible against a backdrop of inky darkness. Rua lay between Conor and Wolf, close enough that their heat warmed her. The grass dampened her front, soaking into her clothes but the wet made the hard earth soft against her ever-skinny body. She may not be on the brink of starvation anymore, but the famine still clung to her and refused to let go.

"You think they'd stop talking," Wolf complained when they heard the Hounds before they appeared around the corner. "It's a stupid mistake to be making."

"You really think you could get Hounds to walk a perimeter for four hours and not talk?" Conor snorted. "They're trained but not *that* trained."

Wolf huffed. "It's unprofessional."

"You were your captain's favourite, weren't you?" Rua asked, tilting her head to watch Wolf.

She shrugged. "I like being the best."

The Hounds came into view and paused in the shadows. The three of them stopped talking. The barn sat alone among green fields on the Síochain's estate, miles from anything, and located far enough away from the manor that the Hounds had to travel the twenty minutes by cart. The isolated location meant that the Síochain had gotten overconfident in his security; no one would dare come onto his land, not this far from the road anyway, and so he had allowed the Hounds to get almost lazy in their rounds. It played to their advantage because never more than six Hounds guarded it at any time. Transporting the food was the biggest problem with no way to access extra carts, and then even if they had more, no way to get them in and out without being spotted.

Rua hated herself for agreeing to wait for two weeks, because after just a few days of watching them, the Hound's patterns became clear. They kept the same hours, changing every four hours with patrols of six, two guarding the door and the other four walking in pairs around the perimeter in opposite directions every fifteen minutes. It would be the most difficult job that they had ever undertaken, but she didn't care.

She just wanted to do something.

The time passing itched under her skin and kept her awake at night. Everyone she passed on the road seemed to glare at her for the inaction. They followed her into her nightmares. She spent her days planning and replanning, trying to figure out how they would get in, load up the food and get out without being discovered. Obviously Aurnia's cart wouldn't be enough. To steal enough food to feed as many people as possible, they would need a whole fleet of carts and more people to load them. They would need to knock out the Hounds to ensure they had time to move the food. Even then it probably wouldn't be enough.

"What if we don't take it all at once?" Conor suggested in a whisper, dragging Rua from her thoughts. "Steal it bit by bit so he doesn't notice."

The itch exploded across her skin like a lightning storm.

"People are starving, dying. How can we ignore that, knowing the food is right there?"

"You'd have to get in and out without them knowing," Wolf said, ignoring Rua's outburst. "If you want it to be a weekly thing, then they can't realise food is disappearing."

"*We're* taking the food," Rua corrected, sad that Wolf still considered herself an outsider. She had saved Oisín and helped Aoife protect him. It was more than enough to gain acceptance.

They both ignored her.

"That makes it harder," Conor mused. "We'd need sacks. We wouldn't get a cart near enough."

"Which means even less food," Wolf hummed.

"And more people dying." Rua listened as two Hounds joked over a cigarette. The tip glowed bright in the dark like a fallen star cupped between two hands. "How long would we need to empty it?"

They fell silent as they examined the large barn. Built with dirty stones and topped with thatch, it could've been mistaken for an oversized house from the road. Except it had no windows and only one door. The only other entrance was a hay hatch at the very top of the wall around the back. A hook swung menacingly from the wall, swinging in the chill wind. As she watched, the Hound dropped the cigarette to the ground, crushed the glowing end and continued on their patrol.

Wolf let out a huff of warm air when they disappeared around the side. "I can climb up into the hatch and find out how much food there is."

"It's too dangerous," Rua said.

"Not for me it isn't," she said, sounding insulted. "Anyway if I get caught, you can just leave. I'll figure something out."

Rua stared, unsure if she meant it seriously. "We don't leave people behind."

Wolf snorted. "Maybe you should."

Steel laced Rua's next words. "We don't leave people behind. Ever."

Wolf nodded, but Rua wasn't convinced she believed her. "Do you want me to check it out or not?"

"Fine. Don't get caught."

"As if," she replied with a grin before slipping away like a ghost.

Rua chewed her lip, waiting until she was sure Wolf was far enough away before she said, "Aurnia doesn't trust her."

"She's too good." He never took his eyes off the shadow of the barn. Wolf didn't appear. "Not only Hounds have trained her."

"Have you heard of anyone else?"

"No one." He pursed his lips, making his cheekbones harsh in the moonlight. "I like her," he finally said. "She's good for you."

She nudged him with her shoulder. "She probably won't even stick around."

"Make her. Give her a reason to. All this shite, Rua. It's not going away." His eyes remained on the barn. A shadow that may have been Wolf, but may not have been, appeared and disappeared back into the dark. "Not for a very long time. You need to find the good where you can."

"That's the most you've said to me in months."

"I've been silent too long. I've let them take too much from me." He cleared his throat. "They're not having my voice, not anymore."

Rua gripped his hand. "I love you."

"I love you too."

She grinned. "I won't tell on you to the others."

His laugh was a gruff bark. "Thanks."

Neither of them jumped when Wolf threw herself down beside them but surprise sprinted over Rua's skin. A fire burned in Wolf's eyes when she glanced at Rua before her face shut down into its blank mask. Rua realised this was how she dealt with anything that upset her.

"There are bags of cornmeal as high as the roof. Cured meat. Packed tight in barrels." She dug her nails into the dirt. "What your friend said is right; there's enough food in there to feed the county for the rest of the winter and probably into the spring."

Rua ground her teeth and allowed her head to drop into the damp grass. "We need more people. More support. People to keep watch on the road leading to the barn. Some to help with getting the food out of the barn and onto a cart." She glared at the passing patrol. "The Hounds will need to be knocked out and tied up. We need help, and I have no idea where to find it."

A broad, warm hand slid across her neck, steadying the painful beat of her heart. With a squeeze of his hand, Conor said, "We'll take it from them, Rua, and then we'll burn their kingdom to the ground."

# CHAPTER TWENTY-FIVE
## WOLF

The force of the blow shuddered up Wolf's arms.

She steadied herself as she twisted away and attacked Conor from the side. He dodged, but she used her momentum to follow him, raining down blows as he frantically defended himself. Just as she thought he would yield, he pushed her back, footwork speeding up and forcing her into the defensive with heavy hits that had more strength than she had. Sweat poured down her back. They ended up chest to chest, at the edge of the practice circle, swords caught between them. Neither willing to admit defeat.

The hairs on the back of her neck stood up.

She reacted without thinking, spinning out of Conor's challenge and drawing a dagger from her sleeve. When she stopped, a blade sat at Aoife's throat and a sword pointed at Conor's chest.

Aoife's mouth dropped open. "How did you even know I was there?"

"Instincts." She withdrew her weapons. "I grew up—" she paused, unsure how to finish the sentence. She swallowed, but it did little to ease the ache in her throat. "—in a bad place. If you didn't trust your instincts, didn't learn to protect yourself, you didn't stay alive."

"What age were you when you learned?" Conor asked, voice soft.

Wolf had noticed him talking more since they had found out about the barn. The small show of strength interested her far more than she cared to admit.

"Five," she replied, hiding her dagger back up her sleeve and handing Aoife the wooden sword they had been practising with. They always used real swords when sparring in the Sisterhood. According to the nuns, it kept them focused.

Aoife and Conor shared a *look*.

Not pity, but it reflected it close enough that Wolf bristled. "I survived."

"Is this why you won't sleep in the cave with us?" Aoife asked in a gentle way Wolf had never heard from her. She had been friendlier since the day at the market; including Wolf in jokes, sitting with her in the evenings, and taking her side when Wolf bothered to give an opinion.

Wolf shrugged.

"You know none of us would ever hurt you, right?"

Wolf stared. "How would I know that?"

"That's fair." Aoife glanced at Conor, a question Wolf couldn't read scrawled across her face.

Frustration made her toes curl. She should be better than that.

Conor shrugged. "We'll get you there." He threw an arm over Wolf's shoulders. "Won't we, Aoife?"

"We'll have you sleeping in the cave in no time." She grinned, and Wolf thought she saw Oisín's kindness in the expression. "Rua figured out the plan."

She didn't appreciate them treating her like a wild animal but she couldn't deny the comfort Conor emitted as he led her towards the cave. The weight of his arm soothed her, and with Aoife closer than usual, Wolf felt protected. The part of herself she had buried a long time ago, the part that craved touch and softness, preened. She imagined setting fire to the need as she left their warm embrace and crawled through the entrance. It had only ever brought her pain.

Everyone was gathered, shuffling under blankets and resting on each other. Only Seán stood apart, arms crossed and face stormy, clearly still annoyed he had been outvoted. He had spent most of the week volunteering for watch and avoiding the rest of them.

Wolf sat close to Rua, watching as she ran her hands through her knotted hair.

Rua blew out all her air in a loud sigh and said, "Conor had the idea that we steal the food week by week instead of all at once."

Outraged shouts filled the room.

"People are dying…"

"This isn't going to make anyone fight back…"

"Told you it was a stupid idea…"

"I know, okay?" Rua started to plait her hair with fidgety fingers. "It's not what I want either, but you've all seen the barn now. There's just no way to get the food out all at once, not without a distraction, a really big one, and enough carts to empty it. There aren't enough of us to do that *and* empty the barn. We'd only get one chance, and we'd be declaring war against him."

"Thought you wanted that," Seán said snidely.

"I want to help people. I want to make sure they're fed," Rua bit back. "This way we can take it a little at a time and share it out, maybe later we can figure out how to take it all." She tied off the plait with a piece of string. "I'm not getting us all killed just to teach the Síochain a lesson. It won't work. We'll just be dead and he'll still have all the power."

"How are we going to do it then?" Aoife asked.

Oisín sat beside her, sorting out his herbs. Wolf would have thought he wasn't paying attention except he nodded when he agreed with what was said.

"Wolf, Conor and I are going to go in and carry the bags up to the hay hatch. Seán will catch them when we throw them down and you guys will run them to cover. The Hounds patrol every fifteen minutes so that'll be our window."

Conor continued easily, "We'll get as many as we can to Aurnia's. I know this isn't what we wanted but this keeps us safe, delivers more food to more people and with practice we'll get better and quicker." Conor watched each of them, gaze heavy. "We have to be smart about this. We have to keep each other safe."

Rua nodded. "Any questions?"

"Am I coming?" Oisín didn't lift his head as he spoke. Just kept filling his glass bottles.

"No," Aoife said at the same time Rua said, "If you want."

Aoife glared. "We have a deal. He doesn't come to the robberies."

"There'll be no fighting." Oisín said. "We're literally running back and forth."

"There's always fighting." She gripped his hand. "I'm older. I get to decide."

He snorted. "By ten minutes."

Something in his voice made Aoife's shoulders relax. "He's not coming."

Rua nodded. "Any other questions or ideas?"

"You're okay with this?" Seán asked Conor.

He nodded.

"Alright, fine." Seán stared down at the ground. "What time are we leaving at?"

"Around midnight," Rua responded. "We're hitting them when they're most tired."

Wolf stared at Seán. "Are you actually okay with this?"

"Don't have much choice, do I? Everyone else already agreed." He pushed himself off the wall and stuck his hands in his pockets with a shrug. Only the crease between his eyebrows told of his annoyance. "It's fine, I'll support them like I always do." He considered her for a moment before glancing at Rua. "Do I have time to go into town? I've to pick up the order of arrow tips from the blacksmith."

Rua nodded. "Will you drop into Aurnia while you're there and update her?"

"Sure. I'll be quick." He threw his pack over his shoulder, the strap slung across his chest. He ruffled Rua's hair as he walked past. "Does anyone need anything else?"

"If Aurnia has any spare coffee or tea," Rua answered, grinning. "We're just about out and we'll probably need it tonight."

"Coffee, tea, update Aurnia, arrow heads." He listed them off on his fingers and waved.

Tired goodbyes called out as he crawled from the cave.

"Another round?" Conor asked, sitting down beside her. "Best out of five?"

Wolf laughed. "Sure, but you're not going to win this time either."

# CHAPTER TWENTY-SIX
## WOLF

Crouching low, Wolf raced across the grass. Rua and Conor were silent shadows beside her. Usually, she completed these sorts of jobs alone and it felt nice to have company. Voices carried over to them just as they reached the barn. She didn't bother glancing at the other two as she paced up the wall, the uneven stones providing easy handholds. Just as they pulled themselves over the edge and onto the wooden platform, two Hounds passed below, chatting and laughing.

"That gives us fifteen minutes until the next patrol. Thirty before Seán is below ready to catch…"

Rua kept whispering but Wolf stopped listening as she crawled to the edge of the landing. Sacks of cornmeal tottered above her in drunken towers. Barrels steadied them with sturdy lines. Skinny pathways weaved through the food. A slim line of moonlight lit the walls and cast shadows across the stacks. Nothing was disturbed. Nothing moved. But the silence settled uneasily, reminding her of the storage shed when Pup snuck up on her. Goosebumps sang along her arms. She waved at the others for quiet, and gestured for them to stay put. Rua started to argue but Conor put his hand on her arm and she acquiesced. Wolf slipped down the ladder, landing on the hard floor soundlessly. The floor creaked to her left and she twisted.

"There!" A woman shouted behind her. "They're in the hay loft!"

Wolf bolted back up the rungs. "Go," she shouted.

Someone grabbed her foot. Rua grabbed her hand. She glanced down. A Hound held her ankle in both hands. For one desperate moment, she was pulled in two directions while trying to keep her grip on the ladder.

"I'm not leaving you," Rua panted.

"How many are there?"

Rua's eyes moved as she counted. "Ten."

Conor had his arm around Rua's waist, supporting her.

"You've got to go," Wolf gasped out as the Hound clutching her ankle gave her another painful jerk.

"I'm not leaving you," Rua snapped.

An arrow flew by them, hitting the beam behind Rua and quivering. Rua still didn't let go of Wolf's hand. The next arrow was close enough to rip across Conor's thigh. He fell to his knees, arms still around Rua's waist. Another arrow embedded itself in Rua's arm and her hold on Wolf weakened.

Wolf ripped her hand free. "Go," she said, eyes on Conor. "Get them to safety."

He nodded, dragging a fighting Rua back across the loft.

Wolf allowed the next jerk to dislodge her, making sure to land on the Hound. They grappled on the ground for a few moments, both trying to get the upper hand, until Wolf managed to get her arm around the Hound's neck. She choked them out until they stopped struggling and then pushed their limp body off of her. She jumped to her feet, and withdrew her sword, glancing around the gathered Hounds.

She withdrew her sword. "Okay, who's next?"

Five Hounds stood visible, squished together between rows of food. She grinned something fierce and threw herself into the fight. The enclosed space made it tougher but that just added to her enjoyment. It took a while before she realised that she wasn't really meant to be fighting back. She had told the Síochain she would get caught, and this was the perfect opportunity, but she had to buy enough time to get Rua and the others far enough away so they were safe. She ignored how wrong that should have been to her.

She twisted and split open a row of cornmeal sacks. It scattered to the floor in waves making the floor uneven and slippy. She would be able to fight, but the Hounds weren't trained for such unusual conditions. Someone was calling orders but she ignored them to concentrate on the soldiers in front of her. The tight rows meant they had her surrounded, unable to hold off one before another swung a sword or dagger. She didn't know if they had been told to take her alive, or if they just didn't care.

She elbowed the closest in the chest, and kneed him in the stomach, kicking him in the face as he fell. A woman attacked, skilled but not as skilled as Wolf. She failed to adapt her style to the cramped space. One of Wolf's tests had included close quarter skills. That had been against five though. Not ten. She took a hit to the kidney and the pain was a sharp drag of a knife. She steadied herself at a crossroads between the stacks.

Five Hounds were unconscious. Five watched her from the connecting paths. Two attacked at once, forcing her to slash back and forth, kicking out when one to her left reached out for her. She ducked just in time to escape a punch to her ear, but the movement left her unsteady and someone kicked her, boot slamming her into the ground. A knee fell on her making her back crack and her ribs ache. They relieved her of all her weapons but the knife up her sleeve.

Rolling her eyes at the incompetence, she allowed herself to be pulled back up and then using the momentum she slammed her head into her jailer's nose. The crack was more satisfying than she would admit to anyone. She kept rolling back, kicking off the ground and tumbling over the crouching Hound, landing on her feet behind him. She kicked hard and he slammed into the two in front of him. Her hands were behind her back, but she had a bloody grin on her face.

Six down. Four to go.

There was no reason to fight so hard except her blood sang and for the first time in weeks, she felt like herself again. Felt in control. She didn't have to hide who she was, pretend she was anything but the killer they had made of her. She dislocated her thumb and slipped her hand free. The Hounds watched her, too wary to approach. Whoever had been giving the orders had fallen silent so she must have knocked them out.

She shoved her thumb back in, ignoring the shot of pain as it rocketed up her arm. They had to come to her one by one in a thin walkway, making the fight easier. She fought them slowly, almost bored with how quickly they fell. When the last one fell, she had leaned against a stack of cornmeal that had managed to survive the brawl.

A slow clapping echoed through the quiet.

"Well, look at you. I'm almost impressed." Liam Cogadh had his hood up but a sharp grin remained visible even in the shadows. He watched her as she rolled her thumb, getting it to click a few times before she felt satisfied it had gone back into the joint correctly.

She glanced up at the hay hatch.

"Your new friends got away. Don't worry. I'll send the Hounds after them in a while." The words were mocking. "What I'm interested in is why you had to knock them all out?"

"A member of the Sisterhood of Righteous Death does not allow themselves to be captured. Not ever."

"Even when they said they would?" He dragged a finger

down the side of her face and it came away bloody. There was something mildly threatening about the action.

She shrugged.

"I don't care about your indoctrination tonight," he sneered. "I want to know how you found out about the barn."

"Same way they find out anything. They met with their informant." The smile dropped from the Síochain's face so fast ice crept up the back of Wolf's knees. "I followed, but they're smart, I couldn't get close enough to find out who he was or hear what they were talking about." A knot twisted up her stomach as she spoke. Like she had betrayed Rua. Conor. Aoife and Oisín. Even Seán. She shook it away because it was ridiculous. She only ever had to protect herself. "He wore your colours and is a man. That's all I've got so far."

He didn't speak for a very long time. So long that some of the Hounds started coming around with groans that did nothing to help the tension that laced the air.

"Well, isn't that interesting? I won't be needing your help after all." He walked away, stepping around the bloody bodies. "I know who the informant is."

"Wait." Panic seared through her. "You'll still sponsor me though, right?"

"Why would I do that, Little wolf?"

Wolf froze, muscles rigid. No one knew her name but Rua's gang. Not even Pup knew she *had* a name. He knew they were coming. He had placed the Hounds in wait. Someone had betrayed Rua. The shock boomed so loudly, she almost didn't hear his next words.

"You failed at a very simple task, and worst, you've wasted my time. You can leave in the morning." This time he did walk away. "Let the Hounds tie you up in case there's anyone lurking around. No point in you destroying the Sisterhood's secret as well as failing me."

# CHAPTER TWENTY-SEVEN
## RUA

Conor dragged Rua from the hay hatch, away from Wolf, and forced her down the wall. She pulled the arrow from her arm. It had barely embedded itself in her muscle but she still winced as blood leaked from the small wound. He was limping, breath coming in uneven gasps. A scream ripped through Rua's head the further they got from Wolf. Before she had broken free of Rua's hold, Wolf had had a smile glinting at the edges of her lips, eyes burning. All she had cared about was getting them to leave.

"Rua, we have to go." Conor sounded frantic in a way she didn't recognise. "We need to warn the others."

He didn't let go of her even as they scaled down the stones, jumping the last two feet. Conor landed with a grunt of pain. They raced across the flat fields, conscious that the alarm could be called any second.

Panic was a noose around Rua's throat.

Wolf could be dying right now, and they were running in the wrong direction. They were doing the exact opposite of what Rua had promised; they were leaving her behind, and Wolf would never trust her now, would never forgive her. Conor still didn't let go of Rua's wrist, refusing to go back when the sounds of a fight echoed from the barn.

Even when she fought. Even when she begged.

When they reached the treeline, she tried yet again to yank her hand free. "We have to go back for her," she hissed. "We can't just abandon her."

The others were staring at them, uncertainty making them quiet. Moonlight leaked in through the branches. They glowed like dark creatures waiting to cast their magic.

Rua trembled.

Seán spoke first. "What's happening? Where's Wolf?"

"Hounds were waiting." Conor refused to loosen his grip as she tried to tug herself free. "We have to leave."

She ignored his words. "We need to go back. Wolf is by herself."

"No." Conor's tone invited no argument. "She told us to go. She knew what she was doing. We're leaving."

Nobody moved. Wind rustled through the leaves. Hounds shouted in the distance.

Conor flinched.

Rua shoved him but he barely moved. "We have to get her."

"I said no. Head out." The words were met with more blank stares, the others unsure how to deal with them fighting. It had never happened before. "Now." Some of the commanding officer he had been sounded in the word. "Go!"

Like he had broken a spell, they scattered into the trees, keeping quiet and disappearing into the darkness. Still, Rua refused to move. They were too far away to hear if the fight had finished, if Wolf had survived. She watched the barn. Stillness settled over the night. Approaching hoofbeats interrupted the calming beat of her heart, making it trip over itself again. A horse trotted up to the barn and the rider dismounted.

Horrified, Rua gasped.

The shadow of the Síochain's cloak made him Death marching to meet his dead.

"We have to go, Rua. Please." Panic tinged Conor's words. He didn't force her though, and she knew he cared about what happened to Wolf as much as she did. Hearing his fear made nausea crowd her throat. "She's a good fighter. She'll be okay. But we have to go now."

Hounds were starting to spread out. A woman on horseback shouted orders and directed search parties. They were going to start hunting for the intruders. Desperate relief that Conor had forced the others to leave flooded her. She kept watching. Just one look, one hint, Wolf had survived.

Finally, Wolf emerged at the point of a sword, hands tied behind her back. Not hurt. Not yet anyway.

"Okay," she whispered. "Okay. Let's go."

\*\*\*

Silence sat heavily on the cave when Rua and Conor arrived back.

Aoife sat buried in her pile of blankets, mouth a thin line. Oisín sat beside her and he examined them, eyes widening when he noticed the blood. He stood, pulling his bag with him and rooting through it.

"I need to stitch these up."

"Rua first."

Rua glared at Conor as Oisín cleaned out the wound on her arm and stitched it up. The pain felt almost soothing, reminding her she was still alive. It took him minutes to wrap it in bandages and move to Conor's leg.

No one spoke until he had finished both of them.

Seán gripped his axe and leaned against the wall near the entrance as if waiting for an attack. Rua didn't know if the cave had always been so big, or if Wolf's presence had really made such an impact.

They had never lost someone before.

*Not lost.* She'd been captured.

Rua didn't know how she felt. She had only just met Wolf, but in the last few weeks, she had become an important part of their small, broken family. Argued with Aoife about stupid things. Talked with Oisín about herbs she had used on the road. Conor and her sparred most mornings. Seán had added her to the wall of pictures. She had saved their lives even when she claimed not to care. Rua just liked sitting with her in the quiet of the sunrise, being with her particular brand of silence. It soothed some of the edges of Rua's hurt. Even though Wolf kept insisting she didn't need a family, she had slotted into theirs like a piece they didn't know had been missing.

When Oisín settled back beside her, Aoife finally broke the silence. "What happened?"

"We got into the barn okay, but Wolf just knew something was off." Rua hated how broken her voice sounded. It hadn't been so empty since she had lost Saoirse, and Conor had helped her stitch her broken heart back into an unrecognisable shape.

"Instincts," Conor said. Only Aoife nodded like it made sense. "She went down to investigate. They caught her when she tried to get back to us."

"She made us leave." Tears made her voice thick and rough. "Conor made me leave."

"If I hadn't, you'd be at the Síochain's mercy as well."

Rua stepped away from him and started pulling the plaits from her hair. Agitation made her fingers rough. "We don't leave people behind." She blinked away tears. "I promised her."

Conor stepped forwards slowly, arms raised and when she didn't move away, he wrapped her in a hug. "We'll get her back. Aurnia will know what to do."

It was too hard to stay angry with him, especially when she knew somewhere deep down he was right, and that Wolf had been right as well, so she leaned into him and allowed a few tears to escape. When she felt like she had control of the ache in her chest, she stepped away with a tiny nod.

Relief lightened the lines around his eyes. "We'll get her back."

She nodded again. "What about the barn?"

"Now the Síochain knows we know it'll be untouchable," Aoife answered. "Do you think your friend knew it was a trap?"

The contents of Rua's stomach hit the back of her throat. "It's the only thing that makes sense." She didn't understand why he had decided to turn them in now. They had been friends for over two years. Working together for ten months. She thought he understood, thought he wanted the same things, but she hadn't asked him about the first trap because he had distracted her with the barn. "None of us would've told, and neither would Aurnia. He betrayed us."

Seán cursed.

Aoife nodded her agreement.

"He doesn't know where our camp is?" Oisín asked, ever the voice of reason. "Because I'd really like to get some sleep before we have to run."

"We're not running. No one knows where our camp is."

"Wolf does," Seán said quietly.

"She won't tell." It shocked Rua how fiercely she believed that. "She won't," she insisted when uncertain faces met her claim. "But we can sort this out in the morning. Talk to Aurnia. Make a plan. There's nothing to be done now. Let's just get some sleep."

It took a long time for the quiet hum of sleep to fill the cave. Rua lay awake, listening as one by one they drifted off. She waited until everyone slept before she snuck out. Her bed was closest to the entrance so it took no skill to get away unnoticed. Weapons still strapped to her body, she started the long trek to the Síochain's estate.

She would save Wolf, and she would do it tonight.

# CHAPTER TWENTY-EIGHT
## WOLF

The cart bucked unsteadily as they travelled back to the house.

Hounds surrounded her, hands resting on swords and eyes never leaving her form. As a prisoner the Síochain had taken personally, they wouldn't allow her to escape, but they had also seen the mayhem at the barn; they knew how dangerous she was. Irritated by their watching, she dislocated her other thumb and slipped free of the restraints. No one moved except for the tightening of hands on their weapons. She popped it back in with a blank face and dropped the rope at her feet. One leaned forward, words already on her lips, but another pulled them back, nodding towards a horse coming up alongside them. Wolf palmed her knife, twisting it so it caught the moonlight, amused at the annoyance and fear in their expressions.

The horse cantered by the cart. "At least pretend to be my prisoner."

"I'm staying in the cart, aren't I?"

The Síochain rode a beautiful black horse with a slow gait that thumped across the ground like a dying heart. For once, his hood rested across his shoulders. The moon etched the lines of his face in harsh light. Stubble traced across his cheeks and down his throat. Dark bags made his eyes grey; emptiness shaped them. With his hood down and his dark hair swept back, he appeared like a handsome, cruel king. Too much power and too little care for those around him. Privilege was a wondrous thing when always on your side. He probably didn't even know how much he owned.

She reached out and scratched the horse's warm shoulder. The animal leaned her head into the pressure, coat coarse beneath the pads of Wolf's fingers.

"Can I ride her?"

Something like pain twisted his mouth, and for one short moment, it made him almost fragile. "You're leaving as soon as the nun is ready."

Wolf's skin prickled with the understanding that he chose to show her these parts of himself. She didn't understand why she had been offered such a tainted gift, and she wanted to give it back to him, but she also wanted to push until she found a weakness to manipulate.

"Oh, right. I failed you." She rolled her eyes and for once allowed him to see since they were being *so honest.* "Because you figured it out yourself."

None of the Hounds were listening. Wolf would have been willing to bet they were actively not listening. Some knowledge wasn't worth having.

He stared ahead, face once again unreadable. "Can't reward failure, Little Wolf."

"Don't call me that." She didn't snap at him but the words were sharp enough to cut.

"Is it sentimental?"

The carefully blank tone made her skin tighten and she couldn't help but snarl, "What would you know about what I deem sentimental?"

"Little Wolf," he hummed, ignoring her outburst except for

a slight tightening of his hands on the reins. "Such a fitting name for someone like you."

"I don't have a name," she replied. He had no real idea that she had chosen a name. This was just another test and she refused to fail by trusting him with such a truth.

He watched her, waiting.

Unease crawled across her skin and she tried to calm the unsteady rhythm of her heart. Even if he had somehow found out her name, he had no idea why she had chosen *that* name; he just saw knives like teeth and blood on her hands. "None of us do."

"Does that bother you?"

She let the quiet clip of hooves and the shifting of the Hounds be her response.

He quirked his eyebrow in a way that was more threat than curiosity.

"I am a member of the Sisterhood," she relented, suddenly and inexplicably exhausted by his attention. "Nothing bothers me."

He smirked, harsh and cruel. "You don't lie half as well as you think you do."

She ignored his spiked words. "How did you even come to hear that name?"

He didn't reply but his shoulders relaxed just slightly.

Wolf asked instead, "How did you know we were going for the barn tonight?"

He tilted his head with amused acknowledgement. "Your interrogation skills need work." Clicking his tongue, he said, "I have spies all over this county."

The easy response shocked her but she didn't let it play across her face.

"Sometimes they feed me so many secrets, I feast. Sometimes they find me nothing but scraps." He tightened his hands around the reins and his leather gloves sang. "They had lots of things to say about you, and how you looked at the red headed girl."

Relief made Wolf weak; no one close to Rua had betrayed her. Her downfall had been bad luck and her trusting nature around too many listening ears. She should have known he would put it together himself. Intelligence burned through him like an unattended fire in a dry forest.

The rest of his words caught up to her and her pulse tripped over itself. "I don't look at her in any way but as a mark."

"You are so young." He laughed; it reminded her of his nights by the fire with Luchán and how he would sometimes allow his nephew to amuse him. "I forget that sometimes. Still so innocent."

Wolf laughed too, a bitter noise she hadn't meant to let escape. "I haven't been innocent since my father dumped me in that place."

"You remember your father." The sharpness of his voice pierced her skin, spilling blood from scars she thought long healed.

"No."

He nodded. "You just know you had one?"

"Everyone came from somewhere." She hadn't mentioned her father aloud in years. Not the truth of him anyway and the Síochain certainly wasn't the person to tell it to. "Anything he gave me is long gone. They made me bleed it out."

Softly, he asked, "And what did they replace it with?"

"Death."

He nodded once, a sharp, bitter shape, and clucked his tongue, speeding up his horse and disappearing into the dark, leaving Wolf to question why this man knew the paths to all of her deepest secrets.

She spent the rest of the ride in silence. She refused to

consider that she may never see Rua again, or spar with Conor. That they would all become a distant memory too. Their loss throbbed in a familiar way, a way which reminded her of those first years in the convent when she still thought her father would come and retrieve her.

When they stopped in the yard, the Hounds watched in confusion as she jumped off the cart and headed to the stables. Having watched how the Síochain spoke to her, no one dared to question it. Emptiness greeted her when she strolled into Pup's room, so she kept going, stopping in the kitchen for some food, and then slipping up the stairs. Preparations for the Masquerade Ball were visible in the crisp, bright decorations hanging throughout the hallways and the shine on the side table as she climbed up onto it, pulling herself up on the beams. It took bare minutes for her to be sitting in the shadows of the Síochain's private quarters, watching him as he wrote at his desk.

Candlelight made him softer.

Wolf didn't like him like this. Didn't like that it made him more human. She preferred him as the monstrous monarch he portrayed. A knock on his door dragged her attention away from how his face tightened more and more as he wrote. She wanted to know what exactly he had figured out in the barn.

"Come in," he called, voice as rough as a last breath.

The nun entered. "You sent for me."

"I know who the informant is. I will no longer need the help of the Sisterhood. You and your protegee can leave after you have delivered this." He folded the letter over and sealed it with wax. "This letter needs to be placed in my sister's hands and no one else's. You will ensure this happens."

"Of course."

"I will not be sponsoring the final test." He handed over the letter with something like reluctance. "She failed to complete my request."

"She will be punished."

Wolf swallowed. Punishment could be anything from impossible exercises to time in the Silence, a room with no windows and no light where no one heard them scream and beg and plead to be released. Her last test had taken place there; torture and starvation without breaking. She had lasted an atrocious three weeks. Longer than the others in her age group but not the longest of any apprentice.

She forced back the shudder that crawled across her muscles.

She didn't want to go back to the Silence.

He nodded, and Wolf thought maybe he glanced up to the corner where she hid. Without a noise, she shuffled further into the shadows.

"Do they all choose to stay? After the final test."

The nun cocked her head as if considering his words. "There have been instances when girls have chosen to leave. We have methods that persuade them not to."

"And the woman who succeeded in leaving?"

"No one has ever succeeded in leaving. She is a rumour created among the younger of the girls. Something of a fairy tale they tell each other."

Wolf's stomach dropped.

The violent swoop reminded her of falling off the high beam when she was six; the world had toppled and toppled around her until she landed with a hard, shattering splat. She placed her palms flat on the wood below her to steady her shaking.

He nodded as if she had confirmed what he already knew. "No one who knows the secrets can leave."

Despite the solid beam beneath her and the steadiness of her stance, the truth of his words made her feel like she had fallen again and hit the ground.

Every silent part of her screamed.

"The Sisterhood of Righteous Death must remain unknown, but it is always better for our apprentices to think they have chosen it." Amusement settled across the nun's voice when she said, "A cell is not a cell if the person doesn't know they are captured."

This time he definitely gazed up at her before tilting his head back towards the nun. "We are all prisoners in someone else's cage. Sometimes it is better to know where the walls are. It stops us wanting more." He handed her the letter which disappeared into her clothes, quicker than even Wolf could follow. "You will leave as soon as possible. Avoid the eyes of my Hounds."

She bowed her head, respectfully. "We will be gone without a whisper."

"Just you. Come back for the girl. I can't risk her slowing you down." For once, the disinterest in his voice sounded imperfect. If it hadn't been Liam Cogadh, she would have thought concern dictated his words. "That letter must be in my sister's hands by tomorrow and I need a reply by tomorrow night."

"I will leave tonight." She tucked her hands behind her back. "The bodyguard is working out?"

"She is young but dedicated." He no longer watched the nun. To Wolf it seemed like taking his eyes off a venomous creature ready to strike. "I will mould her into something worthwhile yet."

Wolf barely heard the words.

The tightness of her throat made getting air impossible. Ringing in her ears deafened her. Numbness swallowed the tips of her fingers. Scrunching herself into as small a ball as possible, she clung to her forearms and tried to remember how to function again.

It had all been lies and she had believed them.

She had thought herself so clever being able to identify

mistruths and yet she believed the biggest one. Of course no one left the Sisterhood. The stupidity of her wishes would drown her. Want had blinded her; she choked on it.

She would never leave free.

Stretching in front of her were years and years at the beck and call of the nuns and the Table and the Síochains, killing who they chose, gathering what secrets they wanted, whispering and playing at polite, until Wolf disappeared, leaving a nameless, obedient assassin.

She sucked in a gasping breath, uncaring for how loud it sounded in the sudden quiet.

"I am sorry to force the truth on you in this way."

It took her a moment to understand the nun had left, and he spoke to her. He sounded sincere in the way a knife would if it apologised while it stabbed her.

"I have learned bad news should arrive at the earliest possible convenience."

It took her even longer to parse out the meaning of his words.

"The quicker you accept there is no life, but this one, the easier it will be. You could be the best of them all, but first, you must choose it. Choose the death they taught you. It is better than mourning everything you have lost."

"Is that what you did?" She had to force the words out. They scraped up her throat and broke her teeth as they fell between her lips. "Did you give up what you wanted to follow their path?"

"I gave up more than you can even imagine."

"Do you regret it?"

He sat silent for a long time, and when he responded, no answer came. "It's time for bed, Little Wolf. Maybe one day we will meet again."

His tone brokered no argument and she knew not to push him.

On the other side of those words sat punishment steeped in violence. Even with what he had given her today, he was still Liam Cogadh and that meant he was as cruel and harsh as the ocean during a storm, and she was a small raft about to be dashed on the rocks. Silence made an uneasy compromise while she tried to remember how to move her body again. She watched him as he stared into the fire, face an abyss of hurt she feared would one day be reflected in her own expression.

She departed like she had every room since she was five, silently.

# CHAPTER TWENTY-NINE
## RUA

I t was easy enough to identify Tadgh.

Wider than any of the other Hounds, he stood taller too. An elk transformed into a man. Antlers forced into swords and shields. Crouching low, she ran along the shadows of the perimeter wall and climbed up it once she saw he was alone. She landed beside him with barely a noise. Still, he swung his sword and she had to duck and tumble to avoid getting injured.

"Tadgh, it's me," she managed to get out before he struck again. She pulled down her hood to show him her face and then fixed it quickly so none of her hair remained visible. Mud still splattered through it but the red was starting to shine through brightly in places.

The sword hovered above for a long moment before recognition softened his features. "*A dhiabhal*, Rua. You were this close to me killing you."

She snorted. "Let's not get ahead of ourselves. I didn't even fight back."

He didn't grin like he usually would. "What are you doing here?" He hissed. "Do you know how dangerous this is?"

"One of mine got taken. I'm here to get them back." Guilt rested on her shoulders; a heavy weight she thought she had grown used to, but now it dragged her down worse than before. She had broken a promise. Failed someone she swore to keep safe. "Did you see a prisoner they brought back about two hours ago?"

Someone shouted up at them.

Tadgh pushed her back and answered, "No, sir. No intruders. Just a cat." He listened to a muttering voice. "Yes, sir. Will be more careful. Sorry, sir." He forced Rua back into the shadows when she crept forward to hear. "Where's Conor? No way he let you come alone."

She shrugged.

"You're an *amadán,* you know that?" Tadgh shook dark hair from his eyes. "You're gonna get caught and then the others will have to come and save you." Broad in his Hound's black, he kept her hidden from wandering eyes. "Who is this prisoner to you?"

Rua shrugged again. "Someone I promised not to leave behind."

"Conor is going to kill you and then he's going to kill me."

Conor had been Tadgh's commanding officer before he deserted. They had been close, closer than either of them would admit, and they had used that to convince Tadgh to help them. He had been too scared to desert with five sisters and six brothers at risk, but did what he could once it didn't put them in immediate danger. Killing Conor's family had kept more people in the Hounds than Rua cared to think about. She didn't blame them; she would do anything to protect her own as well. When the Síochain leaned on someone, he knew exactly what buttons to press until they were begging to be compliant.

He checked around again before whispering, "I don't know much. When they got back, no one would talk about it. The Síochain spoke to her in the cart so they very carefully didn't hear a thing. I think she's in the house. I don't know where."

"How do I get in?"

"Stables over there are probably the best." He pointed as though stretching. "Watch the new stable hand, she managed to stop an intruder by herself last week."

Rua leaned up and kissed his cheek. "Thank you."

"Please be careful." He gripped her shoulders with hands so large they reached down to her shoulder blades. "If anything happens to you, Conor will skin me."

She nodded, and disappeared back into the dark.

She paused in the shadows at the bottom of the wall when two Hounds strolled past her, steam rising from cups in their hands, and then raced to the stables. Sneaking across the yard seemed almost too easy when everyone faced outwards. Maybe she would tell the Síochain before she slit his throat. The thought made her stomach churn; she wasn't a killer, no matter how much she tried to convince herself. That wasn't a problem for tonight though. She had to get in, save Wolf and be back before the others even noticed she had left. Better to ask forgiveness than permission. Rules her mother had passed down when teaching her how to steal.

The stable held only horses, stomping in their hay and watching her progress with little protest. The side door led to a bedroom, and she paused in the shadow, watching. Certain no one waited in the dark, she crept over to the other door but froze when she noticed one of the beds piled high with blankets. Saoirse used to do the same on cold winter nights. They would hide under a tent of blankets together, building whole worlds and tearing them down with their words. She forced herself to ignore the reminder.

Saoirse was long gone. Wolf needed her. Wolf she could save.

A skinny hallway led to an oversized kitchen, stocked with food, beer and warm fires. She would kill to be given a chance to feed people from here. Anything to allow them the warmth and homeliness of a home cooked meal and a safe haven. Anger choking her, she raced up a steep staircase without meeting anybody. The hallways were empty and she moved through them softly. The entrance hall rose above her, reminding her of the cave. Tapestries added colour to the dark mahogany but failed to make the house welcoming.

Quietness hung like a gilded frame; only someone with too much space and not enough people would be able to own such a calm and silent home. Shadows stretched out as the night lightened with the day's slow ascent to wakefulness. She didn't have much time. She edged along the wall, unsure how to find the cells. Bullying herself for not asking Tadgh. Her pulse was a galloping horse that almost masked the near silent whisper of someone landing behind her.

*Almost.*

She twirled around, dagger already drawn.

Wolf stared at her with a blank face that was for once from shock rather than an overt control. "What the hell are you doing here?"

"I'm here to rescue you." Rua stepped forward, gaze sweeping over Wolf to check her for injuries. "Did you already escape? Am I late?" She grinned but it fell from her face when she saw how Wolf's mouth slashed across her face in a harsh, pale line.

Wolf grabbed Rua by the shoulders and dragged her into an alcove. "You idiot," she hissed in a tone far more threatening that Tadgh's. "Why would you come here?"

"We don't leave people behind." Rua's back hit a wall and still Wolf crowded closer. "I promised you."

They huddled in the shadows, so near Wolf's body heated Rua's cold skin. Rua reached up and pushed a strand of hair behind Wolf's ear. She tensed at the contact but didn't move away. Rua had noticed that Wolf reacted badly to casual, soft touch and she wanted to smother her in it until she no longer flinched away from kindness.

She gripped one of Wolf's wrists gently. "Are you okay? Did they hurt you?" A slither of pain snaked across Wolf's expression; a betrayal so extraordinary and obvious Rua felt her gut clench. "Wolf, what did they do?"

"They lied." She sounded wretched. Like she had contracted an illness in the last few hours. "They always lie."

"I don't understand." Unease scraped her back with sharp nails. "Did you escape already?"

She shook her head. "It doesn't matter. You can't be here. You have to go."

"But you're coming with me?" Rua gaped when Wolf's eyes filled with tears. She placed her hands on Wolf's shoulders, rubbing her thumbs in soothing circles. "Wolf, what's going on?"

"I wish I'd never met you," Wolf whispered, voice as sharp as any of her blades. "I wish I'd never come here. Everything is worse than ever."

Hurt made Rua breathless.

Wolf must have realised what she had said, because between one inhale and the next, her blank mask fell back over her features. "You can't be here. *Má aimsíonn siad thú,*" she trailed off when a stair creaked.

Rua blinked at her words. If they find *you.* "Wolf?"

Someone coughed; an intentional noise in the otherwise silent space. "What have you brought me, Little Wolf?"

Recognising the voice, Rua went cold.

"Nothing, I brought you nothing." Wolf stared at Rua, eyes wide. For the first time since Rua had met her, she looked a little bit scared. "It's a kitchen hand, lost. I'll show her the way back."

Liam Cogadh clucked his tongue. "I already told you you're not as good a liar as you think. Although I suppose you did get this one to believe you."

Wolf's grip on her arm tightened. "I'm sorry," she whispered.

The apology made no sense to Rua.

"Now," he said coldly.

Only compliance followed that tone, and Wolf knew it. She stepped back from Rua. Without her as a shield, it suddenly hit Rua what a mess she had made of the night, of the week, of the whole month.

Trusting Wolf was the worst mistake she had ever made.

The Síochain examined her with cruel, cold eyes. "So you're the woman who's been causing me so much trouble? Barely a scrap of a thing, aren't you?"

She took a step forward, slipping her dagger free from her sleeve. Wolf stopped her with a hand to the chest. Rua stared at her, confused, and the Síochain laughed, a cruel sound that made her skin crawl.

"Wolf?" She asked again, but she already knew, the betrayal tasting like bitter ink on her tongue.

"What do you want me to do with her?" Wolf's voice held nothing. All the life she had gained the last few weeks had seeped away like colour fading from autumn leaves.

The Síochain studied them both for a brief but probing moment. "I'll take her to the cells. Not that I don't trust you, but we did talk about how you look at her, didn't we?"

Without any hesitation, Wolf relinquished Rua to the Síochain's waiting hands.

# CHAPTER THIRTY
## WOLF

Rua had come to save her.

Wolf didn't know what to do with the knowledge. Part of her burned furiously. She had been telling Rua for weeks she needed to *plan* and *think* instead of rushing into danger. The others couldn't have known she had come. None of them would allow Rua to behave so completely without reason. Trying to steal a prisoner from the Síochain's cells needed more than one person. She wondered how she got in, *who had let her in*, but Pup would have to figure that out.

Each time she thought of finding Rua in the hallways, of her examining Wolf for injuries, her skin tightened over her muscles almost pleasantly, but the memory of Rua's betrayed expression when Wolf had handed her over to the Síochain soon erased that. She didn't like how it made her stomach churn like before a particularly bad punishment. She didn't know what to do with any of the revelations the night had shared. Usually she would spar and let the violence steal away any doubts or misgivings. She couldn't do that here; not just because it was dawn on a long night, but because the Hounds would see her.

Instead, she went back to Pup's room and curled up under her blankets, forcing her mind to empty, a skill she used often to forget the blood and the punishments and the pain, and allowed the waiting arms of sleep to embrace her for a few hours.

She woke before the door handle twisted fully, blade in her hand, sleep already forgotten.

Pup watched her for a long moment before she sat on the other bed. "You caught an intruder last night?"

Wolf heard what she didn't say. *Caught, not killed.* "Where do they have her?

"The third cell. Furthest from the exit. Hardest to break free of."

"You're getting better at asking questions without actually saying them out loud." Wolf made herself sound bored.

Pup shrugged one shoulder. "The Síochain has been questioning her the last few hours. He's finally left her alone. I haven't had a look at her yet. Maybe I'll pay her a visit myself."

"And what am I to do with this knowledge?" Wolf refused to let an inch of her uncertainty show. Now wasn't the time for games with Pup. Not when she felt so out of control.

"Whatever you want." The smirk told her that Pup knew exactly what Wolf would do. "I'm going on my rounds. In case you're wondering, she's revealed nothing, and he hasn't hurt her too badly."

The *yet* remained unspoken.

When she left, it took Wolf moments to roll to her feet. Maybe if she explained she meant none of it personally, it would wipe the memory of Rua's hurt from her brain.

***

For no reason but the discomfort of the prisoners, the cells were dark, wet and freezing. Stone shone with mildew and damp. Slits lined the walls opposite the cells, allowing frigid wind to cut through the space like a sword through bone. Wolf never revealed discomfort, but she knew torture intimately, and something like this drove a person wild. So effective too, with no way to escape the weather. She passed an empty cell, and then the one with the same two bodies as before, huddled together for warmth. A set of dark eyes watched her as she walked passed.

Not dead, then.

The thought made her heart trip over itself. She pushed the emotion aside and stopped in front of the last cell. Rua curled into the corner of the cell, hair covering her face, chains around her wrists and ankles. She seemed smaller, like the Síochain had already stolen something from her, but when she gazed at Wolf through curtains of hair that hid her face, she realised that *she* had stolen from Rua and that felt worse than a thousand slow cuts.

"Are you alright?"

She snorted and pulled at the chains on her hands. They clinked when she jerked them forward. "Oh, sure. I'm perfect."

"I didn't want to hurt you." The truth of the statement shocked Wolf. It grew and blossomed in her; not just physically but emotionally too. Wolf never meant to cause a scratch of harm to this strange, vibrant, beautiful woman. "I had a job to do."

"Who are you?"

"I can't tell you."

"Is your name even Wolf?"

She wanted to say yes, but now, back here, she had to be nameless again. "I don't have a name. None of us do."

Rua leaned her head against the wall, hair still covering her face, and shivered as a gust of wind blasted through the cell. "Aurnia was right not to trust you."

The value of Rua's trust was only realised once she'd lost it. "I can get you a blanket."

"No, I'm good."

"You're not good, Rua," Wolf snapped. "You're in so much danger I can't even... Why did you come for me?"

"I thought you were..." she stopped.

Wolf hated that her hair still covered her face. She needed to be able to read her expressions to understand.

"You were more at the cave." The words were spoken hoarsely as though forced out of a tight throat. "You're so small here."

Wolf blinked sudden tears from her eyes. She never cried and now she had twice over this woman in less than twelve hours. "What about the others? What will they do without you?"

"They'll move on."

The lie blared from the words like she had screamed it. Wolf knew they would come after her, after them both, and would be caught as well. She didn't want the others here, beaten and broken like Rua, chained to the walls and shivering in forced discomfort.

"Why couldn't you let me go?"

"I made a promise. You might not understand what that means but I sure as hell do."

Rua finally let her hair fall from her face.

The Síochain had destroyed it.

Cuts from a sharp knife lined her cheeks. Both eyes were swollen and black. A split lip made her teeth crimson. Blood painted her pale skin until it matched her hair. Wolf realised the Síochain had cut up her fingers and down her arms as well.

Bright, righteous fury surged through Wolf nearly knocking her back. No one would ever hurt this woman again without first dispatching of Wolf who would always, always stand in front of her. An instinct so foreign she didn't understand at first that she felt *protective*.

She tried to push it away, because she would be leaving soon, and this woman would never be hers to protect, but it was too late. A fire already burned low in her gut. Nothing like when she found out Pup hadn't been told of her life being attached to the Síochain's, worse than the first time she knew with certainty that her father wasn't coming back, or the day after the first test when she had sworn to stay alive no matter what. This felt bigger, more violent, softer, warm. Almost too much for her to contain inside her. It would consume her and burn away all the parts the Sisterhood claimed ownership of. It didn't feel like that would be bad. She would let it take all of her if it was needed. She would allow anything once Rua remained safe.

"You were one of mine." Rua stared at her as if trying to figure out why Wolf had betrayed her. "I don't leave mine behind."

The fire roared. "*A dhiabhal*, Rua."

"That should be my new name since you all are saying it so often."

"Don't joke about this," Wolf snapped.

"Why not? You already won," she spat. "What's left to do but laugh?"

Wolf knew the sensation well. "I won nothing. All I wanted was you safe. Them safe. I never win, Rua. I follow and follow and follow."

She kicked the metal bars separating them, and spun away, hating showing even that much emotion. She thought she had landed when she learned of the Sisterhood's lie, but now she realised she still fell, twisting desperately to try and find the ground. She needed the jolt of the landing to wake her back up from this nightmare.

"Why'd you do it, Wolf?"

"He told me to."

Rua scoffed. "And you obeyed?"

"Where I'm from, if you don't obey orders, pain follows instead."

"They hurt you."

Wolf hated how softly the words were spoken. All her silent

parts were still screaming, the noise ratcheting through her. She didn't know how to quiet them again.

"They're going to keep hurting you too," Wolf finally managed to reply. "There's nothing I can do to stop it."

"There's always something."

She didn't reply. Just walked away.

It didn't stop her from hearing Rua's final words.

"I never took you for a coward, Wolf."

# CHAPTER THIRTY-ONE
## RUA

The lock scraped open and Rua jerked awake from a fitful sleep. Pain sliced across her ribs and she gasped. None of the injuries were deep. They were shallow cuts designed for the most pain. She peered over at the bars swinging open, and for one barely alert moment, she hoped Wolf had come to save her, but then the Síochain strolled into the cell. He wasn't alone. Luchán strolled in behind him, resplendent as a boy prince.

Her Luchán. Her mouse. Her friend.

She wanted to refuse to believe he had betrayed her at the barn, but standing there, with the same striking features of the Síochain, the family resemblance clear in the cut of his jaw and the dismissive mouth, she had a sudden sinking fear that she had misjudged everyone she'd ever aligned herself with. She forced her stiff legs to straighten and crossed them at her ankles. No pain showed on her face. They would not see her hurt. Arms braced across her chest, despite how it made her fingers scream, she watched them coolly.

Luchán wore casual clothes, expensive in how simple they were, in the heavy material of the long sleeved jumper, the thick trousers and the perfect shine of his boots. The difference between him by the lake and him standing in his home were obvious; there he stood less sure of himself, a stranger in her land, but here, where he lived with his destined power, he swelled larger and larger until his presence felt almost as claustrophobic as the Síochain's.

It only took a quick examination to know he hadn't betrayed her; the horrified set of his mouth and the quick blinking of tears from his eyes told her as much. She remembered Wolf then and reminded herself she already knew her betrayer. No matter how painful it was to believe. She hoped the others were safe. She wished she'd left them a note. They would be losing their minds trying to figure out where she went. Maybe Tadgh had gotten a message to Aurnia. Maybe they knew. Maybe they would let her go. She almost laughed at the impossibility of that.

Not one of them would leave behind their own.

The Síochain's words dragged her from the truth of that realisation. "This prisoner broke into the house yesterday to murder me."

Luchán stared at her, horrified.

"No. I didn't." Talking hurt but this man wouldn't steal her voice. "I came to rescue a friend."

"How did that work out?" The Síochain watched Luchán as he spoke.

When he realised, Luchán schooled his face into an imperfect copy of Wolf's blank mask. The result made it too easy to read the fear in the twist of his mouth and his anger in the tightening around his eyes.

"Why did you bring me here, Uncle?" Luchán failed to remain impartial; his voice was saturated in his unease. "Isn't this a job for Roisin?"

Rua wondered at the uselessness of his training as he failed to hide his emotions, and then wondered if it was because he cared about her too much. She hated how unstable his voice sounded. Like it would collapse at any moment. Refusing to risk his exposure, she channelled Wolf and forced cool arrogance into the set of her mouth and scorn into her eyes as she considered the men.

"Why did you bring this man to visit?" She forced herself to sound bored, hiding her fear under layers of nonchalance. "I told you last night I wouldn't talk."

"She's been stealing from the Table." The Síochain acted like she hadn't spoken. "We need to discover who her informant is."

"To betray the Table means death," Luchán said it by rote, a phrase so often spoken that it had clearly lost its bite. "No one in this house would betray them."

"And yet my life has almost been stolen twice now."

"More's the shame they failed," Rua muttered.

By the glint in the Síochain's eyes, he heard her but deemed it unimportant to his lesson. "We know the penalty of betrayal, nephew. We grew up learning about the power the Table wields."

The Síochain's mask was not imperfect. There was no way to tell whether he really was just educating his nephew or if he'd figured out that Luchán had betrayed him and the Table by helping Rua. But that was impossible. Only she and Luchán knew.

A dagger glinted suddenly in the Síochain's hand and he handed it to Luchán. "Whoever has been helping her seems to have forgotten that to betray the Table means *death*. No forgiveness. No mercy."

The pain and fear from the night before roared to the surface. She swallowed back her pleas of *no more*, and said, "If he comes near me, I'll kill him."

The Síochain laughed. "Such words from a trapped mouse."

He twisted a dial in the wall that dragged her up by her chains, forcing her to stand and then hang from the stones by her wrists. It hurt worse the second time. Especially now her injuries were already like cold ice pressed for too long against her skin. The gashes on her wrists burned and the pain in her shoulders stole her voice for a second. A scream crawled up her throat but she refused to make a noise; the only way to ensure she wouldn't beg or cry, or worse, reveal a secret she'd sworn never to tell.

With a second knife, the Síochain cut her top to a little above her lowest ribs. "Ask her who her informant is. When she refuses to answer, which she will," grudging respect leaked into the words, "cut her. Nothing too deep. We need her to stay alive until my interrogator returns."

"If she's not going to answer us, why are we torturing her?"

He snorted. "This is hardly torture, Luchán. This is barely violence. You must learn the truth of being the Síochain. You cannot expect the Hounds to do your dirty work." He leaned against the wall and crossed his arms. "Go on then. See what it feels like to have this power you are to inherit."

Luchán walked towards her, a horribly broken expression on his face. She knew him well enough to read the apology there.

When he had blocked her from the Síochain, she whispered almost silently, "It's okay."

Tears in his eyes, he asked who had betrayed the Table, and when she didn't reply, he sliced her skin. Again and again and again.

# CHAPTER THIRTY-TWO
## WOLF

The bedroom door slammed open.

Pup stood in the doorway, hands gripping the wood so hard, her fingers were almost transparent. "They're torturing her." The words landed between them with the violence of a punch. "The Síochain and his nephew are torturing her." She glared at Wolf, eyes straining wide. "Say something," she spat.

Wolf shut her eyes and forced herself to stay calm. "What do you want me to say?"

She had been lying on Pup's bed, staring at the ceiling and allowing Rua's words to settle into her bones. Coward was an accurate description. Accurate when applied to the Sisterhood as well. They never stood in the light of day and declared a moral stance like Rua did. They hid in the dark, hid behind the stone walls of the convent, hid behind disguises and masks and poison and swords. They followed the Table in whatever road they led them down.

Wolf was so, so sick of following.

She rolled over, and forced herself to stand, recognising the conversation needed to be had on her feet.

When Pup glared at her, she said, "It isn't our concern." It tasted like the worst kind of lie because it was the sort you wanted to believe for yourself.

Pup stepped into the room and shoved her into a wall. Curious, Wolf allowed the violence to happen.

"You have to save her," Pup whispered, determined and bitter. "Get her out of there. And don't give me any Sisterhood shite." She wrapped her hands in Wolf's shirt but it felt more like she needed Wolf's body to hold herself up rather than it being a threat. "I heard what that nun said last night about no one getting to leave and you've had one foot out the door since I met you, *Wolf*."

She didn't bother denying the name or the truth. Mostly she was impressed Pup had not only got the read on her, but had stayed hidden from her in the Síochain's quarters.

"What does she matter to you?"

"Nothing." Something broken shattered the word. Not a lie, but not the full truth either. "But she doesn't deserve this. You know she doesn't."

Wolf blinked at this raw, unhinged version of Pup. All control and obedience gone. Maybe this was really her, who she would have become, if survival hadn't been her only aim.

"You want me to do what exactly?" Wolf asked. She didn't speak softly but it wasn't as harsh as it would have been before. "Give up my place in the Sisterhood for a woman I met a few weeks ago?"

"No." Pup gave her a frustrated shake. "I want you to use that *loyal to only yourself* bullshit you spouted at me from the beginning. Get her and yourself out of here."

Wolf tilted her head and studied her; Pup shuddered with the force of her emotions, her practised calm long forgotten. Paleness made the red of her hair loud. She leaned into Wolf, body damp with sweat despite the chill, and lips a thin line of frustration.

"You gonna come with us?"

The offer shocked Pup into stepping back.

Wolf thought maybe she had made up her mind to leave the minute she saw Rua broken and beaten in the cell. She thought maybe it had been when the nun had said no one ever left, or when the Síochain called it a kindness to be told, or when she learned that the woman who chose never to return didn't exist, or the day she knew her father had abandoned her. Maybe it was after the first test, or the first time she searched for comfort and found cruelty. Her whole life had been building to her leaving, and all Pup had done by slamming into the room was help her find solid ground again.

Pup shook her head. "My place is here. I *earned it.*" Speaking of her survival calmed some of the wildness from her eyes. "I earned safety away from the famine. I'm not going back out there to fight for scraps again."

"There's no safety here, Pup."

She sucked in a shuddering breath. "It's better than out there. Trust me."

Wolf nodded. "Loyal only to yourself."

"And maybe a little bit to you," Pup replied grudgingly.

A small, genuine smile broke free of Wolf, and then she grimaced. "If I do this, they'll never stop hunting me."

"If you don't, you'll never be free."

Agreement thrilled through Wolf. She would not allow the world to become dull and grey again, would not allow Rua to be stolen from her, would search out beauty like her father had told her to. She refused to be a coward. She would no longer follow a master she hated. Fear was not an unfamiliar emotion but it had stopped controlling her long ago.

She nodded, "I'll free her. I'll get her to safety."

"And you'll stay with her." She sounded desperate again, and broken; a sin she needed penance for. "You'll *keep* her safe."

Wolf put a hand to her shoulder, and found her trembling worse than before. "How do you know her?"

"I don't. Not anymore." She glanced away from Wolf's searching eyes and blinked until hers held no more tears. "But you're the only one I would trust her with. Please, Wolf. Keep her safe."

Unsure, Wolf nodded.

"No. You have to say it. You have to swear to me on… On your…" she trailed off.

"I'll swear on the memory of my father." Wolf held eye contact and kept her voice steady. "I swear to you I will stay with her and keep her safe."

Pup wiped her eyes with the back of her hands. The action made her younger and so much more vulnerable. "You gave me a name," she whispered. "If you ever need to get in contact, use it."

Wolf nodded. "Same."

"When will you take her?"

"Tonight. I'll free her tonight."

# CHAPTER THIRTY-THREE
## WOLF

**W**olf waited until the house slept.

She strapped her knives to her body, way more than she had been carrying the last few weeks, and felt better with the weight of her sword on her hip, her long daggers on her back. She dressed in the Sisterhood's garb; heavy trousers designed for easy movement and to slow a knife, a tight, long sleeved top and a light, flexible corset to protect her ribs and organs. She had hidden her bag under Pup's bed when she had first left to find the thieves. It felt like a lifetime ago but it also felt like something slipped into place when she put on the clothes she had grown up in.

Pup plaited her hair and tied it into a bun. The boots she slipped on last were as soft as summer grass and made movement easy. Her promise to Pup trilled through her. She had only ever been ordered. Only ever followed. Never asked. Never trusted with something precious.

Now though, she would lead Rua to safety.

When Wolf got to the cell, Rua wasn't alone. The Síochain's nephew knelt beside her, crying. He had washed Rua's injuries and was now wrapping them in bandages. He kept up a constant stream of apologies as he did. Rua ran a hand through his hair, comforting him.

"I'm so sorry, Rua," he babbled, voice hoarse as he whispered "I should have stood up to him. I should never have done it. I'm so sorry."

Rua shushed. "You couldn't. Not after everything. Not yet."

"No," he hissed. "What I did to you. I'll never forgive myself. I'll never make it up to you."

Wolf stepped from the shadows and tilted his head up with the tip of her sword. "Is there a reason you're here, Luchán Cogadh?"

He glared at her with slitted eyes. "Who are you?" His commanding voice sounded so similar to the Síochain's that she almost considered answering.

"Wolf." Rua said her name like a curse. "Let him go."

She dropped her sword but kept it out.

"Is there a reason *you're* here, Wolf?" Rua glared at her, wincing when Luchán tied off the bandage around her stomach. "I thought you had to run back to your masters."

Wolf hated the disgust in Rua's expression, hated how it made her stomach curdle and her hands damp. Locking away her emotions and forcing herself to focus, she said, "I'm here to rescue you."

Rua straightened up. "What did you say?"

"I've decided being a coward is not for me." She tried to make it sound casual but she couldn't help the bit of pride that slipped in. She was actually leaving the Sisterhood. She almost grinned at the rush of adrenaline.

Luchán glanced between them, and back to Rua. "You know this girl?"

"She's who I came to rescue." Bitterness soaked the words. "She didn't need it."

"Do you trust her?"

Rua studied Wolf for a long moment. "I trust that she's telling the truth right now. I don't trust her though."

Wolf kept her face blank, refusing to show how much that hurt.

"You should go with her." He wrapped up her hands, wincing as she hissed. "Someone is coming tomorrow to question you. You won't survive it. *Imigh, le do thoil.*" Go, please.

The old language seemed to convince her. "Help me up."

He lifted her gently, and Wolf handed her a dagger. "Are you okay to use that?"

Rua took the knife, wincing as she grasped it, but otherwise ignored the question. "Don't let him know you were here." She ran her fingers through Luchán's hair again and a burst of heat clenched Wolf's stomach. Rua shouldn't know this boy. She certainly should not be risking more injury by touching him. "If you need me, you know where to find me."

Wolf suddenly realised exactly why he had come to help Rua. "You're her informant?"

Luchán and Rua exchanged wary glances.

"Wolf," Rua warned.

She ignored her. "You have to come with us. The Síochain knows who you are."

"That's impossible," Luchán responded. "There's no way."

The wind pounded on the stones and bars, demanding they pay attention to it. Wolf peered out of the cell to make sure no one used the sound of the weather to mask their approach. Pup kept watch near the entrance but there was only so much she could do without being caught.

"He figured it out in the barn," she grabbed his bicep and shook. "You'll hang for this. He already sent a letter to your mother."

"I'll get a slap on the wrist and more training." Luchán brushed aside her hand but his eyes shot to Rua's bandaged stomach with a sick expression. "Get Rua out of here."

"To betray the Table means *death*. It doesn't matter who

you are. He will not risk the rest of his family to protect you." Wolf pushed Luchán, frustrated. "You cannot be this naive. You grew up in this like I did. Or did you not get punished when you failed?"

Rua put a hand on Wolf's shoulder, calming in a way that wasn't controlling. "Luchán, she's right. It's time. We both knew one day this would happen."

"I can't just leave my family."

"Your privilege won't protect you now," Rua said gently.

Wolf needed a weakness. Something only he and the Síochain would know to prove she was truthful and trustworthy. Frustrated at how much easier this would have been when she had Rua's confidence, she forced herself to think, remembering those nights in the Síochain's rooms.

"Uncle Liam won't protect you no matter how much you make him laugh."

Luchán swallowed audibly and she knew she had him. He considered the bandages again and nodded. "Okay. Let's go."

Wolf led them from the cell, intentionally hiding the two sleeping bodies as they walked past. Rua would want to take them too but Wolf didn't think she could manage all of them. She had already chosen who to save.

Luchán supported Rua. Each step made a quiet whine of pain escape her pale lips. They crept along the dark walkway, and disappeared down steps that led to a dank set of corridors running under the grounds. It led to the tunnel that Pup had hidden from the Síochain. The three of them could use it to escape. The tight quarters made Wolf nervous—she would be able to protect herself but not the others in such a small space— but the tunnel broke free close enough to the trees that they would be able to run into the shadows, invisible even on the most moonlit night.

They moved slower than she would have liked but Rua

couldn't go any faster. The entrance to the tunnel had just appeared in dim light when a knife suddenly sliced through the sleeve of her top, grazing her bicep, and planting itself in a wooden beam in front of her.

Wolf spun around, dragging the other two behind her.

The nun stood in the darkness, shaking her head. "I expected better from you, apprentice. It will bring me such joy to rid the Sisterhood of your failure."

The nun unsheathed her sword and struck.

# CHAPTER THIRTY-FOUR
## WOLF

The blade swung in a tight arc. Wolf moved instinctively, taking a step back, grateful she already had her sword in her hand. She threw it up and met the nun's sword in a clash of violence. She pushed her back with a harsh shove.

They circled each other.

Wolf's heart pounded a ferocious beat against her ribs. The nun struck again, spinning away from Wolf's attack and forcing her into the wall. Wolf ducked and twisted. The blade scraped across the wall where her head had just been. She raised her sword to strike again but the nun countered easily.

Wolf stayed in front of Rua, while trying to force the fight up the corridor and away from them. Luchán had Rua shoved behind his back; the wounds must be worse than she told them if she willingly let someone else fight for her.

"Is this how poorly we trained you?" The nun taunted, turning the fight around to retrieve her dagger from the wood. "All that arrogance and barely the ability to parry blows." Her eyes shone almost black in the dim light, and she paused, sword in one hand and dagger in the other. A predator in their natural habitat. "You always were pathetic, weren't you? Seeking approval from anyone who would give it to you." She shot forward again, a blur of movement.

Wolf barely felt the slice of a dagger down her cheek. Blood made her lips wet. She swung her sword up quick enough to prevent another blow. Another slice cut along her neck. She stumbled back and the nun stalked forward. Wolf had more skill than this, moved faster than this, but with Rua watching, she choked, helpless and afraid, reduced to the scared child she had once been.

The nun grinned, teeth like fangs. "How did you pass any of your tests?"

The words were weapons too. They hit Wolf in places she failed to ignore.

Wolf pushed forward, attacking with more energy, forcing the nun into the defensive and away from her friend. The nun laughed, cruel and giddy, barely out of breath. Wolf heaved in another gulp of air. It hit her all at once; how heavy the sword felt, her clumsy movements, and the tiredness that already bit at her muscles.

Watching her like a hawk would a mouse, the nun laughed. "Figure it out yet, little apprentice?" The nun twirled the bloody dagger between her fingers. "The Sisterhood doesn't play fair."

She had cut Wolf with that dagger. Three times.

Hours of training with Conor and Aurnia should have made her stronger. Should have made her quicker. Fitter. Better. But they were too honourable. They took on their opponents through skill alone. The nun knew how good Wolf was, and had decided to make the fight unwinnable.

*Bás Tostach.* Silent death.

The thirteenth test had been poisons. Eight girls in a circle. Each had to consume a poison and name it from their symptoms. If they succeeded, they got the antidote. If they failed, they still got the antidote, but they also got two months in the lab of the poisons expert, testing each of the new concoctions she created. Wolf got all eight right. She'd also had to test *Bás Tostach* on herself. She knew the symptoms well; sweats, shortness of breath, weakness in her limbs, slurred speech, dizziness and unconsciousness. If she didn't receive the antidote soon after she fell unconscious, she would die, but as a creation of the Sisterhood, only the Sisterhood had the cure.

Wolf was already dead.

Knowing that, she attacked more violently. "Luchán, get her out of here," she shouted. "Get her to safety."

"Not without you," Rua screamed.

A quick glance showed Luchán pushing her towards the opening and Rua struggling weakly against him.

"Go, Rua," he shouted. "I'll help her. Go."

For once, Rua went.

Luchán tackled the nun from the side and they both fell over. Momentarily safe, Wolf leant against the wall for a brief second, gasping. Shouts echoed down the passage. Hounds trampling down to investigate. She had no urgency left; Rua had escaped and the soft kiss of death whispered along her skin. Luchán fought the nun messily, desperation more than skill, but his bigger body was an advantage that kept them both on the ground. With a grunt, he finally knocked the sword from her grip.

"Wolf, go! She can't hurt me without the Table's permission."

Wolf watched them and nodded. The nun parried blows but didn't try to injure him.

She pushed herself off the walls, body heavy. If she saw Rua one more time, it would be okay. Dying would be okay. She crawled into the tunnel, hot and heavy. Dirt fell into her eyes and mouth. Dragging herself along, exhausted, she knew she couldn't make it. The tunnel was too long, too dark, too steep, too much. She had decided to give up, accept the grave, when two hands gripped her wrist and dragged her out.

Rua gasped in pain but helped Wolf to her feet. "Where's Luchán?"

Blood still poured from the slash across Wolf's cheek and neck. She tasted copper on her lips. "We have to go, " she managed.

"Where's Luchán?"

"He saved me."

"I have to get him. I left because I thought… I shouldn't have…" Rua went to climb back down the tunnel and Wolf grabbed her wrist in a loose circle. "You can't."

Rua tried to free her wrist but neither of them had much strength left. "I have to."

"The Hounds got him. The nun has him." The words were hoarse and shook like a foal learning to stand. "They're going to be after us. We have to go."

"But," she froze, lost and unsure.

"Rua. Now." The world spun, swooping under her and making it hard to stay upright, but she kept hold of Rua's wrist and pulled her towards the forest. "Can Aurnia hide us?"

When no answer came, she dragged them forward anyway, moving only because Rua allowed it. Wolf didn't think she had any real strength left. Leaves smacked their faces as they raced past. Branches cracked underfoot. Wolf ached; her stomach and her face and her joints. All rioting against the poison in her system. She had hoped she still had time to make up for her last mistake by getting Rua to safety. But the rough shouts and determined orders echoing behind them told her she didn't. Hounds were already following them.

"Rua. Please." Wolf stumbled and fell into a tree, forcing herself up as she did. "We gotta keep going," she slurred.

"What's wrong?" Stopping, Rua examined Wolf's face. "The cut, it's dark around the edges, almost black. What did she do to you?"

"*Bás Tostach* on her dagger. Poison."

"Silent death? I've never heard of it." Rua wrapped her arms around Wolf's ribs to keep her steady and threw Wolf's arm across her shoulder. "Wolf, tell me about it. Keep talking to me," she pleaded.

"Mix of poisons. Make you sick. Slow. Dead." It took her longer and longer to form each word. "Dizzy. Tired." Wolf's pulse stampeded across her skin.

"Aurnia will be able to help you, okay?" Desperation soaked the words. "Stay with me until then."

"'M sorry, didn't want," she stopped talking, tongue fat and heavy.

"Wolf!"

"Hurt you." She stumbled again but Rua's grip kept her upright.

The Hounds sounded closer. Wolf knew she should care but it all felt so far away now. She swallowed back a sob as fear became a vice around her stomach. She didn't want to die, not now she had finally found something worth living for.

"Father, I found it."

"Found what? Wolf, found what?" Rua sounded annoyed and Wolf didn't want her to be angry with her.

"Beauty," she whispered. She ignored the whispering voice telling her she shouldn't be saying the words. "*D'aimsigh mé thú.*" I found you.

Rua seemed to choke. "We're almost there, Wolf. Please keep going."

They moved in silence, Wolf resting more and more on Rua. She almost cried with relief when Rua crept them in through a small gap in the fence and helped her to the inn. Rua banged on the door, and Wolf begged her to be quiet. Or she thought she did. She wasn't sure if her words were working any more. Her head hurt so much.

Aurnia swung the door open, eyes wide. "Rua?"

"They're after us."

As if on cue, the warning bell rang out, alerting residents that a search would be taking place. Wolf winced as the noise sliced through her brain. Aurnia rushed them inside, leading them to the pantry and pushed aside two heavy barrels. Wolf leaned against Rua, glad they had stopped. Her eyes were going dark at the edges. She shut them.

A hand smacked her face and she forced her eyes open.

"Not sleeping, nun, 'm awake." The words slurred more than she wanted. "Don't hurt me, 'm ready."

"Wolf. Wolf."

"My name. You can't." She fell back and tensed when she knocked over a vase; shards of ceramic shattered on the floor. Wolf whispered, "Don't punish me, 'm sorry."

When she knelt down to clean up the pieces, the ground rushed up to meet her and Wolf let the darkness claim her.

# CHAPTER THIRTY-FIVE
## RUA

Rua shot forward and managed to catch Wolf before she hit the ground. She lowered her gently, hands screaming with the touch. Crouching over Wolf, she ran the pads of her fingers over her skin, worried about how clammy she felt.

"Don't die, please don't die," Rua whispered and then shut up when the sound of boots echoed across the yard outside.

Aurnia lifted a section of the floor, shining a light into a tiny space that would just fit the two of them. "Get in and hope she stays alive long enough for me to help her." Cold fury shook the words in a way Rua had never heard from Aurnia.

Rua lowered Wolf into it. Banging started on the door.

Aurnia practically pushed her in and slammed the floor closed. The barrels scraped the wood as they were dragged back into place. Aurnia's footsteps softened as she walked over to the kitchen door. Muire called down about the disturbance.

Wolf's breath barely grazed across her cheek.

Rua held Wolf's hands, even though it made her fingers scream.

"Why are you knocking at my door at this late hour?" Aurnia's voice demanded answers in the same way the Síochain's had. Power could be wielded by anyone with a strong enough spine.

"Two prisoners escaped the Síochain's cells tonight."

"And you think they're here?" Muire asked in a kinder but more judgemental tone than Aurnia. Aurnia wielded power. Muire wielded disappointment. "It's just us and some guests upstairs. We'd ask you not bother them though."

The Hound sounded young. "I have to check every room."

"Sure, you might as well come in then," Muire sighed. "Is your friend going to stay in the shadows or are they coming in too?"

"I'll come in," someone replied, grumpier than the first but no less young.

Muire hummed. "I'll prepare some apology drinks for the guests. You can search the kitchen and then the bar while I go wake them."

The floorboard above Rua's head creaked. She locked her muscles and hoped that her breathing only sounded loud because of the tiny space.

The grumpy Hound asked, "What happened there?"

"I got a fright with the banging on the door," Aurnia said. Pieces of ceramic scraped across the wooden floors. "I knocked it over."

"Is that blood?"

Aurnia laughed, but it sounded strained to Rua's ears. "Sauce. Spilled that too."

Rua gripped Wolf's hand tighter. Slits of moonlight illuminated the dark. Wolf's eyes moved back and forth beneath her eyelids. She whimpered. Rua smacked a hand over her mouth.

"What's that noise?"

"Mice, probably. Always infested in the winter. Everyone trying to escape the cold; mice, people, Hounds." Aurnia's voice sounded right above Rua's head. "Now you've searched the pantry, would you like to see the bar?"

The conversation moved away.

When she glanced over, Wolf's eyes were open but her pupils were so wide the black had stolen the irises. She stared at Rua without seeing her. After a moment, she shut them again. Rua refused to cry, refused to pray, refused to beg.

"She's going to survive," she whispered to the dark over and over again.

The search took forever. Wolf's hair stuck to her head with sweat. Paleness made her more skeleton than person, aggravated by strips of moonlight through gaps in the wood, basking her in unforgiving white. Even after the Hounds left, the guests refused to be shuffled back to bed, merrily drinking free beer and bantering with Muire, laughing about the inconvenience of being woken so late. Time crawled as Rua lay in the dark listening to Wolf die. Finally, the barrels were dragged back. She shoved the hatch up off her.

Aurnia gripped the edges and stared down. "What happened?"

She sat up and ran her bandaged hands over Wolf's hair. "*Bás Tostach* on a dagger."

Aurnia hissed and glanced at Muire. "Help me get her up."

They carried Wolf to the table and Rua followed behind them and wrung her hands at her uselessness.

"It's poison," she said.

"I know what it is," Aurnia snapped. "Muire, I need my box. It's under the bed." When Muire rushed off, Aurnia wiped down Wolf's forehead with a cold, damp cloth. "Oh, *mo leanbh*, what have they done to you?"

Rua stood by the door to avoid looking at Wolf and listened to the commotion outside. Clearly not everyone was as accommodating at being woken in the middle of the night. Violence hummed on the night air. The march of Hounds echoed through the streets. Doors slammed open and shouts of anger called out. She stepped further into the shadows when two Hounds passed close to the entrance of the yard.

"Rua, get away from there," Aurnia hissed.

Rua nodded and moved closer to the table. Bile rose up her throat. Wolf had shrunk down since that last night in camp; sitting by the fire, bantering with Aoife over the flames. She had made Conor smile when she insulted Seán's axe skills and then taught him an easier grip. Rua had watched them all and something had lightened in her chest. As the fire died, and the others left them to go to sleep, they sat side by side, not talking. Just being together. Rua didn't think she could bear to lose her for the second time.

The betrayal had torn through her, but she had watched Wolf in that place, cowering back without even realising, making herself smaller, and Rua knew it hadn't been a choice. Someone as arrogant as Wolf would never make herself less unless she absolutely had to.

Muire appeared with a black wooden box.

Aurnia opened it, eyes expertly glancing over labels. "This is not just *Bás Tostach*. It shouldn't act this fast." She picked three vials and mixed them together in a bowl, diluting them with water. "Hold her up. I need her to drink this, and quickly, she doesn't have much time left."

Rua and Muire each took a shoulder and supported Wolf as Aurnia helped her to swallow down the rancid smelling concoction. Wolf thrashed violently, but once she had swallowed it all, she settled. The tension left her muscles and she slumped into Rua, breath steadier than it had been.

"I added a sedative to help her sleep." Aurnia's voice sounded distant and her eyes lost to some other place. "She should be okay."

When Muire touched her, she shuddered and gazed at her as if confused. "Stay with me, *mo stór*."

She squeezed Muire's hand. "Let's get her up to the spare room and then we can talk."

Rua watched, chills scuttling across her skin as the adrenaline faded. "How did you know to do that?"

"Because I come from the same place Wolf does." Aurnia's eyes blazed. "I was a member of the Sisterhood of Righteous Death."

# CHAPTER THIRTY-SIX
## RUA

Rua sat down heavily as the exhaustion and pain caught up with her. She knew she should offer to help them carry Wolf upstairs, but her body had nothing left to give. The adrenaline had faded, leaving her with a hollow chasm where her energy had once been. Aurnia's words shuddered through her but they had no real weight to them. She didn't know what the Sisterhood meant for either Wolf or Aurnia. All she knew was what she had seen; Wolf, so helpless, so petrified, it made Rua want to scream or cry. Every part of her ached, and now her heart did as well. She lay her head on the table and listened to the women return.

Muire ran her hand tenderly over Rua's head. "Oh, *mo leanbh*, what did they do to you?"

Rua would have laughed at the repetition of Aurnia's words if everything hadn't seemed so hopeless. She shrugged.

"Bath?" Muire asked.

Before she answered, Aurnia said, "It'll help clean the wounds."

"And ease the pain."

Not needed for the conversation, Rua let them whisper to each other about herbs and temperatures as she tried to banish Wolf's terror from her head. When Wolf had handed her over to the Síochain, it had been so easy to dismiss her, mark her as unworthy of Rua's friendship, but having watched the nun taunt her, seen the sick fear on Wolf's face, how desperate she had been to keep Rua safe, and the barely coherent whispering about beauty to her dead father, Rua couldn't see her as a willing participant, not now she had seen her as a victim.

The rush of water interrupted her thoughts. She rolled her head sideways to watch them make up the bath. The smell of lavender and chamomile floated over to her, mixed with parsley and mint.

"Healing herbs," Muire said, motioning her to stand.

She pushed herself up, wincing as her fingers throbbed. Aurnia peeled off her top, unwinding the bandages as Muire motioned for her to lift each foot. They stripped her quickly and without comment, but shock still shaped their expressions. Only the crackle of the fire broke the silence. When she was naked of both her clothes and Luchán's hastily applied bandages, they helped her step into the tub and she lay down. The warm water stung painfully, but then it began to ease the horrid ache in her muscles.

"What happened?" Aurnia asked, before she gently pushed Rua forward and poured water over her hair. Muire washed her arms with a soapy sponge, her dark skin illuminating Rua's paleness.

"I wanted to protect Wolf." She choked on the truth. "I didn't want to put the others in danger to do it."

Aurnia clicked her tongue in soft rebuke.

"I know I have to trust them. But they shouldn't have to die for me." An unshakeable truth Rua had built her life around; as true as the sky being blue and frost being cold. "No one should have to die for me."

"But you'd die for them?" Muire asked.

Rua nodded miserably. She didn't know how to explain it.

Sometimes, before she had managed to steal enough food to satisfy her stomach, she would get so hungry, she would just stop noticing it. The hunger would seem almost distant, present but ignorable, and she would do what she needed to do without acknowledging it. She knew now the hunger would never leave her, had settled into her bones and would always be there, no matter how far from the famine she got. If she had children, they would know this hunger. Her children's children would know of this hunger.

It was irrevocably part of who she was.

Dying for them, refusing to let them die for her, felt the same.

After Rua had dragged Saoirse to the workhouse when she didn't want to go, and Rua would hold that shame close to her heart forever, she had decided that no one would ever die as a consequence of her actions again. She voted Wolf in. She insisted on robbing the barn. She let go of Wolf's hand. She had to get her back.

The two women shared a look over her head in a language she didn't speak.

"You got into the Síochain's estate?" Aurnia prompted.

"Tadgh helped." Rua shook her head. "Actually he told me not to be a fool but I still did what I wanted."

Muire grinned. "Can't be changing nature."

"Yeah, probably." She couldn't dredge up a laugh. "I broke in, found Wolf, but she told me to leave. She tried to make me go. The Síochain found us."

Both sets of hands paused on her body.

She took a shaky breath. "Wolf handed me over to him. I don't think she really wanted to. She came to explain and then later to save me. She fought a woman who spoke about a Sisterhood. What is it? How did you know she was part of it?"

Neither spoke for a long time. Another silent conversation

happened over Rua's head.

"I have my own spies, Rua, and I needed to know where they were keeping you. I knew who the nun was the minute she was described to me."

"You were going to come for me?"

"You are not the only one who fears losing people."

Rua couldn't find the words to reply to the rebuke.

When Aurnia finished scrubbing her hair clean, and had rinsed it free of suds, she said, "Lie back there and let me tell you a story."

Rua did, pleased when Muire added another pot of hot water to the bath. Everything that ached was soothed and safe again. No one could hurt her here. Not with these two women.

"My parents sent me to the Sisterhood at three. There, they train you to be an assassin for the Table." Aurnia spoke softly, staring into the flames. Muire took her hand. "You are given fifteen tests over fifteen years, and if you pass them all, you become a member of the Sisterhood of Righteous Death. They send you to do their bidding; spying, murder, infiltration and protection."

"How did you escape?"

The question startled Aurnia. "At nineteen, I met Muire and fell in love. I realised I didn't want that life. I was nothing. Muire made me real."

"You made yourself real, *mo stór*."

They kissed softly over Rua's head.

"It took me a long time to plan my escape, and when I did, I made sure no one would ever come looking for me." She sat perfectly still, meeting neither of their eyes. "There are some things even I wish to forget. It took a long time to exorcise the stains from my soul. All you need to know is that I escaped." She snapped her attention back to Rua's face. "If Wolf is a member of the Sisterhood, if she is an apprentice, then they will never stop hunting her."

"She said she was glad she found me," Rua whispered.

"I will talk to her. Make sure her intentions are honourable." Aurnia helped her stand. "Dry off and I'll apply a tincture to your wounds. It will help them heal quicker."

Muire wrapped her in a towel and pulled her into a warm, brief hug. "Don't do that to us again. We were worried sick."

"I promise."

"Conor will be here in the morning." Aurnia crushed herbs in a bowl and added some water. "At least this will stop us from having to sneak into the Síochain's house."

Rua froze. "You weren't."

"Of course we were," she snapped. "What did you think would happen?"

She stared down at the towel on the floor, refusing to answer. Her mind supplied all the ways her rescue could have gone wrong.

"Rua," Aurnia's stern tone forced her to pay attention. "I am more skilled than all of you put together. Do not think of doing something like that again without my input, do you understand?"

Rua nodded.

"Good. Now this is going to sting a bit."

When her cuts were tended, they brought her up to the same bedroom as Wolf. It wasn't one of the guest rooms. Instead, it was a secret room, hidden behind a piece of wall, and made even less accessible by a sideboard that had to be pushed aside to access it. Aurnia moved the sideboard and swung the wall open. Wolf lay unconscious in one of the beds. Rua crawled onto the second one and they watched her tuck herself in.

"Try not to make any noise, okay? The Hounds are still looking for you."

Muire smiled gently. "We'll bring you breakfast in the morning."

"How long will Wolf be like that?"

Aurnia shook her head. "Hopefully she'll wake up sometime tomorrow. She'll be exhausted but her system should've cleared it by then."

"Sleep, *mo leanbh*." Muire squeezed her toes. "We'll be right next door."

Rua nodded, eyes already heavy.

When they slid the wall closed, she reached over and took Wolf's hand, fingers resting over her slow and steady pulse. She fell asleep to the rhythm of Wolf's heart.

# CHAPTER THIRTY-SEVEN
## WOLF

Wolf couldn't move.

She was back in the Silence, trapped in the dark again. She tried to force her muscles to shift. Nothing happened and she swallowed a whine. Terror played strings up her spine. Rats nested in the corner, shuffling the straw and scraping the ground. A thick, heavy spider ran up her arm. She wanted to swipe it off but her hand wouldn't obey her. She didn't think it had been long since she had eaten, but hunger gnawed at her stomach. Cold stone seeped into her bones. Damp air made her skin slick. Every part of her body ached; her neck struggled to support her head, her hips begged for soft bedding, and her skin thrummed a beat to match her pulse. The dark covered her eyes, an unbreakable black that no light breached.

Some part of her brain knew she was dreaming but she still couldn't move.

The door exploded open, making her blink and blink and blink to clear the tears caused by the searing illumination. She thought maybe she had been here for a month. She thought maybe she had been born in the dark and lived in the dark and would always be in the dark. The nun stared, eyes flashing. Wolf stole in a heaving breath.

The nun hissed, "He was never going to keep you, Little Wolf."

Wolf blinked. Liam Cogadh towered over her.

"You never were a good liar, were you *mo Mhac Tíre Beag*?"

She sobbed at the name, her private name, said with such disdain.

"Quite the loyal little thing, aren't you? Do you have a single original thought in that useless skull of yours?"

More memory than dream, she knew her lines. "I could show you some of my more original thoughts, *a dhuine uasail*, if you like."

"We do not speak that language here."

"*Ní labhraítear, a dhuine uasail.*"

"There you are."

Wolf couldn't move. "Who is my father?"

The smile that traced his lips promised cruelty. "He is a man long dead, but you knew that, didn't you?"

She nodded. "Did he love me?"

"More than you can ever imagine." The Síochain spoke but Rua's voice came out instead.

The Síochain faded into the shadows. The door closed.

Wolf couldn't move.

Somewhere, a hand gripped her wrist, measuring the beat of her pulse. Wolf held onto the sensation of skin on skin.

Outside her rioting body.

Outside this nightmare.

This memory.

This fear.

Somewhere, Rua held her wrist. Somewhere, she slipped her fingers along the delicate skin there. Somewhere, she anchored Wolf to her body. Somewhere.

Wolf couldn't move, but she felt a little less alone in the darkness.

# CHAPTER THIRTY-EIGHT
## RUA

When Rua opened her eyes, her fingers still clung to Wolf's wrist.

It took her a few moments to remember they had broken free. Relief was a spike of adrenaline. Warmth enveloped her. Used to hard ground in the cave, the bedding cradled her throbbing body. She blinked awake and stared around the room. It had been dark when she had gotten into bed but now a small window at the very top of the wall cast sparse light. Stone shaped the walls. The thatch roof sat visible above her, uncovered unlike in the bar where a wood ceiling kept in the best of the heat. The only pieces of furniture were the beds, squished together with barely a foot between them. They were shoved into the corners of the room, leaving only a small space at the bottom.

Conor leaned against the wall, watching her.

In the tiny space, every inch of his anger was visible as it tightened his eyes and made his lips as harsh as a winter frost that would catch up with her no matter how hard she ran. She ached, had slept curled in a ball like she had in the cell and had dreamt of monsters and knives and nuns with sharp teeth. When she shifted, a spasm of pain jolted across her skin. It must have shown on her face because Conor's fingers gripped his biceps so hard they turned white. She winced at how awful she must look, bruised and scabbing with thick streaks of Aurnia's tincture smeared across her skin. It hurt too much to sit up so she stretched her body out, wincing as fresh pain spasmed through her. She refused to let go of Wolf.

Stumbling through the forest with Wolf dying, watching her fall to the ground, hearing her struggle to take in even shallow breaths in the dark under the floor, meant Rua needed to know she was alive, needed the pulse of her heartbeat beneath her fingers.

"I'm sorry." Her voice sounded like she had choked on stones. "I'm so sorry."

"What the hell were you thinking?"

She rubbed her thumb over Wolf's pulse. "I had to save her. I didn't want any of you to get hurt."

"Oh, you hurt us, Rua," he growled. "Never doubt that."

She swallowed. "Conor…" An ache throbbed in her chest and her eyes pricked. She blinked.

"Seán woke first but he fell back asleep. Do you know how much he's beaten himself up for not noticing you'd slipped away?" Conor's voice could have frozen water on a summer afternoon. "Aoife has barely spoken in days. Oisín is running himself ragged trying to look after everyone."

"Conor…"

"Don't you dare," he snapped. "We lost two people in one night. *You made us* lose two people in one night. Did you even think—" he paused, seeming too angry to even formulate the words. He stared at the low roof and took several deep breaths. "—Did you even think what it would do to us to wake up and find you gone? Not a note in sight. You're lucky Tadgh has a whip of sense and managed to get a message to Aurnia." He held her eyes for several long seconds before she had to look down. "You go on and on about us being a family and then leave us to go after Wolf. We all wanted to save her. We just needed a plan."

He took a shuddering breath and silence settled between them.

Conor finally broke it. "Rua, you can't keep doing this to us. Throwing yourself into our fights. Leaving us behind. Thinking you're unimportant. If you died—" He ran his hands through his hair but she saw how they trembled. "—how do you think we would cope? Do you think any of us would be okay? Haven't we lost enough already?"

She nodded, small and stupid.

"And look at you. Oisín is going to… " He coughed, clearing his throat with a rough bark. "*A dhiabhal,* Rua, what did they do to you?"

She glanced down at her bandaged hands. "How much did Aurnia tell you?"

"Not much. She said you had to face up to what you did."

"That seems about right." She sat up, ignoring the pain. She didn't meet his eyes, fidgeting with her blankets instead. "The Síochain wanted answers. This was the easiest way to get them. He's got Luchán. My friend. He's going to kill him and there's nothing we can even do."

"Your friend is the Síochain's apprentice?" Conor rubbed his forehead. "No wonder you couldn't tell us. How did you know you could even trust him?"

The question, and the realisation that Luchán had been captured, that she had been captured, that Wolf had almost died, slammed down on her. Great, gulping sobs exploded from her, making her chest hurt and aggravating the wounds on her face. It had only been a few days but she felt like everything had changed. She had messed it all up so badly, had hurt everyone and saved no one. Not even Wolf really. Aurnia had done that. Rua always failed people; her parents when she didn't steal them enough food to keep them alive, her sister when she dragged her to the workhouse, the others when she had left them behind, and Wolf, whose heartbeat pulsed faintly beneath her fingers.

"I'm so sorry, Conor."

He walked forward, shuffling up beside her on the bed, and wrapped his arms around her, gentle enough that it didn't hurt. She put her legs over his and curled into his chest. She finally let go of Wolf's wrist so she could grip his shirt.

"You can't keep pushing us away with one hand and trying to protect us with the other." He rested his chin on her head, enveloping her. "You're just going to end up with a world of hurt."

"I already hurt," she whispered into his chest with a wet giggle.

He sighed but it sounded relieved. "You're prematurely ageing me. I'm twenty three and I have grey hairs."

"Wolf almost died." She tightened her grip on the rough material of his shirt even though it made her fingers scream. "I had to drag her the last mile and the Hounds were after us and everything hurt and all I wanted was for you to be there."

"I'm here now." He ran his hands through her hair, gently unknotting it. "I'm not going anywhere so you better not either."

"I promise," she whispered and then again in the old language so he knew she meant it.

When they let go, both had to wipe their eyes.

Conor kept her pressed into his side when he said, "Tell me what happened."

It took longer than she expected to chronicle it all. She had to stop a few times while he questioned her, or when she cried. He stiffened when she mentioned how Wolf had handed her over, and only relaxed when she explained how she had then saved Rua.

She nodded. "Aurnia says her and Wolf are from the same

place," she finally finished. "That they're trained to be assassins for the Table."

Conor nodded, examining Wolf's prone form with sharp eyes. "I'll talk to her with Aurnia when she wakes up." He disentangled himself and shimmied down the bed, sitting horizontally with his feet on Wolf's bed and his head resting against the wall. He stared back at her. "You need to get back to camp."

She shook her head. "Not without Wolf."

"Yes without her," Conor growled.

"Why?"

Exhaustion made his grey eyes stark in his face. "For so many reasons." When she didn't reply, he said, "The others want to see you. It's dangerous in town with the Síochain searching for you. I'd feel better if you were safe back at camp." He listed them off on his fingers. "You need to heal. If the Hounds keep doing raids that wall won't hold up to their scrutiny."

"They already searched here."

Conor continued as if she hadn't spoken. "We need to question Wolf without you here. You're too close to her, Rua. You can't be objective." He cupped her cheek with his giant hand, skin rough. "I need you to be safe with the others, okay? I need Oisín to check you over and tell me you're okay. Do you understand?"

The guilt of what she had put him through, probably put all of them through, hit her like a galloping horse. They had thought she was dead. Thought they had lost her. With their families gone, all they had was each other, and Rua had run off in the middle of the night without even a word.

She nodded. "I'll go back to the camp."

"Just be prepared." He grinned but it didn't lighten the shadows in his eyes. "The others are all going to want to have words."

# CHAPTER THIRTY-NINE
## RUA

They hid her in a barrel that stank of stale beer and wet wood. The cart moved back and forth as Muire navigated the crowded streets. Rua had her knees curled into her chest and her head resting on them. The pile of hay hiding her tickled her neck. As a hiding place, it wouldn't stand up to investigation, but they had filled the first few barrels with a vile concoction of slop bucket, old beer and hay. Aurnia hoped it would stop anyone from going past them. Rua hid in the one furthest back, body already seizing up from her contorted position.

The cart stopped, horses whinnying and barrels knocking against each other.

A Hound called up, "You're early with the barrels this week, Muire."

"Couldn't stand the stink." Muire laughed. "Usually not stopped though."

"Síochain has us searching for two escaped prisoners. Can you take a look at these portraits? See if you recognise them." Paper rustled and the Hound continued. "The raid probably woke you up two nights ago?"

"Oh yes, the guests were thrilled. We had to give them free

beer. Refused to go back to sleep." Muire hummed. "I don't recognise either of these. Are they local?"

"Apparently. Every Hound in the county is searching for them." The woman snorted. "Waste of time if you ask me. We have enough trouble with the starving masses. Don't mind if I search these, do you?"

"Go ahead," Muire replied, sounding as easy as anything. "Just try not to stand too close. Had a sick guest and ended up using the barrels to save everyone else from the smell."

Rua's elbow slammed into her ribs as the cart swayed under the woman's movement. She tried to keep her breathing steady as she waited to be discovered. The thought that the Hounds had her image made her skin crawl. Portraits of wanted people were sometimes seen littering the walls outside the Hounds quarters at the edge of Scíth but they were never given out to individuals. She didn't think she had been such an annoyance to the Síochain that he would go to so much trouble to find her. They had always been more careful than that.

A lid opened followed by a grunt of displeasure. "What did he eat?"

"Nothing he got from us anyway," Muire responded, humour lacing the words.

"They all stink like this?"

"Indeed they do."

Another barrel opened. Rua nearly wretched from the pervasive stink. It reached up her nose and coated her tongue and throat, making her stomach protest. She swallowed convulsively and wrapped her shaking hands around the back of her head. She refused to go back to his cells.

The cart shook again as the Hound moved through the barrels, sniffing as she did. "I'm definitely not paid enough for this. Anyone asks, I checked them all."

Muire laughed again, loud and hearty. "Of course. You'll be in after your shift?"

"Sure where else would we go?"

Muire called her goodbyes and clicked at the horses.

The cart pulled forward with a jerk that had Rua gritting her teeth. As much as Rua hated it, Aurnia liked the Hounds to drink in the inn because it allowed her gossip she wouldn't already be privy to. Before Rua had met Luchán, eavesdropping on them got her the best information about shipments and so she had accepted it as part of her life.

Her heart lurched at the thought of Luchán. She never thought he would be so selfless as to sacrifice himself for her. He always joked his brains would get him out of any situation. She wished she could run her hands through his hair and sooth whatever pain he had experienced.

Rua ached; her hands, her legs and her heart.

As the cart trundled down an uneven road, she closed her eyes and fell into an uneasy sleep. The sudden stop jolted her awake. Adrenaline made her breath sharp gasps until she remembered she had escaped. The lid lifted. Light blinded her. Muire helped her up, and Rua stretched the ache from her bones before climbing out of the barrel. She lowered herself off the back of the cart with Muire's guiding hand.

Once Muire made sure she was steady on her feet, she said, "Rest, *mo leanbh*. Make sure Oisín checks you out."

Rua nodded. "They're going to be angry."

"Only as much as they need to be."

She grimaced. "I better go." She gave her a quick hug, inhaling her scent of fire smoke, stew and hay, before retreating into the forest, wiping her eyes as she did.

A fog drifted over her as she slogged her way home through wet leaves and sucking mud. Chilled fingers traced over her skin and she pulled the jumper Muire had given her closer. There would be no one on watch; they never bothered in the fog. No one would find the cave and they wouldn't see them approaching anyway. She paused at the entrance. For the first time since they had found it, it didn't feel welcoming.

She forced herself to crawl in.

The main cave sat empty and dark. They kept it that way in winter when the light travelled too far on the heavy nights. Hollow silence permeated where lively noise should be. She had done this. She had taken the joy from this place, stolen the trust.

She walked into the side cave and coughed. "Hey."

Nobody spoke for a long moment and then everyone moved at once. Aoife stood, staring at her with her hand on Oisín's shoulder. His mouth swung open as his eyes darted over her body. Seán moved towards her but stopped halfway across the cavern.

He finally stepped forward and wrapped her gently in his arms. "You're hurt."

"I'm okay," she replied, hugging him.

"So he didn't kill you then?" Aoife said, voice wretched with tears.

Rua shrugged. "He tried."

Oisín freed himself from Aoife's grip, and walked over, untangling Rua from Seán.

"Let me see you." A crinkle of worry creased his eyebrows together and Rua wanted to rub it smooth. "Clothes off. Let me have a look."

They watched silently as she revealed herself; bandages covered Rua from her armpits down to her hip bones. Both her arms were wrapped up and most of her fingers. Aurnia had left her face clear so they had already seen those injuries but they all blanched at the sight of her.

"*A dhiabhal*, Rua," Seán said, voice tight.

"He had questions." Guilt was a sharp blade slammed under her ribs. "I didn't want to answer them."

Seán wrapped one arm around Aoife's shoulders. Aoife reached up and gripped his hand. They were a united wall, protecting her from the outside world, close enough she could feel their body heat. Rua felt some tension relax in her shoulders. She hadn't thought she would see them again and the fear she had felt in the cell reared up again. She swallowed it down.

"I'm going to have to take all of these off," Oisín said gently. "How high do the cuts go?"

She motioned to the top of her ribs, just under her breasts, and he unrolled the bandages like a terribly wrapped loaf of bread. When he reached the top of her injuries, he tied off the material and examined her bare stomach.

"Aurnia has already done most of the work," she managed. His fingers were cold where he trailed them across her skin. She shivered.

"Sorry." He blew on his hand to warm them up. "I'm going to clean off this tincture and leave them to air. I'll do the same with your arms. Aoife, will you get me a bucket and some water?"

He unwrapped her arms, taking the bucket from Aoife when she handed it to him. She returned to Seán and he gently washed Rua's skin. Standing made her dizzy but she didn't interrupt him. Just leaned slightly against the wall. Observant as ever, he grabbed her a stool.

"These cuts aren't deep," he said with an unasked question.

"He made his nephew do them. Luchán Codagh. He's the one who's been feeding me the information." She ignored how they all stiffened. "The Síochain found out. I think he was testing him. But Luchán would never willingly hurt me."

Oisín sounded hoarse when he said, "Your arms are worse."

"The Síochain did them himself."

Seán stormed out with a stream of curses. Something crashed in the other cave.

Oisín hissed when he saw her fingers.

"He wanted me to understand what power my hands held and what it would be to go without them."

"Okay." He let out a long shuddering breath. "Aoife, will you come with me to refill the bucket?"

Aoife studied him for a second before nodding. "Yeah, of course." She threw her arm around his shoulder, whispering in his ear before they had even left the cave.

Alone, Rua leaned against the wall and let herself feel the pain.

Shouts echoed in from the other part of the cave. Rua pushed off the stool and stormed into the cavern. Aoife and Seán were screaming at each other. Oisín stood between them, arms up to stop them getting physical.

"HEY!" Rua's shout silenced them. "What's going on here?"

"Oisín needed a second because seeing his friend so beat up was damn hard," Aoife aimed the last part at Seán. "But this *amadán* wouldn't give him any space. Kept getting in his face to get back to you."

"She's hurting and he's out here having a break."

Aoife took a step forward, and Oisín pushed her back. "I'm fine, Aoife."

"Everyone back in the side cave." When no one obeyed, Rua shouted, "NOW."

They moved but they were clearly angry about it.

Oisín watched them from beside Rua. "It's been like this for days. Conor had to pull Aoife and Seán apart like four times."

Rua nodded. "I'll talk to them. Find out what their problem is."

Oisín looked at her strangely. "We know what their problem is. You left."

# CHAPTER FORTY
## RUA

When she came back in, the room was divided. Aoife and Oisín together on one side, and Seán alone on the other side. No one spoke. She glanced at each of them, noting how exhausted they looked. Blankets and books littered the floor haphazardly, making the cave messier than usual. Like someone had thrown everything around and had only half bothered picking the mess up.

"Table." No one met her eye. "Now."

They shuffled over unwillingly, with scraping stools and huffs of annoyance before everyone settled. Silence in a place that rarely knew of it was a disquieting thing. Rua's stomach clenched with guilt.

The long table in the middle of the space had been built by Seán; he'd gotten the wood from fallen trees Conor had found for him, and the stools from the left over trunks. They rarely used it for eating, but sometimes they had sat there and planned robberies, or played games when the weather made it impossible to leave the cave for days at a time. They had carved their initials into the surface, along with little doodles. This was their home, and this table was a representation of everything they had spent years building.

Rua sat. "I'm sorry I left."

Aoife snorted.

"Aoife, I really am sorry," she said quietly.

"Why didn't you wait for us?" Seán asked.

She expected the question, but since her conversation with Conor, her answer felt woefully inadequate. "I didn't want to put you in danger. I didn't want to risk you."

"Rua, you know that's not fair to us." Oisín tapped the table once. "We've been saying that to you for months."

Flashes of too many conversations hit her all at once; Aoife snarking about staying in her own fight, Oisín upset as he stitched her up again, Conor warning her of the dangers of paying attention to everyone else and not enough to herself. Aurnia telling her it was her weak spot, easily manipulated, and Seán rolling his eyes at her attempts to explain why she needed to protect them.

Even Wolf, who had only known her a few weeks, had spotted it almost straight away.

She nodded. "And Conor has reamed me out. I know how wrong I was. I promise."

"Not worth much at the moment," Seán muttered.

Aoife nodded. "Your word is about as useful as a famine potato right now."

That hurt but she understood. Trust was like ice on the lake; it seemed as tough and as beautiful as glass until someone put a foot through it. It never froze the same, always lined with cracks that showed the damage.

"I'll tell you everything that happened the last few days." She managed to keep her desperation out of her voice. "Wolf is at Aurnia's. She was poisoned and she hasn't woken up."

They stilled.

"Will she be okay?" Oisín asked, looking like he was ready to bolt to Aurnia's and examine Wolf himself. She could see him going through poison antidotes in his head.

"Aurnia helped her. She said it would just take her a few days to get it out of her system."

Conflicted, he finally nodded. "I need to finish cleaning your injuries."

"Some air will do them good." When he allowed her the point, she glanced around the table. "Wolf saved me. She nearly died trying."

"But?" Aoife asked, able to read Rua too well.

She took a deep breath, stealing herself for the next part. "But she isn't who she said she is. She handed me over to the Síochain."

Seán stiffened and snapped, "Did he put you in the cells? You know where they are?"

She glanced over, startled by his aggression. "Yeah, he kept me there, but I couldn't see much. I was alone in the last one."

"Did you at least try to learn the layout?" He watched her with dark eyes. "It might give us an advantage."

"I think so," she answered, unsure of this new level of anger radiating off him. "I don't know if that's what's important right now though."

Seán nodded stiffly and looked down at the table.

"And Wolf?" Aoife pressed, a furrow between her eyebrows.

"I don't know the full story but she works for him. Worked," she corrected. "She's part of a group of people who are loyal to the Table. They kill people."

"The Table have assassins now?" Aoife muttered. "Well, that is just fucking wonderful."

"Was there anyone else in the cells?" Seán demanded.

Rua glanced at him confused. "Not that I saw. But, you know, pretty busy being tortured."

He nodded a curt shape and averted his eyes. "Why was Wolf here?"

"I think she had to find out who my friend was."

"And it's Luchán Cogadh?" Aoife snapped. "Could you be playing anymore with fire?"

"I trusted him."

Seán snorted. "And so which one of them betrayed us at the barn? These *trusted* friends of yours? Which one of them told him we'd be there?"

"Neither," Rua said, and then realised what the words meant. "Whoever betrayed us is still free."

Seán sounded exhausted when he spoke, "So we have to move?"

They all stilled as the weight of Seán's question hit them.

"No. Only we know the location of our camp. Even if someone found out what we were planning, they couldn't know where we live."

The words sounded like a lie though. Someone had told the Síochain about the robbery that night. Someone was working against them and she didn't even know where to start looking. She pushed aside the suspicions and smiled weakly.

"Luchán doesn't know where it is and Wolf saved me. She got me out of there. She's on our side." Rua hated that it sounded like begging but she needed them to believe her, to believe in Wolf like she did. "Aurnia says that once you desert, there's no going back. She's one of us now."

Aoife cocked an eyebrow. "Are we going to vote on that?"

"No."

The others stared at her.

Before anyone spoke again, she said, "Because we already did. Wolf is one of us. She just took the long route to figure it out."

"She got you tortured, Rua." She had never heard Oisín's voice so cold. "She betrayed us. Betrayed you. Handed you over to the Síochain. How can you even be sure this isn't another ploy?"

"Aurnia and Conor are going to interrogate her when she wakes up."

Some of the tension eased out of the room.

"What did he do to you?" Seán said.

"He asked me how I was getting my information. Asked me who you all were."

The cell, the blade, his rough voice; the memories were as sharp as if she was still in the room. She could smell the damp and mildew, hear his footsteps as he strolled to her cell and feel how warm his fingers were when he held her chin. The heat of his breath on her skin as he leaned closer to examine Luchán's efforts. Hunger as it gnawed at her stomach like before. A memory of red hair she had probably hallucinated.

She sucked in a shuddering breath and forced it down her tightening throat. "Asked me why I thought I had a right to steal from the Table."

Seán asked quietly, "What did you say?"

"*Níl Béarla agam.*" I do not speak English.

Silence fell, and then like a storm breaking, they laughed.

The sound eased some of the worst of the ache across Rua's skin.

"*A dhiabhal*, Rua." Aoife sounded awed. "That's almost impressive."

Rua's mind was still only halfway back from the Síochain's clutches but she forced a grin. "I just kept that one thought in my head." She blinked away sudden tears. "I was so afraid that I'd tell him something and get you all killed."

The silence suffocated the remnants of the laughter.

Seán stood up and gently wrapped his arms around her. "*Amadán.* Only you would be scared for us when being tortured."

She leaned into him. "I really am sorry."

"We better get you looked at and put you to bed," Oisín chided. "You're probably exhausted."

She nodded and accepted Seán's help to stand. Oisín checked and rewrapped her injuries quickly and efficiently. When they all followed her to the main room, she knew something was up, but she didn't have the energy to complain.

"Where's my bed?" She asked, noticing her pile of blankets missing from near the entrance.

Seán said, "Over here."

Rua's blankets had been moved to the farthest corner of the cave, and were surrounded by all the others. "What's happening?"

Aoife shrugged. "You don't really think we're letting you anywhere near there, do you? You're gonna have to climb over us to sneak out again."

Rua wanted to argue but tension and exhaustion weighed heavily on their stiff shoulders and in the bags under their eyes. They were all poised for a fight so she just nodded and crawled into her bed. Seán lay down by her feet, Aoife and Oisín were by her shoulders.

"What are you doing? It's early."

"None of us have slept much," Oisín replied.

"We could use an early night," Seán said.

Aoife shushed them loudly.

Rua giggled, and then Seán joined in, and soon all of them were laughing so loudly it echoed around the cave and back to her. She didn't think she would ever see them again. She wanted to cry from happiness.

After it had been quiet for a while, Oisín asked, "What do we do now?"

It took Rua a minute to answer but she knew they were listening. "Now, we save Luchán."

# CHAPTER FORTY-ONE
## WOLF

Wolf opened an eye halfway and examined the room. She didn't remember much. The cell and Rua. The tunnel and the nun. Nothing else. Blankness waited instead. Trying to remember made a sharp pain shoot through her head. She lay on a bed, but not in the stables with Pup, or in the cells with Rua. Someone sat on the opposite bed reading, but she didn't want to open her eye too far and alert them to her consciousness. Her knives were gone and the thought she had been unconscious around this person when being weaponless made nausea churn her stomach. She swallowed convulsively to stop herself vomiting. She couldn't fight it when the darkness dragged her under again.

Nightmares waited. She tried to fight them off, desperately aware she was asleep, and so if she tried hard enough she would wake up. Shadowed ghouls chased her, screaming and scratching her skin. She raced down winding corridors searching for something, for someone. She opened a door. The Síochain towered above her, snarling. He transformed into a wolf and bit her, sharp teeth easily slicing through her delicate skin.

The terror forced her awake with gasping breaths.

Candles lit the room, casting long shadows she wanted to hide from. She reached for her knives again and winced when her fingers met empty skin. Still too weak to sit up, her eyes darted around, and her breath caught when she saw Conor. He sat on the opposite bed, a book open beside him, and watched her warily. She scanned for exits. She could just make out the outline of a door opposite her and a circular window above the beds that she could probably get through if she needed to.

Satisfied, she asked, "Where's Rua?" The words sounded like a cart driving over stones. "Is she okay?"

His eyes widened a little at the questions. "Why?"

"The nun attacked me. I can't remember what happened." Wolf raised a shaking hand to her forehead and wiped sweaty hair from her skin. "Is she safe?"

Conor nodded. "She's back at the cave with the others."

"And Luchán?"

"The Síochain has him."

She swallowed and shut her eyes, guilt a new sensation she didn't particularly enjoy. "Luchán jumped on the nun. Made me go because she wouldn't attack him. I had to leave him, Conor." She needed him to understand. She wasn't quite sure why. "I had to keep Rua safe."

He leaned forward and squeezed her hand. "How are you feeling?"

She took stock for a moment and then muttered, "Like death."

"Aurnia said that was normal of *Bás Tostach*."

A memory blinked at the back of her mind. "The nun poisoned the dagger."

"Seemed you saved Rua." A hardness settled on the words like weights. "After you had given her up in the first place."

She tried to push herself up; her arms trembled and failed her. She already knew the effects of the poison intimately from her tests, she had not needed a second go around.

Letting herself fall, she shrugged. "You were a Hound. You have a tiny idea of what training I went through."

"I deserted."

"Technically so have I," she shot back.

He nodded his acquiesce. "What's your plan now?"

"Protect Rua." The promise made her feel important, and motivated. The memory of Pup's desperate and devastated expression made her chest ache. Wolf wished that she had come with them. "I'm going to keep Rua safe," she repeated.

Breathless fear followed the words; she had deserted the Sisterhood, she finally had her freedom, she would be hunted for the rest of her life.

Freedom stretched out bigger than she expected. She had been told what to do her whole life. Knowing what the next day held, where her next meal would come from or where she would sleep at night were decisions she had never had to concern herself with. Not when the nuns decided all of those things for her. Not when all she had to do was follow.

She wouldn't follow anymore.

Cold anxiety made her stomach tumble over itself and the promise felt like a reaching hand in a drowning ocean. For the first time in her life, she didn't want to be alone. She wanted to stay with Rua and her weird, dysfunctional family. Even if Wolf didn't really understand why they were a family or how that was a good thing. She just knew that being around them eased the quiet ache she carried. The only thing Wolf had ever known was chaos and violence. But Rua needed protection and Wolf could protect.

"You betrayed us."

Wolf took the words like a punch. "I had a job to do."

"I don't know if the others will allow you back."

A sudden ringing in her ears deafened her. "You can persuade them."

"I don't know if I want you back." Conor laughed an unfriendly sound. "Most of what I care about has been taken from me. You almost allowed someone else to be stolen." The words shook and his eyes burned. "It's not an easy thing to forgive."

"I don't know how to make it better." Tiredness crept back over her, dragging her eyelids down. "I don't want to—" She refused to shut her eyes. She had to keep him in her sights.

Conor watched her struggle and then said in a tired voice, "Go to sleep, Wolf. I'll keep watch."

Something about his voice soothed the sharp edges of her panic. She allowed her eyes to shut. "Don't let anyone—" The words trailed off and she fell asleep.

\*\*\*

Conor's voice broke through the haze of her dreams. "She says she wants to protect Rua."

"Do you believe her?"

Conor huffed. "I'd have believed her more before all of this. Everything she's done, if we ignore her handing Rua over to the Síochain, has been about protection. She's saved Rua's life a few times now."

Wolf wanted to say something, agree with him, prove herself, but sleep was slow to let her go, and her tongue felt like moss stuck to a stone.

"That's a big thing to ignore," Aurnia scoffed. "But it's not an easy thing to walk away from the Sisterhood. We aren't designed to be able to. If she chose it, if it isn't some trick, I would be willing to give her a second chance."

"She can't come back to camp. Not yet. I need to be sure before I risk them."

"Rua won't like it but you're right." The floorboards creaked and she felt the heat of their examination. "She's just so young. I forget sometimes how much hardship I faced before I left."

"Haven't we all?"

"Why don't you get some sleep?" She spoke like she was soothing a wild animal. "I can watch over her."

"No." The firmness startled Wolf and she woke a little bit more. "She doesn't trust people when she sleeps. She trusted me. The least I can do is respect that and be here when she wakes up."

Wolf's chest ached with the words.

"We're just next door if you need anything."

The wall locked back into place with a quiet *snick* and the other bed groaned.

"I know you're awake."

She blinked her eyes open. "How do you know about the Sisterhood?"

"You'll have to ask Aurnia."

"Can I see Rua?"

Conor studied her with a piercing gaze but didn't answer her question. "How are you?"

She stretched out her limbs, noticing how they trembled from the effort. Fatigue burrowed into her bones which made it hard for her to think. She yawned and her eyes watered.

"Sore. Tired. Foggy still. I'm probably going to fall asleep again soon." She scrubbed her hands over her eyes. "I hate this."

Dark bags shadowed his eyes. "Did you want to be there? Be part of this Sisterhood?"

"My father sent me there at five." She hated revealing her soft underbelly but she forced herself to keep talking. "Later than the others. We're meant to join at three. Maybe that's why I'm defective."

"Defective?"

"Never believed the lies. Never wanted their promises of

secret glory." Her voice grated, rough with thirst, and he held a glass of water to her lips. She drank it gratefully, still unsure of the gentle kindness. When she finished, she said, "I decided I wanted to leave by eight. I first killed someone at eleven." At Conor's widened eyes, she explained, "Poison in a glass. They needed someone that wouldn't be noticed. Someone small and fast and smart. I poisoned his wine at a feast. He died in front of me."

"What is it you want?"

That had always been the easy answer. "Freedom."

"From the Sisterhood?"

"From everyone." She knew he would have something to say about it. Just like Rua did. "People make you weak, make you vulnerable, slow you down. I just wanted to be alone and safe."

"That's not how it works, Wolf."

She shrugged and stared at her hands. Tremors made her fingers quake. "All I know is I'm twenty and the only person I have ever loved left me in hell. People abandon you, try to kill you. They hurt you, or exploit you. They betray you. They fail you." She clenched her hands into fists so she wouldn't have to acknowledge her weakness anymore. "I betrayed Rua. I betrayed all of you. But I swear I'll make it up to you, and then if you want, I'll leave and you'll never have to see me again."

"What if she doesn't want you to leave?"

"When she finds out who I am, what I've done? She won't want me. No one would."

# CHAPTER FORTY-TWO
## WOLF

Aurnia sat on the end of her bed with a tray resting on her lap when Wolf woke up next.

Conor nodded when she met his eyes. It helped calm the thunderous beat of her heart. She didn't understand it, but she knew that even angry at her, no one would hurt her while he had watch. She understood now why Rua stayed near him so often.

Aurnia watched the exchange with a quirked eyebrow. "Can you sit up yet?"

Wolf nodded and forced her body to comply. She didn't know how many days she had been unconscious, but she wouldn't continue being weak, and even though her arms trembled and her shoulders ached, she managed to push herself up and lean against the headboard.

"Stubborn as anything," Conor muttered.

Aurnia settled the tray on her lap. "Eat. Bone broth. It'll help."

Oily and heavy on her tongue, it eased the pangs in her stomach. "Thank you."

She waved away the thanks. "We need to talk."

"We do," Wolf agreed. "How do you know about the Sisterhood?"

"Not quite what I meant," Aurnia replied but she still answered. "They trained me."

She choked on her soup. "You're her? You're the woman who escaped? They said you were a lie. A fairy tale we told ourselves." Questions Wolf had held close to her heart bubbled to the surface and exploded free. "Why? How haven't they found you? What did you do?" She smirked. "No wonder you were so good in the sparring ring."

Aurnia smiled a little but it held no amusement. "I destroyed any records they had of me. I killed the three nuns who tracked me down. I went to the Table itself and promised divine retribution if they didn't let me go."

Wolf gaped. "You met with the families?"

"Met is a strong word." She gestured at Wolf to keep eating. "I broke into their rooms while they were sleeping, revealed their weakest spots, and told them if they didn't order the Sisterhood to release me, I would tear their kingdom apart."

Wolf swallowed. "How?"

"I was motivated."

Conor took a shuddering breath and they glanced at him.

"You're both a little bit scary. I just want you to know that."

Aurnia squeezed his hand. "Thank you," she said sincerely.

He laughed and the tension left the room.

"I can't do that," Wolf admitted.

"It wouldn't work twice anyway and it wouldn't work for you. You're not as good as I am."

"I'm the best."

Aurnia scoffed, amused, and patted Wolf's knee. "You're good, loveen, but you're not the best."

Disbelief made her mute.

"They allowed me to go free because I was leaving the life," Aurnia continued. "No," she sighed. "They let me go because they knew I would take as many as I could down with me, and they knew that was too many to lose at once." She glared at Wolf. "You, on the other hand, are knee deep in a rebellion they have to squash. They're going to make you an example to all the other little assassins. Nothing good waits for you if they ever capture you again."

Wolf nodded. "But they think I'm dead. No one survives that poison." A bubble of hope burst in her chest. "They think I'm dead."

Aurnia glanced at her. Sadness made her mouth thin. "Wolf, they're searching for two people. Without your body, without proof, they'll assume you survived."

Wolf stared up at the ceiling, heart a wretched mess, but she nodded. "They trained us better than dying by poison," she said, bitterness staining the words.

"They did."

Disappointment flooded her. Considered dead was always better than alive and hunted. She had a promise to keep and it would have been easier if she didn't have to look over her own shoulder for shadows as well.

"You can't leave Rua." Conor said, clearly misinterpreting her disappointment. "You may not have made this mess but you sure as hell helped to aggravate it."

"Me?" The rest of Aurnia's words caught up with her. "I'm not knee deep in anything."

Aurnia glared. "Are you being intentionally obtuse? You and Rua are in this together. Would you really leave her to figure this out by herself?"

A shudder passed through Wolf at the thought of Rua fighting without Wolf protecting her back. "She'd get herself killed." The promise felt like a secret, but with another person. She had only ever had secrets with herself. "Rua isn't rebelling anyway," she finally said. "She's just stealing food."

"Is this really how short sighted the new apprentices are? How disappointing."

Wolf scoffed but she closed her eyes to think it through. "Attacks across three counties. Rua is stealing food. Word is spreading." Wolf hated being tested. "She's the spark that's going to burn the country down."

"The country or the Table. Something has to change."

"Eat your soup," Conor chided and then glanced at Aurnia. "It's going to get bad, isn't it?"

"Depends," Aurnia replied. "The rebellion is nothing but luck and opportunities at the moment. No one is in charge. No one is sure who wants it and who doesn't. People feel powerless. How do you change society on such a scale? How do you destroy your system of government for something better?" Aurnia shrugged. "It's going to get bloody and violent and awful. It's why they're keeping us weak and poor and building meaningless roads to nowhere. They can't let us know how unstable their power really is; how it only exists if we all buy into it."

Conor snorted. "No one is buying in anymore."

She nodded. "The famine has gone on for too long. The anger is a riptide and someone is about to be dragged under."

Wolf finished her soup and bit into a warm, buttery roll. "You think Rua did all this?"

"No. What Rua is doing, what you're all doing, is giving people hope again. We're managing to get food to all six counties now. We're not feeding everyone, but we're feeding enough for people to realise that there is a better way."

"Feeding the troops is always the biggest concern of any army," Conor said.

"Exactly. You make them strong again. You ignite that anger. You release them on the Table. Uprising."

"Death," Wolf snapped. "To betray the Table means death."

Aurnia laughed a loud, bright sound. "So young." She leaned forward. "Listen here, little assassin, and let me tell you a secret. No country is infallible. No ruling class is undefeatable. All that propaganda, all those rumours of power, are just that. Rumours, lies, whispers, wishes, words. Held together with our fear and our belief."

Wolf swallowed. "We could destroy them?"

"Every single one of them."

# CHAPTER FORTY-THREE
## WOLF

A pounding on the inn door broke their contemplative silence. Before they moved from the beds, they heard the crack of the lock smashing and the shouts of Hounds as they filled the kitchen. Chairs crashed to the ground. Doors slammed in the hallway. The room must have been over the kitchen because Wolf listened as the Hounds arranged themselves, heard the drag of swords as they were drawn from sheaths.

"You check upstairs," the woman in charge ordered, voice carrying easily through the wall. "You two into the bar. You two check the stables."

Aurnia stood, listening at the wall. "I can't go out now. They'll see." She froze when the Hound's boots tramped up the stairs, knocking against the wall as they did and making an unignorable ruckus.

"What are you doing?" Muire asked, voice steel. "You've already checked our premises."

Aurnia's shoulders turned to granite.

"And now we're checking again. You have a problem with that?" The Hound sneered. "Because the Síochain has given us permission to lock up anyone who resists."

"Has he now?" The words held the edge of a sword swinging.

"I won't take that tone from an innkeeper." There was the noise of a scuffle and the wall tipped slightly. "What's behind that wall?"

It took a moment for Muire to answer. "The bar staff sleep there sometimes. It's empty at the moment."

"Open it. Now."

Wolf reached again for a knife that wasn't there.

"Now," the Hound grunted, and banged on the wall. It curved slightly under the force. "Have you guests?" At Muire's affirmative, he shouted, "Everyone up. Now."

The disgruntled sound of guests being woken up, the slamming of doors, and the shouts of the search seemed to distract the Hound, his footsteps echoing up and down the corridor. None of them moved; aware only Muire and a thin wall separated them from being discovered.

Silence fell again except for the thud of heavy boots. "I won't ask again. Open it."

Aurnia blinked to life, glanced up at the small round window, and then at Wolf.

"There is always an exit," she whispered in response to the question on Aurnia's face. Another test. "Conor will have to help us up."

"Boost me. I'll help Wolf and then you follow us," Aurnia hissed. "Hurry. She won't be able to stall for much longer."

The Hound's hand slammed on the thin wall. "Why haven't you opened this yet? Where's Aurnia?"

"Out," Muire snapped. "Not here."

Aurnia groaned quietly. "I need to get out there before she gets herself hurt." She pulled Wolf up off the bed, quickly but with care.

Pain seared through her.

"Out?" The Hound sounded louder which meant he must

have moved closer to Muire to threaten her. "It's the middle of the night."

"As far as I know there's no curfew in effect," Muire replied easily. "Unless we missed it?"

The Hound snorted. "No curfew, but certainly some suspicious behaviour."

Muire hummed.

"Boost me," Aurnia snapped at Conor.

Wolf knew Aurnia would be able to climb the wall if she had to, but the tone from the Hound was violent at best, and murderous at worst, and he would rip the wall open soon if Muire kept delaying. Conor braced his legs and leaned against the wall, cupping his hands and holding them out for Aurnia to step on. He lifted her up, and she gripped the ledge of the window, stepping up onto his shoulders and flipping open the lock. The window opened inwards, and she pulled herself up onto the ledge.

"Don't make a sound," she whispered.

Conor steadied Wolf. She took a breath, pushed down all the weakness, and forced her body into compliance. She stepped onto his hands, using the wall to keep herself balanced when she stepped onto his shoulder. She gripped Aurnia's hand and the woman pulled her up onto the thatch. A long beam stretched across the roof. Wolf dragged herself along it, body trembling and dropped down, invisible from the ground.

"Stay down," Aurnia snapped at Wolf. "What are you doing?" She whispered down to Conor.

"Hiding the traces of us," he muttered.

Up high, the Hounds were much louder. Wolf could hear raids happening all over Scíth. There were fights breaking out; scuffles and brawls sounding in shouts and bodies hitting the ground. The thatch itched. It caught in her hair and found spaces under her clothes to tickle her. The cold was a bitter bite along uncovered skin. A bright moon illuminated the shine of armour through the streets.

She could hear the murmurings from the hallway but was too far away to make out any words. Conor finally appeared in the window, just barely managing to drag his body through the small space. Aurnia closed the window behind him and gestured for him to lay down. He lay beside Wolf, his body hidden by the thick beam.

"I have to get down there. Do not let yourselves be seen." She crawled over the thatch and disappeared over the side of the building.

Neither of them spoke for long minutes. Wolf took Conor's hand when she saw it trembling. She didn't know his story, but she knew the expression of a person about to break, and Conor was shattering slowly. The window shuddered and opened slightly. Conor gripped her hand.

"Take your hands off me," Muire's voice reached them easily which meant she had finally opened up the room.

"This bed looks slept in," the Hound snarled.

"I told you. The girls sleep here when they are too tired after they've been working in the pub." Muire sounded like a tired teacher explaining a simple concept. "We don't change the beds every time."

The man grunted. "Fine. But we're not going anywhere until you tell me where your wife is."

"I'm right here, loveen." The word held none of the easy affection she had given Wolf. It held a threat, waiting. "Let go of my wife. Now."

"You can't give me orders. I'm a Hound."

"And I'm the owner of this inn and if you want any of your crowd to be served again you'll back away before I make you."

"I'm fine, dear," Muire replied easily. Wolf could hear the

relief in her voice though. "If he had really hurt me, I would have broken his fingers."

"You can't speak to me like that," he growled.

Aurnia snorted. "Get out of my inn."

Before he responded, someone called the all clear.

They heard the Hounds leaving, heard the wall sliding shut, what sounded like Aurnia giving the Hound in charge some trouble about her soldiers, and Muire calling the guests into the bar. Finally, quietness settled. When she was sure no one was in the yard, Wolf crawled over to the window and lowered herself back into the room. She dropped onto the bed, shudders ripping through her muscles. Conor followed and fell onto the opposite bed, letting out a whoosh of air.

"Are you okay?" she asked tentatively.

"When my sisters died, I could do nothing," he said in a voice thick with tears. "I had to watch him slit their throats. The only reason I'm alive is because Tadgh helped me escape the cells." He wiped his eyes with the heels of his hands as if trying to erase the memories. "Standing by when one of my own is in trouble, it's not a thing I do lightly." He shook his head. "Are you okay?"

She nodded. "Can you close that window?"

Even in the few minutes it had been open, the temperature had dropped and Wolf could see her breath. Shouts from around the town reached them; it seemed like a lot of people were unhappy with the midnight search. Conor stood, and balancing on the edge of the beds, he shut it. He sat back down, leaning against the wall.

"You should go to sleep," he muttered. "I'll keep watch."

"You need sleep as well."

"Later." Staring at the wall, he barely seemed aware of where they were, and Wolf knew he was lost in his remembering. "Go to sleep, Wolf. I'll wake you up when I need to."

# CHAPTER FORTY-FOUR
## RUA

A shuffle at the entrance to the cave woke Rua up.

She shot up and groaned at the dart of pain. She forced herself to stand, freeing herself from her pile of blankets. Oisín refused to let her do anything but rest, *Rua, a dhiabhal,* until her wounds were at least properly scabbed over. She withdrew a knife and watched, heart pounding, to see who would emerge from the gap.

Potent relief struck her when Conor pulled himself forward. It made her realise how worried she had been that she had let something slip to the Síochain, or worse that Wolf had told them everything. Even as she thought it, she remembered Wolf's face that first day she'd brought her back to the cave; the crease of her eyebrows, the determined set of her lips and the promise written in her eyes that she would never give up their home.

Rua had trusted her then but she didn't know what she thought anymore. She knew now Wolf wasn't unflappable and untouchable. Wolf would probably disagree with her assessment. Claim she was never frightened. Rua knew different. Knew just how scared Wolf was. Knew maybe just how scared she was as well. She wasn't sure what to do with either bits of knowledge.

Conor grinned when he saw her, but between the dark

circles under his eyes and the drawn pallor to his skin, it didn't help him look any less wretched.

She grabbed his forearm, giving it a squeeze. "When did you last sleep?"

He curled his hand into a fist and rubbed an eye before running his fingers through his hair. It made him look oddly young. "I've gotten a few hours here and there. I kept watch over Wolf."

"Is she okay?"

"She's weak, exhausted, but Aurnia says she should be back to normal soon."

"*In ainm Dé.*" Relief made Rua's shoulders uncoil. The smile fell from her lips when she finally looked at Conor properly; exhaustion sat heavily on his shoulders, making him look so much older than he was. She took his hand. "You need to sleep."

"Where are the others?" He asked, allowing her to pull him over to the blankets.

"Washing, watching, around. I have to rest according to Oisín." Scorn filled the words to bursting.

Conor laughed. "No harm." He lay down, leaving enough space for her to curl up beside him. "Go to sleep, Rua. I'll tell you everything when we wake up."

*** 

When she did open her eyes, hours later, warm and safe in his arms, Conor stared at the ceiling. Wrinkles etched his forehead and his mouth pulled down into an unhappy frown. She turned around so her body faced him and gripped his hand.

"Did you sleep at all?"

"For a few hours. The others are waiting for us." He squeezed her hand once before letting go. He sat up and cracked his back. "Your face is already less ghoulish. Well, back to the normal level of ghoulish."

"Thanks," she snarked.

He laughed and stood, helping her up as well. "Let's get this over with." He sounded so weary, her heart ached for him.

"You're awake," Oisín grinned when they walked in. "How's Wolf?"

"Better. Managed to get out of bed yesterday. Aurnia changed her hair colour, and they changed her clothes, and she's lost some weight, so they're hoping it'll be enough for her to be able to leave the room as soon as she's feeling better."

"What colour is her hair now?" Rua asked.

"Dark blonde."

Rua tried to imagine that hair on Wolf; the dark hair had been so stark against her pale skin. She wondered if she would look softer without it and ignored how her heart skipped at the thought.

"What has Rua told you?" Conor asked, settling onto one of the stools.

Rua joined him at the head of the table. "Everything."

He nodded. "Alright. So. The question is, are we accepting Wolf back or not?"

"What?" Disbelief made Rua louder than usual. "Of course we are. We already voted once."

Conor glared at her, mouth a harsh line. "Rua, you don't get to force this on people." His tone brokered no argument. "She's a risk. She's going to bring a lot of people down on us. A lot of *well-trained* people. Everyone has to vote. It has to be unanimous."

"I want to speak to her before we do," Oisín interrupted.

"It's too dangerous right now," Rua said.

Seán snorted. "We can sneak in during the night. We can use the back entrance. We can all hide in Aurnia's. We are just as dangerous as they are."

"Stop trying to protect us, Rua," Oisín said. "It's not your

249

job." He spoke gently but the words still sliced through her skin like the Síochain's knife.

She nodded and bit down on her tongue to stop her arguments escaping.

"It's late enough now," Conor said. "Let's eat and then we'll head out. Rua with me. Thirty minutes between each group leaving. Hounds are doing random sweeps. They raided the inn last night, so keep your eyes open and stick to the shadows."

Oisín glanced at Rua. "Let me check you out before we go. Then you rest until we leave."

"I'll plait your hair, coat it in ash. That should hide the red," Aoife said, following her brother from the room.

"You're okay?" Seán asked Conor.

"Wrecked." He ran his hand over his face. "Nothing a few quiet days and some sleep won't solve."

"Seems unlikely with this lot." Seán grinned. "I'll get you some coffee instead."

Conor shot him a grateful smile. It fell off his lips as soon as Seán left.

The tension was clearly not in Rua's imagination then. "Why are you making them vote again? I thought we'd agreed she could stay."

"I'm not having this argument with you."

"Conor!"

"NO," he exploded. "You almost got yourself killed. You almost got us killed, because don't doubt for one minute, we wouldn't have followed you into that hellhole. You do not get to keep putting yourself at risk, and you sure as hell don't get to keep putting them at risk." He stood and ran his hands through his wild hair. "There are consequences when you go off by yourself, consequences to us and to you." His eyes were dark with grief. "I need you to grow up, Rua. Stop seeing the world in such unchanging realities and learn that we're all living in the grey."

Conor stormed from the room and Rua heard him scramble out of the cave.

She stared down at her hands, and bit her lip to stop the tears from falling. She knew what he said made sense, but separating the world into right and wrong, do or don't, help or ignore, made it so much easier to exist in. Keep moving forward. Keep helping. Keep saving people. She had forgotten about her responsibilities to this new family she had been building, this new place they called home. She had forgotten the trauma they had all suffered in her selfish quest to be unselfish, to save everyone. Stark truths were easier than the messy shades of grey that meant she might lose someone again. Might end up carrying another death on her shoulders. She knew he was right. She just wasn't sure she was brave enough to change.

# CHAPTER FORTY-FIVE
## RUA

**M**ore Hounds patrolled Scíth than ever before.

Crouching low, they raced around the edges of the town, keeping to the shadows and pausing when the Hounds passed close by. No laughter. No banter among them. Rua wondered what exactly the Síochain had said to put such a fear in his soldiers. The streets were empty of any people. Quiet permeated the night air but not the normal calm of a settled night. This dark held a tension that wrapped its arms around the small town and tightened. Claustrophobia notched up and up each time a patrol completed their rounds. Curtains twitched and stilled.

They made it to the inn undiscovered.

It didn't stop Rua's heart from trying to beat free of her chest.

Time slowed as they waited in the closed bar. Muire made tea on the fire. Rua watched out the window. They arrived together, hiding in the shadows and sneaking into the inn easily. It took them a few minutes to settle as Aurnia checked on each of them, ensuring they were safe and healthy. Muire checked them as well as she handed out the hot drinks. When Wolf emerged from the darkness by the staircase, silence fell.

Rua's breath caught. Wolf's hair hung loose around her

face. The lighter tones made her pale skin warmer. She had bitten her lips red. Two raw and jagged cuts laced her cheek and her neck. She had lost more weight. Rua wanted to sweep Wolf up into her arms and feed her until she stood as strong as before. She looked almost ethereal in the candlelight. Her face held the carefully neutral expression Rua had first seen on it. She hated it. She wanted to hug her, or welcome her back, but Conor's words sat heavy on her shoulders, and she knew she had to allow Wolf to show everyone who she really was.

Still, she moved over so Wolf had room to share her bench. The warmth of her knocked away some of the chill Rua had been carrying since the cells. Wolf's hand settled down beside hers, not touching, but close enough she felt the heat of it like a whispered secret. Scant comfort, but comfort nonetheless.

"You all know who I am now?" The words were resigned and her voice hoarse with pain. Black bags swallowed her eyes.

A nod worked its way around the room like a wave.

Wolf seemed to have no idea what to say or do. A first for her. She had always been so confident in every situation, and for once, Rua knew she wasn't faking it. She saw how Wolf's fingers trembled.

"They just have some questions," Rua said when the silence stretched to breaking. "They need to know they can trust you."

"They?"

"I already trust you."

Some of the tension left Wolf's body. She glanced back at the rest of them. "Ask away."

No one spoke for a long moment and then Oisín said, voice cold, "You handed over Rua to the Síochain. Why?"

Wolf swallowed. "Because I had to."

Candlelight shadowed his face, but Rua saw the anger and worry in the curve of his mouth, in the way he fiddled with his cuffs, and the fine line digging into his forehead. "Why?"

"I protect the Table. I protect the Síochain. I have to do what he says. He says jump. I ask how high. I follow. I obey. I do." Bitterness coated her words. "I *had to* obey."

"I doubt that somehow," Aoife said. "You've never done anything you didn't want to do in camp."

"It's not the same."

"Why not?" Seán asked.

"Because I have to do what they say." An underlying anger hid in the words; Rua didn't know if it was directed at their questions, at having to explain herself, or because of what her life had been. "Because to betray the Table means *death*. If I hadn't handed her over, we'd both be dead."

"That's not the reason though," Oisín said.

She shook her head. "No. I handed her over because I was meant to. I didn't like it but there isn't much in my life that I do like."

Seán shifted to get Wolf's attention. "What happens now you've betrayed them?"

Wolf shrugged. "Death if they find me—but they won't find me," she finished coldly. "I'm never going back to them."

"How bad was it?" Aoife asked.

"Very."

"You are brought there at three. Trained brutally." Everyone swivelled around to look at Aurnia. "You have to complete a test every year from the age of six. At twenty one, you are made a full member of the Sisterhood of Righteous Death. But you start killing much earlier than that."

"I was eleven."

"Ten," Aurnia followed.

Rua swallowed. Before she had found out the Síochain had intentionally starved people, not once had she considered killing someone. Any of them. Yet, Wolf spoke of it with such ease, startling in its casualness.

"You were one of them as well?" Seán asked.

Aurnia nodded. "I got out."

Rua glanced between Wolf and Aurnia, understanding the respect between them. "Can Wolf stay?"

"Can we trust her?" Oisín asked. "I'm not stitching one of you up again because she suddenly remembered where her true loyalties lie."

"I'm not risking my brother on a maybe," Aoife agreed.

Conor leaned against the door, arms crossed. "I'm not risking anyone for Wolf, but I do believe she's serious about joining us, and I do believe she's left that place for good. I vote yes."

Rua blinked as relief surged through her. With those words some of the tension had already leaked from the room, and Rua knew it would be okay. No one trusted her at the moment but they all knew Conor would do nothing to hurt them. She wished she knew what he and Wolf had talked about when they were together. She squeezed her hand into a fist and released it, letting her fear evaporate with it. She had really thought Conor would vote no.

"I vote yes," she followed, even though she usually voted last.

Aurnia tapped her biceps. "I vote yes."

"Same," Muire said from behind the bar.

Oisín considered Wolf for a long moment. "You swear you'll cause no intentional harm to any of them again?"

Wolf nodded. "I swear."

Oisín glanced at Conor and Aurnia, bottom lip caught in his teeth. He peered at Aoife and she shrugged, waving her hand in a gesture that told Rua that she would do whatever Oisín decided. "Fine. I vote yes."

"Same. At the very least she can teach us some things."

Everyone watched Seán.

"It has to be unanimous," Conor reminded him.

Seán glared at Rua. "You couldn't have wanted Aoife? She's right there."

Aoife snorted. "Not interested."

Heat flooded her cheeks and Rua ignored Wolf's probing examination. "Well?"

"Yes." Seán sighed. "She can stay."

# Chapter Forty-Six
## WOLF

When Seán agreed, a knot loosened in Wolf's throat. The thought of losing these people hadn't become real until they were all in front of her, furious because of her betrayal. She didn't understand *why* but she felt like maybe she needed to keep them, to be part of what they were, this confusing and brittle family, and not just because of the promise. The realisation was so terrifying, so precious, so easily broken, she locked it up somewhere she would never have to acknowledge it again. Wolf hoped the shuddering breath she released was quiet but she saw how Rua watched her intently. Observation wasn't a new sensation in her life. It was the most normal thing she knew. But it had never come from a place of concern, and she knew the difference in the way it didn't make her skin prickle and her rage flare up.

"What now?" She asked to kill the uneasy silence settling over the room like an unwanted blanket on a warm night.

"We need to save Luchán." Rua gripped the bench but didn't look at anyone as she spoke. "I know how dangerous it is but we can't just abandon him."

"I agree," Aurnia said. "We don't leave people behind. Even the Síochain's nephew."

Rua nodded, relief showing in how she released the bench. "Have you heard from Tadgh?"

"Not a word since he got the message through about you." Aurnia paused and glanced at Muire. "You'll be okay with them for a few hours?"

Muire's lips pursed but she nodded. "Be careful. Do not get caught."

"As if I would." She laughed. "I'll be back soon. Stay here and stay quiet. We've no guests in, thanks to the Hounds, but that doesn't mean you're all safe."

"Where are you going?" Conor asked.

"To talk to Tadgh, of course."

Wolf stood. "I can come with you."

Aurnia snorted. "*Mo stór*, you can barely stand. You need to rest. Rua, help her back upstairs."

Rua nodded.

Wolf sat heavily, knees weak. She hated this, hated that her body had become a stranger when last week it had been her closest ally and most finely tuned weapon. She knew from her last recovery that all she needed was another few days and she would be back to normal but it felt different from last time; then she revelled in having a precious few days free from the other apprentices in the convent, but this time, she was stuck in bed when people needed her help.

"I'll make up some food to keep you all going," Muire said. She pointed at Wolf. "You sleep. We'll wake you when she gets back."

Aurnia kissed Muire and slipped from the room.

"Let's get you to bed," Rua said.

Wolf glared at her outstretched arm and trooped across the room without any support. She had made it down the damn stairs and to the bench without any help, she would make it back to bed the same way. Still, by the time she lay down, her limbs were trembling and her breath came in short gasps.

"Can I get you anything?"

She shook her head. "Make sure to wake me up as soon as she gets back."

Rua nodded and turned to leave.

"Thank you," Wolf muttered, cheeks burning. "For trusting me."

Rua shrugged. "You got me home. It's the least I could do."

Wolf wanted to say more but her brain fogged up and her limbs were sinking into the bed like bread into a bowl of soup. Sleep was one opponent she couldn't win against.

\*\*\*

It felt like minutes when someone shook her awake.

For a moment a dark figure towered over her, blocking out the light of the candles, and she had no knives, and she couldn't protect herself, and then they shifted, and Conor gently held her bicep.

"Aurnia's back."

"Where's Rua?" She asked, with a sleep-thick voice.

"Sleeping. She's recovering too. Up you get." He helped her up, arm across her back, steadying her. "You okay?"

"Better than a few days ago. Will be even better tomorrow."

"One day at a time."

She smirked. "Something like that."

Quietness had joined them in the bar. Rua was curled up under a cloak, asleep. The others were resting, but no one else slept. She glanced out the window. The night had darkened further. The moon and stars were barely visible in the void-like sky. Wolf worried for one terrifying moment that she would slip off and fall into the nothingness. She blinked and the sky was just the sky again. Hounds still patrolled but it seemed to be less than before; a lighter night duty while the majority slept. Such a lack of vision annoyed Wolf. Attacks rarely happened in the middle of the day.

She turned back to the room when Aurnia coughed.

Rua shot up, dagger in her hand, reminding Wolf that she still needed to get her knives back. She understood not having them before, politely played along with the *don't give the traitor weapons* plan, but they had voted her back in and she needed blades now she had a giant target drawn on her back in blood.

Rua blinked and put her knife away. "What did you find?"

"Tadgh was asleep." Aurnia grinned. "Surprisingly he wasn't pleased to see me."

The smile held something feral that made Wolf settle in her skin. She had felt it on her own face too many times to be anything but comforted.

Wolf asked, "Did he have any useful information?"

"The Síochain's apprentice is locked in his room. No torture. No punishment. Not yet." Aurnia sat, glancing around the room to be sure they were all listening. "Tadgh thinks, and he insisted that I tell you that this is just gossip from the ranks, that they're waiting on a letter from the capital."

"The nun already returned. She would have brought the letter," Wolf clarified.

"It's not an easy thing to decide to kill your child."

Aoife tapped the table. "What do you mean kill your child?"

"You don't know how the Table works?" Wolf scrunched together her eyebrows.

"We know what Aurnia told us which was apparently less than she knew," she said pointedly, glaring at Aurnia. "But the Síochain was more important than the Table and it's not like they want us to know anything about how they govern our country into the ground."

"Sorry," Wolf replied quickly, still aware of how little time had passed after the vote. "I didn't know. I grew up in the convent and respect for the Table is the first thing they teach us."

Aoife shrugged, but the annoyance faded off her face. "It's fine."

"I told you enough to keep you safe but now..." Aurnia trailed off and glanced at Muire.

She shrugged and then nodded. "You might as well. They're in too deep not to know."

"The Table is simple," Aurnia continued like she hadn't shown uncertainty for the first time since Wolf had met her. "The eldest child takes the seat. The youngest becomes Síochain. Everyone else becomes an adviser to the eldest. Only the eldest is allowed to have children to continue the tradition. Three is the least. If they don't, the second can offer up their children to continue the tradition.

"The Síochain's have to give up any children. The others do as well unless the eldest doesn't have enough children. To the Sisterhood, if they are girls, and to the Hounds, if they are boys. No question of legitimacy or power grabs."

"It works *because* they are family. They are bred into it. Absolute loyalty to the family name and the Table," Wolf finished.

Conor raised an eyebrow. "So, you both have Síochain's as fathers?"

"No," Aurnia answered. "We don't know who our families are. The nuns buy babies, steal babies, and are given babies. We could be anyone's."

"You don't know who your family is?" Aoife asked.

Wolf shrugged, refusing to think about warm arms and a lilting voice.

"So when we're talking about Luchán," Rua interrupted. Wolf got the impression Rua had saved her from the uncomfortable conversation. "His mother or father, whoever is on the Table, has to decide how to punish his betrayal."

"Mother," Wolf answered. "And to betray the Table means death."

Aurnia nodded. "They know what they have to do, but killing strangers for your beliefs is a lot different than your own child."

"So we have some time?" Seán asked.

"Very little, but some."

Conor shifted. "What else did Tadgh say?"

"The shifts are changing every four hours. Four Hounds to every unit. Sweeping the wall and around the estate with almost no breaks in between. I can attest to that. It was almost a challenge to get in."

Wolf laughed, glancing around when everyone stared at her. "What? That's funny."

"She is correct. I am hilarious."

Muire coughed. "Of course you are, dear."

Aurnia grinned at her wife before she continued, "The preparations for the Masquerade Ball makes it harder to sneak in. He said they're checking every cart that enters and leaves the estate, and there are more Hounds patrolling, but it's our only option. The ball itself is in a few days but I would hesitate to wait that long."

"Nothing else?" Conor pressed.

"Well, I planned to tell you later," Aurnia said with a smirk. "Tadgh did insist I make sure to tell you he said hi. Very important to him that I passed that message on to you."

Conor flushed. "Oh. Okay. Great."

Rua giggled which seemed to give everyone permission to join in.

"Shut up," Conor said. "Nothing is even happening."

"Sure," Seán managed between laughter. "Just a friendly hello between friends."

"So friendly, he forgot to extend it to the rest of us," Aoife agreed, which started everyone laughing again.

Confused, Wolf asked, "Are Tadgh and Conor…?"

"No," Conor practically shouted. "We were just in the same regiment. I was his commanding officer. Nothing happened."

"But you wanted it toooooooooo," Aoife sang.

"We were friends. That's all."

Misery saturated his features so Wolf decided to change the subject. "How do we get to Luchán?"

The room fell silent as the seriousness of the situation settled in again like a raincloud on a sunny day. Wolf felt almost bad about stealing the levity away but the grateful look Conor shot her warmed something in her chest.

"I'm not sure yet," Aurnia answered. "Tadgh said there are patrols inside as well. He doesn't know where Luchán's room is but he thinks it's somewhere over the east end of the house. He emphasised that everything he knew was idle gossip."

Rua rubbed her eyes. Tiredness leaked from her every movement. "What are we going to do? We can't just leave him there."

Wolf bit her lip, considering her next words and decided they were worth the risk. "I know the layout pretty well but I might also have someone on the inside who can help with the patrols," Wolf admitted. Tense silence fell. Wolf saw the moment they started doubting again in the averted eyes and drawn lips.

"How do we know we can trust this mysterious person you have literally never mentioned before?" Aoife snapped.

"You voted to keep me in," Wolf replied quietly.

"And?"

"Which means you've decided to trust me." She kept her tone easy but irritation tightened her skin. "So trust me. I'm here. I've given up everything I've ever known to stay with you all. Ask Aurnia. They don't make it easy to leave. They don't make it something we even consider. Two people have left," she gestured between her and Aurnia. "Two out of hundreds. There is a reason I am standing here and not back at the Síochain's estate. Either trust me, or don't, but make the decision now. I still have time to run. Get off this godforsaken island and go somewhere far, far away. Make your choice, Aoife, because I am not going to prove myself to you over and over again if you are going to just keep throwing it back in my face."

Wolf let out a shuddering breath; she had never allowed herself to lose control like that before and she felt almost giddy with the adrenaline.

She really was free.

The room was deathly silent as they all processed her words. Rua had a smug grin like she had just been waiting for this moment. Wolf rolled her eyes at her. The grin widened into something softer, and more private.

"Fine," Aoife said, dragging Wolf's attention away from Rua. "*A dhiabhal*, fine."

Wolf nodded. "I'll try to get a message to her."

She knew Pup checked the ivy on the gate every day and she thought maybe she would help, or at least be able to give Wolf more information from within the house; where they were keeping Luchán, what the patterns of the Hounds were, and what the Síochain was saying.

She refused to risk Pup though.

The nun had to believe her loyal to the Sisterhood, or she would be in danger as well. Wolf might not agree with her staying, but she would respect her decision.

"When will you be fit enough to go?" Rua asked.

Wolf glanced at Aurnia who nodded. "Aurnia can place the letter tonight. Collect it tomorrow. She'll know if it's a trap, but I don't think this person will betray me."

Rua glanced between Aurnia and Wolf.

"We need more information before we even try to save him," Conor agreed. "Let's see what Wolf's friend can find out."

"Okay. Everyone. Bed." Muire clapped her hands lightly. "As much as I'd prefer to keep you all here, it's probably better if you go back to the cave. Aurnia and Wolf will sort this out and we can meet back here tomorrow at the same time if there is a response. Seán, you can come tomorrow to check?"

"I've got an order of wood I need to pick up anyway." He stood. "Leave the same way?"

Conor nodded. "Thirty minute breaks. You all go first. We'll go last."

"I want those two close to me for the moment," Aurnia said, pointing at Rua and Wolf. "They need to be staying in beds."

Conor nodded, and Rua agreed with a small smile.

Relief flooded Wolf at not having to say goodbye to Rua yet. Having her close meant she was safe. Wolf sat back on the bench and watched the others put on heavy jumpers and scarves.

Rua joined her after a second. "Are you okay?"

Wolf allowed herself to move slightly closer than before to soak up as much heat as possible. "Are you?"

"Alive."

"Same."

They grinned at each other and Wolf's heart tripped over its feet.

"Do you think that says anything about us?" Rua mused.

"Only that our standards are probably too low."

"Probably." Rua reached out and traced the cut on Wolf's cheek.

At the touch of Rua's fingers, Wolf's heart fell over and refused to get back up.

"Does it hurt?" Rua's words were as gentle as her touch.

She wanted to shake her head but didn't want to dislodge Rua's hand. She wanted to answer but her tongue was suddenly too dry and heavy to form words. Wolf shrugged and swallowed, hoping her voice didn't break when she said, "It's okay. Twinges sometimes."

Rua nodded and dropped her hands, fingers leaving a trail of warmth behind them.

Wolf flushed, probably as red as Conor had been. "Oisín was angry at me."

"He's protective."

"Aren't you all?"

Rua laughed a little bitterly. "Maybe a little too much sometimes."

Not knowing how to respond, Wolf let silence fall between them.

She noted every detail of the moments they sat beside each other. Rua's warmth. The scent of leaves and damp and winter cold. Ash had coloured her brown jumper black at the shoulders but streaks of red were visible by her neck. She breathed so silently, Wolf checked to make sure her chest rose. Despite the itch demanding her to move closer, they didn't touch. The bare inch separating them might as well have been a cavernous drop to Wolf's desperate fingers.

She hated it a little. She longed for more.

"Be safe," Conor whispered, interrupting Wolf's rioting thoughts. "I'll see you tomorrow."

Rua nodded.

"Tomorrow," Wolf agreed, basking in having Rua to herself for a few precious hours, and shying away from the feeling like a spider from a flame.

# CHAPTER FORTY-SEVEN
## RUA

Rua woke the next morning, curled up on her side and facing Wolf. Wolf had slept the same way; a pair of parentheses reaching for each other. The nightmares had been knives and blood and tearing daggers on sensitive skin. Each time she had gasped awake, Wolf had been watching, light blue eyes reassuring.

As always, Wolf had woken at the same time Rua had.

"Why are you okay sleeping beside me?" Rua wanted to reach for her and feel her pulse beneath her fingers again. She wrapped her hands in the blanket.

"I don't think you're planning on murdering me." Wolf shrugged lazily. "My body is too tired to fight it."

Rua smirked. "And if I tried to murder you?"

"I think you'd learn that *try* is as far as you get." Arrogance shaped her expression. "You wouldn't be the first to have tried and failed."

"So sure of your skills," she snarked with a grin.

Wolf shrugged one shoulder and glanced away from Rua's searching eyes. "My skills are all I have."

The smile fell from Rua's lips. "Yeah."

"Don't be sad for me, Red." She rolled onto her back and stared at the ceiling. "No one else is."

"Luchán calls me Red," Rua replied, heart aching. Everything she'd done to protect him had failed. "We have to save him, Wolf."

When they had gone to get ready for bed, Wolf's knives had been sitting on her blanket, and now she played with one of them. "We will."

The words were spoken with such confidence, Rua couldn't help but hope. "Are we resting all day?"

"Probably," she said with a tired grin. "Hopefully my friend will have written back with some information."

They startled when the wall slid back suddenly. Both of them brandished knives.

Aurnia burst into the room. "Rua, they're in the square."

"Who is?"

"Luchán and the Síochain." The edges of her eyes tightened. "They're going to hang him."

"No." Rua's heart plummeted and her stomach roiled. She swallowed down her bile as she threw on her jumper and boots. "We're meant to have more time."

She pushed past Aurnia and flew down the stairs, racing through the tavern and out onto the street. It was dense with crowds, making it difficult to fight her way through to the market square. Hounds were visible but none of them noticed her. They were too busy guiding people to the gallows. Rua couldn't remember the last time it had been used. They mostly deported people now.

Vomit hit the back of her tongue.

"People of Scíth," Liam Cogadh called, voice as rough as an axe on wood. "There has been a betrayal of the Table, a betrayal to the families. To my family. One that has come from within. Someone has been stealing food."

Whispers broke out across the crowd as Rua pushed herself forward, desperate to get to Luchán. People had come from all over and were shoved together in an almost impenetrable wall. She swallowed back frustrated tears and kept forcing her way through whatever gaps she found.

"My nephew, your future Síochain, has betrayed the Table. And to betray the Table means death." There was no break in his voice. No care shown for his nephew. "Bring forth the traitor."

Two Hounds dragged Luchán onto the stage. He had two black eyes and a split lip. His hands were bound. Rua kept pushing through the crowd, desperation a clogging weight she had to swallow around.

"We cannot save this man from his crimes but you can stop more offences committed in your name. Tell me who is stealing food and I will reward you all."

A murmur spread through the crowd like wind through the trees.

Rua felt more than one pair of eyes watching her. She tried to push forward again, but a hand wrapped around her wrist, dragging her away from the square. She couldn't fight with so many bodies pressed in so close. Couldn't even reach her knife.

The side alley was empty and she palmed a knife, spinning around. Wolf stared at her, expression placid. She tried to break free but Wolf's grip was unshakeable. No matter how hard Rua fought, Wolf wouldn't let her go.

"Rua, stop," she finally snapped. "Now."

Rua ignored her, kept trying to pull her wrist free. Wolf threw her against a wall. When Rua tried to push away, Wolf shoved her back and braced her arm across her chest, a knife pressing into the soft skin under Rua's jaw.

"What exactly do you think you're doing?" Wolf asked, voice as chilled as the morning ground.

Rua stared, almost speechless with the helpless rage burning through her. "I have to save him," she gritted out. "I need to give myself up."

The laugh sounded hard and cruel.

She didn't recognise this version of her friend. It reminded her too much of the nun in the tunnels. Rua blinked and looked away from the cold eyes to the entrance of the alley; people were crowded at the bottom of it, ignoring them and staring at the stage. The Síochain's voice rose and fell in the rhythm of speech but she couldn't make out what he said. The crowd stood deadly silent except for one crying child. She wished someone would comfort it and then comfort her. She ached for her family; for the safety of her mother's hugs, for her father's hand on her shoulder and her sister's warmth beside her in bed.

Rua forced herself to meet Wolf's eyes again.

"What do you think happens if you show yourself?" Wolf's face remained expressionless. They could have been talking about the weather for all the emotion she put into her words. "He dies. You die. And then everyone else dies."

Rua glared. "It's not right."

"He knew what it meant when he got involved with this little rebellion of yours," she spat, knife digging in slightly and making Rua hiss. "He knew the risks. Do not take that choice from him. Do not steal that honour."

The word shocked her; Rua had never considered it a rebellion. She just thought it was the right thing, the only thing she could do, after everyone else had died, and everyone surviving continued to starve.

It took her a few tries to force the words out. "No one should have to die for me."

"And yet they will. Over and over again."

Rua blinked away tears.

"But," Wolf whispered, lowering her knife and taking Rua's hand between hers. "Many people will live because of you as well."

Neither of their hands were soft, too many hours practising

with a blade, but it was a comforting warmth on a suddenly freezing day, and Rua clung to it. She never wanted this. Too many people had already died because of decisions she had made. Too many people lost because of her reckless need to help.

She swallowed back the lump in her throat.

"The least we can do is bear witness to his death." Wolf linked their fingers together and led her back to the crowd. "That is the only thing we can give him now."

The Síochain's voice echoed through the square. "*Chuig an mbord.*"

They had missed the rest of his speech.

"*Chuig an mbord,*" murmured the crowd like a rising flood.

The Síochain pulled the lever. The trapdoor opened. The rope went taut.

Luchán was gone.

# CHAPTER FORTY-EIGHT
## RUA

Rua emptied her face of any emotion until she appeared blank, hollowed out. She followed Wolf back to the inn. Wolf's hand was warm in hers, helping her to stay present as they fought their way back through the packed streets. Hounds watched the heaving crowds with searching eyes but Rua still had ash black hair and Wolf's was dirty blonde. Nothing like their descriptions. But still, they needed to get out of sight.

Wolf moved them with a swiftness that belied the relaxed way she laughed with strangers and allowed children to scoot ahead of her. The act needed no more work; Wolf had transformed herself into a peasant, into a famine child, into an onlooker.

Inside, Rua screamed.

Nothing yet had managed to quiet the roaring instinct deep inside her that made her war against how unfair it all was, the instinct that forced her to get up every morning and fight. If she had a choice, a real choice, she thought sometimes, she would take disinterest over caring. It had to be easier than feeling so damn much. She screamed at the loss of her friend. Two years they had known each other. Worked together. Studied together. Sat by the lake and discussed politics. Read. Ate. Laughed. It hadn't always been this *rebellion*. They had been children once. She thought maybe they still were. Children playing at thieves.

It no longer felt like a game.

Inside, she screamed at never again meeting Luchán and skimming stones, never again running her hands through his hair, or receiving comforting forehead kisses when he instinctively knew she needed gentleness. She felt like she had been screaming somewhere deep inside herself since she lost her father, and then her mother, and then her sister, and now Luchán.

Rua followed Wolf and allowed her grief to gnaw at the remains of her heart. She glanced up to see red hair disappear into the crowd. It seemed like an omen sent by her sister. Maybe someone else would die today and nothing would stop it. She cut off those thoughts with the slice of a blade. A long time had passed since she had remembered her grandmother's stories of curses and fae, banshee calls and Death's waiting arms. She didn't have time to dwell on fairy tales. Someone had already died. No need to make up stories of more grief to come.

She wondered briefly what the Síochain felt watching his nephew die. To kill his own blood seemed like something only a monster would manage. Any children he did help create were lucky to be taken away from him. The bitterness around the thought was drowned out by the knowledge she had garnered the fateful night Wolf had been poisoned; she wouldn't wish the Sisterhood on anyone. Not even that bastard's children.

Wolf placed her in a chair by the fire. She didn't remember getting to the inn.

Aurnia stood by the door, and when Wolf shook her head, her face hardened. She crossed the room to the dresser and emerged with a letter.

"Rua, this was left for you." Her hand rested briefly on Rua's shoulder, a quick squeeze of comfort. "A girl delivered it. Said Luchán asked her too."

"What did she look like?" Wolf held the paper as if expecting it to attack them.

"Said her name was Pup and that's all you would need."

Wolf nodded. "We can trust her."

"Your friend?"

Wolf nodded again and handed the envelope to Rua.

She took it with numb hands. Only one page waited inside. Ignoring how her hands shook, she translated the familiar code, scribbling it down on the page as she did. She skipped the beginning, knowing that sentence by heart even in the cipher. Instead, she focused on the middle three sentences. It took her only a few minutes to finish. Luchán had kept it short and simple; the message too urgent to be drowned in heavy language.

*He has a spy in your camp.*
*The execution is a distraction.*
*He plans to take them and hang them at midnight at the ball.*

Rua stood so suddenly her chair fell. The noise echoed loudly through the quiet room. She thrust the note at Aurnia and took the stairs two at a time, hating how it made her body ache. She grabbed her sword and daggers. It didn't shock her when Wolf joined her, layering weapons over her body. They raced back downstairs.

"Back entrance. I can't leave. The Hounds are already suspicious after the raid," Aurnia practically growled with frustration. "Get them back here."

Rua nodded and ran.

They made it out of Scíth with no trouble; the streets were still full but not packed, and they used the cover of the crowd dispersing to get them out of town while the Hounds were distracted and inattentive. As soon as they were clear, they raced down the road, covering the long distance quicker than she ever had before. Her lungs burned by the time they reached the forest. Wolf moved steadily and silently beside her, but the strain made her lips thin. She was still recovering as well, and yet, she appeared as calm and steady as ever. Rua drew comfort from that and slid into the shadows of the trees.

The closer they got to the camp, the slower they moved until they were soundless. Even the carpet of leaves was left undisturbed. Quiet had settled over the forest. Not the comforting tell of home, but the agitated silence of bad news and unhappy households. They crept towards the clearing, swords in one hand and daggers in another, and Rua's heart beat so fast she thought it would explode in her chest.

No movement lifted the stillness.

They inched closer, pausing at the very edge of the clearing.

Hounds lay dead on hard ground. The scent of copper and thick plumes of smoke polluted the air. The blood rolling in rivets across their land broke Rua's patience. She sprang from her hiding place and raced through the bodies towards the cave. Billowing smoke poured out when she pulled back the bushes. She fell back coughing. Heat from the flames inside made her skin burn when she tried to get closer.

"They're not in there," called a wet, weak voice. "He took them." A gasping, choking cough followed the words.

She twirled around. Seán lay half covered by a dead Hound. Wolf lifted the woman off him and knelt beside him, pulling up his top to expose a vicious wound slashed across his torso. She hissed.

Rua stood, frozen. She couldn't do this. Couldn't lose another person.

Wolf glared at her. "Rua. Help your friend. I need to find something to stop the bleeding."

She stumbled forward and fell to her knees, grasping his hand. "What happened?" Tears wet her face.

He gave her a small smile. Crimson coated his teeth. "It's my fault." He coughed again. Blood dribbled down his chin. "He has my sisters," he slurred.

Wolf's hand paused from tearing up the Hound's uniforms. "Where?"

"In the cells. Two of them. He said I had to tell... the robberies... I told him about the barn. I didn't tell him about Aurnia, I promise. I said we..." He sucked in a rough breath, but it caught funny. Hacking coughs ripped through him.

Rua wiped her eyes with the back of her hand. "Why didn't you come to us? Tell us? We would've helped."

"Too late now." Regret and pain shaped the grin. "You have to save them."

Rua didn't know if he meant his sisters or the others. Either way, it was an easy thing to promise. "I will."

He screamed when Wolf put pressure on his wounds with a ball of fabric. "Don't. Please. I'm done."

She nodded, and Rua noticed her hands were trembling.

"I'm sorry." The words were barely the faintest whisper now. "Save them. Please," he murmured and shut his eyes.

Luchán was gone. Seán was gone.

Everyone was gone.

# CHAPTER FORTY-NINE
## WOLF

Wolf watched as Rua sobbed into Seán's bloody chest, not knowing what to do. She had never seen such unbridled grief. Rua had Seán's bloody shirt clenched in her fists as she gulped back tears and choked out apologies. Her shoulders shuddered. Rua crouched closer, feet losing grip on the blood soaked ground.

"I'm sorry. I'm so, so sorry," she whispered.

They couldn't stay here. The Hounds would be back to pick up their dead soon. Wolf wrapped her arms around Rua's waist and pulled her up, clutching the crying woman to her chest.

"We have to go." She murmured into Rua's hair. "We have to get back to the inn."

"No." Rua broke free of Wolf's grip, facing her with a ferocious expression. "I won't just leave him for the crows. I won't allow *his* soldiers to hurt him anymore," she hissed.

Wolf knew she meant the Síochain. At least Rua was with it enough to realise the Hounds would be back. Wolf gazed around the clearing at the bodies and the puddles of blood. The sight disgusted her, not because of the death, but because of the destruction of their home. Thick smoke leaked from the cave like the mouth of a dragon. Wolf knew it would be visible from the road, a beacon calling in the forces.

She thought for a second, then nodded. "Grab his legs."

They carried him over to a deep ditch. It sloped into the ground, too shallow to be a grave but far enough away from the battle to hide him until they had time to come back and bury him properly. They placed him down gently. Tears still streamed down Rua's face but she didn't falter as she helped Wolf to cover him with leaves, dirt and branches.

"*Tá tú saor ó bhaol, a chara. Codladh sámh.*" You are safe from harm, my friend. Sleep well.

Wolf blinked away unexpected tears. "We have to go, Rua."

Rare doubt prickled beneath her skin; she had seen the two women in the cell and chose to save Rua over them. It seemed impossible now that such a split second decision would cause such harm. She had always lived with life and death choices but this was the first time she had seen the consequences of them. Rua spoke so passionately about saving others, about the importance of each person's life. Wolf had never understood before. She had learned that life was a commodity easily destroyed, as cheap as the dirt underfoot. This was the first time she had realised that maybe saving people had more value than taking their life.

They raced through the forest, aware that the soldiers could be back at any time. Slipping around the edges of Scíth, avoiding anyone that would question their blood soaked clothes, they made it to Aurnia's without notice. Only when they stood in the warm kitchen did it hit Wolf what had happened.

Luchán was dead. Seán was dead. The others were to be hung.

Aurnia caught sight of them and raced from the bar. "What happened? Are you hurt?"

They were covered in Seán's blood; her hands, her chest, Rua's face and arms. It had dried a dirty red, flaking as they moved. Wolf rubbed her hand across her chest. Blood had never bothered her but she had never had the blood of a friend on her skin before now.

"Seán is dead," Wolf said, shocked at how hollow she sounded. "The others were captured."

Aurnia sat heavily.

"He wants to hang them on New Year's Eve as part of the ball. Probably to signal a fresh year with no troubles," Rua spat, bitterness making her words hard to hear.

"The ball is the most protected time of year on any Síochain's estate. It will be impossible to sneak in." Wolf leaned against the wall, settling into the quiet part of her she used when she waited. Allowed herself to become as still as a statue. Locked away any distractions. Made this become just another job. "We need to attend as guests."

Aurnia examined her sharply. "How will we get tickets?"

"We are thieves and liars," Wolf answered, exhausted by the obvious test. "We take what we want, and if we can't take it, we lie."

Rua stared at her. "What do you mean?"

"I can make forgeries of the tickets. I've seen them before."

Rua grinned, bright and harsh.

"We'll need ink and high quality paper. I can get that." Aurnia considered them both. "Wolf, you know the estate? The ways in and most of the Hounds?"

Wolf nodded.

"Write it all down. Everything you remember. Where the cells are. Where the Hounds will be placed. How we can get out." She glanced at Rua and Wolf knew she was questioning if Rua could hold it together long enough to save the others.

Rua seemed to know what Aurnia was thinking as well because she bristled. "What do you need me to do?"

"I have weapons. Clean them. Sharpen them. Get them

ready." She pointed at Wolf. "You're still weak and you," she said, gesturing at Rua, "look like you've gone three rounds with a rampaging horse. Rest. Stay hidden. The Hounds are still looking for you."

Wolf nodded, accepting the truth in the words, and glanced down at herself. "I need a bath."

After they had bathed in one of the empty guestrooms and changed into spare clothes donated by Muire, they sat at the kitchen table and planned with Aurnia. Muire would stay to mind the bar and keep up appearances, claiming Aurnia was sick. They knew who would have tickets; landlords, merchants, rich business owners and whoever else the Table favoured. They needed to be sure they would be able to blend in with them, so they needed dresses to match the finery of the other guests, but it helped too that the ball was a masquerade. Names weren't placed on the tickets, a failing in security that still made Wolf scoff, so it would be easy enough to sneak in with the fake tickets. They would need three between them. They only had two days.

"We can use our wedding dresses. I can make a third with the leftover material from them," Muire said after she'd shut up the bar for the night. Candlelight made her face a harsh, unforgiving thing and Wolf thought maybe she understood why Aurnia had chosen her over the Sisterhood. "I'll have them by the morning of the ball."

Aurnia nodded. "I'll have the paper and ink by tomorrow afternoon. Will that give you enough time to make them?"

Wolf nodded. "Once I do one, you'll be able to copy it."

"The Sisterhood trained us well," Aurnia agreed.

Wolf nodded but once again felt that helpless scratch under her skin that the others were in danger, were probably being tortured like Rua had been, while they sat and planned.

As if pulling the thoughts straight from her head, Rua

snarled, "So, we just wait now?" Rua's voice sounded harsh from the tears she had shed. "You expect us to just sit around while our friends are hurt?"

"That's exactly what I expect."

Wolf sat up straighter as Aurnia's voice took on the tone of a nun.

"We can rest," Wolf said. Rua would be easier to protect if they were both healthy. "Let's go to bed now," she said to Rua. "It's been a long day."

Rua's expression hardened, and it seemed like she would fight back, but then like all her strings had been cut, she slumped and nodded. "Sleep would be good. Finish this monstrous day."

Wolf nodded and led her up the stairs to bed.

\*\*\*

She woke to darkness and silence. Something had disturbed her. A small rock tapped the window of the guest room they had claimed. She stared down at the yard. Pup stood in the moonlight, fretful and violent. Throwing her sword over her back, Wolf hurried down to her.

"How did you get out of the estate?"

Pup shrugged. "Easier to get out than in. How is she?"

"Two of her friends died today. The rest are on the executioner's block." Emotions roiled beneath the surface but Wolf remained externally calm. "She's not great."

"Tell her they're okay for now." Pup kept glancing around, one hand on her knife. Somewhere in the distance, the beat of hooves sounded. "They're in the cells with two women who claim to be sisters to someone called Seán?"

Wolf nodded. "I left them there when I got her out. I could have prevented all of this." The sting of truth had yet to diminish; small acts could change the course of everything, were worthwhile just for the doing.

"We both could have prevented all of this," Pup snapped. "Now we just have to live with the consequences."

Wolf pushed them into the shadows when she heard the chatter of Hounds out on the street. "Why are you here, Pup?"

"I need to know what you're planning, how I can help."

"Why?"

She shrugged.

"Not good enough. We already lost two people today. I'm not risking Rua. You want me to trust you, you have to give me a good reason."

"I can't. If I tell you the truth…" Pup shook her head. "You'd have to tell Rua and I think maybe I'd want you to."

Wolf thought about it. "Give me your name. Your real name."

Pup hissed. "You always know the exact place to hit."

"They trained me well."

Cigarette smoke scented the cold air. Neither of them spoke until they were sure the Hounds had passed. Wolf studied Pup; heavy bags sat under her eyes telling Wolf she had been sleeping less than before, and her mouth drooped like a disappointed crescent moon. She seemed to have aged since the promise. Once again, Wolf wondered who Rua was to her. She knew Pup had been nothing but honest the whole time she had known her; she had helped in every way she could. She deserved to be trusted in return.

Wolf broke the silence, "We're going to go to the ball. Forge the tickets, cause a diversion, and break them out. Unless the tunnel is still an option?"

"They collapsed it."

Wolf nodded. It's what she would have done. "Are there any Sisterhood members there?"

"Just the nun."

An owl hooted and they both paused to watch it take flight.

Inky darkness coated them in easy cover. Wolf wished she could cut a cloak from this night and use it to disappear.

"I'll help how I can," Pup said. "But I won't reveal myself."

"Why are you staying with them? If Rua means so much to you, leave. Come with us. Help us in the light."

"The choice I made, she'll never forgive me. And I don't want to be forgiven. It was my choice. I would make it all over again if I had to." She stepped out of the shadows, suddenly illuminated by a bright path of moonlight. For one blinding moment, she was Rua, and then she moved back into the dark, and was herself again. "My name is Saoirse. Tell her if you want. She won't believe you."

Wolf watched as she scaled the wall of the inn and disappeared into the dark.

# CHAPTER FIFTY
## RUA

Aurnia woke them the next morning with a sharp rap on the door.

One glance at Wolf told Rua she had barely slept. When she raised an eyebrow in question, Wolf just shook her head and left the room. Rua followed quietly. She had no energy to find out what was wrong with Wolf. It took all she had to keep her anger under control. Took all she had not to race to the Síochain's estate and free the others herself. All that mattered now was getting her family back, and then making sure nothing like this happened again. She knew what Conor had been trying to teach her, knew they thought she should let them risk their lives, but she wouldn't, not now, and if they insisted, she would leave and go out on her own. She would never risk them again. Not for her *rebellion*.

She scratched at the ash in her hair, irritated by how it made her scalp itch like crazy. She huffed when Muire gestured at the chair in front of the fire but sat anyway, allowing her to run black through it again. Wolf watched with a longing coating her face like light rain. Rua wondered if she wanted the softness that Muire's hands promised, and then she wondered if she had ever had that type of gentleness before. Rua desperately wanted to run her hands through Wolf's hair. She wanted to show her every type of soft touch.

"What now?" She asked the room to stop that train of confusing thoughts.

"I've to open the bar," Muire replied. Aurnia appeared at the bottom of the stairs and she kissed her. "Aurnia is going to get the ink and paper for Wolf. You two are going to sit here and review what Wolf wrote down yesterday about the estate and the manor."

When Rua sighed, Wolf stood and grabbed some paper.

"I'll talk. You write." She waited until Rua nodded and then sat at the table. "Grab some rolls and cheese. I'm still hungry."

Listening to Wolf talk about secret exits, the manor layout, and how many Hounds there were, soothed some of her frayed nerves; there was something calming about how she discussed everything in the same neutral tone no matter what the topic. The planning passed the morning, and although it did little to calm the thrum of anger beneath her skin, Rua admitted to herself the rest had helped her body recover from the past few days. The memories from the hanging, from Seán's bloody face, still dug into her stomach like a shard of glass, digging and slicing towards her heart. It didn't matter if she ignored it, it kept slicing away little parts of her. Two people she trusted, she cared about, she *loved*, were gone. The part of her that screamed was hoarse with the pain.

Aurnia finally arrived back late in the afternoon. She held up thick parchment, thin, delicate quills and bottles of gold ink. "Had to go halfway to Ríthe to get this but it should be good enough to pass inspection."

Rua rolled her eyes. "Well, at least that's one part of the plan done. Unless they don't look good enough and the Síochain catches us."

Aurnia snorted. "Still in good form then?"

Rua shrugged and stood to get away from her searching eyes. "Wolf, do you want lunch?"

Wolf stared down at the maps they had been making of the manor, tapping the quill against the wood. It took a long moment for her to drop it and look up.

"Do either of you..." Wolf stopped talking, seeming suddenly frustrated with herself. "Do either of you know a Saoirse?"

Rua's hand jerked to the hilt of her dagger. "Why?"

"I asked Pup her real name last night." Wolf's voice barely carried across the room. "She said I could tell you but you wouldn't believe me. Why wouldn't you believe me?"

Rua stared at Wolf, heart pounding and stomach churning. "You're sure she said Saoirse?"

Wolf nodded.

Rua gasped, hands trembling when she pulled at her hair. They came away black with ash. "What does she look like?"

"Red hair. Shorter than me." Wolf watched her with her piercing blue eyes. "Young. Maybe nineteen. Sort of like you, I guess. Same eyes."

Aurnia held up her hand to stop Wolf. "Rua, you don't think it's really her, do you?"

"Really who?" Wolf demanded.

"My sister."

Clues Rua had ignored or brushed aside as impossible slipped into place; the pile of blankets on the bed in the stables, the glimpse of red hair she had thought was a hallucination in the cells, another one at the market before she got the letter from Luchán. The world tilted and swooped before settling over this new truth.

Saoirse was alive.

Grief washed over Rua and she thought her knees might give out. So much time had passed. She had lost so much, but to have her sister back, to have one tiny part of her other family back, would be like the first gasp of air after nearly drowning.

"Why didn't she stay?" Rua's heart thumped in her ears. "Why didn't she find me?"

Wolf hesitantly said, "I don't think she knew you were alive. When they had you in the cell, when Luchán interrogated you, I think she found out then." Wolf gripped the quill so tightly Rua was sure it was going to break. "I think she thought she was alone and did what she had to to survive."

A sob tore its way up Rua's throat and she nearly suffocated on it. "In the workhouse, I got really sick. Almost died. When my fever broke, the woman who had helped me told me Saoirse was gone. I was too sick to question her word choice. But gone doesn't mean dead, does it?" Horror crackled across her skin like fire. "She was in the Sisterhood all this time?"

"She thinks you won't want her back."

Rua laughed an ugly sound. "I would kill to have her back."

"Maybe you won't have to, *mo leanbh*." Aurnia's calm was a reaching hand as Rua drowned. She grasped onto it gratefully. "We'll save her along with the others."

Rua could hear the caution in Aurnia's voice but she didn't care. Relief was a soothing balm on all of her hurts. "Aurnia, she's alive."

Aurnia's eyes darted between Wolf and Rua. "We'll get her back."

Rua rushed over to Wolf and wrapped her arms around her briefly. "Thank you."

Wolf nodded but sadness lined her eyes. "Of course." She glanced at Rua, and away again. "I better get started on these," she said, waving the parchment and ducking her head so Rua couldn't see her face anymore.

# CHAPTER FIFTY-ONE
## WOLF

The morning of the ball, the last day of the year, rose clear and sunny. The bite of cold in the air and the fog hanging over the distant mountains did little to kill the cheer circulating around Scíth. Even now the people of Éirely had hope that the new year would bring a fresh start. Listening from the window to the calls of delight and the children laughing, to the plans for gatherings and the happy greetings, made Wolf itch. She didn't understand how in the face of such destructive forces, people managed to find joy in their days.

Rua still slept.

Wolf didn't bother waking her and she ignored the soft ache as she watched the gentle rise and fall of Rua's chest, how the knots in her hair sprawled across her pillow and one of her fists gripped the sheets. She didn't want to leave this strange and beautiful woman, but she knew once Saoirse returned, she would have no reason to stay.

The promise was just an excuse and she hadn't realised it until Pup revealed her name. She knew Rua would want to follow Pup, would want to find her, and the knowledge made her stomach churn. Jealousy was such a stupid feeling. Regret as well. Wolf felt both of the emotions when she thought of Rua and her sister reunited, of Pup being Saoirse, of no longer having to keep her promise because Saoirse would do it herself. She had finally found someone that was truly beautiful in the least expected place and now she would have to give her up. Freedom meant having no one to answer to but herself. It meant carving out her own space in the world, *alone.*

She dragged herself away, body aching but less than the day before, and went downstairs. Muire had three dresses hanging from the wall. They made Wolf's heart yearn. She ran her fingers over the silky soft fabric and examined the detailed embroidery. They were each a different colour; black, navy, and purple. Stars fell down the skirts from the waists, and flowers lined the hems. The skirts and corsets were separate. Their masks matched the dresses and would cover most of their faces.

She recognised two from the picture on the wall. "You got married in these?"

"I was a dressmaker in Ríthe when I met Aurnia," Muire smiled softly. "While she fought for her freedom, I made us these from stolen material." She rubbed the material of the navy dress between her fingers. "I had some material left over that I've been using to store them in. The skirts tie around your waist. The corsets are reinforced. Back then she wouldn't wear something without being sure she could fight in it."

"They're beautiful."

Muire nodded. "They are that. I'll do your hair but you'll need to bathe, apply perfumes. Smell like a lady."

"I've done this before," Wolf agreed. "Never as a rescue though. Always to kill someone."

"Well, you're not going to have to kill anyone anymore."

Wolf snorted. "Sure, I'm not."

"*Mo leanbh,*" she replied softly. "You don't have to do that anymore."

"Okay." Wolf rubbed the skirt through her fingers, liking

how the smooth material flowed like water. "Will you be okay alone in the bar tonight?"

Muire sighed but didn't push it any further. "We have three women who help us when we're busy. They'll be there and I can visit my poor sick wife regularly to keep up the ruse. I'll be fine."

The day stretched out in front of her like a bleak, empty canvas. Wolf missed Conor most, but the loss of any of them hurt like a knot in her gut. "Do you think they're okay?"

"I hope they are but the state of you and Rua when you returned." She shook her head and went over to the counter. "Let's get you fed."

Wolf didn't know if she did it on purpose but Muire kept them busy all day. She made them both bathe for as long as it took to clear the dirt from under their nails and the creases in their knuckles, and where it had embedded in their skin from the forest. She muttered about them being wild while she made them scrub and rinse and scrub again. After, they covered their skin in oil that smelt like lavender and roses.

"I don't think I've ever smelt so floral," Rua whispered.

Wolf huffed out a quiet laugh. "I don't think I've ever been so clean." She gestured at her pink arm as proof. "I think she took some of my skin off."

Rua smiled, small and weak. "Are you nervous?"

"No." Wolf would allow no doubts to cloud her judgement tonight. "We're getting them back."

When Rua didn't reply, Wolf studied her face. Muire had covered both their bruises with powder and rouge. Unless you searched them out, Rua's injuries were invisible. They had long gloves to cover the cuts on Rua's arms and hands. It soothed something in Wolf to see how much easier she moved as well. Wolf already felt better from the poison, still weakened but not weak.

Realising she had been staring, she tore her eyes away and said, "I refuse to lose anyone else."

"You were sure about Luchán as well."

"Rua," Wolf gripped her healing forearms gently. "We are getting them back. Failure is not something I'm interested in. Not again."

"You were the best in the convent?"

"I *am* the best, and we will save them."

Rua loosened up just a tiny bit with her words. "Okay."

Muire bustled back in with the dresses. "I have to open up the bar soon." The skirts rustled on her arms. "There are no weapons at the ball but you won't be searched. It's too undignified for the guests. Even so I didn't want to risk it, so I built an oversized hem." She held up the navy skirt. "You can fit your daggers in there. It won't be much protection but some weapons are better than none. The skirt ties at your waist and you'll be able to strap your swords to your thighs. You'll wear trousers under it and remove it when you need to. The corsets will protect you if you're stabbed, but I would really prefer it if you didn't get stabbed, okay?"

They both nodded.

"Get dressed while I check on Aurnia. The cart will be ready in an hour and we still have to do something about both of your hair."

They got dressed silently; Wolf in her Sisterhood garb and Rua in her robbery gear. The corset sat heavily over her thick black top. She struggled with the silky ties at the back until Rua pushed her hands away and set about tightening them. She stood so close her breath tickled the hairs on the back of Wolf's neck and made goosebumps dance along her skin. Neither of them spoke. Wolf didn't think she had any words left when Rua trailed her fingers along a bare patch of skin above her shoulder blades.

"All done."

Wolf swallowed on a dry throat. "I can do yours now."

Rua nodded.

Wolf's heartbeat played across her skin like a flute. She trembled and it had nothing to do with the *Bás Tostach*. The fabric felt as soft as ever as she threaded each side of the corset together. Rua shivered, and Wolf realised she was as affected by Wolf's breath on her skin as Wolf had been by Rua's. It settled the quaking fear inside her as she finished tightening the top.

"Thank you."

Finding it suddenly impossible to meet Rua's eyes, Wolf picked up her skirt and wrapped it around her. She didn't understand the feeling. It felt like someone had lit fire to a bottle of alcohol and let it burn until the glass shattered and the flames exploded. It seared every part of her being, this unexplainable urge, and she didn't know how to put it into words, and didn't know what she should do about it. All she had learned about attraction had come from a book and a scathing lecture on how to abuse the trust of people by using her attractive face against them. She didn't want to do that to Rua. She didn't know what she wanted to do or say to Rua.

They finished getting ready in silence.

# CHAPTER FIFTY-TWO
## RUA

The Síochain's estate was transformed.

It glowed in the moonlight. Lanterns hung from the walls. The tinkle of laughter and cheerful voices simpered on the air, and drums played a steady beat behind the walls. Torches lined the road, illuminating their carriage in an orange glow. Hounds stood between each torch; dark sentinels on watch. They were an impressive and intimidating sight as they glared at the mixture of carts, wagons and carriages that drove past. Their swords shone sharp in the light. When Aurnia's cart reached the top of the queue, a Hound took their tickets and inspected them. Seconds ticked by without a word. The more time that passed, the more Rua convinced herself that they had already failed.

He scrutinised them all once more before nodding. "Enjoy your night," he muttered gruffly.

The guard by the open gate beckoned them through.

"Oh, we will," Aurnia charmed before driving the horse forward with the reins.

Although the night's chill left goosebumps across her skin, people milled around the yard. It looked nothing like when Rua had crept across it when she had tried to save Wolf. Memories of the cell surfaced like ripples on a lake but she pushed them away. She couldn't lose herself now. She needed to save the others, and her sister.

Holly hung in garlands across the dark walls. More torches sat under them, highlighting their red berries. Dresses of all colours made the dull space look like a field of wildflowers. Servers walked the crowd with trays of alcohol and food. Their cart was guided around the edges and someone took the reins from Aurnia. They climbed down and she petted the horse goodbye, knowing they might never see it after tonight. The exit they hoped to use wouldn't allow the horse to accompany them, and even now, escape seemed like more of a jagged hope than an actual plan.

They walked the edges of the party, warmed by the giant bonfires in the corners. The crowd moved like a living organism heaving as the cold wind made sparks fly off the fires. Shadows crawled up the walls. Rua stuttered to a stop when she saw the hastily built gallows sitting by the entrance to the manor. Five ropes swung in the lamp light. Conor, Aoife, Oisín, and Seán's sisters. She swallowed on a painful throat.

"Move," Wolf whispered.

Rua dragged her eyes away when she saw other guests staring at her.

"Get to the ballroom," Wolf said with a gentle shove.

Rua nodded, stumbling up the steps.

People swarmed the halls leading to the ballroom, warming up and fawning over each other's finery. Mulled wine and the chill winter scented the space. Wolf's hand rested on her lower back, a warm weight steering Rua through the crowd. The celebration in no way reflected Rua's world. She felt sick. Food was plentiful. No one here had known a day's hunger in their life. Laughter and good cheer were in easy supply, ready to be picked from the air like canapes off a tray. The masks were disorientating; flashing of shining white and satin black, some with jewels and others plain, slitted eyes and wide fake ones. They peered from the darkness and mutated in the tall flames, appearing like banshees screaming for death in the flashing light.

Hundreds of candles lit up the ballroom. A band played in the corner; a jaunty song which would have had Rua and her friends performing a jig together, but the rich just stood around, chatting. Probably about their successes. Rua didn't think it was possible to hate anyone more. They had passed crowds of starving people trying to get closer to the estate as they travelled from the inn. Held back by Hounds, more than one bled.

She ignored the taste of bile as it hit the back of her tongue and scanned the room for any hint of Saoirse. A canopy of masks and oversized gowns, glittering jewels and fake smiles assaulted her vision but no flash of red. No hint of her sister. The heat made her cheeks burn. Wolf tensed suddenly beside her, and Aurnia caught Rua's wrist.

Liam Cogadh strolled in, every bit the ruling lord. He wore dark pants and a pale blue jacket. A navy shirt shone under it, the same colour as Wolf's dress. Whereas Rua had thought earlier how the dress brought out the blue in Wolf's eyes, this just forced her to acknowledge how cold his eyes were as he scanned the room. She froze, remembering how his breath felt on her skin as he sliced her open. Remembering how he had taunted her and made Luchán hurt her. Remembering how blank he had looked as Luchán died in front of them.

*A dhiabhal,* she hated him.

"Welcome to my home." His voice sounded like stone on stone. It held no comfort, no guilt. "I hope you are all enjoying the final night of another successful year. Rents are up. Food is plentiful. The Table is succeeding."

Polite clapping filled the room.

"Do they know what state the country is in, or are they really that naive?" Rua whispered to Aurnia.

"I think they believe what they want, and see even less. They're successful and comfortable. They assume anyone who isn't just isn't working hard enough."

"Nun," Wolf whispered when another woman walked into the room in a pitch black suit.

Rua watched as Wolf stepped back almost unconsciously, hiding half behind Aurnia. Just one small step but it told Rua all she needed to know about how Wolf felt about her role in the Sisterhood.

"Both of you stay away from her." When they nodded their acquiescence, Aurnia asked, "Rua, are you sure about searching out Saoirse?"

Rua glared.

"Don't look at me like that," Aurnia snapped. "This is a large place."

"She'll be in the rafters," Wolf whispered. "I can get her."

"No," Rua snapped.

Jealousy flared up, a fierce burn at how easily Wolf had spoken of her friendship with Saoirse. Wolf trusted no one, and yet, she had trusted Saoirse with what seemed like no effort at all.

"She's my sister." Rua tried not to care that Wolf knew her sister, knew who she had become, because Saoirse hadn't come back to Rua, to her actual family. If anyone was going to save Saoirse, it would be Rua. "Aurnia, you're going to create a distraction?"

Aurnia snorted, and Rua took it as an agreement.

"Wolf, you know the manor best so you'll go and find the others. Aurnia will meet you at the gate behind the stables. I will too when I find her." They already knew the plan but it eased something in Rua to say it again.

Aurnia glanced between them. "I don't like either of you going off alone."

"We'll be alright," Rua reassured her. "Just make sure the

distraction is big enough that no one thinks to check on the prisoners."

Something feral set across Aurnia's face. "Just make sure you get out quickly."

"Why?"

"Because I'm going to burn his damn house down."

# CHAPTER FIFTY-THREE
## WOLF

Once the Síochain and the nun were caught up with the crowd, Wolf led Rua out of the ballroom. They walked casually down the packed hall, arm in arm. The chattering scratched on Wolf's battle ready nerves. They manoeuvred around the guests, pretending to admire the art hanging on the walls as they strolled through the gathered onlookers.

"The tapestries are magnificent," Rua said. "Let's go see if we can find more."

Wolf knew it was an act, and knew they had succeeded by the indulgent glances shot their way, but she wondered what it would be like if it hadn't been another game she had been forced to play. She suddenly wished the soft satin of Rua's gloves and the warmth of her arm promised more than violence to come. It made her chest ache, knowing she had to let her go, knowing she had to give her back to Saoirse and leave.

Pushing away the distraction, she grinned easily as they strolled away from the crowd. "I'm sure there must be some this way," she replied, forcing a giggle from her mouth. "Probably just as beautiful."

As soon as they turned the corner, she dropped Rua's arm. "Pup seemed pretty set about staying," she muttered, pulling them into a small sitting room. She untied the skirt from around her waist and dug her daggers out of the lining. She dragged off her gloves and tucked the knives into the sheaths on her arms. She threw her mask at her feet. "Are you sure she's even going to want to come with you?"

Rua untied her own skirt, and after freeing her knives, she grabbed both skirts and masks and hid them inside an empty coal bucket.

Ignoring Wolf's question, she asked, "Corset?"

"Extra padding."

Rua nodded. "I'm her sister. She's my *family*. Of course she'll come with me."

Wolf knew her well enough by now to hear the doubt in her words. "A night like this, she'll either be in the rafters probably close to the stables or by the Síochain."

Rua nodded. "That's the other side of the manor to the cells." She strapped the weapons to her body. "I might not be able to get back to you."

Laughter tinkled up the hall and they both froze. No voices followed.

"We'll meet you outside then."

Rua grabbed her hand. "Don't you dare die."

"I won't if you won't."

The grin Rua threw over her shoulder was bright as she disappeared from the room.

Wolf stood for a second, listening to the sounds of the party before she shook herself free of her melancholy. She checked she had her swords and daggers in easy reach, and left the room, going straight to the cells. They had obviously closed off this part of the manor because only silence and darkness met her. Not even the candles were lit. She crept soundlessly, listening for any change on the heavy air. The walls muffled the sounds of the party making it seem like she was the only person alive in the whole world. She liked it better this way. She preferred to hunt than be hunted.

Halfway to the cells, she heard voices behind her. She threw herself up on a sideboard and then pulled herself into the rafters, concealing herself just as the Síochain and the nun appeared around the corner. Annoyance flared through her at the messy mistake; she should have been in the rafters since she had left Rua.

"I'm sure I saw her and her little red headed friend as well," he growled. "Go check the cells, and when you're done, check the Hounds are still patrolling the manor. Catch them and return them to their rightful places."

"Even the deserter?"

He paused and towered over her. "I thought the Sisterhood had ways to make people loyal?" The chill of his words could have frozen a heart still in its chest.

"We have ways, *sir*." The nun said *sir* like she meant to say *bastard*. Wolf had never seen a nun show so much emotion. "Of course we can make the deserter loyal again."

Wolf's stomach clenched. She had never given them loyalty. She wouldn't start now.

The Síochain nodded. "Check the cells. I have guests to attend to."

They disappeared in opposite directions.

Wolf knew she should be brave and face the nun, but her body was still recovering from the poison; Aurnia had said to avoid her, and just seeing her had Wolf's heart smashing into her ribs in loud, painful thuds. She knew she had been trained better than allowing her fear to control her, but she didn't want to go back and be made loyal. Gulping, she numbed every part of her, quieted the tiny voice that wanted her to run away and never come back, and headed for the Síochain's office. Rua had told her to stay safe. It felt like an easy order to obey.

She travelled silently across the rafters. There were few Hounds patrolling the hallways. The ones she did pass were too wrapped up in their own conversations to notice her. She dropped down into the Síochain's office. Glowing embers cast long shadows across the dark walls. The place felt larger without his oppressive presence. Her boots made no noise as she strode across the floor. There were no papers on his desk but she had spent enough time watching him over the past few months that she knew where he kept his most important documents.

She knelt in front of the locked drawer and rooted out her tools for opening locks; they were hidden in the bottom of her Sisterhood corset and it took her two tries because she fumbled over the shiny fabric of her gown's corset. The lock was well oiled and fell open quickly under her skilled fingers. Papers stuffed the drawer. Some were livestock reports, others were food production, workhouse shortages and occupancy were next, and food shipment deliveries. Codagh had a massive port town which accepted ships from their closest neighbour. Wolf thought it would make more sense for a busy port to be part of the capital city but fairness stated that no county held more power than another. The Table sat dead centre on the island surrounded by Ríthe.

Wolf quickly read the schedule in her hands; every shipment, in and out, for the next six months. It was exactly what Rua needed with Luchán gone. She stole a piece of paper out of the drawer and transcribed the details as quickly as she could. Once she was finished, she folded the papers up as small as she could and tucked them into the hidden pocket on the inside of her trousers. This wasn't the first time she'd had to sneak out important documents. She put the documents back in order and tucked them back into the drawer.

She had just stepped around the desk when the door handle turned, sounding loud in the quiet room. Knowing she had no time to hide, and needing a reason to be in here that wouldn't draw attention to the desk, and what she might have found there, Wolf grabbed some loose papers off the top of it and threw them on the fire. At least this way, he may not realise they had the schedules until they had managed a few robberies.

"I'd have thought petty vandalism would be beneath someone of your skillset."

She forced herself not to react as she faced the Síochain. "Anything to make your life slightly more difficult."

He laughed. Not the almost amused laugh from before. This was cruelty wrapped in noise. "You have no comprehension how difficult you have made my life."

She swallowed. "I'm not going back there."

"No one escapes their destiny, Little Wolf, and when they try to, they die."

"Like Luchán."

"That fool of a boy should have known better." Again, he showed her the roiling storm beneath his calm exterior. Bitter grief soaked his words. "*You* will know better."

"Why do you even care?"

He laughed again; weighty and uneven. "I care about order. About rules. About laws. I care about how we hold this country together by making sacrifices that the poor, snivelling peasants can't even imagine." He stepped towards her and she saw how he quivered with unchecked emotion. She had never seen him so out of control. "I care," he snarled. "Because if I didn't get to keep you, she definitely doesn't."

Wolf took a small step backwards, pulse a trapped bird. "What are you talking about?"

"Have you still not figured it out, *mo Mhac Tíre Beag*," Liam Cogadh sneered. The name tore over her skin. "Do you still not recognise me? I knew who you were the moment I saw you in the yard."

Wolf couldn't move.

Overwhelming grief drowned her, dragging her under, and she wasn't sure what to say. She had imagined this moment so many times. She had practised the words, over and over on dark, lonely nights when she ached right down to her bones. They all seemed pointless and worthless now she faced the truth of her heritage.

Liam Cogadh was her father.

"Why?"

"Why what?" The burning light made a monster of his face; shadows hiding his eyes in darkness and the embers glow glinting off sharpened teeth. "Why did I give you up? Why did I keep you the extra two years? Why am I telling you now?"

The dismissive tone ignited her rage as easily as any attack would. She withdrew her sword. "Stop talking. I don't care," she swore, meaning it mostly for herself. "I have a promise to keep."

Wolf attacked.

# CHAPTER FIFTY-FOUR
## RUA

The noise of the party faded away as Rua slipped towards the stairs. She knew the kitchen would be packed but she hoped she could sneak through without anyone noticing. Wolf had explained to her about the rafters that she could use to traverse the space. Servers passed her with trays of food and drinks, but she kept to the shadows and they hardly glanced her way. The few who did barely looked at her before letting their eyes move on; everyone who worked in the Síochain's estate had long learned to keep their noses out of his business. Her heart thumped like the drums in the yard as she followed the darkened hallway.

A couple giggled behind her, shoes clipping on the wooden floor like heartbeats. She held herself close to the shadows and waited until they disappeared into a room together. She didn't think they had seen her but it still took her a long moment to move again. She studied the rafters, thinking maybe she had seen a shifting shadow.

"Saoirse?" She whispered, tapping her fingers on the wood behind her to calm her nerves. She couldn't spend too long searching, couldn't abandon the others again, but Rua refused to leave her sister here. "Saoirse, please."

There were no good choices when it came to family.

She crept down the hallway. Light spilled from the staircase like a puddle of gold. Three Hounds appeared so suddenly she had no time to hide. They froze when they caught sight of her. They stared at her, taking in her trousers and many weapons. No one spoke for the longest moment. She withdrew her sword and braced herself for a fight.

"What do we have here?" Forced amusement didn't hide the shock beneath the words.

"An intruder," a woman on the left said. "Capture her and throw her in the cells." When no one moved, she hissed, "You saw what he did to Tadgh. Do you want to be mistaken for traitors as well?"

A grunt behind her alerted her to two more Hounds. Surrounded.

Rua's breath caught. "What did he do to Tadgh?"

The shadow behind her shifted. She threw herself against the wall so she could keep them all in her sight at once.

The Hound scoffed. "He threw him in the cells with the rest of them. He's probably going to hang him with them."

The woman grinned. "Not enough rope."

The others jeered and laughed.

"You can't really want this." Rua winced; she sounded like a child and these guards were all at least ten years older than her. "What they're doing to the country, to *our* county. You can't want this."

"Doesn't matter what we want," said a man to her right as he withdrew his sword. "Stopped mattering the day we put these uniforms on."

He surged forward, but she was faster. Dodging his swing, she punched him in the nose, gratified when she felt bone crunch beneath her fist. She sidestepped his next punch but got caught on the side by someone else's sword. The force of it almost pushed her off her feet and she had to step back to steady herself.

The corset did what Muire had wanted though and protected her from serious harm but she knew by the power that shuddered through her body that it would bruise.

"Keep it down," another man grunted. "If we disrupt his party, it'll be our heads on the chopping block."

Two of the larger Hounds attacked again. They parried sharp blows with her, as she held them off with a sword and dagger. Tiredness already weighed her down with the speed of the fight but she refused to give in. She pushed forward again, but while she was distracted avoiding an attack from the front, someone grabbed her hair and pulled her to a broad chest. A cold blade pressed against her throat.

"Got her."

Rua struggled but the hold stayed strong. "Just let me go. I have to find my…" She trailed off when a person dropped lightly from the rafters.

"A dhiabhal, Rua." Saoirse's voice soothed her like a balm on burned skin. "Can't you just leave well enough alone?"

A ragged cry tore free from her throat. "Saoirse. I thought you were—" The man holding her shook her roughly and she stopped talking.

"Let her go."

Someone snorted. "We don't take orders from little girls."

Saoirse lashed out, attacking the two closest Hounds in a flurry of controlled movement that reminded Rua of Wolf. The Hound holding Rua dropped his hand and she wrenched herself free, slamming a foot onto his boot and twisting to hit him in the groin. While he gasped for breath, she pulled down his head and let it collide with her knee. He dropped to the ground, unconscious.

Rua twisted and fought the woman closest to her. She fought without confidence, unsure and young, clearly fresh out of training. Rua felt almost bad with how quickly she dispatched her and by the time she had finished Saoirse had already knocked out the other three.

Saoirse huffed. "Grab their legs, we need to get them out of the hallway."

She refused to look at Rua. Barely acknowledged her presence as they laid the Hounds out. Saoirse walked back to the closed doorway, body leaning into it, and listened as another stream of servers passed by. Only then did the tension fall from her shoulders.

She finally faced Rua.

Moonlight illuminated her in white light. She had gotten so much older; had lost the haunted expression she had carried after their parents died and had gained enough weight to almost pretend she had never known starvation. There were ropey muscles across her arms and shoulders. She had the same weapons as Wolf. Rua wanted to cry. She wanted to laugh.

She smiled, splitting her face.

Saoirse withdrew her sword and lifted Rua's chin with the tip. "What the hell do you think you're doing here?"

# CHAPTER FIFTY-FIVE
## RUA

"Saoirse?"

She jerked at her name and the steel breached Rua's skin. A droplet of crimson dripped down the shining metal. Both of them watched it stain the blade. Saoirse gasped when it hit the hilt and tore the sword away from Rua.

She glared at Rua. "What are you doing here?"

"I'm here to rescue you." Rua glanced at the Hounds spread about the room. "Not that you apparently need the help. Why didn't you come find me when you found out I was alive?"

"Are you joking? Didn't Wolf tell you anything about the Sisterhood?"

Rua leaned against one of the seats when her knees felt weak. Saoirse had been in that horrible place all this time and Rua had left her there to play house in the woods. She gazed around the room, shame making it impossible to meet Saoirse's eyes.

A couch lined the wall underneath bookshelves. A fire roared in the fireplace and the candles were lit in their little glass containers. Leather warmed in the candlelight made the room welcoming but the dark walls and high windows invited in the cold. Rua imagined the Síochain brooding in here on a cold winter night in this room larger than their whole house had been.

Saoirse clicked her tongue, impatiently. "This isn't a game. You could get me killed."

"Come with me." Desperation drenched the words and Rua didn't care. She wanted to touch her, to feel her solid weight and convince her brain of the truth. "Come home."

Saoirse flinched at the word *home*. "We don't have a home anymore." Voices echoed down the corridor and she stiffened, listening. When the noise faded, she said, "You have to go."

"I'm not going anywhere without you." She took a step forward, hand outstretched. "Saoirse, where have you been?"

Saoirse stepped away from her reaching fingers and leaned against the door, arms folded across her chest. Tension made her face a stranger.

Rua saw how her fingers trembled. "Saoirse, please."

"Stop calling me that," she snapped. "I'm not her anymore. I'm not anyone." She tightened her hands on her biceps, knuckles almost protruding from her skin. "I survived, Rua. I thought you were dead. Thought everyone was dead. I buried her with you."

She went to open the door, clearly done with the conversation and Rua rushed forward, grabbing her hand.

"No. You're not leaving." She squeezed Saoirse's hand, covered in calluses and rough skin just like hers. Neither of them had lived an easy life and she ached to take away the pain from her sister. "I won't let you leave."

"Take your hand off me," Saoirse snarled. "You are not in charge of me anymore."

"I'm not losing you again."

Saoirse pushed her back and spun around, drawing her sword again. "I am not the child you knew. We are not sisters, not anymore. Let me go." A hint of pleading soaked the final words.

Rua shook her head.

"*A dhiabhal*, Rua. Do you always have to be so goddamn stubborn?"

"You're the only family I have."

Saoirse snorted. "Don't let the people in the cells hear you say that. All they've talked about was how you were a family now and how you and Wolf would save them," she sneered. "How do you always manage to collect people?"

Guilt thickened Rua's next words. "You met them?"

"I watched them. I didn't speak to them."

"Come back with me," Rua begged, eyes watching how tightly Saoirse held onto the hilt of her sword. "We can be together again."

She stared at Rua, eyes hungry. "I thought you were dead."

"I thought you were too," Rua begged. "Please."

Saoirse shook her head. "I've commitments here."

Rua scoffed. "Protecting the Table? Protecting him?"

"Your little rebellion is going to get you killed. The Table will not fall. It is too big to fail." Saoirse stepped forward and raised her sword. "I won't let you drag me down with you. This is your final warning. I won't interfere with your rescue but I will not protect you if you meet him."

"Da would be ashamed of you."

She flinched. "Ma would say I'm making the smart decision." She stepped forward again. "Either leave or fight me. Those are your only options."

Rua blinked back tears and withdrew her sword. "If I knock you out, I'm bringing you with me."

"If I win," she hissed. "I'm staying here."

She struck hard and fast. Rua fell back, barely able to defend herself. Saoirse wasn't as fast as Wolf, and the blows were sloppier, but the speed and strength she showed outmatched everything Rua had. Rua threw herself into the fight, barely managing to step over the stationary bodies and avoid furniture.

Rua forced Saoirse back using her greater arm reach to create space between them.

"Saoirse, please."

"No." Metal grated against metal. "You have no right to ask me to join you."

They fought like they were children again and didn't know the consequences of their actions. Fought like their parents were shouting at them to stop and share. Saoirse knocked Rua's sword back and stepped on her foot. Rua responded by kicking her knee. They grabbed hair and jerked clothes and pinched skin. Rua fought with a desperation she rarely felt, needing to win, needing to knock her out so she could protect her, keep her safe.

"I'm not letting you fight this alone," she shouted, defending herself from vicious attacks. The clang of swords screeched through the room. Rua feared they'd attract someone soon. "I have to keep you safe."

Saoirse broke free and stumbled back. "You have no right to say that to me. Not after I followed you to hell, and you abandoned me there."

Rua froze, and the force of Saoirse's next blow travelled up her arm. "Is that what you really believe? That it's my fault?"

"You left me to fend for myself. And I have." She panted, sweat a slight glow in the candlelight. "Do not dare ask me to follow you again."

Everything Conor had been trying to tell her suddenly made horrible, painful sense and she gasped like she had been thrown from a horse. She kept forcing people to bend to her will, kept trying to keep them safe, or stop them making their own decisions, and it had gotten her nothing but broken trust and damaged pride. As much as it made her stomach churn and tears burn in her eyes, she had to trust Saoirse's decision for how she wanted to live her own life.

Saoirse's life. *Not* Rua's.

"Okay." Rua swallowed away the nausea and tears. "You have to make your own decisions. Fight your own fights." She stepped away, sheathing her sword.

Saoirse studied her suspiciously.

The expression was so familiar, Rua wanted to laugh. She wanted to sob.

"Really?" She didn't put her sword away yet.

Rua nodded. "I will always be here. Come back whenever you want. But this is my fight." She stepped forward cautiously. When Saoirse didn't react, she wrapped her arms around her in a fierce hug. "I love you, little sister."

Saoirse sobbed into her shoulder. "Thank you," she whispered before pulling away, and without looking back, she ran from the room. The open door allowed Rua to hear the desperate screams that suddenly echoed through the manor.

Rua ran.

# CHAPTER FIFTY-SIX
## WOLF

L iam Cogadh moved with the speed of a nun.

Wolf threw everything she had at him; every sleepless night, every time she cried, the pain and the hurt. She struck like she could show him every time she had thought herself unworthy because he had left her. He had abandoned her in hell and she had survived without him. She always survived without him. She fought viciously, pushing him back with the strength of her hits. As soon as she thought she had the upper hand, he switched easily into offence and shoved her back. She walloped into a wall. The breath left her lungs in a whoosh. She held her sword in front of her. She hated how her arms trembled.

"You left me," she growled, avoiding the swing of his fist.

"I had to for the family." He wasn't even panting. "You are not the only person I love."

"You never loved me. You never loved Luchán," she screamed. "Or is that what being loved by you gets?"

He took a step back as if her words were a blow he couldn't defend himself from. "You will never understand the choices I've had to make."

She strode forward. "I never want to."

The fight was brutal; she punched and scraped, bit and

pinched. No attack was below an apprentice. He fought just as cruelly, playing to the weaknesses left by the poison and his years of experience, taunting her with how fast he moved and attacking in a way that told her he wouldn't stop until she gave in. She would not give in. They fell apart when the first scream sounded out.

"What did you do?"

She smiled through bloody lips. "Burned your little kingdom to the ground."

Smoke coated her tongue. Burning wood made her eyes sting. The single scream mutated into a roar of panic, of clattering feet and crackling fire. The air weighed heavier now, harder to force into her lungs, and she knew she needed to get out of here as quickly as possible. The others were still in the cells, locked in a burning building. She twisted away from him and raced for the door.

A heavy fist landed on her shoulder and hauled her back. "You're not going anywhere. You're going back to the convent. Punishment awaits you, Little Wolf."

She snorted even as she fought to free herself from his grip. "I am never going back there."

"Of course you are. I told you to learn your place. Accepting who you are means letting go of any unnecessary ties. Those people make you weak." He shoved her head hard against a wall and the room went black for just a second. Her sword dropped from nerveless fingers. "They're making you forget who you could be."

He dragged her from the room, one hand wrapped in her hair and the other tight around her wrists. She was still weak from the *Bás Tostach*, and he was much stronger than her, but she refused to give in, refused to be stolen from Rua. The others were still trapped in the cells and she had to save them. She stomped on his toe. He hissed and shook her so hard and for so long that blackness stole her eyes again.

When they reached the entrance hall, a mass of bodies were trying to force themselves through the too small doorways, trampling people and crushing others against walls. Flames roared free of the ballroom, and despite her shock, Wolf mourned the beautiful tapestries. The Síochain huffed at the scene and pulled her back the other way.

"We'll go by the cells," he hissed. "You can say goodbye to your little friends before they burn."

His words made her fight harder, made her struggle against his grip until she thought maybe she would be free. He shoved her into the wall again, slamming her head against unforgiving stone. She was dizzy now, her head pounding. The cells were blessedly clear of smoke because of the wide, open windows. Screams echoed across the courtyard. Somewhere in the distance, horses panicked and neighed.

The cacophony of sounds hurt her spinning head. She wanted to shut her eyes. The world kept swooping under her. She felt like she had been poisoned again. The cool stone against her cheek forced alertness back to her. She pushed off the wall and slammed into him. He lost his grip on one of her hands. She grabbed a dagger. It sliced through the hand reaching for her. He let her go and she twisted, slamming into him again. She kicked him in the gut, winding him with a gasp.

"Where are the keys?"

He snorted.

She gripped his shoulders and banged his head against the wall, and then punched him twice. Once in the stomach and then the mouth. He spat blood.

"Where are the keys?"

She knew he wouldn't answer, knew by the bloody grin he shot her, so she crashed her fist into his temple, knocking him unconscious. She let his body fall to the floor. Footsteps behind her dragged her attention back to the door. Pup raced towards her, missing something vital if the slump of her shoulders and her wet eyes told the truth. There were shouts from the last cell but they were hidden by a bend in the corridor.

"Where's Rua?"

"She let me go. My stubborn, always knows what's best, sister actually let me go." Wonder eclipsed the desperation in her voice.

"Pup…"

"Please don't ask me to stay. I can't. I—" she stopped talking and stared down at the Síochain. "Did you kill him?"

She shook her head and blurted out, "He's my father."

Pup blinked.

"Don't tell anyone."

"Like I have anyone to tell. I have to get him out of here."

Wolf nodded. "You'll come back to us?"

"Someday. Maybe."

Wolf nodded and gestured to the shouts carrying up from the cells. "I have to save them."

"I have to save him." Exhaustion leaked into her voice. "I'll tell them you were already gone when I got here."

Wolf pulled her into a short but vicious hug. "Don't you dare die."

Pup shrugged. "Haven't so far." She grabbed the Síochain's wrists and pulled him towards a window. She shoved him out, seeming to barely care if he hurt himself because of the small drop. "I won't be able to distract them for long. Rua is coming. If she asks, you didn't see me."

"Be safe," Wolf muttered as Pup followed the Síochain out the window.

Rua came pelting out through the door seconds later.

Smoke billowed in after her making Wolf's eyes water. "Wolf? What happened to you?"

She shrugged. "Got ambushed. We have to get the others out." The flicker of flames were visible in the hallway Rua had just emerged from. "Let's go."

# CHAPTER FIFTY-SEVEN
## RUA

They raced across the stone and skidded to a halt in front of the same cell Rua had been held in. She swallowed down panic as memories tried to flood her brain, focusing on the bodies crowded together on the floor.

"Rua!" Both Conor's eyes were darkened with bruising and a harsh wound stretched from his forehead to his jawline. Rua knew instinctively it would scar and her stomach churned. Tadgh's head rested on his leg and Conor's hand threaded through the strands. Tadgh's jaw was swollen and he had his arm clutched to his chest.

"Are you okay?"

Aoife and Oisín sat wrapped around each other but they smiled up at her. Two women huddled together in the corner a little away from the others. Rua's heart stumbled when one of them stared at her with Seán's eyes. Smoke seeped along the stone like fog.

"Didn't doubt you for a second," Aoife said.

Oisín snorted.

The bigger of the two women glared at them. "Where's my brother?"

"Where's Seán?"

Rua swallowed. "He didn't..." She blinked away sudden tears.

"We need help getting out of here," Oisín interrupted, saving her. "I'm fine," he muttered, flapping away Aoife's supporting hands. "We're all able to move but we'll be slow. I patched them up but I had nothing but my hands and some rags."

Wolf coughed into her elbow. "We need to get them out now." Bright flames illuminated the stones until they glowed. "The smoke will get us before the fire."

"You burned the place down?" Conor asked, supporting Tadgh. They were a quilt of bruises and dried blood. "I'd say good work but we're still trapped."

"You were meant to be out by now." Wolf rooted through her corset and pulled out two long, thin metal tools. "I can unlock it. Just give me a minute." She hissed when she touched the metal. "It's hot."

Rua watched the flames struggling against the stone, saw them set alight the wooden roof and felt the heat pouring off the metal bars. The straw lining the cell's floor sparked alight almost immediately. Smoke billowed from the door in dark clouds. The wide, open slits in the stone stole some of it away but not enough. The air burned on each inhale and caught in Rua's throat.

"Rua, grab that water." Oisín gestured to a bucket in the corner. He started coughing and it took him long seconds before he could talk again. Still wheezing, he managed, "Wolf, we need your knives." She handed him two without question. "Cut strips off your clothes. Enough to cover your mouth and nose. Rua, wet them and we'll tie it around our faces. Now," he ordered when no one moved.

Rua handed over a third knife and took the first piece of material from the bottom of Oisín's top.

"Soak it in the water and tie it around Wolf's face."

"You first," Wolf said, startling everyone.

He shook his head. "You have to stay awake to get us out."

Rua did what he said.

"Now you, Rua."

Rua baulked but complied even as her instincts warred against it. She had decided when she had let Saoirse go. She had to allow them to make their own choices. She tied the wet material tight and felt the ease in her airwaves. Once she was sure the piece wouldn't move, she worked quickly wetting the different pieces of fabric. Soon they were all partially protected from the smoke.

Wolf growled in frustration and slammed a hand into the cell. "The metal's too hot. It's fused together. I can't open it."

She froze when she heard tears in Wolf's voice.

"What are we going to do?"

"I don't know. I..." Rua stared into the cell at her family, huddled together and watching her for solutions. "I don't know..."

Wolf shook the bars and hissed when her hands came back blistered. Sweat pooled in the base of Rua's back. Her ears burned in the growing heat. She dropped to her knees as the smoke got lower. The others followed, crawling as close to the bars as they could.

"You have to leave us," Conor said. "You have to get out."

"No," Wolf growled. "We don't leave people behind."

"This time you might have to." Aoife clutched Oisín's hand. "You came for us. You don't have to die for us."

Rua choked back a sob. "Don't make me do this. Please."

Aoife tucked her head into Oisín's neck. "We'll be okay," she whispered, just barely audible over the roar of the fire around them. "We'll be together."

Tears streaked Wolf's face but her voice was steady when she said, "No. Think. There is always an exit. Always."

"Wolf," Conor started but Tadgh, still collapsed into his side, groaned and interrupted him.

He coughed and croaked out, "*Púdar dubh*. Hounds armoury by the stable."

"What's that?" Oisín asked.

Wolf grinned. "Explosive."

Conor nodded. "Go." He somehow managed to grin but Rua read the fear in his eyes. "We'll wait here."

Forcing a grin at his terrible joke, she followed Wolf out the window.

The courtyard heaved with people; the panic had spilled from the manor and flowed into every inch of the yard. Party guests were choking on the black air, ash lining their faces. The Hounds were battling the fire but they were also fighting the starving peasants, drawn closer to the mayhem. Horses trampled people. Swords glinted in the light. The thatch of the stables burned. Hot air made it difficult to take full breaths. Without the wet cloth, it would be unbearable. Wolf led them around the mayhem to the stables.

"Rua! Wolf!"

Rua spun to the familiar voice. "Aurnia! Get a cart and a horse. Under the cells. The others will need help walking."

"Where are you going?" Blood streaked along one of her cheeks.

"*Púdar dubh*," Wolf answered, with a sharp edge to her words. Rua thought it might be worry. "They're trapped."

Aurnia nodded and didn't keep them any longer.

As they neared the Hound's quarters, Wolf withdrew a dagger. Rua did the same. Adrenaline slipped over her skin like a coat of armour, ensuring she would have enough energy and focus to finish the night. She blinked a few times to clear them from the stinging wetness. They crept past the blistering heat of the burning dorms to the entrance of the armoury. Wolf held up her hand. They paused. She glanced around the open door of the armoury.

She held up three fingers, pointing one to the right, and two to the left.

Rua nodded. Wolf counted down from three.

They attacked from behind and the first two fell quickly under their blows. It took little effort between the two of them to discard the last one. They searched the shelves, throwing swords and armour to the ground. Rua rooted through the bottom and Wolf climbed to the higher shelves to check there. It probably took less than a minute but Rua's heart pounded *too late too late too late* in her ears. Most of the shelves were empty, the weapons in a pile on the ground, before they finally found a bag of *púdar dubh*.

Wolf gripped it. "Let's go."

The violence in the yard had ratcheted up as more starving peasants arrived. A fire that big in the middle of winter would attract the homeless and destitute for miles. The Hounds were focused on them, rounding them into groups to arrest. Party guests huddled together, fearful and injured, easily separated by their fancy gowns. Flames took over the horizon. The heat burned across her skin as they skidded around the edges of the disruption and raced over the yard. She could see the too large windows of the cells when a rough hand grabbed Rua's hair, dragging her back into a hard chest. A dagger touched her throat.

"Let me go!" She struggled but froze when the blade scraped her skin, drawing the wet touch of blood. "Wolf!"

Wolf skidded to a halt, spinning to face them. She stumbled and froze. "You can't have her."

"You have your place in the Sisterhood, apprentice." Liam Cogadh's breath was warm on Rua's cheek as he growled the words. "If I have to kill her to remind you of that, I will."

Sharp metal pierced her skin. Rua tried to breathe as shallowly as possible. "Wolf, go. The others are dying."

"I can't leave you. I won't." She wouldn't take her eyes off

Rua. "Please don't do this." She inched forward and the blade dug further into Rua's neck. "Okay," she held up her hand. "I won't move. Just let her go and I'll go with you."

"Don't you see how pathetic she's made you? How they all have?"

Wolf shook her head. "You're wrong. They make me stronger."

Pride made Rua's heart sore.

"You're nothing like the woman you were in the yard when I picked you," he snarled.

She took a tiny step forward. "Please."

The Síochain laughed, an unpleasant noise. "And have you run the minute my back is turned?"

"I won't. I promise." A desperation Rua had never heard before coated Wolf's words. "Anything you want." Her eyes darted over the Síochain's shoulder and back so quickly Rua didn't think he noticed.

"Come on, Little Wolf. This game has gone on long enough." The dagger pressed further into her throat. "I already told you, if I can't have you, no one can."

Wolf nodded and stepped closer. "I'll stay. Please."

Blood wet Rua's neck. She gasped and the knife dug deeper. Tears leaked from her eyes. She wanted to stop them but they fell without permission. He had his arm across her chest, pinning her arms in place. He held her too tight to his body for her to shuffle free. She couldn't risk stepping on his foot in case it resulted in the knife being lodged in her throat.

"Wolf," she begged.

"I know. I know." Wolf had frozen, muscles strained to fight but holding herself back. "Do you trust me?"

"Always."

"Now," Wolf shouted.

Wolf darted forward, pulling the knife away from her throat

just as something heavy thumped him from behind. They both fell. The knife clattered free from his hand. Rua rolled away from his prone body. Wolf kicked the Síochain until he stilled.

Rua pushed herself off the ground and grabbed her away. "Wolf, I'm fine. I promise."

Wolf blinked and then pulled Rua up into a hug, warm and fierce. Her whole body pressed against Rua's and still Rua wanted to be closer. She wrapped her arms around her waist and gripped the corset, burying her face into Wolf's neck.

An explosion rocked through the yard forcing them apart.

Eerie silence fell for one moment before the screams erupted, louder than before.

"We have to get the others."

Rua nodded.

They raced away from the Síochain, neither bothering to look back.

# CHAPTER FIFTY-EIGHT
## WOLF

Wolf wanted to hug Pup.

Watching her hit the Síochain with a water pale, saving Rua when Wolf couldn't, made it tempting to ask her to come with them. They could keep the promise together. Rua had room in her life for both of them. She wanted Pup to choose them, but she wasn't ready yet, so Wolf led Rua away, making sure she didn't notice Pup dragging the Síochain to safety. To be part of the Sisterhood meant being able to live in the most vibrant grey; complex and confusing decisions were made too often not to see the world as one large problem to solve, to see people as allies or enemies, but never friends.

Pup was her friend now. Wolf would respect her choice and wait for Pup to save herself.

It took too long to push through the crowds and get back to the cell. Aurnia waited for them beside a cart and a snorting horse. She didn't say anything, just crouched and linked her hands. Wolf stepped onto them and pulled herself up into the cells. Leaning down, she helped Rua up.

Horrific heat met them. Flames devoured anything wooden. A thick beam blocked their path, burning. They crawled under it. Wolf felt her skin blister. She hoped the explosive in her pocket didn't react to the temperature. Smoke had settled like bruised clouds. She couldn't see her hand in front of her face. Coughs heaved their way out of her chest.

Rua gripped her hand. "Conor? Aoife?" No one answered. "Oisín? Tadgh?"

"Rua!" Conor coughed on the word. "You've got to get us out of here," he wheezed, the words barely carrying over the cackling fire.

Wolf could just make him out in the smoke, surrounded by the others.

"Back away from the bars," Wolf ordered. She layered the lock in *púdar dubh* and poured some into it as well. Carefully tucking it back into her pocket, she picked up a flaming piece of wood and stepped back, pushing Rua behind her body. "Ready?"

"Ready," Conor shouted.

She lit the powder.

The explosion threw them both back into the wall. Rua groaned beneath her. Wolf pushed off her, checking with a glance she was okay, before kicking the damaged bars out of the way.

"Go," she ordered. "Now."

They struggled over to Wolf. Blood and ash dirtied their faces. Tadgh slumped unconscious in Conor's arms. Aoife and Oisín supported each other as they limped from the cell, followed by Seán's sisters. Coughing added to the ruckus of flames and the groaning of the house. The heat's touch was almost unbearable. Tears streamed freely down Wolf's face, mixing with sweat and grime.

"We're almost out," she promised as she helped them from the cell, passing them to Rua who guided them to a window. "Jump. Aurnia is waiting."

It took long seconds to get everyone out. Sweat blinded Wolf's already stinging eyes but she double checked this time to make sure no one had been left in the cell before running to the window.

Rua waited for her and they jumped together.

Aurnia helped them up onto the cart and took off as soon as they were safe. No one spoke. Not yet. They slipped through the yard, unnoticed in the mayhem. As they approached the gate, the manor exploded in a wave of heat. Half of it fell in a roar of flames. The Hounds were too overwhelmed in the panic to notice the cart slip out. Even if they had stopped them, ash covered their faces and clothes. They would never have recognised their prisoners.

Seán's sisters huddled together. Aoife sat close to them and whispered something Wolf couldn't hear. She wondered what would have happened if she had just taken them the night she had saved Rua. It might have saved them all, saved Seán. Maybe even Luchán.

She took a breath and allowed the guilt to settle in her. She had learned a long time ago to live with the consequences of her actions and this was just one more choice to add to an ever growing pile of regrets. Too much had happened tonight. Too many revelations. Too many goodbyes. Knowing who her father was, that he had chosen the Table over her, over Luchán, felt like a twisted knife to the gut, a wound that wouldn't stop bleeding.

She understood now how important her actions were. That the Sisterhood had tried to take that power away from her. Told her that without them, she meant nothing. Wolf knew better now; every action she made had consequences in the world and she could use that power for good or bad. She knew now what side of the story she wanted to be on and understood a little better what family really meant as well. She would do anything for these people around her, would go back to the Sisterhood to keep them safe even though it was worse than death. Dying for them would be easy, but they would never let her, would fight for her every inch of the way. They would come for her just as she had come for them.

Suddenly exhausted, she lay her head on Rua's shoulder and closed her eyes. She wouldn't sleep, not until they were all safe, but she could try and escape the blinding exhaustion for the journey home.

*Home.*

With these people, she was already there.

# CHAPTER FIFTY-NINE
## RUA

R ua stared at the sunrise, allowing the searing light to burn away her tears. It had been three days since the Síochain's manor and the ball. Sleep had long abandoned her and she felt dizzy with exhaustion. The doubts about letting Saoirse go were a constant drip in the back of her mind but she refused to give them any real weight. She had chosen her path, and Saoirse had chosen a different one. Just because it led her away from Rua and straight into a wolves' den didn't mean Rua had the right to force her to come back. She knew she had made the right decision letting her go. Even if she had to remind herself of it often.

Today though, they were going back to the Síochain's estate.

Rua leaned back and the floor beneath her creaked.

Wolf shot up in the other bed, dagger in her hand. "*A dhiabhal*, Rua." She rubbed her eye with the fist clutching the blade. It made her seem younger and far from the violent assassin she had been raised to be. "Why are you awake?"

"Just thinking."

"She's okay," Wolf replied, already knowing Rua too well. "She's a survivor."

Rua nodded.

The sky reminded her of the fire; billowing reds and golds shooting across the navy and illuminating buildings in its glow. Ice glinted in the light making the ground look like the twinkling stars that were slowly being swallowed by the sun. She managed not to jerk when Wolf appeared beside her, movement as silent as ever.

"Nightmare?"

"Fire and knives and blood and Luchán."

Wolf nodded. "Nuns and darkness and pain and Seán."

Rua took her hand and squeezed. "Today will be a good day."

"I know."

They stood shoulder by shoulder, staring out at the sunrise in silence. Wolf had laced her fingers between Rua's and the warmth felt like it was melting through her skin and into her bones. She stepped closer so that their bare skin brushed. She gazed over at Wolf; her face, calm in a way Rua had never seen before, shone with the golden light of the rising sun. Probably feeling Rua's eyes on her, she glanced over.

Rua kissed her.

Wolf's gasp felt like an arrow through Rua's heart. She almost pulled back but Wolf followed her, capturing Rua's lips between her own. They were rough with dry skin, and the best thing Rua had ever felt. They parted slowly, sharing breath for a long moment before fully pulling back.

"Wolf," she whispered.

She shook her head. "Come back to bed. We need sleep before the meeting." Rua let her lead her back to bed. Warmth seeped over her skin when Wolf climbed in behind her, nudged her onto her side, and wrapped her arm around her waist. "Go to sleep. I'll keep the nightmares away."

With her warmth beside her, Rua slept.

When she woke, she was tangled in Wolf; their legs, their

arms, even their hair had joined together, until they were breathing the same air. Rua's stomach flipped at being so close to Wolf's chapped lips. She moved, waking Wolf as she did.

"Sorry."

Wolf grinned. "Light sleeper." She had already shrugged off tiredness like an unwanted coat. Alert eyes tracked every movement on Rua's expression. "What time is it?"

"Breakfast, I think."

Wolf nodded, but neither of them moved.

"You slept?" The *beside me* remained unspoken, but she knew Wolf would understand her question.

Wolf shrugged. "Guess I trust you."

"Oh. Okay," she replied coolly but a bright grin stole over her face. She changed the subject quickly, feeling exposed under Wolf's gaze.

"About last night—"

"We'll figure it out. Together."

Rua nodded and hid her grin in her pillow. "Everything's organised, right?"

"They're all ready to go." Wolf tucked Rua's hair behind her ear, her fingers lingering on her throat. "Ready to face them?"

She swallowed, skin burning where Wolf's fingers rested, and nodded. "Might as well."

Wolf laughed. "Let's go."

It didn't take them long to get dressed and make their way down to Aurnia's kitchen. Everyone, but Seán's sisters, were already eating. Wolf grabbed a roll and shoved herself beside Aoife and Oisín. Rua sat beside Conor. Most of them were healing okay but bruises and burns still littered the visible skin. Tadgh had been in bed since they had gotten back. Aurnia sat at the head of the table, writing letters while eating. Muire sang as she set up the bar for the day.

"Everyone will be there at two?" Rua asked.

Aurnia nodded. "Got the final confirmation today."

"It'll be fine," Conor said, handing Rua a bowl of porridge. "Eat."

"How's Tadhg?"

"Better." He shrugged. "Complaining about being stuck in bed so that's something at least."

She gripped Conor's hand and squeezed. "Is he okay coming today?"

"We need him. He'll help convince them to come to our side. We're both well enough liked that it might help."

"Everyone loves you," Aurnia interrupted with a smirk. "How could they not, Conor?"

He rolled his eyes but it didn't quite cover the pleased quirk to his lips. "Thanks."

"So how are the sleeping arrangements?" Aoife asked Rua, laughter in her voice. "Came in to wake you up for breakfast, and there you both were, in one bed, and the other just sitting there, empty."

Rua flushed.

Wolf just shrugged and kept eating her bread rolls and porridge.

"This is where Seán would remind you that Aoife was right there," Conor said with a sad grin.

Uncomfortable silence fell. They had buried him near the cave. His sisters had built a cross out of twine and branches. They had lined the grave with rocks. Aoife had sung. They spat out the proverb at the end, *chuig an mbord*, and followed the words with a shot of whiskey from a bottle Aurnia had given them. The oath sounded more a promise of revenge than the taunting disrespect it had become during the famine years. None of them had felt much like talking after.

They had searched the cave but the fire had destroyed everything.

"We'll go in twenty minutes." Aurnia interrupted the painful silence with a no-nonsense tone. She received more than one grateful smile. "All in one cart. We won't be bringing anything back today. My stocks are full enough and we need to show them that we want unity across the counties."

"We can trust them?" Rua asked for maybe the hundredth time.

"Yes." The full stop made it clear Rua shouldn't ask again. "Now, Oisín, are you happy for everyone to go today?"

Oisín nodded. "No excess activities. No hauling around sacks. No fighting." He glared at each of them to punctuate his words. "If they can stick to that, then yes, it'll be okay."

Ignoring Aurnia's glare, Rua asked, "You've been in touch with Roisin?"

Conor nodded, amusement crinkling his eyes. "She'll meet us there with a few trusted Hounds. I can't guarantee we're not walking into a trap but I'd like to believe we can trust her. She cares about her soldiers and she wants to know that Tadgh is okay. That I'm okay."

Oisín stared at him curiously. "You were under her command?"

"We trained together. She was two years above me. She's the youngest captain in the country."

"That'll play to us," Wolf interjected. "Most people who joined the Hounds in the last few years did it to escape the famine. That's why their numbers have grown. The younger the member, the more likely they are to listen to us."

Conor nodded. "Agreed. Most of the talk during training revolved around how glad they were for food and how glad they were to be able to protect their family."

"Even though in the end most of them couldn't," Aoife finished. "That'll help too."

Aurnia nodded. "Everyone meet me in the yard in five

minutes. Either this works or we end up dead by this evening."

"Inspiring," Muire said, walking in from the bar. "I'm brimming with confidence."

Aurnia kissed her cheek. "I'll be back tonight."

"Of course you will, dear."

Rua followed the others up the stairs to gather weapons and extra layers to protect against the chill fingers of winter. Climbing onto the cart was an exercise in restraint for each of them, still injured and trying to hide it from the others. Tadgh suffered the worst, needing Wolf, Aurnia and Conor to help him up. He was pale and sweating by the time he sat, burying his head in Conor's neck.

The ride back to the Síochain's estate was quiet. The house appeared like a shadow on the horizon, still smoking in the weak sunlight. Blackened foundations raised from the ground like broken teeth. Ash coated the ground, the grass and the trees surrounding it, spread by the wind. Smoke scented the air and caught at the back of Rua's throat. Oisín handed out pouches of water as more than one of them started coughing again. There were no Hounds visible on the gates, nor on the checkpoints around the boundary fence.

Rua took that as a good sign.

It didn't take them long after that to reach the barn. They were the first ones there. Wolf quickly unlocked the doors and shoved them open. The food stood proud in the shadows. Rua swallowed back a sob. She hadn't realised how worried she had been that it would be gone until this moment.

Aoife gasped behind her.

"Told you it would get them to hear us out."

Aoife nudged her shoulder. "Knew there was a reason I trusted you."

Rua grinned, hearing Aoife's forgiveness in the words.

Aurnia came up beside them. "I want the doors shut so they

have to listen to us. Rua, get up on the cart. You'll be standing beside me with Conor. Everyone else stands in front of it. United front."

Closing the barn door, they set themselves up and waited.

The first tread of hoofbeats sounded soon after.

# CHAPTER SIXTY
## WOLF

"Y ou dragged us halfway across the country, Aurnia." The stranger had clearly once been a strong, burly woman, but with sagging muscles and hollow cheeks, she had clearly suffered in the famine. "This better be worth it."

When the woman had been at her peak, Wolf would have considered her a threat, but now she doubted it would take more than two or three moves to take her down. She peered over at Aoife and saw a matching smirk. Wolf glanced away before she grinned too brightly.

Wolf knew how serious this was. They needed these people to agree. Personally, she just wanted to sneak into Ríthe and slit the throats of anyone who sat at the table, and the throats of anyone who supported them, but even as she thought it, she knew it was wrong. A power vacuum would be more dangerous than the Table still existing.

Politics, Wolf understood. Although, the blade always made more sense.

Aurnia called for quiet over the uneasy wave of noise washing over the crowd. "We called you here for a reason. I'm assuming you didn't miss the destroyed manor on the way down?"

Broken conversations burst out.

"Our Síochain has fled the county," Aurnia said over the crowd. "We drove him out. We're not giving it back."

A gasp travelled over the gathered crowd of about twenty people; a mixture of farmers, inn owners and merchants. The most powerful people among the poor, ones with the most sway in their community and the most connections. Aurnia had chosen her network well.

Few of them were real threats. They were fed better than most of the starving masses, but they were still weak and mostly unarmed. Wolf didn't even think any of them would be of any use with a sword. These people dealt in words, in stories, relationships and conversations. They held a different power but one Wolf had been trained in. She guarded Rua anyway, hating that she stood on the cart further from her reach. Knowing the others were ready for the first sign of trouble eased the tension in her shoulders. Liam Cogadh had been wrong; having people watching her back made her stronger.

"The Table has been lying to us." Rua's voice rang out like a morning bird. "They have enough food to feed us all but they're allowing the famine to continue."

"No one would allow this suffering to continue," someone shouted.

Wolf snorted.

Rua hopped down from the cart, nodded at Wolf. They walked over to the doors and dragged them open together. Usually Rua's flair for the dramatic irritated Wolf but she did enjoy the quiet gasps that followed the reveal. The tension ratcheted up in the small clearing.

Wolf stepped closer to Rua.

"This is why we called you here," Rua shouted into the stunned silence. "Why we told you to bring your carts. Why we invited you, the most well connected and the best-placed, to deliver this food to the people who need it, the people who are starving in your counties. Starving because the Table allows it—" Rua paused as her words hit home.

Wolf thought she was spectacular.

"They're lying," Rua shouted. "We have to stop them."

Silence fell for a long moment before someone asked, "Where did the food come from?"

"The Table sent it," Rua snarled. "Liam Cogadh *chose* not to give it out. Your county will have its own barn stuffed full of food. They know we're starving and they don't care. They know we're dying," she screamed. "And they don't care. It's time we made them."

Wolf smirked at the shocked quiet that fell.

"How?" Roisin stood rigid, five Hounds at her back. She didn't take her eyes off Tadhg, sitting on the ground and leaning against the wheel of the cart, bruised and exhausted. "How do you plan on making them care?"

Rua considered her for a long moment before she answered. "We're going to burn their goddamn kingdom to the ground."

The explosion of noise that followed reminded Wolf of the cells. She shook the image away and leant back against the cold wood to watch the argument. They broke into groups, shouting over each other and snapping out opinions. Most of the bickering was based on fear or selfishness, not wanting to alter the status quo if it already benefited them, and not wanting to wait if it didn't.

Half were for rebellion. The other half were against it.

Ignoring the uproar, Roisin strode away from the gathered Hounds and crouched in front of Tadhg. Conor leapt off the cart and knelt, talking quietly to them both. Roisin's expression grew tighter the longer they spoke. The other Hounds stood at the edges, watching the crowd. Two had their hands on the hilts of their swords, faces unsure.

Wolf found the commotion interesting. She had never seen this sort of democracy in action. No one talked back to the nuns in the convent. She didn't join in but she listened to the differing points of view, arguing against them in her head. She had learned to know both sides of any argument, to always be prepared to switch if she had to. Something she knew would take a long time to forget. She had chosen now but she still wanted to know what the other side said, wanted to know how to fight against them. Too long after the proclamation did silence fall.

The gruff woman stepped forward. "How do you plan on doing it?"

Aurnia glanced at Wolf, head tilted. Wolf was so, so sick of being tested.

Still, she said, "We take their food and we feed the nation. Build loyalty to our cause simply by being the ones with the supplies. We take their Hounds," she nodded at the gathering of soldiers who were watching her. Some even nodded back. "We destroy their assassins, the members of the Sisterhood of Righteous Death." Adrenaline zinged through her when she said the name out loud. "We drive the Síochains from their manors and into the capital. We starve them. We wait until they are too weak and too scared to fight back and then we take that from them as well." She withdrew her sword. The noise of it being unsheathed rang through the clearing. "We kill them if we must and build our own country on their bones." She shrugged. "Or we give them a fair trial and a fair punishment. The point is we decide."

Unease spread across the crowd at her words.

"And who are you?"

She didn't know who shouted it, but it felt like another test.

"I'm Wolf," she declared, more real than she had ever been. "I was a member of the Sisterhood of Righteous Death. I think it's time they stopped hiding in the shadows and revealed themselves, don't you?"

# CHAPTER SIXTY-ONE
## RUA

Rua knew these strangers didn't understand what Wolf had done, how she had made herself real in that moment, but Rua did and it made goosebumps flitter across her skin like a round of applause. Rua stepped forward and gripped Wolf's hand. Wolf gripped it back like a lifeline she needed to stay grounded and present.

Rua had never been more glad that Wolf had come into her life and had led her here. Standing on the edge of rebellion, on the verge of saving her country, she had never been more scared or more sure she was doing the right thing. She knew her parents would be proud, and knew somewhere even Saoirse was proud.

It helped having Wolf's hand in hers.

"For now," Rua shouted to calm the noise. Silence fell over the group like night, slowly but without argument. "All we want you to do is empty this barn and get as much food to as many people as necessary." They had the shipments that Wolf had stolen but they had all agreed not to reveal them yet. "We need each county to have a place where we can contact them and someone in charge. Aurnia is ours."

"That's it?"

"For now," Rua repeated. "We work together. This is not about ending up with another Table. We work *together*," she repeated. "No one knows who is in charge, except the six heads of each county and the people working with you. We need to keep this quiet for as long as possible."

"What about them?"

Roisin stood with her Hounds. "I'm with Aurnia. This is my county. My soldiers are with them. This is their county too."

The Hounds around her gave varying nods of agreement.

"Not one of us is loyal to a Table that burns people out of their homes." Real pain seeped into Roisin's words and Rua saw suddenly how hard it had been to take orders from the Síochain, how scared they had all been after Conor had deserted. "We were just sick of starving."

"So you sold out your country?" Someone shouted from the back of the crowd.

The sneer infuriated Rua. "No." She took a step forward. "That is not how this begins. Not one of us hasn't done something worse to survive. Not one of us has clean hands. We fight because it's right. We fight against a greater evil than all that we have done. We are in this together or we are going to fail. Am I clear?"

The quick agreement settled something in her chest.

Aurnia called the crowd to order again and directed people into the barn.

Emptying it would probably take days. Rua watched until Wolf pulled her back, and she realised she had clutched Wolf's hand so tight the knuckles were rolling beneath her fingers. They walked together to the tall grass and sat down, watching. Conor had helped Tadgh over to the Hounds who were examining him and checking his injuries. Aoife and Oisín were sitting on the cart, legs swinging as they joked about something or other. Aurnia spoke to five others; they must have been volunteering to be the county leaders. A chain led from the barn to the carts. The atmosphere had relaxed so much it was almost festive. Everyone knew how much good the food would do.

She missed Seán and Luchán, a constant ache that throbbed behind her breast bone. She hoped neither of their deaths had been in vain. Hoped with everything she had that they would lose no one else before this finished, but she knew, like it was written across her bones, that they would. She hoped Saoirse was safe. Hoped she saved her before she became another loss.

Wolf nudged her shoulder, dragging her from her thoughts. "Good speech."

Rua laughed. "Thanks."

Wolf leaned into Rua, her body a long line of warmth. Rua wanted to bury herself in it as the ground froze her bones. The air rang with bird song.

"So this is what we're doing now? Rebellion?"

Rua nodded. "Rebellion." The word still felt foreign in her mouth but she thought she would get used to it. "Save my sister."

"Save Pup," Wolf agreed.

Rua heard the protectiveness in her voice and knew Wolf would fight as hard as she could to save Saoirse. It helped calm the frantic pacing of her heart. She gazed over at Wolf.

Wolf already stared back.

"*Le chéile?*"

"Yeah," Wolf replied, easily. "Together."

# ACKNOWLEDGMENTS

The acknowledgements are the first thing I read in any book. I love seeing who the author thanks, who helped put the book together, and all the work that went into it. I've been planning these acknowledgments for years, writing and rewriting them in my head, and now, sitting at my desk — on my couch but close enough — I have no idea what to write.

Firstly and always, I have to thank my family. My parents who have supported me, always. Sinead, who is a best friend and a sister wrapped up in one. She is always there when I need her and I appreciate it every day. Matthew, who is funnier than he had any right to be and always manages to cheer me up when I need it. Ger, who always keeps me company at family parties when we are both hiding in the corner. My wonderful nieces who are easily the best thing that have ever happened to me. My extended family — my aunts, uncles and cousins — who are wonderful and entertaining and a joy to have in my life.

I have too many friends to name so I have to apologise in advance for everyone I miss. Just know I love you and appreciate each and every one of you.

Courtney, who has been there for every step of this journey, who has encouraged me, grown with me and has been the best company a lonely writer could ask for. My Big Smoke friends; Eve, Olivia, Aisling, Kevin, Niamh and Ciara who have offered support, feedback, and encouragement every step of the way. Big Smoke, of course, cannot be mentioned without thanking Nic and Claire who gave me so many opportunities to learn and grow as a writer and supported me every step of the way.

Amy, the best friend anyone can ask for. Growing up with you has made everything better, and definitely more fun. You are one of the best people in my life; I am so glad to know you. Amy, my *other* Amy, who is always there when I need something, always supporting me and listening to me rant, and, most importantly, always willing to get ice cream with me when the need strikes. Kate, who very often keeps me sane and grounded. Elaine, for being one of the kindest people in my life and for always listening to me ramble. Lef, Ciara, Laura, Liz and Cathy for making me laugh, for supporting me, and for being my friends for more years than I'm willing to count.

Thank you to Alison for helping me make sure my Irish was as correct as it could be. Every mistake is my own. Laurel Sills who did an amazing job copyediting the book, and Lorna Reid who formatted it wonderfully. And to Hampton Lamoureux for the wonderful book cover.

And finally, you, dear reader.

You do not know what it means to have someone read your work, and then stay to read the acknowledgements. I appreciate every single one of you.

Hopefully I will see you again. Hopefully when I release my next book.

Fran xx

# ABOUT THE AUTHOR

Frances Quinn is a chronically ill writer from Dublin. She has a BA in Philosophy and Sociology, MSc in Business Management, and MSc in Climate Change: Policy, Media and Society. She spent a year living in New Zealand, travelling there for the Rugby World Cup, and has also travelled around Europe and America. She is an avid music fan, reader and *very* amateur painter. When she's not hanging out with her friends, she's babysitting her nieces. She spends an incredibly large amount of time resting.

Instagram: franquinnwrites
TikTok: franquinnwrites

If you enjoyed this book, please consider leaving a review.

Printed in Great Britain
by Amazon